PRAISE FOR
TONY SMALL AND LORD EDWARD FITZGERALD

"[*Tony Small and Lord Edward Fitzgerald*] is a fascinating and well-told story of the American Revolution in South Carolina—and of its ramifications across racial and national boundaries." —**Walter Edgar**, author of *South Carolina: A History*

"The author brings to life the challenges and opportunities that the American Revolution brought to African Americans in the South in this engaging account of a free black man's wartime experience and postwar friendship with a British officer he rescued from the battlefield." —**Jim Piecuch**, author of *Three Peoples, One King: Loyalists, Indians, and Slaves in the Revolutionary South*

"[*Tony Small and Lord Edward Fitzgerald*] is a marvellous piece of historical recuperation, based on scrutiny of documentation. Its two Parts, one 'creative nonfiction,' one historical notes, present a remarkably convincing and original literary form, the principal outcome of which is to record black achievements and experience in their own right. This is a major and important work." —**Bernard O'Donoghue**, Wadham College, Oxford University

"At one point in this compelling narrative as the reader is absorbed into a story that needs to be told, we read, "Others shot quick glances at someone they reckoned would be their weakest link. [*Tony Small and Lord Edward Fitzgerald*] deserves much more than a quick glance. The history contained in this book is solid. The story concerns a challenge to "quick glance" studies in the real world of Africans in the diaspora, and readers are fortunate indeed that Robert Ray Black is the sort of imaginative historian who has forged a bond between us and an otherwise neglected hero." —**Joseph A. Brown**, SJ, Ph.D., Professor, African Studies, Southern Illinois University, Carbondale

"A courageous blend of history and fiction." —**Professor Kevin Whelan**, University of Notre Dame

Tony Small and Lord Edward Fitzgerald

CREATIVE NONFICTION OF
BLACK AND WHITE BROTHERHOOD IN STRUGGLES FOR
FREEDOM DURING THE AMERICAN REVOLUTIONARY WAR
AND IRISH UPRISING OF 1796–98

ROBERT RAY BLACK

With notes, appendices, and maps
Cover Ilustration by Joseph Winkelman

A Revised Version of Fortune's Bond © 2019, with Corrections and Additions

ISBN: 978-1-64704-276-9 (Paperback)
ISBN: 978-1-64704-284-4 (Hardback)
ISBN: 978-1-64704-275-2 (eBook)

Published by Cymbee Press LLC
1021 O'Connell Drive,
Bozeman, MT 59715.

Distribution by Bublish, Inc. in Mt. Pleasant, SC
Printed on acid-free paper.

For Friends in the Lowcountry of South Carolina

Modern illustration by Joseph Winkelman of Tony Small's rescue of Lieutenant Lord Edward Fitzgerald after the Battle of Eutaw Springs, 8 September 1781, as recorded in the register of the 19th Regiment of Foot. Draper Manuscript, 6VV321. Thomas Sumter Papers, Lyman C. Draper Manuscript Collection, 6VV321, State Historical Society of Wisconsin. Quoted in Thomas Moore and Martin MacDermott, *The Memoirs of Lord Edward Fitzgerald*. London: Downey and Co., Limd, 1897, p. viii. https://archive.org/details/memoirsoflordedw00moorrich (Accessed 07 August 2019.) Exhibit 1, below.

Tony Small rescues Lord Edward Fitzgerald
after the Battle of Eutaw Springs, 1781.

S o close, indeed, and desperate was the encounter, that every officer engaged is said to have had personally, and hand to hand, an opportunity of distinguishing himself, and Lord Edward, who we may take for granted, was among the foremost in the strife, received a severe wound in the thigh, which left him insensible on the field. In this helpless situation he was found by a poor negro, who carried him off on his back to his hut, and there nursed him most tenderly till he was well enough of his wound to bear removing to Charleston. This negro was no other than the 'faithful Tony,' whom, in gratitude for the honest creature's kindness, he now took into his service, and who continued devotedly attached to his noble master to the end of his career." Draper Manuscript, 6VV321.

Synopsis

U ntil publication of this book, virtually nothing was known about Tony Small, the African American from South Carolina who helped further an existing revolutionary spirit of liberty in Ireland as much as Lafayette did in France. For the first time, Robert Black brings Small to life in a work of creative nonfiction that includes his influence upon Lord Edward Fitzgerald, the military commander in the United Irishmen's revolution against British rule in Dublin between 1796–1798, whose life Small saved at the Battle of Eutaw Springs in 1781.

Much is known in Ireland about Lord Edward, but very little is recorded about his time in the Southern Campaign of the Revolutionary War from June 1781 until May 1782 in South Carolina. The book identifies twelve battles in which Lord Edward probably participated with the British Army's 19th Regiment of Foot and narrates plausible events surrounding them until the British evacuate Charleston in December 1782.

Tony Small is a real person, the main character in the book. Everyone else when named in the book is also a real person, and most are black. The book records the names of over two hundred documented African Americans who may have participated in the battles and creates a fictional narrative for many of them. They have names in place and time and play dramatic roles as real people other than as historically nameless "Negroes." Some, like Tony's lover Ruth, are given particular prominence. Their voices and Small's in Part I give fictional context to moral, social, and revolutionary realities during

America's first civil war. The appendices, notes, maps, and exhibits in Part II firmly anchor fictional detail to historically recorded facts.

The book necessarily contributes to new revelations about the Southern Campaign. For example, the Battle of Quinby Bridge prior to Eutaw Springs sees the future military commander of the Irish Uprising fight at spitting distance against some of the greatest military figures in American history—Francis Marion the Swamp Fox, Thomas Sumter the Gamecock, and Light Horse Harry Lee.

Tony Small and Lord Edward travel from South Carolina to the West Indies, Ireland, Gibraltar, Canada, England, and France where Lord Edward's republican sympathies lead him to resign his commission and, later, join the United Irishmen. The nephew of the Duke of Richmond and great-great-grandson of King Charles II marries Pamela, the illegitimate daughter of Louis Philippe Joseph d'Orléans, also known as Philippe Égalité. Tony Small, Lord Edward, and La Belle Pamela bring to focus the American, Irish, and French revolutions as they affect the personal fortunes of each. Few accounts of the Age of Romanticism admit so strong a roll of a black person.

In a common struggle for freedom, one for blacks and one for Ireland, Tony Small and Lord Edward are more inseparable friends than master and servant for seventeen years before Lord Edward is captured and killed. Tony and his Irish wife Julie continue their devotion to Lord Edward's widow Pamela after she flees to Belgium. The Smalls move to London where Tony dies around 1804.

By bringing to light the story of remarkable figures in eighteenth-century American, Irish, Canadian, English, and French history, the book is unequaled as a record of mutual respect and devotion between two men that begins on the level battle ground at Eutaw Springs. It also creates an account of African Americans not as mere slaves or free black men and women who do manual labor, but as soldiers and patriots of the highest order to help establish the new republic.

CONTENTS

PREFACE

⟋⟍

While this book is mainly about Tony Small, a free black from South Carolina, it tells three stories—one of Tony, one of Lord Edward Fitzgerald, and to a lesser extent but nonetheless significant, one of dozens of historically documented blacks who did participate or could have participated on either side of the twelve battles in which Lord Edward fought during the Southern Campaign of the American Revolutionary War. It is written in two parts to tell a good story and to popularize two virtually unknown historical figures—the one solid and steadfast in his influence on his noble friend, the other an adventurous Irish revolutionary whose real military and romantic life itself reads like a work of fiction.

Part I is written in a creative nonfiction genre, imaginative and colorful, with roots in historical fact. Part II backs up the story and is full of historical notes, appendices, and maps, some previously unpublished, that are fundamental to the story of Tony and Lord Edward in South Carolina. It includes, for example, a section on Tony's identity as well as a list of black individuals by name who in most historical accounts of the Southern Campaign—and throughout early American history—are simply identified collectively and, regrettably, dismissed as nameless "Negroes." Readers who are happy to accept Tony's story in Part I as pure fiction must at the same time find place within the story for the historical notes in Part II. Together the two parts bring to life an amazing, riveting story of *Tony Small and Lord Edward Fitzgerald* that extends from the new world to the old.

What Survives Today?

O n upper King Street throughout the 1940s and '50s in
Charleston, South Carolina, the black manager at the Belk-
Robinson Department Store routinely gave free clothing to
the poor. Marion Alexander Stroble, father of deputy U.S. marshal Fred
Stroble, was among those who collected the clothes from the department
store for distribution on behalf of Morris Brown A.M.E. Church and
Mother Emanuel A.M.E. Church. The manager was known by the name
"Lord Fitzgerald." How he got the name, whether it came from nowhere or
was preserved by the black community in the Lowcountry as a remnant of
distant events surrounding the great Irish patriot Lord Edward Fitzgerald
and the black man who saved his life in the Revolutionary War, is lost to
history. Lord Edward arrived in Charleston with the 19th Regiment of Foot
on 3 June 1781. Tony Small saved his life after Lord Edward was wounded
at the Battle of Eutaw Springs on 8 September 1781. On 5 May 1782, after
eleven months and at least twelve military actions during the Southern
Campaign of the Revolutionary War, Lord Edward Fitzgerald sailed from
Charleston harbor with Tony Small. After tours of duty in the West Indies
and Canada, Lord Edward returned to Ireland with Tony. Inspired in part by
Tony's presumed accounts of African Americans in South Carolina in their
struggle for freedom, and from experiences in St. Lucia and Canada, Lord
Edward renounced his peerage and commission in the British Army and led
the unsuccessful United Irishmen rebellion of 1796–1798 against British

rule in Ireland. After Lord Edward's arrest and death in 1798, Tony died in London about six years later. With roots grounded in the Lowcountry of South Carolina, Tony Small helped further an existing revolutionary spirit of liberty in Ireland as much as Lafayette did in France.

PART I

Creative nonfiction of black and white brotherhood in struggles for freedom during the American Revolutionary War and Irish Uprising of 1796–98

Chapter 1

TONY'S WORLD

The lean, muscular young man hears sounds he is waiting for. Crows, wrens. The odor of tea olive hangs in the morning mist. His two brothers beside him begin to squirm and roll around. A faint light creeps in the one-room cabin which is no bigger than the vestibule of the two-story brick plantation house a hundred yards away. The glow from embers in the cabin fireplace mingles with the morning light enough for him to make out shapes of six others still in bed. Mud between the logs does not always keep out cold drafts, but it is early summer now. He moves quickly to beat the morning sun to the top branches of his favorite live oak. He doesn't know if he can slip out the door and get by his mother's careful eye. He tip-toes a short distance from the cabin before breaking into longer strides. His mother smiles and pulls the covers over her shoulders. Chores can come later at the springs at Eutaw.

Rain slacking off. Got to hurry before breakfast. Good fatback, grits, biscuits. No one to meet me today. No telling where she is. I'll have my great oak for myself. Just as well, even better. The rain has to slack off so I can see the herons and egrets and deer. All kinds of critters. They won't move around in a lot of rain. And all that lies on up the road, too. All I can see. Not all the way to Charleston, but a long way still. Long-leaf pines, swamps and marshes, sweet grass and rice fields. Rice fields. Hard work for some of my best friends. I want to see what's stirring around today. Maybe some Brits in their fancy red coats.

A half hour later, he looks down to see his mother standing under the tree. She is not a typical middle-aged woman worn out with heavy labor in the field. Rather, she is striking for her beauty and composure which, time and again, she calls on to watch her liveliest son through one adventure after another. She is taller than her husband, but not heavier. Both acknowledge that Tony takes after her good looks and shares her personality. She looks up and nods her head slightly up and down as she smiles at the young adult high above, moving nimbly over the branches of the live oak.

"I knew you'd try to slip by me again this morning."

He looks down at her, fists on her hips, one holding an apron which she has not yet put on. She continues to smile as she ties it—after another swish at a mosquito—with long shapely fingers which could easily stretch the length of a full scale on a piano.

"You're my favorite scout, Tony Small, but you're way too big a man to slip by anybody, and sure not by your momma. I see all your tricks." They both laugh in a way that starts the morning right.

"Now get down out of that tree and go eat your breakfast and tend to those horses right away. That tree'll be here when you get back."

Tony climbs down from an enormous branch, stepping on another that hangs so low it touches the ground. His favorite tree is several hundred years old. The very top branches are too small to hold anything but a bird or squirrel.

"It's the best place in the world, Momma. You can see way off. Everything coming and going your way. Higher the better. So when are you going to go with me to see those other big oaks by the ocean? I hear you and Daddy talk and talk about 'em. A mile around at the trunks."

"Stop that right now and get on with you, Tony Small. You're late with those horses. Your daddy'll go with you someday, but not till he's good and ready. Miss Maggie may need him to do some work down that way toward Charleston. They're sure not a mile around, though. Now you move along. Maybe thirty feet."

Tony walked with his mother back toward the family cabin. His father met them on the way to his job in the fields where he worked side by side with enslaved blacks. Tony and his family were the only free blacks on Maggie McKelvey's Plantation. Shorter but more muscular than Tony, Tony's father was the most important black man on the place. He knew how to deal with overseers without being obsequious. His strength lay in keen eyes that could immediately focus on the person or object directly responsible for the issue at hand. He saw the punch line of a joke coming long before anyone else, and sometimes laughed so loudly that clay-footed listeners could not even hear it when it finally arrived. He could see irony where there wasn't supposed to be any. Regardless of circumstances of life on the plantation, he showed no sense of resignation. He was respected by most in an age of disrespect.

"Well, Tony, looks like your momma caught you again." He poked Tony in the ribs. "One of these days you're going to fall out of those oaks. Their branches are too weak to hold a big boy like you. You're getting too big now to climb so near the top. You're the only man who can even get that high. You're even too big to sneak out of the cabin so nobody sees you."

His mother continued to walk alone quickly toward the family cabin, her mind set on chores. Tony and his father talked a little more about what

Tony was going to do that day. They parted after a while, and Tony continued walking back to the family cabin, still about a hundred yards away. He wasn't thinking about his chores. He was just thinking.

·•◦))✦((◦•·

Big blue herons flying by. I wonder if they are as curious about what's out there as I am. If they're happy and satisfied with the way things are going. Probably are. That's the future out there. I know that. They can see more and more as they fly higher and higher. Since they're still flying after seeing what's there, I reckon what they see must not be too bad. Deer, too. I can tell by their bedding in the woods that they know how to make the best of everything even though they can see only what I can see level on the ground.

·•◦))✦((◦•·

Tony laughed to himself at the idea of deer climbing trees. He looked over at the stables in the barn, which was about the same size as Maggie McKelvey's brick house. He secretly spent some nights in the barn with Ruth. There they made love and shared secrets and news about whatever was going on at other plantations along the Santee River. His mind stuck on Ruth as he smiled and continued to walk back toward the family cabin.

People in the other five cabins began to come out into the morning sunshine and head to work. They usually went in a group, but some laggards were just finishing their breakfast of biscuits and gravy. They chattered among each other, more so than usual, sometimes whispering. One or two threw his hoe away as they walked along, then ran back and picked it up and laughed.

There was no avenue of oaks along which the cabins would ordinarily be built to impress visitors with the wealth of the owner as they approached the plantation house. The cabins were simply lined up in a row along a side road leading to the brick house. Most were the same size, about eighteen by twenty feet with plenty of head room. Most had two windows in the front, one door, a fireplace, and a dirt floor. Bright blue colors were used to trim some of the door frames and windows to keep evil spirits away. Not at Tony's family cabin, however, because Tony's father said if the devil wanted to drop by, he would, no matter what. Tony laughed again to himself, this time about the devil slipping through a window that somebody forgot to paint. He pictured a deer with a paint bucket and smiled.

Tony's family lived in one of the best cabins, about one-third larger than the others. For most of the year, his mother cooked outdoors. To wash clothes she lit a fire under a big pot and stirred the clothes with a wooden stick. She used one of the two churns on the place to make butter. She kept a bucket just inside the door always full of cold spring water. Everybody used the same ladle. A large bowl to the side of the bucket was used for washing up.

Setting out from his cabin after breakfast, Tony saw Miss Maggie McKelvey at a distance, standing on the porch of her brick house waiting for him. Everybody called her Miss Maggie even though she was a widow. The two-story house had two chimneys on each end and was on piers which made it look all the more imposing. Miss Maggie was about the same age as his mother but shorter and heavy-set. Her skin was more wrinkled, too, with liver spots that showed through her dark tanned skin, like all her Irish kin. She had hands the size of a man's. The story around the place was that in the early days she used to switch places with her husband as he, then she, pulled a plow, just like a horse would. That was before they got enough money to buy horses and blacks.

Tony liked Miss Maggie because she pretty much always saw both sides of everything, even some things from the black side. She always seemed to be doing something important and not just bossing around other people and overseers. She had to be ahead of any trouble on the place ever since her husband James died and left hundreds of acres and dozens of enslaved blacks in her hands. It was Tony's job to help her with everything but his enslaved friends.

As he approached, Miss Maggie wiped her hands with three or four quick slaps and brushed off her apron with a few more. For a second, flour dust almost blocked his view.

"You ain't late, Tony. I just need you to get an early start this morning, every morning for a while, I guess. We need to have things all tidy and prompt more than usual 'cause there's so much stirring around these days."

"Lot's going on, Miss Maggie. I can't figure it all out."

She looked off into the distance, pursed her lips and puffed away dust still hanging in the air. "Well, let's get that tackle all cleaned up."

"Done it already."

"Harnesses and saddle oiled good, but not too slippery."

"Done that two days ago."

Miss Maggie smiled broadly at her favorite black man on the place. "Well, I reckon you can tell what I'm thinking before I'm thinking. We're kind of all in this together, Tony. I mean in what's coming up from Charleston, and down from the midlands, too. News is spreading like there's a run on tomorrow. A bunch of British landed in Charleston. We got to take care, you hear?"

"Yes, ma'am, I heard about all that."

He went straight to the barn where Maggie McKelvey kept a horse that Tony loved. The barn had only six stalls, a loft, and a work place in the front, doors at either end. It was bigger than most barns, about fifteen hundred square feet, and nearer to the brick house than the cabins. Like the cabins, it was made of cypress, unpainted because it didn't need to be, and built to last a hundred years. Two wagons sat under an extended roof on one side, kind of like a garret. Tony opened the barn door facing the house and promptly tripped on the baseboard running along the ground. A few steps farther on, still just thinking, he bumped his head on a stalactite flat iron used to build rice dikes that was hanging from the ceiling, along with farming implements in need of repair. Eagle put his head over the door of his stall.

"Well, Eagle, you were just waiting on that, weren't you, ole boy? Starts your day better than the rising sun, don't it?" Tony acted like he was giving Eagle time to answer.

When he needed to make minor repairs on harnesses or wagons and the like, Tony had enough tools hanging from the beams and on the walls or scattered in dusty corners ready for occasional use. He never used the saddles, only the reins hanging on the wall. From above the stalls, he could easily pitch hay down into the troughs for the horses.

"Throw it down where the goats can get it, 'cept we ain't got no goats. Just making everything plain and simple for you, Eagle. Wow! I love to see those little specks of hay dancing in the morning light." Eagle moved around, bumping his big rear end against his stall.

"Hold on there now, big boy. I want to have a look at that hoof. Easy, easy." He reached up to slide the halter over the solid brown horse's head and ears and gently pushed on one of his flanks.

"You wouldn't be so easy to move around if I hadn't been right here when you were born, Eagle. You know from all that poking my fingers in your mouth and nose and ears when you were born that it don't hurt none. I was the first smell you had, too, other than your momma. That's an old trick for you big horses, Eagle, poking you and letting you smell us right away. Lets you know you're in good hands that'll take care of you the rest of your life. And if I couldn't have been there when you dropped, I'd have asked 'em to let you drop in a bundle of my old clothes so you could get my scent right away." Tony went through the same verbal litany each morning with Eagle to let them both know that another day was dawning. Sometimes he tripped on the baseboard of the barn door on purpose.

"Now let's have a look at that hoof." He squinted closely at a mark that presented no lasting concern and let the hoof drop with a loud "womp."

"You're going to be fine, Eagle boy. Just fine. Maybe in a few days I'll jump on and we'll fly away again, just like *Belle-With-A-Rope-On* did one time in Greece, way back when. I know all about it. The Sinklers told me." He gave Eagle a good healthy slap on the rump. "I'll be back after a few more chores and have another look at you, then if we have time, we'll ride out toward Belvidere."

Tony had two more looks at Eagle's hoof before riding out. In the early afternoon as they passed swamps and marshes, he occasionally pulled up on the reins. "Now, Eagle, ain't that the prettiest sight you ever saw? Look at that big cypress trunk. Whoa! Watch out for those knobs sticking up. You know that better than I do. Just look at all that, the way it was when Indians were here. Nice and peaceful and full of snakes." He laughed out loud and jiggled the reins and made a clucking noise to get Eagle started again.

"Let's don't go all the way to the Sinkler place, Eagle. Ain't good for your hoof. I just want to spend as much time outdoors today as possible. Don't know what it is. Just feel funny. Don't you? Sure wish Ruth was here."

Tony gave his horse a friendly slap on the neck with his cupped hand to make a loud sound. "You got big ears like a marsh tacky, Eagle.

"Now look at that great blue heron. Wow! What a beauty. White ones, too, settling their big bodies on the littlest branches of the tallest trees. I don't see how they don't fall off. You're already high as you can get, Eagle. You're eighteen hands, something I bet you already know.

"Lots of birds stick with just each other their whole life long. Herons do. You can see 'em nesting together all the way from the springs at Miss Maggie's to the Santee."

Tony got off Eagle and let the reins drop. "We got to get some more sweet grass for Momma, or she'll think we've just been riding 'round dreaming again, which we've been doing. She's determined to finish a basket for Miss Maggie."

Tony pulled out a big knife his father gave him. After finding the best stand of sweet grass he could easily reach, he leaned over, took a big hand full of it near the ground, and cut three large swaths. After bundling them with cords he had in his back pocket, he managed to hold the sweet grass under one arm as he got back on Eagle. Without a clucking noise from Tony, Eagle began to move as soon as he felt Tony's full weight on his back. Tony looked over at one of his favorite fishing spots as they began to set off back to Miss Maggie's.

"Not today, Eagle, got to get back. You don't want to mess with gators, do you? Not like last time. They're fast as lightning."

Eagle suddenly stopped in his tracks.

"Come on, now. Come on. Gitty up." Tony slapped the reins a few times. "What's wrong with you? Gitty up, Eagle," He began to dig his heels into the horse's sides. He reached up and slapped his ears and popped his neck with the cup of his hand. "Ha! Gee! Let's go. Gitty up. Why are you stopping all of a sudden? You feel funny, too? Your hoof still hurt?"

Tony slipped off and looked down at his hoof. He quickly jumped back. "Whoa, now, big boy. Hold it right there. Easy, easy. I got it, Eagle."

With one quick slice of his knife, Tony cut off the head of a timber rattler that Eagle kept firmly under his hoof.

"So that's why you wouldn't budge, ain't it? You're my faithful friend, Eagle. You tread on that ole snake, didn't you? He's a big-un. Mean, too. One killed Cuffy's little brother last year, remember?"

Tony swung back on Eagle's broad back and gave him a big hug around his neck. "Now let's get out of here before some of his friends show up. Nobody wants to skin and eat him back home, anyway."

As he approached the brick plantation house about thirty minutes later, Tony looked over at his little private garden which he kept in Miss Maggie's palisade garden next to the brick house. He could cultivate what he wanted to in his little garden. That meant not only vegetables but as many flowers as he could manage to take from other Lowcountry plantation gardens or get out of the woods. And weeds.

"Whoa, there, Eagle!" Tony said in a strong voice to impress Sayey who was working nearby in one of the other gardens kept by other blacks. She was about Tony's age, late teens or early twenties, and seemed somehow to keep a child-like appearance in spite of working in the fields ever since she could walk. She had on a bright yellow dress.

"You're all dressed up, Sayey—and stealing my prettiest flowers. Caught you again, didn't I?" Tony smiled at his good friend. "That's a pretty dress, Sayey. You're going to get it dirty."

"Tony Small, why are you putting all those weeds in your garden as fast as the rest of us can dig 'em out of ours? You're putting 'em in Miss Maggie's, too. I've seen you, lots of times. I got a mind to tell on you someday, Tony Small."

"Weeds are as pretty as any other flower. They're all flowers. And who says who's a weed, anyway? You're not a weed, are you, Sayey? Not the way you look today, for sure."

Sayey rolled her eyes and made a funny face. "Tony Small, you're going to say whatever you want to say and do whatever you want to do and put up a good reason for it, too. Even if nobody but you believe it."

"What if some of those weeds got loose and took off and ran away from the garden? What would you do if you got up one morning and—what do you know?—all your little pansies with little feet ran away, right along with those weeds?"

"Pansies with little feet?" Sayey burst out laughing.

"Now there's a pretty little flower," Tony said, pointing to one almost tall enough to touch Sayey's yellow dress. "I'll call it a 'Sayey.'"

"That's a weed, Tony Small, and I'm about to chop it." They both started laughing again.

"I think it's so pretty that I'll come back and pluck it and put it in my garden and Miss Maggie's palisade garden, too. You know I like to help Miss Maggie take special care of her garden even if it means making a few changes now and then. She's mighty proud of that garden."

"She doesn't even know you're doing all that. That's a weed and you know it. You go on now, Tony Small, and let me get on with my chores."

On his way back to the barn, Tony saw one of the overseers yelling at two of his friends and threatening to whip them. The overseer was a foreman known around the area for his steely eyes and skinny frame that looked like he had no hips, like a snake. His skin was about as dark as the blacks' and rumor had it that he had black blood. He stared at Tony riding toward them. His hands were always the first thing Tony looked at. Then his shifty eyes, but this time the overseer was careful to keep his big straw hat down over his eyes. Miss Maggie hired him only because nobody else wanted him on their place. The pickings were as slim as he was.

"What's Stepney and Cuffy done this time?" Tony asked in a light-hearted way, hoping to calm the situation and avoid a correction. He turned sideways on Eagle's back and smiled broadly without looking at either of his friends. "The sun doesn't know it ain't summer yet. Everybody's beat down just standing still."

"You stay out of this, Tony Small," the overseer yelled as he quickly turned back toward the two field hands. "You two rascals messed up one of the dikes. You could have ruined the water flow in the rice fields. And you did it on purpose, too. I'd whip and sell you both if Miss Maggie would let me."

He abruptly turned back toward Tony, still mounted on Eagle. "Now, Tony Small, you get out of here—thinking you can just fly in here and make things right for your two buddies. You're worse than they are. They know their place. You don't. You may be free and have mixed blood, and you got a few muscles in your arms and back, but you're still just a black to me and everybody else. Now get out of here before something accidentally happens to you. I'll tend to these two myself without you hanging around. And I do mean hanging! Now get!"

"Gitty up, Eagle." Tony quickly pulled the reins of the horse toward home and slapped the reins on the side of Eagle's neck with a loud pop. Talking back to the overseer at this point did not even cross his mind. A break on a dike could endanger the entire crop, too. If Stepney and Cuffy messed up one, on purpose or accidentally, that was serious, not ever enough for a correction, but still serious. Inland rice fields were crucial to Upper St. John's main industry and had to be properly maintained at all costs.

Out of earshot, Tony looked back and said, "Eagle, you ain't got boundaries, do you?"

Tony Small could pass as handsome in any society. About five feet, ten inches tall, taller than most South Carolina men, he had enough height and weight to convey a commanding presence in the company of blacks or whites, even for a young man in difficult situations. But only to a point. *Who* he was didn't matter to most white folks. *What* he was—a black man—to all white folks was all that mattered to them. There were limits beyond his control to both reason and friendship, but, like his father, Tony was not resigned to that fact.

He rode Eagle to the barn, took off his bridle and sat down for a long time, thinking about the good feeling he had earlier that morning and how quickly he lost it. After a while he walked back toward his cabin. Without a word, he handed the sweet grass to his mother. She knew something happened but didn't ask. He turned and walked away.

"Now, gitty up, Tony," he said to himself as he left his mother. "Tread hard on that ole rattler. Let's go see what extra chores Miss Maggie has for me today."

Maggie McKelvey was again standing in the door of the brick house, the way grandmothers do when they somehow sense that someone is coming. No visitor ever surprised her. She had her hand on the door frame to keep it from closing shut all the way, but closed enough to keep most of the flies out—one fly, in particular, the size of a small roach. She acted as if she had not heard about Tony's row with her overseer, but the overseer had already sent somebody to tell her, to beat Tony to the draw, and Tony knew it.

Shaking his head to clear it and squinting his eyes in the late morning sun, Tony stood below the steps leading to the porch in front of the door, just as he did earlier that morning.

"Eagle and I didn't get over to Belvidere this morning, Miss Maggie. I didn't want to hurt his hoof any. We didn't see anybody as far as we went.

"Seems like lots of white folks have gone from around here. If they were here abouts, they'd be coming to ride Eagle this morning. Sometimes looks like everybody living twenty miles of here wants to ride. Even folks who just own land with no house on it come by because they hear how good Eagle rides. Lofty, Fish Eye, and Iron Side, too."

Miss Maggie let him talk on to keep the subject of the overseer from coming up, but she wasn't smiling.

"One of the Sinkler brothers came by last week, but I ain't seen him lately. I asked him where the name of his place Belvidere came from, and Mr. James said he didn't really know, just came with the land when they got it."

"Be good to all our guests, Tony—I know you will," Miss Maggie said, all too familiar with Tony's love of names for everybody and everything. She turned to go back indoors.

"Even if folks are from Belmont, Blue Hole, Limespring, Numertia, Brush Pond, Black Jack, and Ash Hill," Tony said.

She looked back. "And especially if Captain Peter Gaillard comes over from The Rocks, or anybody from Walworth. You take good care of all of 'em." She then stopped, turned around and took a step or two on the porch, away from the door. She calmly watched the roach-sized fly zip inside before the door shut. She looked at Tony. She was dead serious.

"Your momma told me to be sure and tell you to watch out for that girl Ruth who's always coming round here to see you all the way down from St. James Parish on the Santee. She's like a heron that flies where it wants to. You're free to go see her, but it's dangerous for her to come to see you, you hear?

"Now I know you and Ruth are sweethearts, but Ruth's not free like you and your siblings and your momma and daddy. Your momma's just trying to be sure you two do the right thing and not just disappear in one of the huts or barns. Or get snatched up by a trader if you get too far afield. You could, you know. And I'm afraid my overseer would be glad to help. I hear white folks talking about you, saying you're real uppity."

Miss Maggie went on in a different, even harder tone. "I know you ain't uppity, Tony, and I know you ain't obnoxious, but I have to tell you to take care that girl always gets back to Mr. Snow. Do you hear me? You listening to me, Tony? She's almost a runaway as it is now. She runs away whenever she's criticized. I'd hate to see anybody hurt her."

"I'll do my best, Miss Maggie. She's mighty head-strong"—and he suddenly lost even more of the good feeling he had earlier that morning from climbing his favorite tree by the Eutaw springs, laughing with his mother, riding Eagle, and thinking about the beauty of the Lowcountry, his garden, and the gigantic oaks near Charleston.

He left Miss Maggie's brick house and began to walk slowly back toward the barn. It was still late morning, spring time, around eleven o'clock. The beauty of the new day took his mind beyond the horizon he saw several hours ago, and he began to get his bearings back.

On his way to the barn, he saw Cuffy working in one of the sheds near the barn, this time without Stepney. The overseer sent him there after cussing him out, but without a correction.

Cuffy had his back to Tony. His powerful shoulders and arms were way bigger than the shirt he was wearing, and his torn serge trousers were the color of the dirt he was digging. Cuffy seldom wore a hat. A chunk of his right ear lobe was bitten off from a fight.

"What happened to Stepney?" Tony asked. Cuffy acted as if he didn't hear. "What happened to Stepney? She's a sweet girl. Was that overseer just making up trouble so he could give her a correction?"

"Shut up, Tony Small," Cuffy muttered without turning around. He continued cutting down a handle to fit an axe.

"I sure am sorry if I made things worse for you and Stepney this morning. You always get the hardest jobs, Cuffy, 'cause you're the biggest and strongest man around."

Cuffy turned around, raised his enormous right fist and shook it at Tony. "Don't try that on me, Tony Small. Shut up and get out of here. What are you up to anyway? You always make things worse for everybody. So nosey. Just wandering around, free as a stupid bird. You think you're better than us folks who have to work for nothing and watch the whip. Work when we're told to. You're just walking around, putting on airs and acting like you don't have a care in the world, talking to that damn horse all the time, don't have real work at all." Cuffy moved his hips side to side in a sissy kind of way. "You're even trying to learn to read and messing with the cymbee."

"I do my work same as you do. I'm just like you."

"No you ain't. You're lighter than most of us, for one thing. You think you're really something. Worse than a high-yellow house servant or that damned overseer."

Angered by his own words, Cuffy suddenly threw down his axe handle and started toward Tony. His first swing caught Tony's left jaw, enough to rattle his teeth. Tony backed away, then dove below the next swing to catch Cuffy by the waist and wrestle him to the ground. The two tussled about, busting lips and noses before four men nearby came running over to break it up.

"Don't think you're free from me," Cuffy yelled as they were dragged apart. "You ain't free from me."

"I won't need to worry none about you, Cuffy. You need to worry about me the next time you tear up my garden. I know it was you.

"And if you had any sense at all, Cuffy, you'd stop messing with that little white girl, Miss Maggie's kin, when she comes around here next time. If any white folks even *think* what's going on, you're a dead black man. They'll have to go to Charleston to find a tree high enough to hang you."

"She's messing with *me*," Cuffy yelled back, louder than he needed to. "She's messing with *me*."

Now that's good enough reason. Got to stay away from Cuffy. Can't get near him any more. Big trouble, and I want no part of it. Ain't afraid of him, but afraid of what he'll bring down on us all. Got to use my good sense because I could be hanging from my tree, just like the foreman said, instead of looking out from its branches. No room to escape from such a mess, either, if I get tangled up with Cuffy. They'll hang us back to back with the same rope.

After returning to the barn and doing more chores with Maggie McKelvey's other horses, Tony rode Eagle over to Woodboo, careful not to go too fast and hurt his hoof again. He also rode over to Wantoot and Pooshee, other plantations near the headwaters of the western branch in Middle St. John's Berkeley Parish. A few days earlier, he looked at Fountain Swamp and Chelsea plantations and into adjacent areas of St. Stephen's Parish, the limestone region. And especially at the springs at Eutaw which were in the same area. He was looking for cymbee water for his mother. She wasn't sick, just wanted some on hand.

He chatted with Eagle along the way to Woodboo. The canopy of big oak branches that leaned over from both sides of the road provided relief from an early June sun that couldn't wait to get the heat going and really show its stuff. After a while, Tony got off Eagle to walk on the soft light sandy roads, brown gold. The dirt helped to cool his bare feet. His trouser cuffs were high enough not to drag in the dirt. If trees with their Spanish moss weren't the best thing about the Lowcountry, Tony thought, dirt roads were. The horse followed him, creating an inimitable image of Lowcountry life.

At Woodboo Plantation Tony hoped to see a cymbee, what some folks told him were Kongo water spirits. Each spring had its own cymbee which looked like a web-footed goose or like a mermaid with long hair, folks said. He had never seen a cymbee, just heard about them. Flora, who ran away from General William Moultrie after Charleston fell the year before, told Tony that she saw one at Woodboo. Others saw them, too, Hercules, Isham and Cadar. No doubt about it, they said. All his life in the South Carolina Lowcountry Tony heard of their relation with the natural environment in both physical and spiritual ways, with both the living and the dead.

"Some say they're like a person or like a python or a gourd, red or black sometimes," Isham said when Tony met up with him at Woodboo. "Or even a spark of fire." Isham was a good friend of Tony's parents and considered himself especially close to Tony. In tattered dirty clothes, he nonetheless was careful to hold himself up in an erect posture whenever he saw the younger man. He seldom got excited about anything, not even hurricanes, but cymbees were an exception. Tony asked him about them every chance he got.

"They're creatures you ought to be afraid of, too," Cadar said, coming from nowhere to join them. He was younger than Tony and distant kin. Like Isham, he wore a shirt made out of a gunny sack. He talked about the cymbee like a child, but in a factual kind of way. Cadar was probably not inventing anything, but Tony could not suppress an incredulous grin the more Cadar talked.

"But they also got good powers, too—from the other world. In this new land here we need the water spirits to survive. My grandmomma told me they're kind of like the undine and the kelpie, the nkisi, the nkita, or the kilundu, back in Africa, but different, too." Cadar distinctly pronounced each of the difficult names and smiled, knowing that Tony was the ultimate wordsmith.

"Grandmomma told me that if I couldn't remember a cymbee's name, it would haunt me till I could. A name's like respect, she said. At night you can sometimes hear a cymbee make a thumping sound 'round the sinkholes. But if you ever see one, you're not ever supposed to talk about it. They'll get you if you do."

"I'm not a scaredy cat like you, Cadar," Tony replied. "You're afraid of the dark. I hear you sleep so close to the fireplace, you're going to catch fire and burn up someday."

"You don't need to be afraid, Cadar," Hercules said as he joined the group of younger men. A big, ageless man, Hercules commanded respect because he respected others, especially the youngsters. Everybody trusted him, including whites. He appeared to be a free man like Tony's father by the way he talked and acted, but he was not.

"They're our spiritual guardians. Give us strength and a feeling that this new land is now ours, too, no matter where we came from. We always want to keep the cymbee." He leaned into Tony. "But remember to skim off just a little from the top of the gourd when you dip into a spring so the spirit of the cymbee isn't so strong that it will give you the ague and fever."

Flora heard Hercules talking, and she, too, joined the group. She put down a basket full of produce and put her hands on her broad hips as if to emphasize her authority on the subject. Flora was a good-looking woman, so the men quickly gave way, happy to have her join them.

"They can heal you in lots of ways," she said and clapped her hands three times for a reason she didn't share. "They're nature spirits that are hard to explain. Mainly they just help and protect us. They're at The Rocks, Wappoo, and Belvidere, too."

All continued to tell Tony about cymbees until late afternoon. It was dark when he got back to the barn at Miss Maggie's and put Eagle back in his stall.

Something to keep in mind. I know the springs and fountains around here have real healing powers. Don't need Hercules and Flora or anybody else to tell me that. They're at the two springs here at Eutaw. They cured Momma. She told me so after a hard time last summer. Said she had female trouble, but the cymbee cured her. I've seen the springs at lots of plantations. White folks know about cymbees, too. They believe in cymbees. We all do.

Several days later, when Tony rode Eagle over to tend to the horses at Pooshee Plantation, he saw Cuffy talking to one of the Pooshee field hands.

"What are you doing over here, Cuffy?" Tony asked in his usual good-hearted way, as if nothing had passed between them, but he braced himself for another rough time. He hadn't seen Cuffy since their tussle at Miss Maggie's.

"I ain't telling the likes of you," Cuffy shot back. Cuffy was dressed better and had a hat on this time. He wasn't dressed for working or fighting. Tony said nothing. He didn't want to fight and could tell that Cuffy didn't either. "You don't need to know. You ain't the kind to know."

Tony looked around and saw several men whose expressions let on that Cuffy's secret was a big one. One of them picked up a small rock and chunked it toward a tree near Tony. It missed. Another, a tall idiotic-looking man Tony was not too fond of, just stared at him with a self-satisfied grin. Another looked at him like he was the littlest in a drove of hogs.

"I already know," Tony said. "Stepney told me."

"No, she didn't."

"Yep, I know. I already know."

"Well, I bet she didn't tell you everything. I have these men and two or three others at Miss Maggie's. While you're messing about looking for water spirits, I'm asking around about something real important. That's a lot more than you're doing, Tony Small, and you don't know the half of it. There's lots going on that doesn't ever seem to bother you one way or the other."

"I can feel there's something going on, too. Miss Maggie, too. People upset at what's coming out of Charleston and from the midlands, and everywhere. Anyway, you've got yourself into another big mess this time, haven't you, Cuffy? A garden's not enough for you to mess up."

Cuffy's big fists knotted up as the muscles in his arms flexed and his back arched forward. He licked his lips to soften them and looked around to see who was watching.

"A garden *is* too little for me. I'm going to plow in some high ground, Tony Small. If being free is a mess to you, then I'm real sorry for you. Nobody's going to be worried about a messed-up garden or a busted dike when things really start happening around here.

"I'm trying to get some of the men here at Pooshe to help us get enough guns for an uprising. That's right. An insurrection. I bet Stepney didn't tell you that.

"No need to get all bug-eyed, Tony Small. You heard me good. Except we'll do what they couldn't do at Stono Ferry. With this war going on, white folks will be too busy to turn away from fighting the British and their neighbors and relatives to deal with us black folks anymore. They'll just let us go. Most of 'em don't even know where we are now. The men folks just up and left the place. Just like them, we can just walk off and get things done if we want to."

All the time he was talking, Cuffy looked at some of the others to get nods of approval, but from their expressions some of what Cuffy was saying was news to them, too. The man who was chucking rocks let a handful drop at his feet.

Pleased with himself for tricking his nemesis into divulging his secret, Tony shot back. "You're crazy, Cuffy. You're supposed to be at Miss Maggie's. You can't just run around free, looking for trouble. Anyway, owners and overseers will drop everything to hold onto their property. That's a big part of what's about to happen. You're valuable property. All the rest of you, too. I'm free, but I ain't safe. Somebody could steal me tomorrow. Y'all know all that, too. White men ain't goin' to be dropping their guns around here."

"You don't get it, do you?" Cuffy folded his big arms. The other men backed off to give the two more room, but Cuffy continued in a less impassioned voice.

"I bet you don't even know what's really happening in Charleston. Miss Maggie didn't tell her pet." The tall idiotic man laughed.

"You don't even know names of who's landed, do you? And you're so proud of knowing things and everybody's name and everything. Well, as soon as Lord Rawdon leaves Charleston for upstate Ninety Six—everybody knows that's what they're going to do—there's going to be lots of guns in Charleston left behind that ain't guarded by all those loyalists and British soldiers that go with him. We're going to get 'em and make for Florida. The Spanish will welcome us as free men. They said so. And women, too. We'll all be free! We're going to take our women folk and children with us."

"That man Rawdon is not going to leave behind guns that ain't guarded," Tony replied, as if he heard of Rawdon already. "You're crazy if you think you can find guns just lying around waiting on you to pick 'em up. And you probably even think the guns are going to show you how to use 'em. Maybe Rawdon himself will help you shoot 'em."

"You can sass me all you want, Tony Small. You're just lucky for a while, but we both know as long as you're black, you can wake up some morning and find yourself in chains. Your color is your chains. No black man or man of mixed blood is free until we all are free. And only guns can make that happen, so you might as well start thinking about how to get 'em.

"To white folks, anybody with color in their skin is no better than a mule. Not even as good as a mule. A good mule costs more than you do. I'm lots stronger than you, so I'm worth more than a mule. You tell everybody that Cuffy's gettin' up a bunch of black men who are willing to fight to get free." The others walked up closer to Cuffy.

"They're two freedoms going on now, Tony Small, and you don't know about either one of 'em."

Tony stood still for a while and looked around without saying anything. He went back to pick up Eagle's reins which had fallen slack to the ground. After he slung himself up on Eagle's back, he started to ride off shaking his head, but he stopped and looked back at Cuffy.

"If word gets out about you, Cuffy, they'll hang you. I'm not going to say a word about any of this. I could get in trouble just by *not* telling Miss Maggie what you're up to. I won't do that, you have my word, but I won't argue with you, either. Just count me out." Then the man of many turns thought of another trick, a quick improvisation.

"Anyway, I'm going along behind Rawdon all the way up to Ninety Six to see the action for myself. It's best to watch every move to see which side's going to win this war. Whoever wins is the only thing that counts, Cuffy. I'm going to fight on the side of the winners. You're fighting everybody.

"I'll see which way to jump when the time comes. My plan beats yours any day. And I won't get hanged for it, either."

"Except you're forgetting one little thing, Tony Small," Cuffy said with an air of absolute certainty. "If the Brits win, they're going sell your black ass to loyalists when they leave, as quick as the rebs if they want to, so-called free or not. To black folks it really doesn't matter which white side wins. To white folks everything is black or white, and you're too stupid to know it.

"And I've already sent word up to Ninety Six," Cuffy continued with a smile. "I just may not hang around Charleston to steal guns. Maybe too hard to get 'em in the garrison, anyway. I got black folks up there in Ninety Six around Star Fort to collect all the guns and swords dead men on both sides leave behind right after the fighting stops and the smoke clears. There's going to be fighting, and black folks aren't going to be sitting around and watching, that's for sure. Then I'll bring guns back to Charleston. So I'm going up there, too, way ahead of you, Tony Small." He turned to walk away, then wheeled around to throw a rock at a tree near Eagle, close enough to make the horse jump.

"You're plum crazy, Cuffy. You're going to get yourself shot up, hanged, or stabbed with a bayonet before this whole thing is over."

—⌢—

Chapter 2

NINETY SIX

"Don't do it, Tony," Ruth replied a few days later in the barn, even before he finished telling her about his plan to go to Ninety Six. "Why are you doing that? Don't go looking for trouble when it's going to find you, anyway. You're just trying to keep up with Cuffy."

Tony raised his head with a slightly supercilious look. Neither moved a muscle until Ruth broke into a great big smile that showed all her magnificent teeth. They both burst out laughing.

"I know you're just talking." He grabbed her in a tight hug and kissed her. "You know why." He hugged her even tighter. "You're just like me. You love to go around picking up facts like trifles left scattered on the ground, just like me. You wouldn't miss a good time packed full of adventure, either. We're both going to find out which side to be on, that's why."

"You're my man, Tony Small. I'll always be by your side."

He pulled her back down on a blanket covering the straw bed where they both lay during the night.

"Well, I guess I'm not always by you side," Ruth said and wrapped her arms around his neck as they continued to laugh.

Ruth was an absolutely beautiful woman, the most beautiful woman, black or white, on all the plantations in St. John's Parish up and down the Santee River. In her, Tony saw as much reason and common sense as any man could see beyond her dazzling physical presence. Her lovely smile, her smooth face and neck and long strong limbs, her arms and legs, instinctively kept men on their best behavior around her, as if lust took a break around her. For Tony, it was more than that. For him, Ruth was a second-self through whom he could think and act on almost any issue or occasion. And whom he could love with equal intensity.

About an hour later Ruth returned to the Snow Plantation on the Santee. The next day Tony waited for her until early afternoon, as planned, but she never appeared. He went by his cabin where his mother packed a sack of provisions for him, enough to get him started. After saying good bye, he reluctantly set out by himself. "I'm sure going to miss her with every step I take. Must be old man Snow locked her up again. Damn that old white man."

After walking about a hundred yards he stopped and looked back to get a good solid look at the place he loved. He saw several of his friends as they went about their chores.

Leaving's a risk, I know. I like it here. I can go in and out of the brick house whenever I want to, if I knock real loud and Miss Maggie says I can. I know how to get along. It's easy getting along with Miss Maggie. I like the house because I like the person living in it. Lots of crazy people around here worship houses whether they're empty or full. The two stories of her house ain't what anybody would call grand, but everybody likes the porch that runs the whole length of the front. It's got cedar board inside, too. Cedar lasts forever. I've seen Miss Maggie climb up and down those steps to the front porch lots of times. Looks like she's not even trying, and she's up and down all the steps inside, too. Keeps

her healthy, they say. That's why she's lived so long. She doesn't much use the garret on the back side. It's all real easy on the McKelvey place, now that Miss Maggie is the only one running it, but something's wrong. Seems like trouble's about to find us pretty soon, so now's the time to get going and catch it by the tail if I can, whether I'm sure I can or not.

⋯⊷✦⊷⋯

"Hey, wait up," Tony yelled to Thomas Blackmore near dusk that afternoon. "Y'all going to Star Fort, Ninety Six, now?" Tony wanted to sound like he knew more than he did, so he added, "even before Rawdon leaves Charleston?"

"You heard right," Blackmore replied, startled by an informed intruder, as he kept talking quietly to the white man walking with him. The short white man stumbled on rocks and clods of dirt in the path as he fixed his eyes on Blackmore and listened intently instead of looking where he was going. Tony almost laughed to see the black guide trying to keep the white man from falling.

"I came down this way toward Charleston to pick up Rawdon's march to Ninety Six. If y'all going on ahead, and it looks like you are, I'd sure like to tag along behind. You're a Black Pioneer, ain't you? My daddy told me about y'all. Both the Brits and rebs have Black Pioneers, don't they? All fixed up in buckskin. I bet you know the backcountry like the back of your hand—wiry enough to get through bushes and briars as easy as a hound."

Blackmore, a tall, thin middle-aged man who bore all the signs of someone who lived most of his life outdoors, stopped talking to the white man, turned back toward Tony, wrinkled his brow and gave him a stern, curious look.

"You're a mighty big talker, boy," he said. "Go on and on, don't you?" Blackmore stopped to knock mud off his shoes with a large stick he was carrying, and almost lost his balance before the white man grabbed his arm. The white man turned toward Tony with the same curiosity, inviting Tony to make his case further. Both knew they could use the eyes and ears of a third person on the long road up to Ninety Six.

"I heard the big Brit Clinton took a liking to you loyalist Black Pioneers, formed companies of y'all to do the dirty work around camps, the digging and cleaning up. Can't carry a gun, though, or at least you're not supposed to, but sometimes I heard y'all do anyway. Been in the middle of just about everything. Showed real courage in all the fighting. I heard about what y'all are doing now, too, I mean going to Ninety Six. But I sure thought y'all were supposed to be on the patriots' side."

"Switched sides. You're a talker. A big talker. Who are you?"

"Tony Small. Why are you working for the British now?"

"Everybody knows a bunch of us switched after Camden. Long as we don't have to fight Americans." He saw Tony was alone. Didn't look like a spy, but you never know. The white man began to fumble in a leather pouch. He pulled out several pieces of paper and looked them over. Occasionally he would look up to be sure he was following the conversation between Tony and Blackmore. The next few days under a hot sun promised a long hard trip ahead, and he was anxious to get going.

"After I take this man to Star Fort, they're shipping me to the West Indies to get out of all this mess," Blackmore said. "Folks around here know that." Tony's big smile grew even bigger as he collected a new fact.

"I don't know why I told you that." Blackmore shook his head and looked more quizzically at Tony. "You can get milk from a toad. More like a hound that keeps his head still before he snaps at a fly buzzing around his head. That's the way you find out what's going on, isn't it? You snap up what's buzzing all around you." He laughed and chomped his teeth a few times, fully captured by Tony's charm.

"And, yes, you can come along, Tony Small, if you can keep up and keep quiet. I know that'll be as much a hardship for you as the road itself. In fact, I want you to come with us. A man of mixed race gives us more cover." Tony nodded at that. "We're on a very fast pace, though. I'll drop off when I deliver you and this white man to Star Fort—don't ask questions about his name or mission. And don't talk to him or me. You've got to stay at Star Fort, if I can get you both inside. It's going to be tricky."

"How are you going to get around Sumter blocking Ninety Six?"

"Good gracious alive, boy, didn't I just tell you not to ask questions? And be very quiet all the way up there. It's a long haul. We won't always be on the road, but it won't be that far from where we are now. How did you catch up with us, anyhow?"

"Came down to the Orangeburg Road here. I heard it went on to Ninety Six." The Black Pioneer just shook his head again as the three pressed on toward Fort Star at Ninety Six.

General Nathanael Greene, commander of the American army in the South, took up a position northeast of Star Fort which lay nearby to the east of the village of Ninety Six. Dick Pickens, better known as Old Dick, arrived with General Andrew Pickens in support of Greene. Andrew Ferguson Jr., arrived with Lieutenant Colonel Henry "Light Horse Harry" Lee. Each black veteran made a powerful impression, one that a raw patriot recruit instinctively recognized as that of a survivor. Old Dick was the older of the two, Ferguson the more experienced. Just looking at them, a young soldier could tell that not much could scare or surprise them. Whenever something even minor occurred, young black troops first looked at Old Dick or Ferguson before they looked at white officers.

It was a clear morning. Bird calls gave away to other sounds to mark a fresh sense of new beginnings in the middle of a series of long days for all arriving patriots. A few critters like rabbits, possums, and coons were still around, the kind that were the last to clear out before trouble starts. Old Dick was sitting on a stump, whittling on a pine stick with his long knife which he always carried. Both he and Ferguson were off to themselves, taking it easy in a little copse of trees. After a while Old Dick threw the stick down and looked around for a piece of oak or cedar worthy of his time. Suddenly he put away his knife and jumped up.

"Don't like to sit down for long. A man gets used to it and wants to do it more and more." He straightened the leather sheathe of his long knife. Ferguson could tell Dick was going to tell another "interesting" story.

Old Dick raised his voice to a few young soldiers nearby. "I'll tell you an interesting story. After the smoke cleared at Cowpens—where Morgan whipped Bastard Tarleton—I went onto the battlefield to look around for whatever I could find." Ferguson had heard this one several times, with more than a few variations, but the young troops had not and began to gather closer to Old Dick. Listening to the war stories of combat veterans was as critical for survival as watching them react in battle. Old Dick didn't talk a lot, so when he did, he expected to be listened to and respected. He ignored a rabbit that burst out from under a sapling and thick brush.

"Dead and dying Redcoats everywhere. This was before they came back to get 'em to bury. Well, they were usually well dressed and pretty well equipped, too, and I sure needed clothes, especially some good boots. No red coat, though." That drew a laugh from other young troops who, to show they were as responsive as the initial group, quickly found a place among the copse of trees. "And you got no 'X marks the spot' white straps across your chest to be aimed at. It's like having a gun sight on your barrel." That drew enough of a laugh for Old Dick to look over at Ferguson and nod.

"I found a young British officer badly beat up leaning against a tree. He was dressed real fine and wore a pair of nice leather boots." Old Dick went over to a young soldier leaning against a tree and began to play out his narrative to everyone's delight. "Well, when I started to take 'em off," he said, jerking on one of the young soldier's boots, "thinking he was dead or ought to be, the man said, 'Surely, my good man, you will not take them before I die.'

"Well, I jumped back, took a-holt of my knife and told him plain, 'They look mighty nice on you, but the general needs 'em, too.'

"'Bring me a little water before I die, and then you can take the boots,' he told me, seeing that he was about near gone anyway, and I didn't have to kill him." Old Dick stared in a mean way at the young soldier and jabbed the air with his knife. The young soldier smiled weakly. Everyone else laughed. "Well, I went over and filled up his hat with water from a stream and gave it to him. He drank most of it and died. Boots fit the general just fine."

The troops, including the young soldier who served as Old Dick's prop, clapped, somewhat relieved that the show was over and content that the old veteran shared one of his best war stories. But nobody in the group thought that the boots made it all the way to the general, an easy confirmation to make when they looked down at the ones Old Dick was wearing.

About an hour later, Old Dick came up beside Ferguson and whispered in his ear, "Seems like we got us a different kind of problem. I just caught a young black fellow trying to hoard a couple of rifles he snatched from some of Colonel Lee's wounded boys. I grabbed 'em as soon as I got suspicious and realized he wasn't going to use 'em to shoot with. He just wanted 'em to keep."

"What are you talking about, Dick? To keep? You ain't talking sense. What young fellow is fool enough just to be here and not be in this fight?"

"Not so loud. He snuck away before I could get a-holt of him, but I think he was up to mischief. He told me he needed those guns back in Charleston for an insurrection, or something like that he's planning. An uprising, he said. Trusted me not to tell any white man."

"Insurrection? Good gracious, Dick." Ferguson grabbed him by his shirt collar and twisted it into a ball. "Keep your own voice down. I hope you shot him on the spot yourself."

"I know. I should've." He pulled back and straightened his shirt. "Nothing can get us all in a real serious mess quicker than if that rascal is found out. We got to keep this to ourselves and shoot that idiot if we see him again. Say absolutely nothing to nobody. Nobody. I mean nobody and I mean nothing. Not even Aaron who's a real nobody. They'll hang us all if we get stuck in the middle of this. I hope that fellow doesn't get caught by *either* side before we get to him. Say he's a spy."

"All you men loyal to the king," Lazarus Jones yelled inside Star Fort, "Colonel Cruger ordered us to dig a trench from inside the walls to the spring. So come on, Ned, let's get to digging. Everybody's got to help because we got to have water to drink and put out fires."

"All right, all right, I'm coming, but life was a whole lot better when I was just a guide for Captain George Martin." A large muscular man with sleepy eyes even in strenuous circumstances, Ned Zanger was especially useful to the British as a guide. Now he found himself pressed into service as a loyalist Black Pioneer to build defenses.

"Don't gripe. I sure wish I still had my team and wagon with the Little River Loyalists Militia Regiment, too, but that ain't now for either one of us."

After making a few bad guesses, they finally found a good spot from inside the walls that was nearest the spring. They began digging under the parapet. The hot sticky mid-June afternoon made physical exertion almost impossible. Once outside, they dug directly toward the spring. The stifling humidity took its toll. More than one or two pick axes slipped out of sweating hands and went flying in the air like chunks of enemy artillery.

"This still ain't working," Zanger said, shirtless, trousers soaking wet. He wiped his face with his wrist. "After digging and setting up this trench, they're still firing at us from their tower the minute they see us pop up. We can't get through their hail of balls. They see us peak around the end of the trench and fire every time we try to run and draw a little water from the spring. I bet they're having a real good time of it."

"The colonel knows that," Lazarus Jones replied. "He's already come up with a new plan to outsmart those rebs. We're not going to be digging anymore—just sneaking out at night now."

"The colonel's new plan is simple," a loyalist officer said as he walked into the conversation. He looked like he enjoyed giving orders more than following them. He spoke in a vulgar way as if to reward the few who accepted his authority. He directly addressed several of the black men without calling them by name.

"Black folks to do everything at night. Some of y'all have to go out there all the way to the spring, beyond the trench, and bring back water. Without water, we can't last more than three days." He paused and looked around. "Do I have any volunteers?"

About that time, they heard a lot of yelling and cheers coming from the parapet of the fort.

"What's all the laughing and whooping about?" Zanger asked. "Volunteer, smellinrear," Zanger muttered under his breath. "Let's get up on the parapet to see."

A dozen or so loyalists were yelling encouragement to a black man and a white man running for their lives toward the gate about fifty yards away. No patriots were giving pursuit, but some were taking aim.

"Hurry the hell up," Tony Small yelled to the white man several yards behind him. He was older and couldn't keep up. "The rebs will shoot you if you're too slow, and Brits will shoot you if you're too fast. Wave that white handkerchief."

"Seems like one of our boys pulled a trick on rebel pickets guarding our perimeter," a voice yelled out over the parapet. "I bet he's a messenger from Rawdon. Looks like he's got a young black fellow with him, and they just got through the rebel lines. Good gracious!"

After the two scurried inside the gate, which was quickly opened and shut, someone shouted, "The white messenger passed himself off as a country bumpkin, and the young black fellow with him as somebody he needed so he could find his way around." Shouts of congratulations and laughter rang out.

"As soon as they got close to the fort, he and the young black fellow took off for the gate like scalded dogs. They left the rebels just standing there, dumbstruck at how they'd been tricked."

Everybody roared laughing again, loud enough for the embarrassed rebels to hear them. Zanger waived over the parapet and yelled out, "Anymore of our boys with you out there? Just send 'em on while you take your afternoon naps." More laughter. A shot rang out that barely missed him.

"He's got word from Rawdon?" Lazarus Jones asked in the kind of voice he normally used only when he was rowdy and drunk. "So, I bet he'll be here any day now."

Tony Small introduced himself to the black Tories surrounding him. Colonel Cruger and other Tory officers were busy questioning the white man who arrived with him. Tony confirmed that Rawdon was indeed on his way. Jones and Zanger were among those who rushed to shake his hand.

"We got a real live hero here with us, boys," Lazarus Jones said and slapped Tony hard on the back.

"Don't know 'bout that. How y'all doing? Who's winning?"

⸻❖⸻

A loyalist officer interrupted and turned their attention back to the job at hand. "We won't be digging anymore. Instead, I want volunteers among you Black Pioneers, especially some of y'all who are real dark skinned, to strip down naked to go out through the main gate tonight and bring back water for drinking and putting out those flaming arrows shot by the rebs from their tower. But you're not going to be walking out like you was on a Sunday stroll. You got to lay low and be dead quiet. And get naked."

"Naked?" Pompey Grant burst out. "Naked? Why naked? I'll do it, but I'm not getting naked." Grant was always the one who the Black Pioneers could count on to say out loud what everyone else was reluctant to say. He was smaller than most but had scars from battle, and bruises from scuffles with other loyalists under Captain George Kerr in DeLancey's Brigade. Kerr gave him a lot of slack.

"'Why?' hell. So they can't see you, of course," Zanger said. "They can't see you in the dark if you're naked. Just don't smile. And keep your eyes closed." More guffaws and laughter, especially from the white officer.

"Sounds like something only a planter would say," Grant mumbled. "Makes the same damn kind of sense to tell a white man to go in daylight so they can't see *him*. Don't the sun and moon shine the same on all of us?"

"You blacks who serve the crown as guides and pioneers know how to get around the enemy ranks at night," the officer continued. "You're smart and you know the land, but this is a little more difficult. They're right there looking down on you from their tower, and some are sentries on the ground, too. You can't be wearing clothes that reflect any light."

"Volunteers? You want volunteers?" Grant asked loudly. "Then I volunteer this here fellow Tony Small. He's the perfect man for the job. He's used to slipping by rebs. He'll just have to put some mud on his high-toned skin—that'll make him as good as the rest of us."

Tony joined in the laughter. "Well, I'll strip down and get naked for King George, but I'll put on the mud myself." He was, for the moment, going to be a naked muddy loyalist. What would he tell Miss Maggie?

Pompey Grant, Ned Zanger, Lazarus Jones, and two other Black Pioneers stripped down and waited for Tony.

"You got a woman, Tony?" Grant asked.

"Sure do, and she's a whole lot prettier than you. Why are you thinkin' about that now?"

"That goes without saying," one of the Black Pioneers said.

"Be sure to take your bucket," Jones said. "Now, who's first through the gate?"

"Follow me," Grant said. "Be dead quiet."

At the rear of the column, Tony kept bumping his metal bucket into the abatis as he and the others negotiated their way to the spring.

"Small," Zanger whispered, "be quiet, damn it." Back and forth they went, completely unspotted, but not without Tony becoming a target of another kind.

On their final trip back to the gate, a faint shadow in the moon light of a rebel sentry appeared only a few feet from Tony.

"I'm seeing things," the rebel sentry said. "Been on duty too long and seeing all kinds of things. Got to relieve myself. I swear I keep seeing a bunch of dark shapes and sizes that look like naked guys in a daisy chain going back and forth to the spring." He stepped farther out and peed close enough to splatter Tony with piss.

"Yep," said the other sentry, "probably just a bunch of wild hogs. It's time for you to rest those eyes."

Loyalists! British sympathizers! I'm finally in the middle of this war. Not sure which side to be on yet, but I'll get to see first-hand what's going on. Cuffy would be envious to see me now, standing right here with these Tories. Ruth, too. But I won't tell Miss Maggie. Maybe I'll tell everybody, depending on who wins this thing and what more freedom I can get. I don't reckon we'll ever get all of it, though, least not in my lifetime. Regular British army soldiers on their way to help. I got to stay alert and watch for anything. Anything can happen, I know. If getting naked with a bunch of sneaky loyalists and pissed on by a reb is the first thing I do for freedom, it's a strange way to get it, but I'll take it as a start.

Loyalist William Cooper looked over the ramparts of Star Fort at noon the next day, 18 June 1781, and could tell that something big was about to happen. Tony Small stood by his side, looking out at a new countryside.

For Tony the midlands lacked the solitude of the Lowcountry. The beauty of marsh lands and inland rivers wasn't there. The birds were different. Critters weren't quite the same, and there were no alligators. Without his moorings in a landscape and wildlife he was used to, he didn't have the luxury of thinking about just one or two things at a time. Now he had to deal with lots of new things all at once, new issues that came with the land itself as well as with the situation at hand. To relieve the stress, he kept an eye out for any kind of weeds or flowers he didn't have at Miss Maggie's so he could take them home when he left.

"The rebels are going to make an assault," Cooper told Tony. "I can see what's coming." A veteran cavalryman with Light Horse Dragoons under Lieutenant Colonel Welbore Ellis Doyle, Cooper slowly shook his head. "Such a waste. This'll be just like Camden. We'll slaughter 'em."

Standing on the parapet not far from Cooper and Tony, Lazarus Jones and Ned Zanger also watched carefully as rebel Black Pioneers and infantrymen on the American side approached the fort as point men in the patriots' assault.

"They'll never make it," Zanger said. "I've got too much experience to give 'em much of a chance against us. Cruger's too stubborn to let us surrender, anyway. We'll just wipe 'em clean as a baby's bottom."

Cooper heard Zanger, laughed and added, "Whether the rebs are coming from one side or the other, they still have to get through the abatis and over our parapet. And they'll never do that before those Irish boys with Rawdon coming up from Charleston get here to help us."

"I don't know about that," Zanger said as he shook his head and just stared at what was happening. "Greene's going to start his artillery any minute now. We can all see rebel officers over there on the right wing getting ready in the third angle of the trench closest to us, and others are getting ready to come straight through the stockade right into the village. They got white rebels perched on the tower and rebel Black Pioneers ready as point men in the infantry. This doesn't look good to me no matter who's coming to help us."

For the first time ever, I'm going to see men come at me with guns and hooks and swords, and they think I'm their enemy. I guess they're mine, too. Real strange to get swept up so easy in this white man's war. Hard looks on both sides. I got to mean to live now. But you can switch some of us and you'd have the same thing happening. Black or white. Just switch a dozen or so from one side to the other and they probably wouldn't know if or when they've been switched. 'Let's sit down and talk about it and call it off. Nobody gets killed.' But who gets the land and who gets to tell who what to do after that? In peace all you think about is dying, and in war all you think about is living. I can hear the screaming already.

Within clear view of loyalists on the parapet, patriot Thomas Carney sprang out of the trench with other rebel Black Pioneers and infantry and ran toward the abatis. "Follow me." A free man from Maryland, Carney was conspicuous for his bravery at the Battle of Guilford Courthouse in March 1781 when he bayoneted seven British soldiers. Now at Ninety Six, Carney found himself leading another attack. "Follow me. You—Evans Archer, Aaron Spelman—go now. Now. You boys got duties of a soldier, just like white folks. Go." The rebel Black Pioneer and infantryman right behind Carney was David Wilson from Maryland, another seasoned veteran who fought at Camden, Guilford Courthouse, and Hobkirk's Hill.

Patriot officers issued grappling hooks and ordered the American assault troops to pull down enough sandbags at critical places along the parapet to allow them to climb over and breach the fortress.

"Get as high as you can in the ditch and grab the bags from the parapets," Wilson yelled as soon as several of the infantrymen cut through a section of the protective abatis around the walls of the fort.

"This ain't working, it just ain't working," Aaron Spelman cried out. "As soon as we make it past the stakes, and get through the fraise, they train their rifles and muskets on us."

Tony realized that he had to do something more than just stand there beside Cooper and watch the action. He left to get a dozen or so sand bags and stack them in position. He helped with water buckets to douse flames on the shingles. During the chaos, none of the loyalist defenders realized that Tony Small did not take up arms against the Americans.

The carnage was horrific. Young men and boys, blown apart by loyalist rifles and muskets. Each time the smoke cleared enough to see what was happening, a fresh look of the dead came into view, the smoke serving as a curtain opening and closing again and again in successive dramatic scenes. A patriot rushing toward the wall to hook a sandbag impaled himself on the abatis.

"The fool is stuck," a loyalist yelled out. "Can't retreat and can't advance."

"Shoot the bastard, a varmint in a trap," another loyalist replied, and several volleys ripped the man apart.

"This is like shooting fish in a barrel," Pompey Grant hollered to Ned Zanger as Cruger's loyalists inside the fort began to pick off one American after another. He took aim at Spelman but missed. "Damn! I like to shoot blacks more than whites."

I'll go with it all. All these other black men on both sides and none of us really knowing how freedom is going to show its smiley face on one side or the other, freedom sticking its head up and ducking down real quick before it gets shot off. Or stuck on an abatis. Right now that's the last thing I need to worry about.

Tony hurried back to William Cooper. A black rebel hooked two of the sandbags, jerked them down, and began to climb over the parapet. Cooper rushed him, and the two black men, patriot and loyalist, became entangled in ferocious hand-to-hand combat. Tony froze. In their struggle, both men fell off the parapet and into the ditch outside the wall without being shot or bayoneted. They continued to wrestle as other Americans gathered around. Each combatant had enormous big shoulders and powerful arms that made them look like twins.

By this time, withering fire was too intense and sandbags were too snuggly placed to allow the high parapet to be breached. Taking a prisoner was all the rebels could do. Cooper yelled at the black rebel who eventually got the upper hand. "Hold on. Take me as your prisoner. I'm done. But why in God's name are you fighting against your own freedom? I'm already free, but you poor patriot bastards have nothing to gain fighting for white folks who want to keep you in chains. Are you crazy? What's your name? 'Stupid'?"

"David Wilson. And you're a prisoner of people fighting for freedom."

"That makes no sense, Stupid. England proclaimed all black people free now. It's written down, notices nailed on every tree and wall. You must not know that. Do you know that?"

At first Wilson ignored Cooper's question, then, curiously willing to continue political discourse in the middle of battle, said, "Those British proclamations aren't worth the paper they're written on. That's what you don't know. You don't know that your so-called British and loyalist friends would just as soon sell you to somebody here or in Georgia or to somebody in the West Indies or East Florida as look at you. They're worse than rebels with enslaved folks. You're the stupid one."

"That ain't true," Cooper shouted and dug his heals into the soft pock-marked ground to stop Wilson from dragging him to the rear. "Black folks are running away all the time—thousands of 'em—have been for a long time even before all the proclamations. Once they get to British lines, they're free. And their children are free when they're born behind British lines."

"My Maryland's my home," Wilson shot back and yanked him harder by the arm. Another rebel grabbed him by the other arm. "My chances of getting freedom are same as yours. Same as with the British. We're on our own. All freedom ain't the same. It's going to be bits and pieces we get, but that's better than your chains. I have to hold out hope that I'll be given lots of freedom if I help fight for Maryland and this new land of ours."

"'Hope'? 'Ours'?" Cooper scoffed.

"Ours!" Wilson replied firmly. "It'll all come some day."

Wilson and Cooper continued to yell at each other over the sound of shots fired from all directions. Shouts of retreat came from the rebel side. Greene's tactics were now doomed to fail—the siege by trenches, by construction of a tower, and by denying water to the besieged.

Suddenly a black patriot jumped out from a trench and ran zig-zag toward another man lying on the ground—a man running in the line of fire to save a comrade.

Black patriot Thomas Carney, the same man who with Wilson led the patriot assault, cried out, "He's been hit. He'll bleed to death." Carney rushed to his friend and master under withering fire, then single-handedly dragged the captain to safety, while dodging loyalist rifle balls whistling in the air and hitting the ground all around him with a familiar thud.

Now I see the patriots are men of great courage, enough to see this whole thing through. I know there's courage on both sides, but an enslaved black man just risked his life to save his white friend and master—and for what reason? Maybe for freedom. Maybe for devotion. I'd do the same for Miss Maggie.

Several runaways in 1779 from William Maxwell's plantations near Charleston were working on Gadsden's Wharf on 3 June 1781. The sultry heat and humidity were doing their worst. The promise of rain remained just a promise, and each labored under the usual practice of seldom looking up. But what was unfolding caught their eye. "Look at those boys staggering off all those ships," Dublin, a big dark man, said. He put down his load, laughed and shouted out to his friend Johnny as the Irish soldiers gradually eased down the gang plank onto the wharf after twelve weeks at sea. Johnny, who was about the same age as most of the troops disembarking, barely looked up. "All those ships and soldiers mean nothing to me. Don't help with my work."

"They look drunk to me," Bella added and joined in the laughter. "They look like they're nursing each plank by plank down the ramp like they do bottle by bottle. I've seen you two look like that many a time." Because she was a very attractive unmarried woman, Bella enjoyed the privilege of free and open criticism of men her age—except those who had no chance with her.

Johnny lifted his head and smirked. "You don't know anything, Bella."

"Well, they can't shoot straight now, that's for sure," a younger, light complexioned man named Billy said. "Like ole man Maxwell. But since I hear those muskets they use seldom hit the target, maybe a little sea sickness might help to straighten up their aim." Pretty soon everyone working on the dock began to comment on what was happening, important enough to excuse a short break from hard work.

"Well, *you* can't shoot at all, Billy," Cain said as he looked up from loading timber to get a good look at the Irish troops. "Nobody's going to let you get near a gun, that's for sure." Cain stood up straight and acted like he had a rifle aimed at Billy who waived him off and spit in his direction.

"He could if they would let him—we all could," Abraham, the oldest of the group, said. "Now best we get back to work before somebody gets into trouble. Billy, you're in bad enough trouble as it is."

Leah, another attractive young woman not yet sullied by heavy labor, glanced over at Bella with a smile on her face, as if to ask permission to have the last word. Her neat and clean appearance belied the fact of her willingness to participate in the hardest and dirtiest tasks. She looked at heavy loads of matériel as they came off other ships and shook her head. "Our boys don't get that drunk. Drunk, but not that drunk. Wonder where they're headed? Ain't any fighting here left to do."

Colonel Lord Francis Rawdon issued orders for immediate deployment of the fresh troops he had been waiting for. A man of average height and weight,

Rawdon nonetheless presented an image of classic commanding authority by his erect military posture and strong voice with an Irish accent.

"We shall take only your flank battalion," he told Major John Majoribanks, who now had to put his cavalryman's sea-legs on horseback. "We shall march immediately to Ninety Six and cannot be detained by slower hat companies. Hat companies, under Lieutenant Colonel Coates, will proceed to our garrison at Moncks Corner to await further orders.

"A short distance from Charleston, at Four Hole Swamp, we'll meet Colonel Doyle and the Volunteers of Ireland, Colonel Watson and his Provincial Light Infantry, and Major McArthur and his troops of Volunteers. I should think a good number of loyalist militia from the Camden district will meet up with the brunt of our troops garrisoned at Moncks Corner, nearly two thousand, with cavalry. The rebel Quaker General Greene won't know what hit him, if he's not already quaking in his boots." Majoribanks politely smiled at the pun.

Lord Rawdon's headquarters were in one of Charleston's largest houses on Meeting Street. A sweet odor of tea olive filled the air as the eighteen-year-old Irish lieutenant walked along the street en route to report for duty. Lord Edward Fitzgerald took a deep breath to get the full effect of one of the new world's favorite odors, ubiquitous in Charleston, and almost strong enough to prevail over the odor of horse manure throughout the town. Flowers and shrubbery in gardens grew along single houses that extended far back from the street with piazzas overlooking the gardens. Cobblestone streets made from ballast used on voyages to the colony ran out into dirt streets with deep ruts.

British headquarters had a broad front façade which faced the street and was not built with a narrow front façade common to single houses. Single houses made after a Barbados design captured the breeze on their extended side piazzas and, dear to the money-minded Charlestonians, reduced taxes levied according to the footage facing the street. Lord Edward walked up the circular staircase to the second floor to Majoribanks' temporary office. Majoribanks looked at his fellow officer of the 19th Regiment of Foot standing at attention in front of him.

"At ease," he said and looked hard at the young man with whom he shared officers' quarters during passage from Ireland. The major stood behind a large mahogany desk and continued to read from an open file. Without looking up he said, "You are not yet nineteen years old, and you have been only recently commissioned. You have been in this regiment only since February, a month before we sailed from Ireland. Now you find yourself in one of our regiment's flank companies."

After continuing to read from the file, he looked up and asked, "Are you in fact so eager for battle that you are prepared for an immediate forced march of two hundred miles?"

"Yes, sir, indeed," Lieutenant Lord Edward Fitzgerald quickly replied in a clear strong voice. "To serve the king, sir. My greatest desire is to distinguish myself as an officer, giving an example to kin and country of my courage and leadership."

Majoribanks smiled at the bold, but not officious, reply of the young lieutenant. He took more time looking over other documents laid out before him, as if they all pertained to Lord Edward. He calmly read from one paper and again looked up at the young lieutenant without saying a work, then returned to read more. This went on three or four times without a word from either man. All Lord Edward could hear was the noise through an open window of horses and wagons passing and a crow offering commentary on the proceedings within.

Majoribanks saw much of his own youth in Lord Edward. He, too, sought fame and glory in the army. He, too, took a commission when about the same age, and he, too, wished above all to prove his valor for king and country. Eventually he spoke.

"It will be an arduous two weeks of forced march."

"I am happy to serve the regiment in the most difficult and urgent of circumstances."

"You are at ease, lieutenant. No need to be so formal now. You and I will see a great deal of action from these rebels. We will be working closely together, along with a few other lieutenants in the flank battalion."

At that, the crow which was annoying both men grew even more raucous. Majoribanks grabbed something that served as a paper weight, went over to the window and threw it at the crow. "Get the hell out of here, you rebel." Turning to Lord Edward and having the laugh he suppressed earlier when talking to the young lieutenant, he said, "There're rebels everywhere, even if they do say Charleston is a Tory town."

After Majoribanks dismissed him, Lord Edward reported immediately to Rawdon. Colonel Lord Francis Rawdon was now second in field command of the Southern Department under Colonel Nesbit Balfour, commander of the British garrison in Charleston. If Majoribanks did not know or care much about the family connections of Lieutenant Lord Edward Fitzgerald, Rawdon certainly did.

After Lord Edward was announced to Lord Rawdon, the colonel returned his salute and bid him be at ease. Like Majoribanks earlier, Rawdon scanned several documents on his desk, looked up and said, "You must know that I think highly of your older brother William, 2nd Duke of Leinster. I am given a favorable report of you through my adjutant-general, Lieutenant Colonel Welbore Ellis Doyle, and I as an Irishman myself am familiar with the illustrious history of your ducal families of Leinster and Richmond." He paused to turn back to documents on his desk. Lord Edward could feel that this was going to be a different kind of report from the one made to Majoribanks and wished for another raucous crow outside the window to divert the colonel's close inspection of his family. Rawdon pulled a page from one of the stacks of paper and looked up again at the young lieutenant. "Where," he asked, "is your place of birth, Lord Edward?"

"Carton House, County Kildare, sir." Lord Edward rattled on to be courteous enough to spill it all out without waiting for direct questions. "I am the fifth son and twelfth child of Lieutenant General James Fitzgerald, 1st Duke of Leinster and 20th Earl of Kildare," Lord Edward replied without any tone of arrogance, but just as a matter of fact. Sensing that his commander's silence meant for him to continue even further, Lord Edward said, "My mother, the Duchess of Leinster, Lady Emily Mary Lennox, was the daughter of the 2nd Duke of Richmond." He hesitated. "The first being the illegitimate son of Charles II."

"And, of course," Lord Rawdon politely added, "through your mother, albeit along an illegitimate line, as fate would have it, she being third in descent from King Charles II. Furthermore, on that note, the fact that Charles Town is named for your lusty royal ancestor does not escape me." With that light touch, both men laughed, putting Lord Edward somewhat at ease but still mindful of the reputation of his superior.

"Lord Edward," Rawdon asked, "What are you doing over here—seeking fame like so many of us? Trying to impress an equally high-born lady who may forgive your penury and marry you?" Lord Edward took that as a light note, but he was wrong.

Lord Rawdon continued in a formal tone of voice. "We are both firmly established in Ascendancy political and military life. I was at the Battles of Lexington and Concord and Bunker Hill, and I count myself fortunate to be alive. One may, however, achieve fame by political means in London and Dublin, where there are no rebel rifles and cannon balls and bayonets."

Then in almost a fatherly tone, as if he wanted to make up for the well-known distance Lord Edward's real father kept between himself and his young son, Rawdon continued.

"I understand that you are despondent over various love affairs." Rawdon pressed his lips together, rubbed his temple and began to nod his head slightly to signal that a limited confession was not out of line.

Before Lord Edward could reply, however, Rawdon continued. "You have powerful social and political connections through your mother's brother Charles Lennox, the 3rd Duke of Richmond, 3rd Duke of Lennox, and 3rd Duke of Aubigny. You must be aware that not many years ago, in 1766 to be exact, he was secretary of state for the Southern Department which included the American colonies. He is an exceptional man. Charles Lennox took the side of the American colonies in Parliamentary debates. Three years ago he even called for removal of troops from the Americas, and he ostentatiously—very ostentatiously—sailed his private yacht through the British fleet in the Solent with what passed for an American flag flapping in the breeze." The senior officer paused enough in his lecture to let Lord Edward know that he may speak. This was rougher sailing than Lord Edward anticipated.

"Lord Rawdon, sir, those are actions of my kin, not mine. I am loyal to the king, as I trust all my kinsmen are, in spite of particular actions taken."

"You are a young Irishman in his late teens," Rawdon continued, dismissing Lord Edward's pledge of allegiance to George III for himself and his family. Instead, he continued what Lord Edward took as a strong lecture that was somehow going to be relevant to Lord Edward's new duties.

"Your pedigree is also political. Your aunt, Lady Caroline Lennox, married Henry Fox, 1st Baron Holland, who under King George II was Secretary for War, Paymaster for the Forces, and in 1755 and 1756 the Secretary of State for the Southern Department. Your political pedigree is remarkable on that count alone, but it continues."

Lord Edward tried to remain at ease, as ordered, but he unconsciously braced in apprehension of what would come next. He glanced out the window, searching for a crow, a gesture that Rawdon saw and met with an amused smile. Rawdon knew as much as he did about his own family.

"I'm especially curious about your first cousin Charles James Fox, son of Henry," Lord Rawdon said. "Charles James Fox is, as you know, an arch rival within the Whig Party of William Pitt the Younger—a man who hopes soon to become Prime Minister.

"Your dear cousin Charles Fox opposes the conduct of the war by George, Lord Germain, and the king's colonial policies as espoused by Francis, Lord North, our Prime Minister. To that extent, like your uncle Charles Lennox, he opposes our efforts here.

"But enough of all this," Rawdon said finally, and allowing just the right amount of silence and looks to take hold, quietly chuckled to himself to let Lord Edward know the necessary litany was over. All apples were shaken from the family tree, and the task at hand for both men now was to hasten relief of Star Fort at Ninety Six.

"Stand at ease, lieutenant. I want you to be my aide-de-camp."

With a hundred and fifty horse and a thousand eight hundred foot soldiers, Colonel Lord Rawdon's column advanced toward Ninety Six. Lord Edward quickly distinguished himself as an eager young officer capable of bold if irrational decisions. On their approach to Ninety Six, an adjunct to Rawdon reported what he saw:

> "It was, indeed, supposed that the American general was not a little influenced in his movements by the intelligence which he had received, that the newly arrived troops were 'particularly full of ardour for an opportunity of signalising themselves.'
>
> "That Lord Edward was among these impatient candidates for distinction can little be doubted; and it was but a short time after their joining he had the good fortune to achieve a service which was not only brilliant but useful, and brought him both honour and reward."
>
> Advancing toward Ninety Six, Lord Edward
>
> "[E]xhibited—or rather was detected in—a trait of personal courage, of that purely adventurous kind found but in romance."

The younger brother of Major John Doyle who was also in the Irish Volunteers, Lieutenant Colonel Welbore Ellis Doyle, Rawdon's senior aide-de-camp, observed his younger colleague Lord Edward in a more-lengthy report to his commander:

> "Among the varied duties that evolved upon me as chief of staff, a most material one was of obtaining intelligence. This was effected partly by the employment of intelligence spies in various directions, and partly by *reconnaissciences*; which last were not devoid of danger, from the superior knowledge of the country possessed by the enemy. Upon these occasions I constantly found Lord Edward by my side, with permission of our noble chief Lord Rawdon who wished our young friend to see everything connected to real service. In fact, the danger enhanced the value of the enterprise in the eyes of this brave young creature. In approaching the position of Ninety Six, the enemy's light troops in advance became more numerous, and rendered more frequent patrols necessary upon our part.
>
> "I was setting out upon a patrol and sent to appraise Lord Edward; but he was nowhere to be found, and I proceeded without him, when, at the end of two miles upon emerging from the forest, I found him

engaged with *two* of the enemy's irregular horse. He had wounded one of his opponents when his sword broke in the middle, and he must have soon fallen in the unequal contest, had not the enemies fled upon perceiving the head of my column. I rated him most soundly, as you can imagine, for the undisciplined act of leaving the camp at such a critical time without Colonel Rawdon's permission. He was—or pretended to be—very penitent, and compounded for my reporting him at the head-quarters, provided I would let him accompany him, in the hope of some other enterprise. It was impossible to refuse the fellow, whose frank, manly, and ingenuous manner would have won over even a greater tyrant than myself. In the course of the day we took some prisoners which I made him convey to head-quarters with a *Bellerophon* message, which he fairly delivered. Lord Rawdon gravely rebuked him, but I could never find that he lost much ground with his chief for his *chivalrous valour*."

No one was happier to see the arrival of Rawdon than black loyalists, but the assault was over by the time he arrived. Greene, including patriot David Wilson and his loyalist prisoner William Cooper, already skedaddled to fight another day, but the patriots—"these half-savage people of Carolina"—left many casualties in their wake. For exhausted defenders of Star Fort, Rawdon's decision to pursue Greene was a decision a leader makes to show that he has to do something, even if futile.

"Good gracious alive," Lazarus Jones said to Ned Zanger. "Now we're supposed to high tail it and chase after rebs who got a two-day head start? Rawdon just got here, and he's already leaving. And we're going with him. It's a stupid thing to be doing." Jones kicked a nearby bench, shattering it into pieces. Tony Small took no position on the matter. He remained quiet, knowing that he would not go with Rawdon, not this time at least.

"I know it as well as you, Lazarus," Zanger said, "and Rawdon knows it, too, and he's even dividing his army to catch 'em. He's taking Majoribanks' foot soldiers and cavalry toward the Broad and Saluda, east of Friday's Ferry on the Congaree. That's what I hear. I've been there with wagons and it's a real trek in this heat, believe me. Either that, or they're heading toward the south bank of the Broad River, or even farther. The sun's going to be beating down on everybody, no matter which way they're going."

Pompey Grant joined them and looked down at the shattered bench that he was accustomed to sit on. Shaking his head in disgust, he said, "That young Irish lieutenant, Rawdon's new aide-de-camp, is leading the way like he's in charge of the whole damn operation. Everybody seems to like him, though. But if he catches up with Greene's rear guard of Lee's Legions and Captain Robert Kirkwood's Delaware Company, he'll be trying to bite a dog he wished he hadn't chased.

"You don't always want to catch what you're chasing. Everybody's too whupped to fight in this heat, anyway." He looked over at Lazarus Jones. "I sure could use a nice place to sit down."

"We'll get no farther than Friday's Ferry," Zanger said. "Chasing after those rebs is as stupid as the rebels trying to dig ditches in our front yard. This whole war is full of stupid."

"Greene knows not to fight in this heat," Lazarus Jones said. "He'll be cooling his heels in the High Hills and getting scouting reports of how we're dropping like flies."

"We'll give up the chase and turn south toward Orangeburg before too long, don't worry," Zanger added. "Those Irish troops have been marching for over a month. I hear fifty died from the heat already. What does it take to get 'em not to dress in wool in the summer and wear red? And not put cross-strap targets on their chests? Yep, this war is full of stupid."

After the siege and assault was ceased at Star Fort and Greene withdrew, Cuffy stayed busy now that he no longer feared Old Dick and Ferguson who withdrew with Greene's army, leaving Cruger and loyalists behind. He never saw Tony and did not even know Tony made it to Ninety Six.

"All this mess from Greene taking off and Rawdon taking off after him so quick is just right for us," Cuffy told a half dozen black men about a hundred yards from the fort. "We can snatch muskets in all this going and coming. And we'll follow Cruger when he marches out, too. Don't bother with Greene's men. They're going too fast. We got a battle of our own out there, don't forget. Get rifles, too, if you see 'em, and paper, gun powder, balls, flint, rods, here and everywhere along the way. Steal 'em in broad daylight, if you have to. They'll be too tired to chase you far.

"There ought to be plenty of guns lying around after all this fighting, but so far I don't see much more than burning buildings, dead bodies, and folks getting ready to leave. Go through everything. Pick the pockets of the dead and almost dead. Be careful. Say nothing, and let's follow Cruger to Orangeburg."

On his own, Cuffy walked toward the fort and began his usual manner of hanging close to loyalist troops. Eventually, he got too close.

"Get the hell out of here before some white man sees us talking to you, boy," a Black Pioneer yelled at Cuffy. "You don't know what you're doing, do you? Well, you're slap dab on the edge of pain, boy. I hear tell what you're up to, trying to start a black uprising. We'll be free after all this, anyway. We're even free now. By proclamation. Now get, and don't touch a single piece!"

Before Cuffy could back away, a shot rang out. Cuffy looked where the sound came from and saw another Black Pioneer loading his rifle for another shot. "You're better dead than doing what you're up to," the Black Pioneer shouted.

Cuffy took off in a zig-zag kind of way trying to dodge a bullet coming his way. The second shot missed. When he thought he was out of range, he started dancing and laughing and acting like he had a rifle aimed back at the Black Pioneers. The first Black Pioneer calmly loaded again and took careful aim. Cuffy stumbled and fell.

"Well, that's the end of one dangerous smart ass," the Black Pioneer said.

Tony Small slipped away from his loyalist friends and looked at the scarred landscape and burnt fort. Without success, a few clouds did their best to block the searing heat. Everything around the fort was shattered. The dirt looked new, it was so dug up and marked with pits and holes from artillery.

Trees without branches looked like tall poles, most of them at a slant. Dead and wounded loyalists were being taken away. If they were dead or wounded, horses were unhitched from artillery or wagons and left where they lay.

Now this mess at Star Fort is finally over. I'm lucky not to be pulled over the wall by a rebel pike. Lucky not to fall over the wall with all those sand bags. Lucky not to get shot. Lucky all around. But I was in battle, even if I didn't take up a gun. I saw friends get killed. Saw bravery. I did my part with getting water to the fort. That's important. Lots to tell Ruth and Cuffy. This war gets stranger every day. It's a funny little duck. Lots of folks switching sides. Brothers, sons, fathers, cousins, neighbors, black and white. Nothing I saw or did so far helps me see what I've got to do next. Even watching and listening to that fight at the parapet didn't help tell me decide which side I'm supposed to be on. I could end up on either side next time around, or no side at all, getting closer and closer to more freedom, real freedom, I hope. But I don't have to go with 'em to chase Greene. Got to get going straight south now and figure this thing out. Got to get to Orangeburg.

Chapter 3

RAID OF THE DOG DAYS

Keeping out of the way, Tony Small followed Cruger southeast from Ninety Six to Orangeburg without seeing Cuffy. After chasing Greene on a circuitous route, including a run-in with the patriot rear guard at Friday's Ferry, Rawdon and his aide-de-camp joined Cruger in Orangeburg. There Rawdon left Lieutenant Colonel Alexander Stewart in charge of field operations, including the six flank companies under Major Majoribanks, and was invalided with a small detachment to Goose Creek en route straight to Charleston. Lieutenant Lord Edward separated from his flank battalion at Orangeburg and went with Rawdon's detachment as far as Goose Creek. At Goose Creek Lord Edward split from Rawdon's detachment and went northeast to Moncks Corner to help his regiment withdraw to Charleston, while Rawdon's detachment continued on to Charleston. Like Lord Edward, Tony still wanted to be in the middle of things and knew his best bet for that was to keep close to the young Irish lieutenant. With the exception of Stewart's army in Orangeburg and Coates' Regiment preparing to leave Moncks Corner, most if not all of the large British eggs in the Southern Campaign were now in one basket outside of the bigger basket of the garrison at Charleston, and Greene, Sumter, Marion, Hampton, and Lee knew it.

A quiet gathering of men and women were sitting around a campfire at the British outpost in Goose Creek when Rawdon's detachment arrived well before dawn. Humidity hung in the air like thick invisible blankets on invisible clothes lines. They could barely see Rawdon's men as they made their way into the camp site. One woman named Phillis stood up and moved forward to get a better view of the shadows emerging toward her. She was a good-looking woman, rather heavy-set but nicely dressed in a long skirt. As she swished away a veil of no-see-ums, her biceps as big as a man's stood out from under her blouse made from a croker sack. The column emerged into the fire light. She took one look at Lord Rawdon, pale, with a crimson stain on his chest, and quietly said to the others in the group, "My, my, he needs some help. Been throwing up on himself. I ain't seen such a sick man in a long time. What a pitiful sight." The others grunted their agreement.

One of the men in the group standing near Phillis observed confidently that the troops would be leaving soon for Moncks Corner. Another claimed they were going straight to Charleston. Arriving with Rawdon, Tony Small overhead the group talking. "Rawdon will be traveling light and quick," he said. "He won't let you go with him."

It soon became clear that British troops stationed at Goose Creek were going to march to Moncks Corner while Rawdon's small detachment would continue on its own to Charleston. As they began to gather their gear, Tony and the other blacks hurried to take positions in the rear of the column going to Moncks Corner, women balancing their children on their hips. Tony saw the young Irishman at the head of the column.

Phillis now knew exactly what she wanted. "I want to go to Moncks Corner with a special guide, one from Cap'n George Martin's Black Pioneers.

I'm pregnant, and I don't need to be running around, but I want my baby born in Charleston. I want to be sure I get there. I hear that every child born with the British is born free, and I don't want this baby to be like my other children. They had to run away with me and their daddy. I hear there's one of Cap'n Martin's guides here."

"Well, we got no choice who's guiding us," Tony told her. "We're all just tagging along behind." Phillis just shrugged as if she were unprepared to hear Tony's remark.

They all began to trudge along behind the foot soldiers, not as quickly as Tony would like, but with quickness the women and children could barely match. The mosquitoes and no-see-ums continued to plague them in the darkness. Brambles along the side of the road grabbed at their trousers and dresses if they wandered even slightly from the well-worn path. Children made whimpering sounds as they stumbled along in the ruts left by wagon wheels and horse hoofs. Mothers somehow kept their babies from crying out loud.

A hot morning sun, eager to get started, rushed out of the chute within an hour after they left camp. Lowcountry humidity wrapped up everyone by nine o'clock. Determination set in as each in turn cared for stragglers.

Finally, they arrived at Moncks Corner. Tony saw the young Irish lieutenant reporting for duty. Tony was at last were he wanted to be, in the company of Coates's Regiment that he heard a lot about already. He had gone from Ninety Six to Orangeburg, to Goose Creek, and now to Moncks Corner, but he saw no action along the way.

That would change. After unarmed black loyalists at Bacon's Bridge and Dorchester, as well as those with Tony from Goose Creek, joined Coates's 19th Regiment of Foot at Moncks Corner, they and Tony listened eagerly for directions before evacuating the British headquarters there and at the outpost nearby at Biggin Church. Those directions came quickly—put everything that could be of use to the rebels inside the church and burn it down. To get the job done, Tony and other blacks quickly walked behind the rear of the regiment as it left Moncks Corner and marched the short distance to Biggin Church near Biggin Creek Bridge.

Other blacks already at Biggin Church were throwing everything troops could not carry into the church. It was hard work, for the day remained hot and humid. The usual army of insects formed their own regiment as menacing as rebel scouts.

"Skeeters in my eyes, can't see 'cause of the sweat. Hell itself don't need anything more than no-seeums," Prince complained as he loaded bundle after bundle of the regiment's excess supplies and baggage onto the empty pews of Biggin Church. A middle-aged man stuck with a demeanor successfully honed in his youth but useless in adulthood, Prince was a carpenter by trade who worked harder at avoiding work than working. His manner fit his name. "We've been working all day and well into the night and nothing we're burning is anything they want. And I don't see any sign of a rebel."

Nancy Peters and her husband Frank were the first to light into Prince. "That's 'cause you're always looking," Nancy said. "The rest of us are working, so we don't have time to stand and look around and listen for what's not there."

"You've got to stop puling, Prince, and get on with it," Frank added. "We don't know what plan the colonel has, but I do know we're not staying here—unless you want to be snatched up again and sent back to old man Bass. He'll deal bad with you if that happens, and you know it."

"Maybe some folks want to be sent back," Ballifo mumbled quietly, as if reluctant to get into a conversation with those he knew would turn on him, too. Ballifo was much like Prince. He confused truth with honesty with the hope it would pass for intelligence. Opinionated, he fell short of clear thinking when it came to major decisions. His judgment on superficial matters was his strength, and what always kept him afloat was that his insipid comments somehow managed to stay within flexible bounds of common sense. Here he was pushing it. He knew they heard him complain many times about his treatment at the hands of the Americans.

"I ain't no Edward Coleman," Ballifo continued. "I wouldn't fight for the rebels like he did. Bunker Hill, Valley Forge, Guilford Courthouse. I think that was against Tarleton about a year ago last May, wasn't it?" No one interrupted him, a good sign to rattle on with more examples to bolster his case.

"I ain't no Thomas Johnson, either. I've been wanting to go home for over a year. First, Lieutenant Mackerill takes me to watch his horses, then he gives me to Lieutenant Warner. It looks like I've been taking care of every damn horse in the 64th Foot after Warner was transferred to Moncks Corner."

"Blah, blah, blah, Ballifo," Frank Peters said. "I'd interrupt you if it meant anything. You don't even listen to folks when you stop to take a breath. You talk about Thomas Johnson. He's a great man, in my estimation. We all know how good Cornwallis treated him as a guide after Charleston fell, even though they made him do it."

"Johnson's a good soldier, too," Prince chimed back in, "I just ain't like him, either. They say he played a big part as a guide for Tarleton's raid on William Washington last April at Moncks Corner before Charleston fell. Well, good for him. Thomas started working for Tarleton a half year before then."

"He's so good a guide and spy that if they ever catch him, he'd better watch out. The rebs'll hang him for sure," Nancy Peters said in an almost casual tone of voice. "I've never seen a hanging, but they say there's not much ceremony to it. They just do it, especially if you're black. Strung up on low branches is the worst, 'cause their little tippy toes can't quite touch the ground, just scratch it like chickens scratching for seed." She laughed a practiced soft hard laugh that few heard.

"Ballifo, I think you just wish you were back at Major Harleston's place for no good reason at all," Nancy Peters continued as she looked sternly at Ballifo and threw a chair onto a church pew. "Thomas Johnson was a free man when he was born on Mr. John Izard's Plantation, and Mr. Izard respected him, too. If he was here with us now at Biggin, he'd be helping throw all this stuff in the church and not complaining one bit."

The column of British soldiers coming from Moncks Corner and the blacks walking behind them, including Tony, finally arrived at Biggin Church in the afternoon of the sixteenth. Tony and the others began to help with the work into the early darkness of the seventeenth.

After everything of value was put inside the church, Lieutenant Colonel Coates ordered the 19th Regiment of Foot to move out in the darkness southeast toward Huger's Bridge and march over the east fork of the Cooper River en route to Charleston. As they all trudged along, Tony and other blacks not pressed into service to carry regimental gear, including records and officers' silver settings, kept a short distance from the rear guard under the command of Captain Colin Campbell. The young Irish lieutenant was among those also riding in the rear guard. Tony heard little about him since Moncks Corner, other than comments about his reputation as a courageous, but reckless, officer when Rawdon's army advanced toward Ninety Six.

After a while, those in the rear of the column looked behind them to see an enormous glow like early daybreak. Some feared an omen of terrible events, but everyone soon realized that Biggin Church was, indeed, burning.

Troops that torched the church caught up with the blacks and hurried on past them to join the rank and file. "I'd rather burn a presby church, instead," one said as he passed, provoking laughter among the others.

At break of dawn along the route toward Huger's and Quinby bridges, Tony saw the same rich verdant undergrowth of hydrangeas, crape myrtle, and tea olive flourishing, just as they did at Miss Maggie's. The great blue and white herons and egrets were the same, too, and the same smaller birds, painted buntings, blue jays, cardinals, and wrens. Amidst all the calm, however, Tony knew it was his most dangerous trip, one even more dangerous than his trek to Ninety Six, and at a time more unprotected than he was inside the parapet at Star Fort. But in the middle of it all—the imminent threat of surprise attack by rebel militia—Tony could not help but be acutely aware of the beauty of his surroundings. The thrill of danger sharpened his sense of beauty as he looked around. He occasionally dropped out of the column to smell the tea olive or get a better look at a particularly impressive oak along the way. He took some bread out of his pocket that he saved from Goose Creek and Moncks Corner and ate it for breakfast. He picked a wild rose that leaned into his hand. He smiled as he felt in it the entire countryside.

·••◦◊◦••·

"We've seen a lot, ain't we?" Old Sandy said to fellow patriot Jim Capers as they sat down to eat supper near Biggin Bridge. "Can you remember all the scrapes and fights we've been in? I can't for the life of me, 'cept maybe the big ones." One of his enormous hands reached toward Capers to give him his share of cornbread and sorghum. Both men carried scars on their arms and shoulders.

Old Sandy and Capers were like Old Dick and Ferguson, although they were not as well equipped with military gear. Each was tough and experienced and devoted to service in the militia. Like Old Dick, Jim Capers served with Marion and had an illustrious history of combat. During his eight years of service, he fought in seven major conflicts and was wounded four times. Old Sandy distinguished himself for saving the life of John Boyce, a patriot soldier whom Bloody Bill Cunningham planned to hang if the Tories ever captured him. Neither doubted their ability to fight and survive in the toughest battles. A drummer, Capers kept his rifle as well as his drum handy at all times. He tolerated Old Sandy's bragging about his own battle experience.

"They're all big to me," Capers replied.

"Well, me, too, but I just can't recall every single one of 'em."

"I didn't say I can remember 'em all, but I pretty much can."

"You sounded like you can't, just like me." Old Sandy looked up and smiled.

"Well, let's say I can and leave it at that. I sure remember Camden. And Savannah, St. Helena and Port Royal."

"I bet you just remember all the fighting no matter where it took place. It's all kind of the same, isn't it?"

"Yep, fighting is all about the same," Capers said. "War is fighting and fighting is killing, but the friends kilt right by you, they're all different. When they die, it's kind of like having the props kicked out from under you one by one, like you were old Noah in his arc when he was building it and waiting for the rain. I mean on dry land before the waters rose. Don't you think?"

"Yep," Old Sandy said. After a long pause, the veteran looked over at his compatriot, then stared into the darkness. "We've heard the cannons roar, haven't we, Jim?"

They did not sleep long. Capers vigorously shook Old Sandy lying next to him. It was four o'clock on the seventeenth, still dark in the early morning.

"I see fire over there. Wake up."

Old Sandy began shouting before he was fully awake. "You're right. Yow, look at that! Those flames are bound to be from the church. There ain't anything bigger around here than Biggin to make a fire like that."

"It's got to be the British burning everything. Those flames are reaching clear to the sky. Lighting up everything like a forest fire."

"That means they're leaving out of here for sure. That's the point. A burning church. My goodness. They slip out from under you while you're asleep. I wonder what the general's going to do now that he's been caught with his pants down." Old Sandy shook his head in disbelief. He began to gather his gear and motioned with his head for Capers to do the same. "Sumter was getting ready to attack Coates at Moncks Corner, but Coates took off before anybody knew it. Got all the way past Biggin Church. I could have done better if I was in command. Those boys sure fooled us."

"Nobody told Sumter," Capers said as he quickly slung a pouch over his back. "The lazy rascals who were supposed to be watching the bridge fell asleep on the job. Wadboo, too. And they were Horry's, Lacey's, and Maham's men, too. Some of the best we got. But I can guess what Sumter's going to do."

"After he knocks somebody silly, he's going to tear out after them," Old Sandy replied and laughed out loud. "With all of us right with him."

"The colonel, too," Capers shouted above the noise of the militia cavalry thundering down the road in pursuit of the British foot troops. "Marion's on his way now."

"Well, I heard Coates has fresh support from Major Fraser, they say about a hundred men and half again cavalry leaving Moncks Corner."

"Somebody's just guessing about that. You don't know. And we'll have to guess which side of the Cooper they're going to take to get to Charleston. Our boys with Sumter, Lee, and Hampton are already covering the road west of the Cooper, so I don't know why Sumter can't figure out that Coates is trying to take the safer route on the east side, storm cross the Wadboo bridge from Biggin Church and head to Huger's Bridge and then cross over Quinby

Creek. Yep, they should put me in command. Put my drum down and put me in command."

"Calm down," Old Sandy said. "Calm down. Quit talking to yourself. We've got our boys all over the place. You always wanted to be a commander, didn't you, Jim? Well, what would you do with all the support Sumter has? Coates has Fraser, but I hear that Thomas Taylor's men are around here somewhere for Sumter, and Wade Hampton's, too."

"I'd be real quick to use Marion's brigade," Capers immediately replied as he took a stick and began to draw lines in the dirt which neither man could see clearly in spite of the glow from the distant flames. "The Swamp Fox's brigade has our best boys in it—the cavalries of Peter and Hugh Horry, Maham, and Lacey, even if they're half asleep."

"And you'd want to use the cavalry of the Virginian, too," Old Sandy said as he grabbed the stick from Capers. "You got the mind of a fishing worm, Jim. Looky here." He began to scratch his own battle plan in the dirt. "Put Lee's Legion onto them before they get all the way to Huger's Bridge." The two men's voices grew louder and louder as they acted out tactical maneuvers of commanding officers, ignoring that they were in the eye of a storm.

"Gimmy that stick back," Capers said and began to draw more lines in the dirt. "See here. Yesterday, Eggleston joined Lee, too, so that now gives us—well, gives us and the Gamecock—about eleven hundred horse of the best fighting force this side of the ocean. I'd put 'em here."

"'This side of the ocean'? What does that mean?" Old Sandy squinted his eyes and wrinkled his face as he looked down at the scratches in the dirt. "'This side of the ocean?'"

"You can be my aide-de-camp, Old Sandy, that's all," Capers replied and joined his friend in a good laugh. When they finally realized they were dawdling and wasting time, Capers threw the stick in the bushes, and they both took off running.

The stage was at last set for what Tony Small was waiting for. Real action. Raid of the Dog Days began with Lee's attack on Campbell's rear guard.

The action at Huger's and Quinby Bridges, and the action at Shubrick's Plantation followed. Lord Edward was in them all, although Tony did not meet him in any of the engagements.

Lord Edward's bravery in Raid of the Dog Days drew the attention of his superior officers, just as it did during his approach to Ninety Six. Major Doyle, head of Lord Rawdon's staff, filed a report on Lord Edward's actions:

> "The nineteenth regiment, being posted in the neighborhood of a place called Monk's Corner, found itself menaced, one morning at daybreak, with an attack by Colonel Lee, one of the ablest and most *enterprising* of the American partisans. This officer having made some demonstrations, at the head of his cavalry, in front of the 19th, the colonel of that regiment (ignorant as it appears, of the nature of American warfare), ordered a retreat;—a movement wholly unnecessary and rendered still more discreditable by the unmilitary manner in which it was effected: all the baggage, sick, and paymasters' chests being left in the rear of the column of march where they were liable of being captured by any half-dozen stragglers.
>
> "Fortunately, Lord Edward was upon the rear guard, covering the retreat of the regiment, and, by the firm and determined countenance of his little party, and their animated fire, kept the American corps in check till he was able to break up a bridge which separated him from his pursuers, and which could not be crossed by the enemy without making a long detour. Having secured safety so far, Lord Edward reported the state of affairs to the colonel; and the disreputable panic being thus put an end to, the regiment resumed its original position."

Along the way toward Huger's Bridge, Tony was eventually pressed into service, not too far behind the Irish troops guarding the rear.

"The wagons keep breaking down," he grumbled.

"They're filled with regimental silver, that's why," a voice replied. "Filled with a strong box of important documents, too. And soldiers' pay. That's what they say."

"We're just stumbling around in the dark. We don't even know where we're going."

"All told, about eighteen miles down this road," another voice replied. "We got to get to Huger's Bridge before we get to Quinby. We're right now about at Huger's."

Suddenly, Tony heard a yell and immediately dove for cover. A ball whistled by his ear and landed with a thud. Mothers and fathers scurried to round up and cover their children.

The attack was over as quickly as it began. "'We're under attack. Stand your ground, men,' that's what Captain Campbell said," Abner Croy told Robert Stedwell after they thought it safe to stand up again. Like Croy, Stedwell came from nearby Bacon's Bridge and was in the rear with Tony. Both were still trembling with excitement.

"At first they all ignored him," Will Waring added. "I heard an officer yell, 'Fire,' and nobody fired a single shot." Waring's spit bounced off a large stone on the ground to emphasize his tough view of the matter.

Croy, a skinny dark little man, looked around for somebody with eyes as big as his. "He yelled, 'Fire!' and nobody did anything. Not one damn thing! And there was even another officer they just flat out ignored."

"That was Captain Bell," Waring said. "I couldn't believe it, either. Why would so many Redcoats refuse to take a stand and fight it out? Lee's dragoons must have scared 'em to death. So they just stood there and let it happen. Now what are we going to do?"

He spat on the ground again, this time not far from Tony's feet. "We're still in the middle of all this. The Brits failed to protect us. The rebs'll take everybody prisoner. Too many Brits to hang. Not too many black folks to sell. There must be about a hundred of us, counting some of those raw Irish recruits they captured, too, the ones afraid to fight."

"Because the main column of the regiment has gone on ahead a little ways," Prince said. He looked around to see if Nancy and Frank Peters were in the group. "I bet this little bunch in the rear didn't think they could resist that many rebels swooping down on 'em. You can understand that. You'd do the same thing. Any soldier would if it meant getting shot for nothing."

"Nope," said Jack, a light skinned man who was quietly listening. He spoke with the authority that attaches to someone who listens before they speak. "The reason those young white Irish boys put down their muskets was because they were plain scared. They never saw a fight before and were just plain scared. I guess they didn't know that rebel militia had the same kind of reputation of being scared, too. And running away, like some rebel militia do."

Nobody knew what to do. Then Ballifo cried out with a whoop and yelled, "Well, if they were scared then, they ain't scared now!" He pointed at men of the 19th Regiment who, at some distance down the path, suddenly began to rally.

"All that stopping and quitting was just a lull in the action." He was almost laughing. "I can tell you that somebody here thought wrong about giving up. Just look at that now. Captain Campbell's got 'em straightened out. He's telling those Irish boys to pick up their muskets and fight. He means it this time."

"Look over there," Frank Peters said. "That's only because that young Irish lieutenant took off back toward the head of the column, telling Campbell and Bell to rally the troops. I saw him with my own two eyes."

"Could have been," Nancy said and nodded to Prince. "And he was mad as a hornet at those troops for giving up at first." If any woman ever looked like a man, it was Nancy Peters who would have loved to have had a rifle.

"But hold up," Tony said as if to pitch in with commentary as authoritative as Jack's. "In spite of that young Irishman's show of force and Campbell's rallying everybody in the rear guard, those troops just had to yield to a stronger bunch of rebels. This whole mess is about the most exciting thing I've seen so far." They all watched in amazement as events continued to unfold.

The action finally ceased. "Well, it's all died down now," Nancy said in an anxious voice, "and the rebels have won this skirmish or we wouldn't be in the fix we're in. Didn't you see the big rebel Lee himself come back to put down the little bit of fight the rear guard had left in 'em? And now we all end up rebel prisoners again, enslaved again, I know it. Lord have mercy. They even captured that nice Captain Campbell."

Frank looked over at Prince before giving his own official assessment. "Lucky for the young Irish lieutenant and a few others who turned around in time to get out of here and back to Coates. Lee would have captured 'em, too. They say Lee wanted everything in the strong boxes. He even left some of his men to keep an eye on the booty his boys got. He should have been rushing toward Quinby Bridge on down the road, but he left men like Armstrong, Eggleston, and Rudolph just to hold onto the stuff in the wagons. I know those big officers when I see them. They're wasting their time. Sumter himself is probably going to be the one who's going to end up with a good grip on that paymaster's chest. Helps pay his troops."

"Amen," they all said loudly.

After leaving Ninety Six, patriot Aaron Spelman came down through Bacon's Bridge to join patriots Jim Capers and Old Sandy after the two left Biggin Church in pursuit of Coates. All three were among the patriots who attacked the regiment's rear guard. The three were also among the troops put in charge of guarding the black loyalist prisoners, including Tony, after most of Coates's men made it over Huger's Bridge and marched a few miles farther toward Quinby Creek.

"Let me stick close to you boys," Tony said to the three, as if he were making a deal that would benefit everyone. "I'm free. I ain't going to run. You look like you've seen all this kind of fighting before."

"Makes no difference to me," Old Sandy replied. "Not much difference now between who's guarding and who's guarded."

"Lots of us black folks bounce back and forth between the two sides, free or not, whites, too," Aaron Spelman said. "You supposed to be a patriot or loyalist?"

"I been both, and they're about the same. Ninety Six taught me that."

"Come on along then," Old Sandy said. Jim Capers just shook his head.

Suddenly, Tony and the others had to jump out of the way of cavalry thundering down the road without any regard of the three black men in their way.

Heavy set and no longer as spry as he used to be, Old Sandy let out a yell. Capers and Spelman muttered curses. Capers took another look and said, "What the ...? Those rebs are all dressed up in British cavalry uniforms. Where'd they get 'em?"

"Stole 'em at Huger's," Old Sandy said, "how else? But that won't fool the Brits after two or three of the rebs get over Quinby Bridge—and then wish they hadn't."

"Wow! Beautiful horses," Tony said. "I never saw such pretty horses, 'cept none of them is a tacky." He continued on, sometimes walking backwards to take in more of the bushes and flowers he passed and to be sure no more horses rode up his back.

Spelman picked the conversation back up. "Ninety Six? You were at the assault of Star Fort? Can't say I remember you. There were lots of us blacks I didn't know. What unit?"

Tony took his time to respond. "Well, I can't lie about it." He looked carefully at the faces of all three. "I can't lie about it. After I got to Ninety Six with a Black Pioneer named Thomas Blackmore, I got caught up on Cruger's side defending Star Fort. Saw everything from the parapet." He paused to take measure of their reaction. "I was with that white messenger from Charleston who tricked y'all and ran to the fort. But I never had a gun, never shot at anybody."

"Well, don't get one and shoot us in the back," Spelman said and laughed. "I know how those things can happen. Property's property to both sides. But you sure did pull a slick one on us." The four men walked on in a group separate from the others, but still within the main column as it left Huger's toward Quinby Bridge.

"Look at that!" Spelman suddenly cried out as they got nearer Quinby Creek. "Look at what's going on now! Redcoats on the other side of the bridge! They look awfully surprised to see us. They're foot soldiers, and our cav..."

"Good gracious," Jim Capers yelled. "More fighting already. There goes Cap'n James Armstrong barreling across the bridge. What in the world?"

"I thought I saw him just a few minutes ago ride back toward Lee," Spelman said, "and now he's back and riding with his saber drawn, right toward that British howitzer set up on the other side of the bridge. He must have gotten his orders from the devil, or he's just plum stupid."

"Good gosh almighty, they'll cut him to pieces if they don't blow him to bits first," Capers said. "Come on, let's get in this. We're supposed to be in reserve with Lee and Hampton, anyway, so, come on, let's help out."

"Wow! A cavalry charge—right over the bridge," Tony cried out. Pointing at Armstrong, he added, "I wonder if he knows his mare's back shoe is gone. Hold on a minute. I'll be damned if the Brits have gone and loosened the planks on the bridge."

"Not enough now to keep that fool-hardy Carrington from riding across, too," Capers yelled back as they all began to run toward the action. "And now there goes Cap'n O'Neal."

"But he stopped," Tony said. "He's not going over. Looks like too many planks are scattered. Redcoats loosened 'em after they got across, but they ain't all thrown in the creek. Maybe we can get 'em and fix the bridge enough to get over and still help out."

"Look here, now," Old Sandy shouted. "There goes a third rebel cavalryman to get all the way across the bridge. Looks like it's Cap'n Macauley from Marion's brigade. I know him. Two of Lee's and one of Marion's over there with only a few men—they might as well be by themselves—and in a real mess, fighting hand-to-hand without any support to speak of. Good gracious alive! They'll be cut off now that the bridge can't be used coming or going. I told you they'd wish they hadn't ridden over that bridge."

"Wait a minute," Spelman said as he squinted to look closely at the fighting on the other side of the creek, about fifth yards away. "Ain't that Redcoat lieutenant fighting by the side of his colonel the same young Irish boy they say was defending the rear guard at Huger's not too long ago? How the hell did he get back here so fast? Now here he is, a-going toe to toe on the other side of the bridge with the best men Lee and Marion got. I bet our colonels are watching this, too. What a sight! What a sight!"

"I can't tell from here who that is exactly," Tony yelled back, "but it kind of looks like him. I reckon I should know. I recognized him when the rebs attacked the Brit's rear guard at Huger's Bridge. Yep, sure looks like him. And he's doing mighty well. This is more exciting than Huger's."

"There go some of Maham's troops to the rescue," Old Sandy yelled out with a loud whoop. "There they go ... but, hang on ... they've been stopped in their tracks. Can't get over the bridge 'cause that howitzer's in place. Damnation! And the Brits are getting more support. Look at that. They're about to get the best of our boys now—all of 'em, Carrington, Macauley, and Armstrong already over there, and Maham's and Marion's men trying to get there to help. Yeeha."

"Naw. Just a few of Marion's men got a little ways over the bridge," Spelman said. "We need to high tail it over there, too."

"But now they're pushed back, it looks like," Capers said. "This all is happening lightning fast, too fast to talk about. As soon as we see something, something happens right behind it. If we're going to get in it, I don't know when, unless when it's over and all the looking is done."

"Well, let's help Lee and Marion get those planks back in place in time to help those boys over there slugging it out," Spelman said. "We all just keep talking. Let's go. Let's get slap dab in the middle of this right now."

"Whoa! There's Armstrong, Carrington, and Macauley, getting out around through the woods," Old Sandy said. "They'll be able to scoot around and get back if they're lucky. We don't need to get over there now, Aaron, and just get ourselves stuck in the mess those cavalry boys are lucky to get out of. They can't get back over the bridge, that's for sure, but they're getting away, anyway, riding through the woods. Planks all gone now."

After they all saw the rebel cavalrymen escape, no one said anything for a while. Then Old Sandy, Spelman, and Capers looked at Tony. "Little rebel children will remember those three boys years and years from now," Old Sandy said. "Yep, sing songs about 'em. I ain't ever seen anything like it. Armstrong, Carrington, and Macauley. Set it to a tune for us, Tony."

"Me? Why me?" I can whistle, but I can't sing."

"A good patriot can do both," Spelman said. The others nodded and smiled.

Tony took a deep breath and was about to give it a try, but Spelman interrupted to be sure his recollection of events was what the others saw, too.

"I ain't ever seen such quick action fighting up close. Never seen such audacity. Good gracious alive! Our boys rode straight into 'em. But Coates and that young Irish lieutenant and some of those other Redcoats, too, stood their ground to hold their side of the creek."

"Our three boys running into that howitzer and that crazy Irish lieutenant!" Tony said as if to satisfy the lot with a verbal comment. "I bet Armstrong still doesn't know his horse is missing a shoe." But he saw the three were still looking at him, waiting, so he quickly made up a jingle on the spot and shuffled his feet in a little dance to keep time:

"Ole Coates's boys burnt Biggin down and took off for Huger.
They lost their fancy silver there and books to Colonel Lee,
Then ran like dogs toward Quinby way and tore the bridge apart.
Our best in all the war saw Brits, cruel men without a heart,
Set up their guns against us rebs, our bravest cavalry,
Who jumped the creek!—Anderson, Carrington, and Macauley.
Palmetto boys and also girls, know well their lasting fame,
And sing of men at Quinby Bridge, ne'er lost without a name."

"Well ... pretty good, I guess," Ole Sandy said, "but it stumbles like a horse missing a shoe. Glad our boys weren't riding it, Tony." The two other men laughed and patted Tony on the back. Reports of gunfire suddenly erupted.

"Wow! Now it looks like more shooting ahead," Old Sandy cried out. "More trouble at the plantation just over the creek."

"Don't you see what's shaping up now?" Spelman said. "Sumter's here now and has joined 'em. The Gamecock finally got here and has joined Marion and Lee and they're going to attack Shubrick's Plantation where the Brits ran to. It's all shaping up. On one side, looks like the Swamp Fox, Light Horse Harry Lee, the Gamecock, Eggleston, Rudolph, Manning, Taylor, Lacey, the two Hamptons and two Horrys, Myddleton, Maham, and Postelle, and a bunch of others. Everybody's there but Mars himself. That's direct conflict in the closest quarters of some of the greatest names we got in the war."

The four men sat down on the ground and waited for an officer to give orders. They were no longer lookers-on. It was a brief time for reflection soldiers instinctively take before battle. Aaron Spelman fumbled with one

of his shoes to get out a briar. Jim Capers crossed his legs and began to take
out his pipe with the certainty that it may be his last smoke. Tony watched
the flow of the creek and the fauna that was mashed flat from the action. Old
Sandy slapped mud off his trousers and slowly shook his head in disbelief.
"Looking straight ahead from Shubrick's on the other side across the creek,
there's nothing less than the best soldiers in the world dug in good, a real
bold commander, and that crazy young Irish lieutenant, who I heard it said
will pluck bright honor from the paleface moon. Reach right up there and
grab it. We won't see anything like Quinby Bridge if we live a hundred years."

Patty Shubrick was in the rear of the British column approaching Huger's
Bridge when Lee's men attacked. Captured by the rebels, she continued
toward Quinby Bridge and ran to the creek in time to see most of the action.
She carried a small croker sack with a little cornbread and sorghum. Near
the bridge Patty could see the plantation now owned by John and Richard
Shubrick, a place she knew well from visits from Charleston with her master
Thomas Shubrick before she ran away. At three o'clock in the afternoon
under a hot sun, Patty saw Coates's Regiment pull back from the bridge and
begin to reorganize at the plantation after rebuffing the charge of Armstrong,
Carrington, and Macaulay. Bug-eyed, hair resting on her shoulders in neatly
platted rows, she looked carefully at the four black men before deciding to
join them.

"Patty," Jim Capers asked after brief introductions, "what kind of
buildings and cabins are on the plantation there? Any good places to hold
up and just take easy shots at us?"

"Plenty of places," she said with her mouth full of cornbread. She offered
what little she had, but all four refused. "Everything is up on a little rise of
ground. You can see that. Can't you see the two-story brick house? Black
folks' cabins, too, all built up in a row, some of 'em made of mud. Lots of big
trees, too. They'll catch a lot of rebel balls."

"It's enough to make it almost impossible to use our cavalry," Aaron
Spelman said. "Sumter will need his artillery for sure."

"You can forget about artillery," Old Sandy said. "Sumter left his artillery back at Biggin. It'll be a long time before Cap'n Singleton's artillery gets here. Meanwhile, we're giving the Redcoats plenty of time to get ready for us. And we don't even have bayonets. Redcoats use 'em as their main weapon—stick and twist. That's why their bayonets are flat, you know, to slide 'em between our ribs. Their muskets wouldn't hit a rabbit a yard away."

"It's worse than that," Capers said. "As good as our militia is with rifles, most of them have ammunition for only about seven or eight shots. At two shots a minute, they'll be out of balls in no time."

Patty listened indifferently to each man's assessment of the situation. Once again she offered what little she had in her croker sack, but this time each man hardly noticed. She sat down on a nearby stump to continue eating. "It won't mean anything to me who wins this mess."

"And Sumter can't wait any longer if he's going to keep Coates from digging in—I mean if he's going to fight before Gould's reinforcements get up here from Charleston," Spelman said. "I hear that's what's happening. From a good black man who should know. That's what's going to make Sumter attack now, even if we're not exactly ready. That's what Greene did when we were at Ninety Six—we gave up on our siege and rushed into an attack before Rawdon's reinforcements got there."

"And that didn't work out so good, did it?" Patty said. "I heard about Ninety Six."

"If we just had a day or two more, it would have," Spelman replied with a dismissive look toward Patty. "Redcoats here have more munitions than we do, and they can load up with buck shot and ball at three to four a minute—bayonets, too, and we don't have bayonets."

"You already said that. It doesn't matter," Old Sandy said. "I've been asking around. I know that Lee and Marion are back from reconnoitering the plantation from upstream. They're not going' to attack a position as fortified as Shubrick's without artillery, bayonets, and plenty of ammunition. They're going to tell Sumter he'd be crazy to attack."

"And it's all against the way Marion fights, anyway. He attacks only when he knows he has the best chance of winning, hits 'em hard and falls back to fight another day. General Greene, too." Old Sandy waited for somebody to say something, but everybody knew that a different opinion meant little to the old veteran, that an opposing point of view didn't even amount to an argument to Old Sandy. "But maybe he'll just go ahead anyway and waste a bunch of lives. I heard that Sumter will wade through pools of blood to win a victory when he smells one—especially when it's not his blood."

"Well, that may be," Capers added, "but I can tell you that Marion's men are down to about only a hundred now. They're deserting and going on back home. Who wouldn't, if you don't have ammunition? Anyway, Lee's and Hampton's cavalry is forming up in the rear, and that means that Marion's infantry is going to be the sacrificial lambs."

"Don't look at me," Patty said. "I ain't got any more information about the plantation than what I already told you. None of that will you do you any good, anyway. You're on your own. I'm going to the rear of all this shooting, whatever kind it is and from whatever direction."

••◦)❉(◦••

"It's started already! Look! Sumter's given the order to attack. Crazy! Crazy!" Spelman cried. "Get out of here, Patty. Here we go with Marion on the right toward the plantation. Look, there's Sumter's men in the center, and there go Taylor's men on the left!"

"Sumter is attacking without his artillery!" Tony cried out.

"Pity us on the flanks," Old Sandy yelled. "We're going to have to hide behind little picket fences, so we'll just be ducks without a pond."

The sudden exchange of fire continued as each man scrambled to find cover. They broke up but remained in shouting distance. In battle, Old Sandy was as nimble as a boy, even if he was slow earlier in dodging British cavalry horses. He dug in and yelled, "I got room for one more, but you got to wash up after yourself."

"As soon as I find a spot, two or three other men are in it already," Spelman shouted. "Thank goodness those raw Irish troops ain't having much luck hitting us, even if we are ducks."

When Capers, Spelman, Old Sandy, and Tony joined Marion's infantry as it advanced across an open field toward a fence about fifty yards from the British position, they could see Colonel Thomas Taylor's men move forward toward a fence enclosure not far from the plantation house. Tony, who remained unarmed, did not advance as far as others with rifles. He saw patriots picked off by Coates's men firing from the second story windows of the house. When Taylor's men ran out of ammunition and were repelled by the bayonets of men under Captain Skerett of the 19th Foot, Marion's men rushed to help them withdraw.

"Look at that," Spelman yelled, by now accustomed to reciting what everybody could see for himself but still willing to point out in dismay. "Sumter's men are over there in the middle of our attack taking advantage of the cover of the cabins, but Taylor's boys are in a real fix now, and we got no cover here except these little picket fences. They got us at their mercy."

Old Sandy yelled over the din of gunfire as if no battle were raging and he could just talk and talk as usual. He acted like bullets never caught up with seasoned veterans until it simply was their time. "There are some brave men dying in this crazy assault. I just heard Major Baxter tell Colonel Horry that he was wounded. I can hardly believe what I heard those two old soldiers say to one another.

"The way I heard it, it went like this. Baxter was getting shot up. 'Well,' Horry said, 'Think no more of it, Baxter, but stand your post.' Then Baxter cried that he can't stand because he was wounded a second time, and Horry told him just to lie down but not to quit his post. And then when Baxter got shot a third time, he told Horry that if he stayed at his post any longer he would be shot to pieces. So Horry yells back, 'Be it so, Baxter, but stir not.' Baxter was shot a fourth time, and I didn't hear anymore from either one of them."

Look at the bloody water bank on the American side of the creek. Men shot trying to cross. The smoke from rifles and muskets give off a sooty odor, like in a cabin when the fire's gone out, except smell of mixed powder and blood ain't like anything else. Can't mistake it in battle but somehow misty, too, like it's raining. Like Ninety Six. No artillery from the Americans, only the British

howitzer. Their muskets and the rebel's rifles left all this smoke. Can't get a clear view of the British side. The ruckus of men scrambling and jumping for cover that just ain't there on the American side. All that fear leaves an odor of its own, too. I hate to see a body get shot up close. Or running his best not to be, but gets it anyway. How much of this mess am I supposed to be part of? Maybe just to remember what I saw and tell other black folks years from now. Tell that black men fought and died at Quinby Bridge and Shubrick's Plantation. Whites won't tell the story.

"Stop, there, young fellow." Cuffy heard the voice of another black man, one of Marion's men, shouting at him. "What do you think you are doing with that rifle?"

The Black Pioneer at Ninety Six missed his target. Cuffy fell to the ground at Ninety Six only to deceive him. Now he was trying to steal more weapons, this time at Shubrick's Plantation. Cuffy held a rifle close to his chest. He fumbled with the hammer and looked to see if there were any powder in the pan, looked to see if it were dry and whether power and paper were stuffed down the barrel with a ball. He couldn't tell, couldn't tell if the man who had it was shot before he got to reload. The ram rod was in place.

"I'm here for you, too. Here to help you. What's it look like?"

"Looks like you're stealing a rifle, that's what."

"Yea, and for a good cause, too, one you should join."

"Join? What are you going on about, boy? I say 'join.' We got enough going on to deal with this one. Now get out of here." The black soldier came up to him and grabbed the rifle out of Cuffy's hand. "'Join?' I say 'join.' Get out of here before I slap you upside the face, knock you silly, you good-for-nothing. You're on the edge of pain, boy. I have a mind to tell the colonel you're slinking around stealing rifles. Line you up and shoot you dead. You're a fool to think any of Marion's men will let go of his rifle, dead or alive."

"They let go if they're dead." Cuffy got ready to fight, closed his fists, licked his lips. He could not tell exactly how many men were nearby, but he knew from the kind of silence everywhere that more shooting was eventually going to happen. If he were going to get any guns, he'd better get them now.

"You a real smart ass, ain't you, boy? If you weren't such a big mean-looking rascal, I'd get some boys over here to whup you good. I'm twice your age, but I can get some help real fast, so you best be moving on. Those rifles are for killing British Redcoats. I heard about you and your so-called insurrection. I say 'insurrection.' Now get out of here. There's no ammunition for 'em, anyway. Now get! I'll hit you so hard you'll never get up. Now get!"

⬦

Quickly withdrawing to Charleston the next day, Coates kept on the short route east of the Cooper River, passing the Chapel at Pompion Hill, the Church of St. Denis and, farther down, St. Thomas Church, west of Cainhoy, before arriving at the garrison at Charleston.

Tony Small and Aaron Spelman looked around after Coates withdrew. "Have you counted 'em all?" Spelman asked.

"Nope, but I heard sixty-sixty—sixty of us killed, sixty wounded. They counted six British killed, thirty-four wounded, and about a hundred captured. Come on. Help me dig some graves, about six big ones should hold 'em all."

Capers walked up to them. "Tony, I'll help you dig some graves. We've been ordered to, anyway.

"It's really disgusting—not just all our boys who died in the foolish attack on Shubrick's, but I mean the low moral that's got to us now. I hear Marion and Lee left in the middle of the night without telling Sumter, and Taylor told him that he wouldn't ever serve under him again. Madder than a wet hen."

Patty Shubrick by this time came up from the rear and joined them again. She exchanged glances with Tony, who took notice of her good looks for the first time. Ignoring him, but straitening her skirt, she said, "But what really ruined Sumter's action here was when we all found out that he paid his own men out of the seven hundred and twenty gold guineas that Lee's and Maham's men helped him get. I laughed out loud when I heard that. Sumter got all the money from the British chests captured from the regiment's rear guard at Huger's. He got all the regimental silver, too, the silver settings stamped with 'XIX' and fancy things that officers use. Lord knows where all that is now."

Everyone laughed, knowing that Patty was about to tell them. "I bet he kept some of the silver for himself and gave it to his wife. And his family will have that silver on their groaning board for years to come—if the patriots win."

"Well, look at the bright side," Spelman said, still laughing. "At least Sumter didn't pay his troops with us black enslaved folks.

"Now with this mess over, we can look out for another one somewhere. And I bet it's going to be back toward Orangeburg again. There's fighting everywhere, but they say a lot of Redcoats are still in Orangeburg getting ready to go somewhere else."

The following month at Orangeburg, a North Carolina man named Morris, who knew roads from Virginia to Charleston, escaped the rebels to join loyalist Captain George Martin's Black Pioneers. He was eager to tell other loyalists about what he saw. Somewhat of a dandy for a Black Pioneer, he usually liked to dole out information gradually just to watch the changing expressions on everybody's face, but this time he didn't horse around.

"Whoever he was, he was fearless. A young Redcoat lieutenant rushed toward one of Lieutenant Colonel William Washington's dragoons. He attacked with a fury like he wanted a single blow of his saber to stand for the entire skirmish and the skirmish for the entire war.

"I saw him break his sword on the back of one of Washington's cavalrymen. They say he did the same thing approaching Ninety Six—broke his sword on a reb's back. When Captain Watts writes his report, I suspect Lieutenant Colonel Washington will want to know who that Redcoat officer was, if he can't guess already.

"I bet it was that brash young Lieutenant Lord Edward Fitzgerald. He's got a reputation as big as Lieutenant Colonel Banastre Tarleton's and in a whole lot less time—Ninety Six, the rear guard at Huger's Bridge, Quinby, Shubrick's, and now Orangeburg."

••◦◦)❦(◦◦••

After Ninety Six, Cuffy disappeared. Weary from following both sides of the war, Tony headed northeast from Orangeburg to Miss Maggie's. He arrived on a beautiful afternoon in late July. A lot changed at the plantation from the time he left without Ruth for Ninety Six in early June, although he could not tell exactly what it was. He thought perhaps his own new experiences caused a change in his perception while the plantation itself remained the same. Perhaps a new sense of wariness about the future that he and Miss Maggie shared six weeks earlier created a fresh perspective for him. He was a new man in a new world. He went to the barn but could not find Eagle or any of the other horses. He saw no one around, and not even the usual critters and birds so common to sight and sound. He headed toward his cabin, but stopped and, instead, went directly to the McKelvey brick house.

"I've seen the ebb and flow of battles," Tony told Miss Maggie when he saw her standing at the kitchen door, right where he saw her before he left for Ninety Six. As usual, no visitor ever surprised her. Her tanned Irish hands were covered by liver spots exposed by the rolled up tattered sleeves of her blouse. Her sun bonnet, never calculated to hide her gray hair, was tied with a string under her chin and sat neatly in place. She was about to take her apron off, but she changed her mind and kept it on and looked at him as if to ask, Where in the world have you been?

"I've seen lots while I've been gone, Miss Maggie, seen great men on both sides. Seen lots of black folks fighting along side whites. I guess you can say I got lots of experience now, but I still don't see what's really going on, especially for black folks."

As always, Miss Maggie let Tony talk on when he was excited about something. He stood up straight, as usual, but now spoke more as a traveler returning from a foreign land.

"Just looks like folks killing each other to see who gets to do all the killing in the future, see who's in charge without thinking about anything else, much less what's going to happen to us black folks after all this mess is over. Whites ain't worried about that now. They all know nothing's going to change much for us. I didn't hear any white man talk about us, except to put us to work."

"Tony Small, you're full of adventure," Maggie McKelvey replied and smiled. "Most of your work was done by your friends when you were gone, if you want to know."

"I reckon I'll take my stand when I figure it all out, but even after Ninety Six and Quinby Bridge—I'll tell you about 'em—I can't tell who's winning or losing. I just hope the side I pick for the reasons I pick it is the winning and good side." He turned his eyes away with a look that did not have much weight to it, then asked, "Miss Maggie, which side do you think is going win this war?"

"We're going to win it, Tony," Maggie McKelvey shot back. Her light green eyes suddenly widened as she focused intensely on Tony. She was no longer smiling. As Tony saw her do many times, she smoothed out her apron with the usual

swipe of her hands, but this time the flour on her hands and apron flew into the air like a shot from a musket.

"We're going to win it, no doubt about it. I know our neighbors Francis and Job Marion, and we've known the Videaus and Cordes for years. They're all good people who love freedom. That's why we all came over here—Irish and French, Scots, English, too, and Germans. Francis ain't going be on the losing side of this war, I can tell you that much."

Tony was not about to share every one of his thoughts about freedom with Maggie McKelvey—and he certainly would not tell her about Cuffy. He nodded politely and began to walk back toward the barn, thinking of getting in touch with Ruth as soon as he could.

"But, Tony," Maggie said in a less passionate tone of voice after he walked away a few yards, "I have to tell you that you and your family and all the others on the place, free or not, or hoping to be free, need to be thinking about clearing out of here. I hear that the British are headed toward the springs. They'll take whatever's left."

"You mean our two springs—the big and small one—right here at Eutaw?"

"It's a rumor now, but a good one, and enough for me to pack my things and move to Brackey. You'd best come, too. Tell your momma and daddy, if they ain't gone already. Rebels done took Eagle, Lofty, Fish Eye, and Iron Side. There's not going to be any work to do around here if there's shooting going on, that's for sure. The British are coming."

———⌒———

Chapter 4

EUTAW SPRINGS

Sometime before September fourth, Tony Small left Miss Maggie's Plantation and raced to catch up with rumors. Stewart and Greene were on the march. This time Ruth came along. She ran away from old man Snow, refusing to be left behind as she was when Tony went to Ninety Six. She envied his being able to join the ruckus during Raid of the Dog Days. She was as keen on adventure and a search for freedom as much as Tony, and they both knew equally well that the clash of armies presented a chance of a lifetime for them. She arrived well before dawn at Tony's cabin, went inside and shook him to get up. This time Tony's mother knew her son was not heading to his favorite oak tree. She smiled at them both, rolled over, and went back to sleep. She and Tony's father were not yet alarmed enough to flee the McKelvey plantation. Tony grabbed his gear and together they headed northwest about thirty miles along the Santee

River toward Thomson's Plantation. There they hoped to see Greene's army coming southeast from the High Hills and Marion's men coming out of nowhere.

"This place is bigger than Maggie's," Ruth observed when they arrived a couple of days later at what they thought was Thomson's Plantation. She sat down on a stump and opened a croker sack with fat back and biscuits.

"Don't you think? Seems dead, though, not many flowers and no vegetable garden to speak of. No tidy picket fence like Miss Maggie's. You sure this is Thomson's?"

"Don't know, but it could be Belleville. That's the name of Old Danger Thomson's Plantation. I know all the names of the plantations up and down the Santee, but I don't know exactly where they are. And I don't even know if this one here is Old Danger's, but whose ever it is, somebody left a mighty big mess."

Ruth began to whistle softly to herself, lips pursed, really just blowing out air, not whistling in the usual way. Not singing, no words, just unconsciously blowing out air with soft, muffled sounds of different notes, the same tune Tony heard a million times before. It sounded like a child's nursery tune that burrowed so deeply into her mind that she could never forget it. She put aside her croker sack and fanned her toes back and forth, heels in one spot, then stopped and wiggled her toes and moved her fingers up and down without moving her hands that rested on her knees.

Ordinarily, Tony loved to catch her like that, when she was happy and oblivious to her surroundings, but this time Tony wasn't paying much attention. He looked up at the sky as if to ask if there were any reason for the solitude in his mind that began to congeal into uncertainty about what they were doing. Were they even in the right spot to see the armies as they headed toward Eutaw Springs?

"Let's move on, Ruth. Ain't nothing here. Let's get on back down the road, back toward the springs. If anything is coming, I'd rather meet it closer to Eutaw, anyway." Ruth put aside her day-dreaming and put on her shoes. They began to retrace their steps down River Road a short distance to Mt. Tacitus, Henry Laurens' Plantation.

"Well, Ruth, it doesn't look like there are many black folks here, either, least not enough to run a place this big. Looks like they all scattered here, too. Nobody's in the fields that you can see. No white folks at all."

Ruth nodded her agreement and looked around Mt. Tacitus for a good place to rest. "Let's spend the night here and then get on back down the road tomorrow. Burdell's Tavern ain't too much farther. You can tell by all the mess that lots of folks were here already. Just like Thomson's. Brits, I bet."

"Seems like we would have run into 'em. We were going up the road from the springs while they were going down it. But we didn't. How'd we miss a thousand men? Bad timing, I reckon. Sure sorry we missed 'em."

At Laurens' Plantation late afternoon commotion created a new sound of men and horses kicking up dust as they headed south along River Road. Tony and Ruth hurried to stake out a spot to watch the action coming their way.

"Hush, listen," Tony said and smiled at Ruth. "We ain't missed a thing. Listen to all that ruckus. You know that sound as well as I do."

"That means only one thing, doesn't it, Tony?" Her big smile showed all her teeth, like she wanted to bite one of them. "Rebels."

"Marsh tacky horses! And the Swamp Fox. That's what he rides. He's coming, Ruth. Marsh tacky horses. Lots of 'em. I love those little horses. I can hear their gait in my sleep. There ain't anything like 'em in the world. Been here since the Spanish left."

"I've seen tacky horses in pluff mud up to their shoulders."

"And they just roll over on their side and scoot and kick and wiggle, small as they are, till they get out." Ruth joined in the fun and mimicked Tony as he acted as if he were on a tacky, leaning over on his side and kicking with one leg as he scooted away from her, oblivious to the men riding toward them.

"Tacky horses are the main reason British troops can't ever catch Marion," Tony said. "Always staying on the move, hit-and-run. It's like the Swamp Fox has a secret weapon that the Redcoats never heard of."

"All four big hooves on the ground in their gait, sure-footed," Ruth added as each continued to talk over the other. "That's how we know they're coming."

"Agile and fast, too. You can tell a tacky by its double main and the dark streak down its back, and its black legs from hoof to knee. On their face, too. They all got nicked ears. I really love those little swamp horses. So do Marion and his men."

"I started riding 'em when I was a little girl. We used 'em for everything—plowing, hunting. They let anybody ride 'em. Feral, but sweet as a lamb."

"They can survive on salt marsh and sweet grass, something the big fancy thoroughbred horses the British have won't ever touch. Marion never stops because they can just forage on the land—no need to haul their own fancy oats. Got nostrils bigger than most horses have, so they can keep going on and on and on. And they don't even flinch when they hear a gun. Lightning doesn't spook 'em, either, like it does Eagle. I love those horses. I love Eagle, too, but tackys are what built the Lowcountry. What's going to save it, too."

Near the front of the approaching column emerged a black man alongside a short white man, both riding marsh tacky horses. Other men, black and white, also rode close by as if to protect the white man from a sniper's bullet.

"I can't tell exactly who's in charge," Tony said, "but I'm guessing that's him they're riding close to."

"Me, neither. They all got rumpled clothes, leather strips stitched together for shoes, and trousers and shirts all kinds of colors. No real uniforms." She chuckled softly. "A sorry looking lot, really. None of 'em knows what a roof is, I bet."

"Maybe, but eyes in the back of their head are part of their uniform."

One of the black men suddenly turned his horse toward Tony. "Is this Henry Laurens' Plantation?" Without waiting for Tony to reply, he said, "Then we're here," and turned back to say something to the short white man.

"We'll camp here for the night," a soft voice responded over the near silence of a couple of hundred men as they began to ride in, dismount, and start setting up camp. The sword of the short white man looked like it was rusting in its scabbard.

"They're not carrying much," Ruth whispered. "I sure wouldn't call this setting up camp." Like Tony, she was amazed as the casual but guarded routine began to play out. The rough lot looked like they never stayed long at any one place, as if the places themselves were lovers who knew they were one-night stands. They began to set out sweet potatoes near fires that seemed like they already knew men were coming and got started on their own.

The black man in front of the procession, still on his horse, rode back toward Tony and Ruth. He was a man of ordinary size and build, but a closer look revealed a confidence in his eyes that surprised Tony. To Tony he looked like a white man, not by his color, but by the way he acted. It was the first time Tony saw a black man—other than his father and Hercules—act that way, fearlessly, not only because he was in the company of so many others, but also by his own sense of well being and purpose.

"Who are you men?" Tony asked and reached out to take the horse's leash. The black man cut him off and turned his horse away.

"Where do y'all come from? Y'all going after the British?"

The black man smiled and looked at Ruth. "Questions. Lots of questions." Without getting off his horse, he asked, "And who are you?"

"I'm Tony."

"And the woman there?" he said, annoyed that Tony intercepted his question.

"I'm Ruth. Tony's free, but I'm supposed to be back at the Snow place in St. James Parish. It's a ways away on the Santee. I know you ain't going to tell anybody I ran away."

He laughed, a big hardy laugh. "Well, you're not going back there anytime soon, sister, or anywhere else, for that matter, so I suspect we can trust you for a while. Glad to meet you. My name's Oscar."

"Oh, Oscar, I shouldn't have told you about running away. Please don't tell on me," Ruth cried and became very agitated. "My master calls me an arch bitch. I know he will beat me bad if he catches me."

Tony looked at her, surprised that she was pouring out every bit of information about herself to a stranger, especially a rebel.

"I hate working for nothing, and I hate not being free, even if I don't go too far from the place. I'm like Tony's horse Eagle. He'll always stay where you leave him, but if you tie him to a post, he'll pull that rope right off the post and walk away. I can't stand to be criticized."

"Nobody will hear it from me. I won't tell on you or Eagle," Oscar said and laughed again, much too weary to get into a stressful conversation. He continued to chew on something, and eventually spit it out. "And not even from the colonel. And not even if you've been hiding her," turning to Tony.

"Besides, I know Jemmy ran away from Colonel John Laurens, Henry's son, over a year ago after the fall of Charleston, and I ain't told nobody about him either. Jemmy joined the British engineers. But I suspect you're not off to join the enemy just yet. And I'm not going to tie you to a post." He smiled broadly at her before riding back to look briefly at the procession of men as they continued to ride in.

Maybe he thinks he's got something on her now. But she is pretty. Plenty grown up, too. Maybe it's her shiny ivory teeth I love, beautiful white teeth that shine like stars. Her hair, long strong legs and arms, she's so beautiful. Big breasts, not too big. But those teeth, that's what's so pretty when she laughs, and she's always laughing. At the right time. For the right reason, or for a good reason you should have thought of yourself. She's the first to see what's funny and smell what's not. She can see it all coming around a corner, like Daddy can. But she's no giggling fool like Stepney. There's something animal-like about her, too. Good animal-like. Her teeth hold me like a vice, shake me like a dog shakes a rabbit. They're what everybody looks at when she's coming your way. She can get herself in trouble, too, she's so fearless. Me, too, real trouble. Got to be careful. But I'd die for her if I have to.

Relieved for the time being and reassured by Oscar's kindness, Ruth looked around at the others coming in. "They're a sorry looking bunch, all right. I bet that's Francis Marion, the short white man over there. I'm guessing because they say he's just average size, maybe a little smaller. Lots shorter than you, Tony."

Oscar returned, got off his horse, and began to take off his saddle. Tony walked up to him and asked, "Is that the Swamp Fox?"

"He doesn't look much like a fox to me," Ruth said, a step or two behind so she could talk more to Oscar. "He's swarthy enough, though."

"Well, don't believe everything you hear about the colonel." He threw a stirrup up over the saddle and gave the girdle a jerk to give it enough slack to unfasten it and at the same time signal that he did not want to answer a bunch of question. He pulled the saddle and blanket off. With strong sensuous strokes, his rough hands smoothed out the blanket with a touch that could feel the slightest burr or spike from the bushes he rode his tacky through all night. He looked up at Ruth and caught her looking at his hands. They exchanged smiles. He laid the blanket out to dry and led his tacky to a nearby spring where others were congregating. Ruth and Tony followed.

"I hear he can be hard on enslaved folks, but he makes good use of us blacks in the white man's fight for freedom," Ruth said.

"He does what it takes, but I don't know if I'd put it that way." Oscar took a corn cob out of his pack and began to rub down his horse. "Now I'll tell you a little about us," he said, after giving both just enough time to prove themselves not to be too great a nuisance.

"We're just now riding in from Parker's Ferry and Cypress Swamp after a two-day ride. No stopping, the colonel's way. Killed a bunch of loyalists in an ambush and took lots of horses. Stewart's cavalry's got blessed little to ride now. The colonel took his revenge on that rascal Fraser for capturing Colonel Hayne. That's the man Rawdon and Balfour hanged about a month ago in Charleston. You probably don't even know what I'm talking about."

"Yes, we do," Tony replied, even though he didn't. "I hear lots of things. Keep my ear to the ground, too."

Oscar turned to Tony. "Now I told you more than you need to know. So where exactly is Stewart and his army?"

"Since they ain't here at Laurens' Plantation, I reckon they camped at Burdell's Tavern not too far southeast of here. By now they're probably farther on to where I live at the McKelvey place at the springs at Eutaw, but I'm a free man."

"Everybody but this woman here claims they're free. Anyway, that's what we heard, too—about where he is, I mean. How far's Burdell's from here? We're going to push on tomorrow before dawn. It may be that this place is too close to Burdell's to camp, and we don't want to get too close to Stewart and all his little Redcoat bastards. Pardon my language, Miss Ruth."

Ruth drew a sharp audible breath. It was the first time anyone called her "Miss Ruth."

"Burdell's is about three more miles going southeast on down Congaree Road," she said after a pause. "Some folks call it River Road, Old Cherokee, but you'll run right into Burdell's straight on no matter what they call it." She looked over at Tony for his approval, then said, "The Eutaw springs are about seven more miles beyond Burdell's. That's where Tony lives, at the springs. At the McKelvey place. And Nelson's Ferry's a step or two from the springs."

Tony was doing his best to listen to Ruth and take in all the commotion going on at the same time. Mainly he just wanted to be able to tell others that he saw Francis Marion.

"Is that really the Swamp Fox?" But Oscar did not answer and, instead, had his eye on a man quickly approaching them. "That's what Tarleton calls him, isn't it?"

Jim Capers came up and said something to Oscar who left immediately.

"Yep, that's him," Capers said. "And I'm me."

Tony lunged at his old friend from Quinby Bridge and Shubrick's Plantation with a good laugh and hug. He quickly introduced him to Ruth as a true partisan and hard fighter, there and at Star Fort, but neither had time for much reminiscing.

"And the fellow you were talking to is his right-hand man Buddy," Capers said. "They grew up together, nearly inseparable. Some call him Oscar. Later tonight, we'll all be moving on to Burdell's Tavern to meet Greene on the seventh. That's top secret, you know, a general's movements. Should be interesting to watch these two men as they get to know each other for the first time. I guess Marion's forgiven Greene for trying to requisition some of his horses, the ones that aren't tackys." He, Tony, and Ruth laughed at the idea of Marion giving up any of his tackys.

"This big battle coming up won't be like the big ones I was in at Charleston, Savannah, and Camden, I can tell you that," Capers continued. "And not Shubrick's, either. This time we have commanders we know will do us right, whether we're black or white."

"There's a bunch of black men with you, I can say that much for you, from what I've already seen," Tony said. "And they're soldiers, not just helping do what's got to be done, not just blacks taking care of white officers."

"Why don't you join 'em, Tony?" Ruth asked.

"Nope," Capers replied before Tony could respond. "We're all veterans and experienced soldiers. I know you did well at Shubrick's with Old Sandy, Aaron Spelman, and me, but I didn't see you with a rifle. What's coming is going to be a really big battle with thousands of men. Don't have time to train a new man. You could end up shooting one of us in the back. It's hard work riding and fighting with Marion.

"But maybe you can follow this thing that's coming up and remember what goes on and who does it. Old Sandy says you've got plenty of good sense. Maybe tell somebody who can even write it all down. But don't get in the way, don't get shot. You didn't at Shubrick's, did you?" Capers laughed and quickly walked away.

Ruth looked at Tony as he just shook his head and pursed his lips in a disgusted kind of way. "Well, I still think you could do some good with a rifle if you could get your hands on one, like Cuffy."

On the night of the fourth, Tony and Ruth cuddled like spoons as they slept on a lumpy straw bed in a barn at Laurens' Plantation. Oblivious to the world around them, nothing meant nothing until the dawn of the next day when they heard footsteps of more soldiers, the snorting of horses, and the clatter from iron, leather, and wood.

Tony suddenly sat up and looked around. "That racket ain't from Marion. He's already gone to Burdell's, and we didn't even know it."

"Stay longer, Tony, dear. You can find out later. This may be our last time together for a while. I know that was you tickling my nose a minute ago. I was just playing possum. Stay longer so I can tickle you, too, sweetie."

"Tempting, but love of war and love of women are as different as tatters and cucumbers." Ruth looked at him as he stood up naked. He turned to her and beat his chest. They both burst out laughing.

"I salute you, too, Colonel Cucumber, but stay longer, dear. Please."

"Anyway, there will never be a last time with you ... loved I not tatters more, or something like that I overheard that Irish lieutenant tell somebody at Goose Creek. Right now, we just both have to put tickling aside and get in the time we're in. I mean grab the moment at hand. Something else I heard." He stumbled as he tried to get all of himself into his trousers.

Ruth started laughing again. "What? Mighty big talk. Nothing's in hand yet, sweetie. Come on, put away your sword for a while."

"I'll make it up to you."

"Tony, dear, there may not be a next time for a long time. I told you. You can make time, but you can't make it up. My grandmomma from Africa says if you want to go fast, go alone, but if you want to go far, go together. We're a team, Tony."

Tony was already out the door. She hurried to catch up.

William Lomack came to a halt with other blacks in Captain Clement Hall's Company of the 2nd North Carolina Regiment. Lomack pulled his rifle off his shoulder as the two approached. Pushing herself in front of Tony, Ruth asked, "Where y'all from?"

Thirty-one-year-old Lomack, a tall and rugged-looking man, looked hard only at Tony and replied briskly, "From the High Hills of Santee, if that's any of your business. Who are you—that's a better question—and why you not helping us get settled? How far to Burdell's Tavern?" The noise of wagons and horses blocked out Tony's reply.

Another soldier, younger and shorter than Lomack, with a more haggard look, came up to ask the same question. "How much farther to Burdell's Tavern?" He put down his rifle and croker sack and extended a rough and powerful hand, a custom Tony was not used to.

"I'm John Artis. This here is William Lomack. He's whupped. We're all whupped, and we would appreciate a little help with provisions for us black troops before we have to move on." He looked at Ruth.

Tony began to help Ruth but kept looking at Artis whose mouth was shaped in an odd way, frozen in an almost mean-looking grin. Like Lomack, Artis acted like he was the man in charge of the van, just behind the white officers. He took advantage of his less-tattered clothes to give an appearance of authority.

"We're amazed at the number of black men coming with you," Tony told Artis. "Where did y'all come from?"

"Well, if it's any of your business, a lot of black men you see are in Hall's Company and Donovan's," Lomack interrupted to answer the question. He lowered his voice and appeared to be more amiable toward Tony and Ruth as he got off his horse. As early light continued to shine on Ruth's face, her beauty began to settle in his mind, and he knew as a consequence he had to be as polite as possible to Tony as well. A chorus of Lowcountry sounds from birds and critters by now added to all the noise.

"I'll show you who they are because you can't tell by yourself, even if you see they're black. You're right if you think there's a lot of black soldiers. I don't have long. Got to move because we're going to be leaving here directly. Most of us are from North Carolina. Lots from Virginia and Maryland, too. Not many black soldiers from South Carolina or Georgia. They should be here but they ain't. Whites there are afraid if they get guns they'll turn around and kill 'em all. Can't get Stono Ferry out of their mind. Georgia's full of loyalists, about as bad as South Carolina. But at least we got a whole lot more blacks in arms than the Brits do. Brits just give us blacks a bunch of lousy jobs to do." Lomack identified only a unit or two and walked away, as if to indicate that on second thought he had no chance with Ruth, anyway.

By the time Tony and Ruth could start lending a hand to feed the men coming down the road, hundreds of white soldiers and officers and more black soldiers began to crowd into the Laurens' Plantation grounds. Among the blacks was a soldier somewhat bigger than the others. Ruth noticed his stern face as he got off his horse and walked straight toward her. Drury Chavers introduced himself. Ruth immediately asked what company he was with.

"Donoho's," Chavers said impatiently, disappointed with the question. "Not Donovan's. Lomack must have told you to look out for his company only." He shrugged his broad shoulders.

"No, yours will do. I just wanted to know. I'm here mainly to help with the food."

"I doubt that," Chavers shot back, "if I can tell much about a woman just looking at her. Wow! What a smile! Do you bite?" He pulled back in a playful gesture that got Tony's attention. Chavers began to shadow box and show off his enormous biceps the size of Cuffy's.

"You're fighting the British Lion, even if it's just for your masters right now," Tony said. A group of black soldiers, who by now joined Chavers and gathered around to eat, overheard Tony's remark.

"Most of us are born free," one of them said, "so we're the same as white folks. We're from North Carolina."

Younger black troops did not want to get into any kind of talk about why they were fighting for the rebels. Jacob Jefferies, Moses Manly, Daniel Mills, Joel Taburn, and Benjamin Reed began to jostle in line to see who would be first.

"My goodness, boys, we're not passing out anything more than food your officers got for you," Ruth teased. "And they ain't got me. Y'all playing around like y'all just want to beat the other fellow to the head of the line to talk to me."

All the men laughed and shoved one another as if to blame the single thought everyone shared on anyone who would deny it. Ruth gave each man hardtack and rum, looking everybody in the eye and smiling as if she were the last woman they'd ever see. Benjamin Reed, the smallest of the bunch and worse dressed, just stood and stared at Ruth as she gave him his portion of food and drink.

"Move on along now, honey." She patted him on his head and pinched his arm. "You're sweet but we ain't got time. You're as innocent as a new laid egg." Everybody laughed.

"He's just nature-minded," an older trooper said. More laughter.

She left her job on the food line and drifted toward a group of Donovan's men. Tony was chatting up two of them whose appearance was so much alike that he suspected, correctly, that they were brothers. Even their length of hair was the same, but it was their massive hands and arms and shoulders that identified them.

"Not only that," Philip Pettiford told Tony, "nearly every man in the Pettiford family in North Carolina is fighting the British—my brother Elias standing over there by the horses and my other brother William who's not here right now but still in Donoho's Company. We're mostly from Granville County, North Carolina. Donovan's is pretty much an all-black company."

"How many members of your family are fighting for their white masters?"

"Well, counting me and my two brothers, about six—us, Drury, and two named George, but only Elias, William, and me are brothers. I think Drury is a cousin. We're all born free. A band of brothers, they call us, and nobody's going to look out for us but ourselves. We're all going to stick together, take care of one another. We're good fighters, all in Sumner's North Carolina Brigade. And I wouldn't say we're fighting for our white masters. We're fighting for ourselves because we're free, just like white folks." He paused to see if Tony wanted to hear more.

"A band of brothers, eh?"

"We're like some of the black folks in Colonel Marion's militia, even though some white folks say some of us ran at Guilford Courthouse. They say Continentals and some militia ran away from the fight after the Brits charged us with bayonets. It ain't like that. It was a draw till Cornwallis shot his own men with artillery. Anyway, white soldiers, just like us, had to spend last summer with General Greene in the High Hills learning how to be good soldiers, kind of like punishment for thinking we ran away or thinking we were cowards."

The short, stocky man looked down and dusted off his light brown jacket. Eventually Philip Pettiford looked up, satisfied that Tony could not possibly improve on his story with further inquiry.

"You can talk about brothers all you want to," a voice behind them calmly said after listening to Pettiford. Tony turned his attention toward a man noticeably exhausted from the long march from the High Hills to Laurens' Plantation.

"I'm James Nickens, Sr. I got nine brothers and cousins in this war. Ain't none of 'em here in this fight, though. Just me. Nine. Pretty much all of us from the Northern Neck of Virginia, and we're all free. Nine's as many as in any white folks' family, and we don't have to do it, either. I mean we're free, but we ain't got much to protect. Only hope for."

"Well, as long as you're breathing down here in South Carolina," Ruth said as she joined them after going back and forth to the food line, "they say you still can have hope."

Tony and Ruth stood in awe as over two thousand men under General Nathanael Greene, including about three hundred fifty Continentals in Brigadier General Jethro Sumner's North Carolina Brigade, continued to march onto the grounds of Laurens' Plantation. They could not talk to all the black men assembled, but they met as many as they could in all the shuffle, careful to stay out of the way of a moving army following officers shouting orders—but not so loudly as to be heard by Stewart's pickets.

"They're like an army of ants," Ruth whispered to Tony.

"And all these little ants want to be remembered. And here comes another swarm."

Out of the two other regiments in Sumner's Brigade, he met only a handful of the blacks carrying arms. One of them was Will Lomax, without a drop of white blood, one of the blackest men Tony ever saw.

"Other than Armstrong's, there are two other regiments here under Sumner," Lomax explained, pleased that someone wanted to know. "Major Reading Blount's and Colonel Baptista Ashe's. And if y'all going to ask if any black folks are fighting, the answer is yes. And don't go pestering me about whether blacks can shoot straight and whether they're going to get scared and run away the first time they see a bayonet. All that Guilford Courthouse stuff was made up by the white folks who ran away, anyway. They're just chickens who wanted company in the roost."

He looked down at the soles of his boots, aggressively putting his hand on Tony's shoulder to keep his balance. Looking at one sole, then the other, switching hands, taking plenty of time, signaling that his grip was also meant to hold Tony until his story was told. Time enough, also, for Tony and Ruth to see that Lomax was very proud of his new boots. Yet another Old Dick boot story.

He took his hand off Tony's shoulder. "I hear there's a William Lomack with Sumner. I ain't him. I'm Lomax from Haiti, a free man fighting with Blount's Regiment, living now in North Carolina. Came here with that youngster Lafayette. I got a mule older than Lafayette. Remember that." He laughed out loud.

"Over there is Absalom Martin who's nearly forty years old and one of the oldest black men in Blount's Regiment. He's from Carteret County, North Carolina. The black man standing to his left is William Burnett, Private Burnett, been in lots of different units since 1777. I don't know a lot about any of the others, but they'll tell you if you ask 'em."

Lomax walked away with a wave of his hand, muttering a pleasantry Tony could not make out.

Ruth drifted off on her own to talk to another group of blacks while Tony listened to conversations among some black men in Blount's Regiment. He approached Absolom Bibby, a short stocky man who looked like someone with a story to tell.

"Right, I enlisted in Captain Charles Dixon's Company of the 3rd North Carolina Regiment under Major Reading Blount just like a lot of other black men did—but just for twelve months. Don't confuse me with Solomon Bibby. Solomon Bibby doesn't carry a rifle. I carry a rifle. He's a waiter to an officer in Captain Edward Yarborough's Company in Blount's 3rd North Carolina Regiment. He tries to make up for it by talking like a philosopher, all profound and such, slop-chopping any conversation he walks into, leaving folks with no dangling nothing to hang onto, nothing more to say about what they were talking about even if it was something that started out with lots of steam. Or even to start up something new. Fact is, he ain't a glob big enough to spit. Philosophy's just a war without bullets. I don't like him."

"Well, I reckon I can tell that," Tony said.

Ruth rejoined Tony. "That black man over there is John Toney. He's a real loner. Everybody likes him though. He's interesting. Said he joined the 3rd North Carolina Continental Regiment under Yarborough and Blount just this year and got in trouble after running away at Guilford Courthouse."

"How's that?"

"He ran home and they got him back and made him a prisoner and made him rejoin Blount's Regiment to fight again. And he's a free black all along."

"Free or not, you can't just turn and run away whenever you want to. Lucky they didn't shoot him."

"Well, that's what he told me. He said more whites run away than blacks, especially if they ain't got any training and ain't being paid or their time's up. Or they have crops to bring in, family matters to deal with, that kind of thing. Lots more whites have those kinds of problems than free blacks do. Most black folks don't have property to care for, anyway. Only family, and they're scattered by their owners."

"Who are those other black men standing with your man John Toney?"

"One of 'em told me his name's Charles Hood. He thinks he's real handsome. Kind of stuck up, but a real nit wit, I can tell. He's in—well, no telling what unit he's in. I think he's really supposed to be in Donoho's Company, Armstrong's Regiment, but I'm not sure. I can't keep up with all this military stuff, Tony. I don't know a brigade from a regiment, and you don't either.

"But I think the other one sitting down, the fat one, the man of mixed race like you, is Patrick Mason, and he's a private in Captain Dixon's Company. You sit down a lot, too, even if you ain't fat. Is that the white in you?" Ruth laughed and poked Tony in the ribs. She had not teased him since they both got out of bed that morning.

"You still glad you left me so early?"

"I don't think a one of 'em has a rifle. Sword either," Tony said as he smiled broadly at Ruth's remark. "I wish it was still morning and I was Colonel Cucumber."

Ruth took Tony's hand as they walked toward another group of soldiers.

Approaching a man who looked lost in his thoughts, Tony asked, "Tell me, if you don't mind, what is it you do? You look like you're in Blount's 3rd Regiment, but I don't see you armed."

Isom Scott was a big, solid black, handsome man wearing clothes more tattered than his face would let on but with shoes as good as the ones Will Lomax wore. He looked at his hands, both the palms and backs of his hand, which were rough and bleeding, and wiped them on his dark trousers.

"Ain't got any orders yet, but if you need to know, my job's to get wood for wagons and gun stocks and things like that." He looked up from his hands and continued with what sounded like a prepared response, impervious to interruption until it ran its course. After that, he would have nothing more to say.

"They tell me to clear roads of fallen trees sometimes, like a Black Pioneer. Some Pioneers carry guns. I want to. They may need me to do that someday. You can get in and out of trouble real fast if you're out scrounging 'round in the woods. Foraging around for taters or kindling. You can't always count on somebody else with a gun to protect you. That's the way it always is."

"Battles ain't won by just folks with guns," David Pugh interjected after hearing Scott's remarks. He was another dark black man but not as big or handsome as Scott. He was chewing on heart of pine and kept squinting his eyes. Tony backed off a little to give him room to spit.

"Black or white folks. There's lots of men needed to win a fight. Women, too." He broke into a big smile at Ruth and coughed. "Right, ma'am? Right? For one reason or another." He looked around for approval that never came.

"We've been with General Greene since he took over after Camden a year or so ago, and I can tell you that his army depends on folks like me doing my job, too. When you're fighting, I reckon you don't ever think much about skin color. Too busy. I'm a saddler in Captain Wood's Company. Got no stomach for battle, especially the kind we lose, like Camden, but that doesn't mean that my job ain't important. Army moves on its belly. Captain Wood says battles are lost or won, depending on if a man has enough food and a good saddle.

"Bullets, too," he added with another silly smile at Ruth as he turned to spit at a column of ants. "Like that."

Tony and Ruth followed the army from Laurens' Plantation to Burdell's Tavern where they met up with Marion's men. There Tony saw more men in one place than ever before. The view of so many people took over his customary view of trees and wild life in the Lowcountry. People were milling around in every direction, obstructing views of plants and animals, barns and fields. Horses were hitched to artillery, not plows. Wagons were loaded with rum and rations, military trappings, and matériel, not farming supplies or produce. If anything got lost, it stayed lost in all the shuffle or emerged somewhere else like a mole or phoenix.

Domination of the land by guns and cannons made him reflect fondly on the forests and inland rice fields, sweet grass, the barn and Eagle, Miss Maggie's palisade garden near the brick house and his parents' cabin, peaceful images where the laws of nature operated. But he also knew that slavery created its own kind of war that subverted the laws of nature, a soulful civil war that was going on at Miss Maggie's before soldiers would ever get near there. Men in arms now changed the natural landscape inwardly toward themselves. Natural laws would be suspended at the first exchange of fire, and whatever took their place would be chaotic and destructive, affected only by light and darkness and rain.

Ruth watched General Greene's men distribute the contents of all the army's rum casts. "Looks like they have to get drunk to fight."

Tony nodded. "Or be fodder."

General Greene gave the order for battle. The first and second lines of the army took the shape of two long side-winder snakes as they advanced in their battle positions through the woods toward eight and a half-cleared acres west of Maggie McKelvey's brick house. The land was gently undulated and presented no obstacles. No rain, yet, but thunder and lightning would start up later in the day before more rain on the day after the battle. Throughout, insufferable heat and humidity would sap both sides of strength.

"Cuffy and I have spent lots of time on the land in front of Miss Maggie's place," Tony said. "I know every inch of it. When we get to the springs, the cleared land is going to let the Pettiford brothers see each other better and stick together."

Ruth shook her head. "I'd just as soon not be at a place that lets Redcoats take a clean shot at you. Tony, I'm going back to Burdell's, and you should, too. Oscar told me it's the best place—too dangerous for a woman here. Said he would try to meet me back there after the battle, if he's still alive. You, too. I bet Miss Maggie's already safe at Bracky."

"You're right, but I'm going on. I'll be all right. I may even pick up a rifle in spite of what Jim Capers says. I sure hope my momma and daddy and my brothers went to Bracky with her."

As she turned to walk away, Ruth glanced back at Tony and shared a look between two people who are far from finished with each other, even as their strong bond begins to be unraveled by circumstances. Both saw great events happening to them as plateaus marking their love for each other, as progressions toward further adventure and closeness rather than as endpoints at which they could settle down and enjoy the fruits of their relation.

She's a free spirit, I know that. She'll do what she wants, get what she wants. I hate to think she's taken a liking to the Swamp Fox's man Oscar, but I reckon she has. She's reasonable. Knows to take care of herself first, so she can account for generations to come. I reckon men are just the past and present and women the future. I hope to high heaven I never lose her.

Tony continued with the American army as it moved from Burdell's Tavern toward Eutaw Springs. He caught up with Marion's men but immediately left them to catch up with Lee's and Henderson's foot soldiers in the van. Still under the assumption that they were marching undetected by the British, the Americans continued their battle formation of two rows, one behind the other, extending hundreds of yards long in the woods on either side of River Road. Tony ended up closest to Henderson's state troops.

"They don't even know we're coming," one of them whispered to Tony.

"You're wrong," Tony said in a loud voice as Henderson's men came to a sudden halt. They all looked up to see about fifty British cavalry riding hard toward them, followed by about three times that number on foot with muskets and fixed bayonets.

"Hell, they're riding right into the middle of us," the same man with Henderson yelled out as the South Carolinians began to return fire.

"We got orders to encircle 'em," shouted Andrew Pebbles. "There goes our cavalry." A fierce fighter, a man who looked like what he was, Pebbles earlier bragged to Tony about being in combat at Trenton, Monmouth, and

Guilford Courthouse. Now he gritted his teeth and looked around to see if the others knew what was happening. Either way, Pebbles was going on with or without them, whether any orders were given or not. "Ae-oh, here we go. Yee-ha, Whu-rah."

The encircling action by Lee's cavalry and light infantry and return fire from Henderson's state troops were the first shots fired by the Americans in the battle. Tony lay low as the entire forest erupted with the sound of small arms. The British charged right into the middle of the entire American army—not just a small detachment of scattered rebels as they at first thought. Within a very short time, a senior British officer ordered a quick retreat.

The loud gunfire drew the attention of another group of British soldiers nearby. They rapidly approached just as the British cavalry and troops under the command of the senior officer were withdrawing.

"They've been digging taters over yonder, and now they come running to help out," Pebbles said as he loaded his rifle. "Well, we can help them find their way out of here, too. Small, you lay low."

"Withdraw," a young British officer shouted. "We can't fight a whole army with just four rounds each. Withdraw!"

"'Withdraw'? Seems like I've heard that voice before," Tony yelled to Peebles as the Redcoats took off. "I think it was that crazy young Irish lieutenant. Same command he gave at Huger's."

"There may be thousands of the enemy just three miles west of our position and advancing at a steady rate," Lieutenant Lord Edward Fitzgerald blurted out to Major John Majoribanks after bolting back to the British line.

"I know, we've heard. Major Coffin already made his report to the commander. Our orders are to take up right flank positions immediately. We are to assume our formation for battle without delay. Along the river, at an oblique angle to the main line, our backs to the water. The deep ravine along the bank will let us retreat back to camp if we need to."

Lord Edward tethered his horse and began to move out on foot, but not before Majoribanks gave more orders. "Hold on. Let's first be sure you know our formation. I've ordered our flank battalion—nearly three hundred men—to take up positions in a pincer-like position at a sharp angle to the British main line. We can attack the enemy's left flank in the event of a charge toward the center of our main line, as well as defend Stewart's right flank. We used this same formation in Ireland during our five years at Cork, Limerick, Kinsale, and Clonmel. Now we're going to use it again. Get the word to Captain Sleigh and Lieutenant Hickman and loyalist commanders. Let's go."

••◦◦≫⁝⁞≪◦◦••

Observing Majoribanks' distinct formation, American Colonel Otho Williams reckoned it as one "having some obliquity to the main line, forming with an obtuse angle." To South Carolina veteran Record Primes, the large number of British soldiers was simply a very formidable sight.

"Redcoats everywhere," Primes said to another black patriot standing by him, "all across our front as far as you can see through these woods." The heavy-set man looked around, checked his rifle. Dry powder in the pan, powder, paper and ball rammed in the barrel. "Well, I fought in tough ones before— Camden, King's Mountain, Cowpens, and Guilford Courthouse—but I tell you, I ain't ever seen this many Redcoats all lined up for me to shoot."

By this time, Tony moved from Pebbles and Henderson's state troops to close proximity of Marion's men opposite the British left front. He squinted his eyes and cupped his hands around them, but he could not easily see individual soldiers fighting opposite the British right. Nor could he see clearly what was taking place along the American front line.

Greene's main attack began. Militias led by Pickens, Marion, Polk, and North Carolinians under Colonel François de Malmedy opened fire along the front line.

George Perkins was in Marion's brigade on the left-center of the American front line. An enormous man equal in combat to any on either side of the conflict, Perkins was positioned about twenty yards from Oscar who was standing by the Swamp Fox. Perkins yelled out over the din to Jim Capers who stood nearby. "Hold fast, Jim. Keep a look out for the colonel and be ready to make an advance if he gives the command. We're doin' fine so far."

A young drummer named Peter suddenly left the side of his master Captain Thomas Shubrick—master of Shubrick's Plantation—and yelled, "He's hit. Jim's been hit."

Perkins saw Capers lying on the ground, barely able to speak.

"I'm still ready. I'm hit but not too bad. Help him."

"Help who?"

"Help the other drummer."

Perkins looked over at the other drummer lying on the ground.

"He's been hit harder than me," Capers cried. "Help him, Perkins."

"No, you, Peter, go help him."

Peter went over to find the other drummer shot through the chest, dead. As soon as he turned around, he saw Perkins fighting hand-to-hand with a British soldier. Without a bayonet, Peter reloaded and fired. The Redcoat dropped dead. Perkins gave Peter a quick glance.

"Oh, Lord, Jim, you've be wounded—one, two, three, four times," Perkins said after he got up and rushed over to Capers. "Two bad ones, and one cut on your head, and a musket ball plumb through your left side, the very ball, I bet, that killed that poor drummer." Tony was never there to help his good friend.

Perkins left Capers and moved closer to Oscar as both looked to their right at some distance to see Polk's and Malmedy's militia faring much worse. British soldiers from DeLancey's First Battalion under Cruger rushed the North Carolina militia with bayonets as Malmedy's men began to give way.

"Reinforcements got to be sent in," Oscar yelled. "The colonel thinks they'll flank us." All attention turned to the North Carolinians coming up from the rear.

Well, well! Looks like us North Carolina Continentals have to go rescue the North Carolina militia and hold the front line," Elijah Bass, a free black from Halifax County, yelled out to Micajah Hicks who also heard the command to go forward. Bass, a handsome playful young man, looked down at his rifle and smiled. "I just hope I get more than a flash in the pan out of this old long wooden stick. It's times like this that I wish I wasn't a substitute, least not for that white coward Mr. Ebenezer Riggan." Bass turned to Isaac Hammonds nearby. "Or, even better, had a fife to play, like you, instead of this here rifle without a bayonet. Hell, if I get shot, I'm going to ask Mr. Riggan to die for me."

"I was born on the Fourth of July," Hicks said above the noise of officers shouting orders to move forward. "That's a big day. It's a big day for us all." He rushed forward. "As good for us as for any other fellow anywhere."

"Not for me," John Toney, a very light-skinned black, yelled back at Hicks as Sumner's entire North Carolina Brigade continued to take the place of Malmedy's militia and advance toward Cruger's Loyalists. Toney was also from Halifax County and in Blount's Regiment on the far right side of Greene's second line. John Toney was trying to keep his mind off being shot or blown to bits. Make enough chatter just to prove you're still alive. Nobody's listening after you're dead. Toney told his story about Guilford Courthouse to Ruth earlier. "It's no big day for me, the Fourth of July, if it's not for all us black folks."

"We both were at Guilford Courthouse," Hicks yelled back. "I didn't run, but I don't think you're a coward, John. And why are you thinking about being black at a time like this when you should be thinking about not being dead?"

"Isaac the fifer," a strong voice from Major Blount's Regiment called out. "Isaac Hammonds, you and the drummer, sound our advance to the front. Mind Lieutenant Colonel Lee's Legion directly in front as we march to their left. And move on farther to the left toward Polk's and Marion's militias. We're ordered to move up from our position on the second line to fill in the gap left by Malmedy's militia on the front. Isaac, drummer, sound our advance, boys. What are you waiting for? Now!"

By this time, Tony Small had worked his way down the line from Marion's position to get nearer the action as the North Carolina Continentals moved forward. Tony met Isaac among the dozens of black soldiers at Burdell's Tavern. He knew him as a man of color, a free black or man of mixed race or a mustee—mixed European and native American, but having no direct African blood in him—from Fayetteville, Cumberland County, North Carolina, who enlisted the previous month in the North Carolina Continental Line. Now Isaac was in the middle of a great battle, fife in hand and nothing else. He knew British muskets would be aimed at him at the first sound they heard, just like the drummer behind Capers who was shot dead by a British musket ball determined to get two for one.

"Why do they always give the fife and drum duty in battle to us black men?" Isaac asked out loud. "Easy answer." He pulled his fife from his belt, brought it to his lips, trembling, took a big breath, and let the shrill sound of the fife fill the air. "Whew, so far, so good."

Blount's Continentals not only had to go around Lee, but also had to go behind Captain Raiford's Company in Colonel Ashe's Regiment that was detached to Gaines' artillery. At least one man advancing with Blount's Regiment, Daniel Overton, realized that he was in the wrong unit at the wrong time and rushed in the direction of Raiford's Company.

"What the hell's going on?" Overton yelled to anyone listening in Blount's Regiment. "Where am I supposed to be, other than lying dead as a door knob?"

"Let him go," Lomax shouted. "Let ole Butt-eye go. He's always making excuses—'but I this and but I that.' They need him on the guns more than we need him, anyway."

"But I wasn't even given orders for *any* place," Overton said and ran away.

At that precise moment, Lomax got hit with a British musket ball.

"Damnation!" he cried out. "Damnation!" He fell while the Americans advanced in the general direction of the McKelvey brick house. John Toney rushed to his aid as Absolom Bibby provided cover. Bibby, who earlier told Tony he was proud to carry a rifle, could fire, reload, and fire again with the best of them—in twenty seconds. Artillery continued to rain down.

The sound of these big guns wraps you up and squeezes you like it owns all the air and doesn't want to share it. You have to breathe gunpowder if you breathe at all. Big crushing sounds one after the other and on top of each other at the same time, crashing in your ears, and like they're trying to find other holes to get

inside your body. I can't move anywhere to stop the shells roaring in. The noise of one close by is so scary that I almost wish it didn't miss. Artillery! Waiting for what's yours. Musket balls are bad enough. But worse are cannon balls flying like big boys laughing, playing, splintering trees, snapping 'em in half. Making meat out of men. Meat is what the balls want most, but they'll take a tree if it's close by and let the splinters and fragments do the job. Parts of men lying around like they were waiting until it's all over when they can be claimed and put back together. Or not claimed at all. I just can't see that fighting is any way to freedom—might as well be naked—but everybody's fighting as if it's the only way.

From his initial position as a camp-follower, Tony Small remained in the thick of the action when he returned to a position near Marion's militia. Blount's men came from the rear and swung behind Lee and in front of Campbell's Virginia Continentals to take the place of Malmedy's men who fell back. It was a chaotic maneuver for Sumner's brigade to make as the militias of Polk, Pickens, and Marion began an orderly withdrawal. By calling up Sumner's Brigade with lots of black men, Greene hoped to plug the widening gap left by Malmedy's militia when it fell back from the muskets and bayonets of Cruger's DeLancey's Brigade. Not only were the men in Blount's Regiment, those he met the previous night—William Burnett, Absalom Martin, Patrick Mason, Isom Scott, Charles Hood, as well as Absolom Bibby—not only were they coming forward as a part of Blount's Regiment, but also men from Armstrong's and Ashe's Regiments, absent Raiford's Company, were joining them and advancing even farther to the left of Greene's front line.

It all looked chaotic. The three regiments of North Carolina Continentals had to go far to their left, not just straight ahead of them. More than a few of the North Carolinians thought it would have been easier tactically if Greene had ordered his Virginia and Maryland Continentals simply to march straight to the front and fill in where Malmedy's line was crumbling. That would make more sense than to order the dog-leg angle Sumner's

Continentals had to take. But, all conceded, Green might want to save the Virginians and Marylanders, his best troops, along with the men from Delaware, for a more propitious moment in the battle.

"If he is saving 'em," Tony said out loud, "I sure don't know if there's ever going to be a better time to use 'em than now. Maybe he first wants to use the North Carolina black regiments as fodder to plug the gap. Maybe he knows they're just good soldiers."

Tony yelled out to George Perkins, "From looking at all the black troops in Sumner's North Carolina Brigade, it looks like Greene—it looks like Greene," he yelled louder, "figures that Ashe's, Armstrong's, and Blount's regiments are better than the white militia. Those white boys collapsed on the front line. Or maybe they're not as valuable."

"Better *and* not as valuable, both," Perkins yelled back.

The rush of North Carolina Continentals continued. Tony recognized some of the men from Armstrong's Regiment as they ran by.

"There's more behind us," Daniel Mills yelled out, and stumbled as he looked behind. "Sumner's now bringing forward his whole damn brigade."

Most of the black soldiers were from North Carolina units, more than those who made themselves known at Burdell's Tavern. They rushed by Tony in the midst of musket shot and cannon ball crashing through trees and underbrush.

Drury Chavers was near the front of Donoho's Company, followed by the Pettiford brothers Elias and Philip, and by the young boys Ruth fed at Laurens', Jacob Jeffries, Moses Manly, Daniel Mills, Joel Taburn, and Benjamin Reed, as well as by men from Hall's Company, John Artis and William Lomack. Now with wild eyes and steady focus, their faces were far different from those Tony and Ruth saw earlier.

Faces of men in Sharpe's Company, Ashe's Regiment, showed signs of extreme exhaustion as they, too, went charging by to fill in the gap. Edward Harris, Jr., John Hooker, and Mingo Stringer looked like fabled warriors heading into their last battle.

"Tony Small, grab a rifle and follow me," Edward Harris, Jr., yelled as he ran by. "This one's going to be a good one—if we can get there in time to hold the line—even if this is ain't the place to train a new recruit."

Mingo Stringer heard just the last part of Hooker's quick remark to Tony as the entire company ran by on the way to the front.

"Go! Tony's like a lot of the rest of us—too smart for Sharpe's shooting. We're rushing into a mess we may wish we had no part of."

Before these three haggard men in Sumner's brigade carried on, a voice yelled, "Or he's just a coward."

"That ain't right," Tony yelled after them. "I ain't afraid of killing and dying," but he did not know if anyone heard him over the noise of battle. He sat down hard on the ground and put his head in his hands. "I don't know what I'm doing. Can't fight and can't remember all those boys' names, anyway, and I don't even know how to write 'em down, and who cares?" He focused on a blurry object that looked like a rifle someone dropped. He looked away at a tree, then a clump of weeds, then back to what still looked like a rifle. "I'll leave whatever it is to Cuffy, not me."

Troops kept thundering by, yelling, screaming. Tony got up. He looked again at what was nothing but a small tree branch, not a rifle at all. A black patriot lay face down a few yards away with his rifle still in his hand. Tony turned him over on his back and picked up his rifle, then put it back down again. Elijah Bass was still breathing.

"Remember me, Tony Small. That's your name, isn't it?" He took in a long breath of air and let it out. "No, never mind. Don't bother. I'm done for. Let it all go." Bass took several more long heavy breaths and moaned.

"We'll fix you up, brother, but you got to let me move you out of here. You're going to get run over one way or another." Tony looked around for help as troops hurried to avoid fallen trees and bushes. He yelled, "Stop, wait, help me with this man here," but his voice was too faint to be heard over the din of battle.

"Tell my Mary that I love her. I know my good friend Ben Richardson will take care of her, if he ain't shot, too."

"You did Halifax County proud, Elijah—the whole regiment proud."

"Some black folks say it ain't so, but I reckon I'm dying here in this mud for my new country, not for just one solitary person and not for just blacks or whites." He took another long breath and closed his eyes. "God, God, forgive us all!"

Tony left him where he lay.

•••◦◦▶▆◀◦◦•••

"Where's your man, girl?" Ruth looked up from swaths of cotton pads she was folding on a table at Burdell's Tavern. A heavy-set white man stood grinning about two feet away. The fat on his arms sagged down like sacks of flower. His nose was so crooked he had to glare at Ruth out of one eye.

"You know, the mulatto you were with when you weren't hanging around Oscar."

"Tony Small's my best friend."

"Did he run away when the army advanced? I bet he did, You should have seen 'em run at Guilford's. Scared rabbits."

Ruth jerked her arm away from his grip up tight near her breast. "You'd best move on yourself. Nobody here's in the mood to see a white man messing with a black woman in the middle of a battle."

"Another time, honey, another time."

•••◦◦▶▆◀◦◦•••

A new weakness developed on the American left front. Henderson's state troops began to take on withering fire from the British right flank. Tony again hurriedly moved farther to his left along the line to get a better view.

"They're in a thicket there," Tony said to a black patriot nearby. "And it's a real thicket, hard to get through on a horse, even walking. I know because I tried lots of times." Beyond, he could see Miss Maggie's brick house and her palisade garden.

Farther to the left of Tony, but within sight and hearing distance, two of Henderson's men, Kneller and Nelson, were yelling back and forth at each other from behind fallen trees. Each seemed to be more agitated than the other. Darker and much bigger than Nelson, Kneller was the more experienced veteran. He was waiving his hands wildly as well as shouting.

Nelson looked as if he didn't quite take in the seriousness of the situation. Rather than reload right away, he kept adjusting his hat after each volley as if to say to himself, "Well done."

"Look out! Be lively! Forget that damned hat. Was that the colonel?"

"Yep, they just got Henderson," Nelson yelled back as he saw Henderson's aide rush to the side of the state troops' commander. "I think he's been hit hard. It's critical, all right. I can tell from here." The effect of the loss of Henderson was immediate. In a pitiful tone of voice, Nelson yelled, "We're still in the middle of this thing. What are we going to do, Keller?"

"Don't know. Nobody's giving orders. What *are* we going to do, Nelson?"

Opposite Henderson's South Carolina state troops, and now well out of Tony's line of sight and beyond hearing distance, Lieutenant Lord Edward Fitzgerald realized the effect British muskets firing from the thicket was having on Henderson's state troops and the entire American left flank.

"They see the advantage we're gaining with direct fire," Lord Edward shouted. "Get ready for the rebels to charge. They can't take heavy fire like this much longer." He looked over at the men braced for fighting under lieutenants William Sleigh and Robert Hickman.

"They aren't moving forward. Changed their minds. Looks like if they do make a charge and fail, they know they'll leave their left flank exposed. We got them just where we want them."

Looking far down to his left toward the American center, he yelled at the top of his lungs, "Hurray! boys. The rebels are crumbling all across their front. The Buffs and Sheridan are forcing a retreat. Hurray! Hurray! Those rebs who rushed up from the rear now wish they had stayed back and run away with the others."

In the midst of all this, a cry went up, "He's hit! Lieutenant Hickman's been hit by a rebel ball."

"I got him!" Nelson on the rebel side cried out, almost loudly enough to be heard by Hickman as he lay dying.

"You sure?" Kneller asked.

"He's down, ain't he? I just rested my rifle on this here log and took real sure aim like he was a squirrel dressed in a pretty red and white suit."

"Well, we're in a mess, but we got us a British officer. That'll show them boys in Pickens' militia how good we are." Keller began to chew on the twig of a sassafras tree.

"That more than makes up for that poor sot Billy Lunsford," Nelson said. He put his rifle aside and sat down on the ground. He took off his hat, dusted it with the back of his hand and blew on it, reached in his coat pocket for his pipe and began to light it.

"Fool, don't light up. Pick up your rifle. We're in the middle of a fight here. There's bullets flying all over the place."

"Not too long ago they shot poor Billy when he was making like a hog so he could get up close to a British sentinel and shoot him."

"Well, I reckon I heard about that, too." Kneller sat down beside him. Overcome with battle fatigue, both were now oblivious to the action swirling around them. It was time for the kind of story Old Dick would tell and the kind Old Sandy told about Major Baxter and Colonel Horry at Shubrick's Plantation.

"Billy wanted to kill at least one British soldier before he went back to his farm in Virginia. One of Lieutenant Colonel Washington's officers told him it wasn't right to sneak up and shoot a sentinel who was just doing his duty, but Billy insisted."

"And it didn't work out the way Billy thought it would," Nelson said. They both laughed as they tried to regain their wits and reload their rifles.

"He didn't get close enough before the sentinel shot *him*. The Brits heard ole Billy hollering like a stuck pig, found him lying out in a field. They dragged him back and patched him up, I reckon just to laugh at him. But there's nothing funny about this here killing. We got us a Brit fair and square. Nobody's going to patch *him* up." Their rifles erupted with fire at the same time.

A cavalry charge came from the American left flank toward the thicket on Stewart's far right flank.

"Again, we've got them just where we want them," Lord Edward yelled out as he turned to Major Majoribanks. "And the chubby cavalry officer at the head of the charge looks a lot like William Washington himself."

"I know, a cousin—second cousin—once removed—George Washington. Virginian. He and the whole bunch of rebels we got here today were at Cowpens, Guilford, Hobkirk. We barely missed him at Ninety Six riding with Pickens. He's the fat fellow Tarleton whipped at Moncks Corner. But a great swordsman."

"He needs a long belt to hold his sword, that's for sure. It takes one that measures more than three hundred and sixty degrees to get all the way around that belly."

Lord Edward paused long enough to have another good look, then laughed. "And he's making the same mistake he made at Cowpens and Guilford Courthouse—getting way too far in advance of his support troops."

"Well, it paid off then," Majoribanks replied. He was not smiling. "Some horse are even exposing themselves to a devilish enfilade."

"Impatiently rushing into a fight won't help him here. And that damned red curtain of a flag his whore gave him, flapping with his 3rd Dragoons. Doesn't he see that he's exposed to us while we're still dug in? The Buffs have good shots at them, too." Lord Edward was talking to himself by this time. Majoribanks stumbled over to another position.

"We'll take stout advantage of this underbrush to tangle up the hoofs of the Americans' cavalry." Lord Edward told his men. "Let them come to us. Take courage. Their horsemen have no support of infantry, and they're all easy targets, ducks sitting in saddles. Shoot 'em down sweet and proper or bayonet 'em for the king."

No black man on the patriot side was more active in military operations than Andrew Ferguson, Jr. Three months ago, he was with Light Horse Harry Lee at Ninety Six. He was whipped as a fifteen-year-old prisoner with a cat-o-nine tales. The man who whipped him was Colonel John Harris Cruger. Ferguson rode with Daniel Morgan and William Campbell, too, and now he was with William Washington's 3rd Regiment of Continental Light Dragoons at Eutaw Springs, no longer held in reserve by General Greene. He would have preferred to be making a charge at Cruger, not at Major Majoribanks and Lord Edward in the thicket.

"We're crazy to think we can ride through this blackjack," Ferguson yelled to a nearby cavalryman. "Even if it did first look like they were pulling back, the Brits are dug in the bushes. We're falling from our saddles on every charge we make. Everybody's getting shot up. We've got to wheel around. We'll be exposed broadside. Enfilade. Get out of here."

As both men retreated, they ran into Hampton's cavalry advancing in a desperate effort to get to the rest of Washington's cavalry before matters got worse and, mainly, to get Washington himself out of the mess he created. But the mess already crawled too far.

"Get him!" Lord Edward shouted to his grenadiers as Washington slashed his sword at the British ground troops surrounding him on his horse. "Get the fat bastard. Knock him down. Capture him."

Lord Edward's men maneuvered around the back of Washington's horse to unseat him without wounding or killing him, yet avoiding his saber. Frustrated, a grenadier lunged his bayonet at Washington's horse. The American cavalryman fell to the ground, pinned underneath his horse and wounded from the fall. The grenadier raised his bayonet over Washington.

"Hold your bayonet!" Lord Edward ordered with a sudden, wild scream. "Hold back." He knocked away the descending bayonet just in time. "This man is the king's captive. The major wants him alive."

Faced with Kirkwood's Delaware Regiment which by now arrived in support of Hampton's cavalry, Majoribank's flank companies withdrew from the thicket and scrambled along the Eutaw Creek ravine to the McKelvey brick house.

"Our orders are to head down toward the palisade garden by the brick manor house," Lord Edward shouted. "From there we can use those fences to provide cover as the Buffs and Cruger fall back toward the house. When we fall back, we can get cover from Sheridan who's already withdrawn to the house, just as Stewart ordered. Move! Pick him up and carry the prisoner! It will take two or three of you to lug his guts all the way to the house."

Following Majoribanks' tactics used in Ireland, Lord Edward relayed another order to his troops. "From our position in the garden we can again catch any advance in a pincer and enfilade the enemy lines. We can rush out to capture their artillery—fools that they are for moving it in so close."

With Washington's cavalry seemingly all but wiped out, Andrew Ferguson, Jr., escaped safely to tell men back at the American line what he saw. "I turned and saw Redcoats surrounding Colonel Washington. I saw a Redcoat bayonet his horse and another try to do the same to Washington, but he was stopped by a British officer who captured him as he lay there wounded under his horse."

The battle shifted into another gear. Greene ordered Campbell's Virginia and Williams' Maryland brigades finally to move forward from their rear positions. David Wilson, the same patriot who followed Thomas Carney in the assault on the sand bags at Star Fort and who captured William Cooper, was among the troops called forward from the rear in Otho Williams' Maryland Brigade. "Move forward, boys. We got to protect the artillerymen. They're firing a three-pounder against the Brit's four-pounder."

From his position near the McKelvey big spring on the American line about two hundred yards away, Tony Small saw Sheridan's men occupy Miss Maggie's empty brick house and fire on the Americans from the windows. Lieutenant Colonel William Gaines and Captain William Brown, 1st Continental Artillery Regiment of Virginia, brought their guns up to knock down the house.

··•◦╳◦•··

Well, there goes all Miss Maggie's pretty flowers in her palisade garden. And all my flowers and Sayey's, too. What a crazy thing to think about when all these men are dying on both sides—me just thinking about her flowers. With luck I could get over to the British line, pick up a musket and fight against the boys I saw at Laurens' and Burdell's. Or I could pick up a rifle here on the American line and charge Miss Maggie's house. What difference would it make? All I know is that the two 3-pounders of Gaines and two 4-pounders of Brown, and even the 6-pounders the rebs got from the British when they took off—all those guns won't have any luck in knocking down James McKelvey's brick house. Mr. James built that house real solid.

··•◦╳◦•··

Chaos firmly grabbed the Americans when their artillery was silenced. Troops manning the guns were shot dead as they tried to push them too near to the house, within easy range of British musket fire. Tony's friends in Raiford's artillery detachment to Gaines' Company—Ellis, Scott, Sweat, and James—were shot up badly by Sheridan's men firing from the second story windows of the McKelvey house.

Through all the smoke two patriots stumbled over rocks and small limbs of trees as they weaved their way toward the brick house. It looked like an enormous fortress a hundred miles away. "We got to get in that house," Agrippa Hill yelled out to David Wilson as they rushed forward helter skelter. "This is worse that Ninety Six. It's like fire raining down on us from the heavens. We don't have a chance till we get inside that house."

"I heard they're a bunch of New Yorkers in there, Northerners like you, but on the wrong side," Wilson yelled back. "Anyway, the door's blocked as far as I can see. Shut tight. Ain't any use. We're blocked out. Every one of us—all, all us boys—got to turn back or get shot at the front porch or door."

Something about twenty yards away appeared through the smoke, something that looked like a big turtle running on two feet.

"Now there goes somebody who knows how to make a safe retreat," Hill yelled. "He's got his pistol out and using a Brit as a human shield."

"Good gracious," Wilson yelled back. "At least we know that won't happen to us. No white reb's going to use us black folks as a shield—wouldn't do any good."

"Unless, the Brits and loyalists hold their fire when they see us, like I hear the Whigs did with ole Miller Sam at Huck's Defeat. You heard about him, didn't you?"

Guns continued to roar as Hill went on as if he and Wilson were sitting around a camp fire, the same way Nelson and Kneller did at the thicket and Old Sandy and Capers did at Biggin.

"Well, Miller Sam and his master were beating a fast retreat when his master dropped his saddle bag. He sent ole Sam back to get it, and just as the Whigs were about to shoot him, Sam took off his cap to show he was black. When they saw that, a Whig yelled, 'Don't shoot him, it's only a Negro.'"

Hill and Wilson's laughter was almost as loud as the sound of cannon and gun shot. They took their hats off, weaving this way and that, falling down on the ground to play dead, and getting up and running again. Tony saw it all and thought they lost their minds in the midst of battle.

Sheridan's men were winning their struggle to hold the impregnable brick house. Many of Tony's friends were either dead or lay wounded in front of the raised porch that Miss Maggie used to stand on and give him instructions for the day's work. The charge by Campbell's Virginia and Williams' Maryland brigades was arrested, in part, for failure by Gaines's and Brown's guns to knock down the house and turn out Sheridan's New York Volunteers. Although still several hundred feet away, Tony could see what was happening at the same time—a completely chaotic tangle of American troops in the ropes, tents, and other matériel of the British army.

Campbell's Virginians and Kirkwood's Delaware men who now had moved from the thicket, and North Carolina Continentals who retreated earlier with Sumner but were now moving forward, tripped and fell to the ground, tangled up with ropes and stakes. Without effective cover inside the tents and none at all outside, they were completely exposed to a hail of fire from Sheridan's men in the brick house and from Lord Edward's men and the rest of Majoribanks' flank companies firing from the palisade garden.

Like Laocoön and his sons, men twisted and turned as if in the coils of a giant snake. Tony allowed himself a bitter smile at the irony of what was happening. While the American units displayed great dexterity and organization in moving through the woods and brush in their approach from Burdell's Tavern to meet Stewart's army, they could not now, as troops advancing while under attack, get beyond the entanglements within the enemy's camp. The camp was on cleared land set up on part of the eight and a half acres at the front and side of the house.

Andrew Pebbles, the man who helped rebuff the British charge led by Major John Coffin at the potato patch two hours earlier, looked around and saw he was about to be chopped up by fire from the house and palisade garden. Pebbles looked anxiously around for his cavalry commander. Yet, Lee was nowhere to be seen when Greene's order from Pendleton arrived to push toward Stewart's rear in back of the house. Lee's second in command, Major Joseph Eggleston, carried out the order to advance from the American's right flank to attack the British left protected by Major Coffin's cavalry.

As Eggleston charged the enemy, Pebbles was shot in the shoulder, hit badly enough to take him off his saddle. A Redcoat made a parry with his bayonet at him. Pebbles put his left hand up to deflect the blow, only to see his thumb cut off with one quick slice.

"Watch the rascal coming back," someone yelled and shot the Redcoat who was trying to make one more jab at Pebbles. "I'm stabbed bad in the belly, too," Pebbles cried out. "It's the worst of the three licks they gave me. God help me!"

"Lee's Legion is sweeping 'em up," the same voice cried out. "Lieutenant Manning's got a Redcoat officer prisoner."

But the battle swung again in favor of the British. Coffin not only successfully repulsed Eggleston's charge, but also took the offensive. A seriously wounded Pebbles retreated. So did Greene's entire army. Stewart moved forward from his command position in the rear and joined Coffin in the chase. No longer under siege, Sheridan left his fortress at Maggie McKelvey's brick house and advanced beyond the palisade garden to join what nearly becoming a route. Majoribanks and Lord Edward advanced from their position in the creek bed and garden.

··•◦❖◦•··

Tony was still with scattered remnants of Marion's men, most of whom had withdrawn, when he saw Henderson's troops fall back. George Perkins and Peter were standing within a few feet of Tony. The Americans' left flank was exposed.

Peter was still shaken from drummer Jim Capers' four injuries and the death of the other drummer who stood behind Capers. Capers, though seriously wounded, struggled to get Peter up on his feet and beat a retreat for the rest of Marion's men.

"Let me help you with him," Tony said. "I got him. You go on."

With Peter in tow, Tony looked around and saw Oscar as remaining militiamen fell back under fire from oncoming British musket, bayonet, and cannon.

"Well," Tony muttered out loud, "Oscar can now go back to see his new sweetheart Ruth, thanks to Brits who can't shoot straight."

Old Dick, as he did at Ninety Six and now at Eutaw Springs, was fighting with remnants of Pickens' militia who had not yet completely withdrawn. Old Dick yelled, "Fall back," but a South Carolinian, Edward Harris, did not hear him or even pay much attention to all the men on his left and right as they withdrew.

Finally, Harris yelled back to Old Dick, "I've seen retreats and advances—Camden and Cowpens, Hanging Rock—but this here is stand-and-fight time."

"You're a fool," Old Dick yelled back. Harris, veteran of seven battles, finally showed good sense and pulled back.

None too soon. Tony looked back to see Old Dick and Edward Harris barely give ground before they saw troops from the entire British right front line. The Buffs and Major Sheridan's, Lieutenant Colonel Cruger's, and

Major Green's troops rushed the retreating Americans in the few remnants of Marion's and Pickens' militia and North Carolina Continentals that replaced Malmedy's men. While retreating, the Americans took on a chaotic charge of musket and the much-feared British bayonet. Joseph Case and Charles Gibson were among those fighting hand-to-hand.

At a farther distance two white patriots were frozen by fear, too sapped of strength to stay and fight or even to run. The two men were hugging each other and the log that lay beside them, their heads buried under the log so they couldn't hear or see. Old Dick and Edward Harris kicked and yelled at them to get up and get going, but they held onto each other and the log, as if reassured that the log offered their only hope for survival.

Nearly half of Sumner's North Carolina Continentals, by far the most troops, died at Eutaw Springs. In Armstrong's Regiment, Donoho's Company, Drury Chavers was killed in action. Benjamin Reed was wounded. The men in Ashe's Regiment, Sharpe's Company, suffered heavier casualties than most. Twenty-nine of Ashe's men were killed in action, but Edward Harris, Jr., John Hooker, and Mingo Stringer in Sharpe's Company survived. Isaac Hammonds, Micajah Hicks, and Moses Newsom also survived. Elijah Bass, substitute for Ebenezer Riggan, was killed in action.

As Greene's army withdrew, for Lord Edward it was time to go on the offensive. He eagerly pursued the Americans, displaying the recklessness he showed at Ninety Six, Raid of the Dog Days, and Orangeburg—not with the discretion he showed in defense of the sweet potato foragers. Like William Washington at the thicket, Lord Edward found himself in a forward position without support.

Storm clouds gathered. Amidst a dark sky the roar of heavenly thunder blocked out the sound of rifles and muskets. Flashes of lightning in split seconds froze the chaos in successive images as men fell on both sides. Retreating Americans saw the young enemy cavalry officer suddenly in their midst, so far ahead of support that he at first looked like he switched sides and was withdrawing with the American army. Furiously slashing his sword at rebels around him, he quickly dispelled that impression.

"Good gracious," someone yelled. "What a fool. He's an officer. Stick him. We don't want no prisoners. No ransom, either."

Other rebels began to laugh at the predicament Lord Edward was in. "Who's got a bayonet?" another yelled. "Unhorse the bastard, and I'll kill him with my knife. Looks like a dandy fellow trying to prove himself. Where's his daddy now?"

"Well, let's give him some glory," another yelled as they all surrounded him and continued to laugh.

Lord Edward reined his horse around so suddenly and with such force that the mount began to fall backwards. This caused him to rear himself up in the stirrups while trying to slash his sword to the left and right. The horse continued to fall backward. Lord Edward was yelling and cursing as loudly as the half dozen white rebels completely surrounding him.

As one of the more eager assailants reached for the reins of his mount, Lord Edward's sword slashed clear through his neck, dropping him in place.

"The son of a bitch is putting up too much of a fight. We don't have time to kill him."

Lord Edward felt a sudden thrust of steel to his thigh. He toppled out of his saddle in excruciating pain. A debilitating, Adonis-like wound that cut near an artery in his thigh.

"Don't kill his mount. Grab the reins."

"He's done for," cried a rebel who by now had gone on about twenty feet beyond. "He's done for. I stuck him good. Leave the bastard be. He's so damned forward of his men they won't even know he's here. Let him bleed to death. He's going die. Let's get out of here. Grab the damn horse."

A flash of lightning lit up the scene again and a crack of thunder made the horse jerk away and run wildly back toward the British line. Curses fell on the man whose job was to hold him.

The last rebel to leave made a move toward Lord Edward's sword. "I'll just take this, if you don't mind, your majesty."

"Quick, grab his boots, too. We got to get out here," yelled another.

"Son of a bitch just tried to slash me," the other rebel yelled back, "him a-lying on his back, too, helpless as a turtle. No time to reload. Come help me finish him off for good. We got time. He ain't kilt yet. We got to revenge what he done already, and we ain't taking anything till he's good and dead."

"Ain't got time for more killing," his comrade yelled back on the run, now with the others some distance away and hurrying to retreat. "Stick him again yourself." Forgetting both sword and boots, the last rebel ran to keep up with his comrades.

Delirious with pain and loss of blood, Lord Edward looked around on the battlefield. He saw only scattered rifles and muskets and men and horses, dead and dying. He began to lose consciousness.

Mumbling to himself through the crack of thunder, he cried out, "This cannot be how it must end. Not defeated and vanquished on the fields of Carolina. Not by rabble. Not without valor. Yet, better this than at the blade of a Frenchman, O my heart! The regiment's honor is at stake. Fortune, keep me alive."

Chapter 5

CHARLESTON

An eerie silence escorted exhausted troops and horses back to Burdell's Tavern. Shuffles and groans replaced Lowcountry sounds of wrens and crows heard on the way to war. A somber gray sky and cessation of artillery were still enough to inhibit any sound of nature. Troops guarding the rear pushed laggards and the wounded to move faster than they could go. Wives, mothers, fathers, neighbors, and strangers helped those who stumbled and fell.

Silence back at Burdell's gave Tony time for reflection. Without Ruth to share his thoughts, he sat down on a log about twenty yards from the tavern door where he could watch what was happening as Greene and his officers began to restore order. He saw blacks and whites and those who shared blood from both races, native Americans, too, shuffling by. All carried the same stiff, straight-ahead stare in their eyes and looked thoroughly whipped as they passed by. One, mumbling to himself, still shaking from hand-to-hand combat, said that he could smell the other man's breath and feel the heat and sweat from his body as both looked each other in the eye and, like worms, wiggled around on the ground trying to kill each other. The odor of war following the troops came from knife, tooth, and bare hands as much as from cannon and musket ball. Like the visual landscape which Tony saw taken over from nature by men in arms before battle, now the odors after battle were equally arresting. The sweet odor of tea olive was long gone.

"Bodies everywhere," he told Ruth the moment he saw her walk up to him. She was waiting for him on the other side of the road and, after columns of troops cleared enough, saw him sitting on the log. "They fought from early morning till way past noon. Hundreds dead or dying or just lying out there so shot up or cut up they can't move, waiting to die. I saw dead bodies propped up on one another's bayonet and stuck that way like they were mocking a stack of arms."

Ruth sat down beside him and gave him a long tight hug. "I ain't too surprised. You're whupped good, too, and all those poor boys. But I reckon that doesn't touch us hard unless we know some of 'em." She looked to see if Tony agreed. He sat motionless, looking at Burdell's main door.

"Anyway, let's wait till the smoke clears, Tony, and maybe this evening when it's about dark, let's go see if we can find some money or silver buttons and things on folks who don't need 'em any more. I want to be there early. I don't want anybody to beat me to anything out there I can use to buy freedom."

Tony raised his eyes, then looked down and slightly shook his head. "Right, but don't you think we ought to have more respect for the dead—give 'em some time to be alone?"

"Alone?"

"Well, if we do see somebody we know, we'll help 'em. Old Dick—Pickens' man—told me he didn't go on the field at Cowpens till the smoke cleared. It's too dangerous now, for sure. We don't know if any of 'em wounded is still strong enough to pull a trigger or make a jab at us with his sword. Redcoats probably running scared all the way back to Charleston, but they're looking back over their shoulder, too. We don't even know if everybody even ran in the right direction and got off the field."

"Well, Peggy Fenwick's been working for Colonel Stewart ever since she ran away, and she says they're off and running. All of 'em cleared out. Peggy got word out to some of the rebel stragglers that the Colonel's already got lots of us black folks cutting down trees to block the road to Charleston. But we could get caught up in all the commotion of what the Brits are doing to get out of here. I sure don't want to get mixed up in all that."

Ruth looked at the men in Greene's army. She got up and walked forward a little, and at the risk of being run over by horses and wagons coming in, sat down on the ground and put both hands over her face and mumbled between her fingers. Her demeanor was different from her unconscious child-like gestures of whispering a tune and wiggling her toes when she first arrived at Laurens' Plantation.

"I spent all day with the rebels," she said as she looked up, "and I'm afraid of some of them, especially one nasty white man who grabbed a-holt of me when I was folding bandages. But I sure don't want to be put to work now for no Brit. Peggy's right. Light Horse Harry and the Swamp Fox are still after 'em good. But the rumor here is that the trees on the road made 'em turn back around Martin's place, still a good ten to twelve miles from Moncks Corner. I just don't want to be treated bad or be made to work."

She scooted back away from the road, knocked off a piece of mud clinging to her dress. "I met Peggy one time. She loves her some freedom. She left old man Edward Fenwick on James Island the year after Jenny Burton ran away from Andrew Burkin in Savannah to join Colonel Stewart, too. That was about a year or so ago, I reckon, but you know all of that. You're not even listening, Tony. I bet both Peggy and Jenny are on their way back to Charleston now with Colonel Stewart. I'll join 'em someday. I just don't want to be made to chop down trees."

A few hours later, they set out from Burdell's Tavern to walk back to the battlefield, Ruth leading the way. "Slow down, Ruth! This tooth ache Cuffy gave me from fighting hurts when you walk so fast, and I'm still plenty whupped. And don't tell me little things are bad as big ones only if they get to you. It's killing me. And don't say it's just part of life, manure and roses."

"Well, so far, it's doing a bad job of killing you. Just don't think about it. You're just thinking up a little pain to hide what's still big. I know you're hurting, but think about all the silver buttons we're going to get. You can bite down on the gold we find to see if it's real, too. That's bound to be a cure."

After dodging the last of retreating American troops and cavalry, they arrived at the cleared land around the McKelvey brick house and looked at all the bodies. Anything in the woods west of the house was less visible. A very late summer sun and a sense of reverence were enough to slow down the pair of scavengers to a solemn pace, looking one way, then another, but seldom stopping for any length of time. The battlefield was still too fresh with blood to admit any animals or birds to scavenge in their own ancient way. An encore of imaginary sounds of artillery and rifle fire and steel on steel played around the dead. A moist soft breeze heightened echoes and carried aloft the cries of the wounded.

"I sure don't like hearing 'em cry, Tony. Let's go faster. If a ghost has any business with me, it's going to have to keep up. Now I don't even know what I'm looking for."

"You're just having a hissy-fit over nothing, Ruth. Calm down. Colonel Stewart must have been in a mighty big hurry to do what I hear the British never do, leave their dead and wounded behind. I see lots of Brits. At least Stewart didn't fire artillery on his own troops."

They walked nearer the house. "But they sure made a mess of Miss Maggie's garden. Look at that, would you? All my pretty flowers and weeds I snuck in there. All chopped up and gone. A whole lot worse than what Cuffy ever did."

They saw several black patriot women and dozens of white patriot women, camp followers and wives and sweethearts on the battlefield looking for their men, army sutlers trying to reclaim what they could. Ruth noticed a white woman at a distance hovering over a man lying on his back on the ground. Then movement and crying as she raised her dress.

"She's sitting on him, Tony. Look over there. Her skirt's up and she's sitting on him. Can you believe that? Can't you see what they are doing?"

"He's dying, Ruth. And she wants a baby to remember him by. That's all. I hope they make it, but I bet they don't."

"A pitiful sight. I didn't know folks could even try to do that."

There was still enough light to make out the images of bodies lying on the open field in front of Maggie McKelvey's house. Both realized the dangers of poking around a body that was still alive or warm and fresh from dying. Not all the blood was clotted and dried. Not all the smoke was blown away by a wind nearly as dead as the flesh it passed over.

"Dead horses everywhere, too," Ruth observed out loud. Then gasping, she uttered quietly to herself, "Eagle. Oh, my, oh, my. Poor Eagle. Never meant to be a war horse." He lay dead, still hitched to a cannon. "Oh, poor Eagle."

"What?"

"Nothing. The British soldiers are all well dressed in their bright red coats. Some have X's on their belt buckles, like 'XIX.' 'Shoot me here.' That's stupid. But they don't have much money on them." She never told Tony about Eagle.

"They didn't make much money to begin with. They had terrible lives. Might as well be enslaved. Look for officers. On both sides. Some of the partisans in Henderson's and Hampton's brigades could also have valuables on them as pay from looting as Sumter's men."

Ruth stopped suddenly as she looked down at a large disfigured black man lying in a pile of bodies, a rifle still gripped tightly in his hand. Cuffy. She quickly tried to move Tony to another spot, hoping that he did not see—but too late.

"That there looks like Cuffy," Tony calmly said. "Miss Maggie's man Cuffy." Tony paused for a very long time and just stood looking at the body. Ruth said nothing. After a while he said, "I'm not surprised. Can barely tell who he is. Can't tell which side he died for, either."

Tony looked up at the sky as if he could tell time by a sun that wasn't there, as if he were interested in time no matter the hour. "I have to tell his momma."

"Y'all never were friends. He was just looking for trouble. Ain't anybody really going to help us black folks, and we really can't even help ourselves." Ruth took Tony by the hand. "I never did tell you, Tony, but I heard they were going to hang him for messing with Miss Maggie's little niece. I mean if they ever caught up with him.

"Are you thinking about whether Cuffy's more of a man because he fought and you didn't? Look at me, Tony."

"Don't know what side he was on, but he has a rifle, not a musket. That could mean the American side. He died for what he believed in is all I'm going to say. We were friends."

Ruth let go of Tony's hand as they continued to walk among the dead. She slowed down her pace for fear of tripping. She began to look more closely at objects to get Tony's mind off Cuffy. After walking farther, in a hushed voice as she knelt down to the ground, she said, "Look, here. Here's some coins in this Redcoat's pocket. He's dead. Won't miss 'em now."

Tony walked up behind her. "Careful around somebody still alive. You never know when a hand will reach up and *grab* you." He laughed as he quickly lunged at Ruth.

"You stop that, Tony Small! You've got no sense to be doing that now. If I can't tell the live ones from the dead ones, I leave 'em alone." Ruth was barely audible and shivered as she spoke. "But it's pretty easy when their head's shot off. Or if they're stuck on up one another's sword."

"Well, all I got so far is a nice red sash," Tony said. "I'm looking for some nice boots."

They continued collecting a few other coins, brass buttons, and belt buckles which they could see by a faint moonlight. Rifles, muskets, and swords lay on the ground, each as fickle as the next. There was no way of telling which of them once belonged to whom. Now the guns alone continued to live, all lying around like whores in Charleston, trying to look attractive enough to entice the next customer. "This one's got a nice stock—like legs," Tony mumbled to himself. "This one's got a good grip—like breasts. This one's got an easy trigger."

"Here's some more buttons stamped with a 'XIX' on them. Some have 'J9' or '63' or '64.' But they ain't silver," Ruth said.

The moon went in and out behind clouds. Uneasiness in Ruth drifted into fear, like a cloud slowly changing shape, the whole sky disappearing like a scroll rolling up. "Let's go, Tony."

Tony began to follow her off the open grounds to head back toward the road to Burdell's Tavern. It was too dark now to see much, and he didn't have time to look at what remained of Miss Maggie's house and her garden that he loved, or even of his family's cabin.

"Wait." Tony whispered. "You hear that?"

"What? I didn't hear a thing. I don't want to hear a thing. See a thing, either. Seen and heard enough. Don't want to smell a thing, either. It's spooky and this whole place stinks. Let's go, I told you. It was a bad idea to come, anyway."

Tony began to follow about ten feet behind. "No, wait, I hear something, I really do. We're going straight toward where it's coming from. Can't you hear a moaning somewhere around here?"

"I've been hearing moaning for over an hour. I tell you it's spooky here. Let's go." She began to walk faster, stumbling on bodies and dead horses.

"Come here. Come here, Ruth. This one's still alive and trying to say something. Can't understand what he's saying."

Both hovered over the British officer in his bright red tunic, white britches, and black leather boots, lying on his back in a pool of blood and mud. One gold epaulette with a tassel was nearly ripped off from his right shoulder. His eyes were closed. His right hand lay on his sword.

"He's asking for water. Talks funny. Looks like a bayonet got him in his left thigh. Or a rifle ball. Probably a bayonet. Lots of blood, though. Barely missed an artery." Tony moved the sword aside with his foot.

"He's fainting in and out for lack of blood, I bet. Let's go, Tony. We don't know him. He's a Brit who's going to die anyway."

"Quick. Run to the cymbee and get water for this poor fellow. Help get his blood back up. Be careful. Hurry back."

"It's too dark."

"This man's probably not going to make it if you don't go to the cymbee for water, Ruth. He'll live if he can get some healing water and we can stop the bleeding. He's sure hurting now. Look at all the blood he's lost. It's shinning in the dark. Hurry. I'll tie up his thigh with this sash I got."

"Tony, cymbee water is in the opposite direction we want to go in. It's back at the boilers, way past the other side of Miss Maggie's house. I'm afraid, Tony. I'll have to walk through all those bodies again, and in the dark, alone.

Then I'll have to come back through the same thing." She plumped down on the ground. "I ain't going."

"Then you stay here and tie up his thigh. I'll go to the big spring."

As Tony started to run away, Ruth said in a hushed voice, "Remember what Hercules said about the cymbee water spirits. Remember to skim off just a little from the top when you dip into the spring, so the cymbee won't be upset at you. They could make things worse for all of us, give us the ague and fever."

There's my favorite tree set against the dark sky. Silhouette. Beautiful. Majestic. Peace and a place to think, my special place as a child and even now in the middle of all what's going on. My tree's an anchor and a compass that says where I am and where I'm going, and I can see something's surely changing. Something new and exciting and dangerous. I'm going to save a life.

After arriving at the big spring and before dipping into the waters with a gourd he found nearby, Tony knew what to say.

"Cymbee, great spirit of flowing waters, give me water, please. Help cure a fallen soldier who means no harm to you and your dwelling place. Help him with your power to heal, oh, cymbee. Help him, please."

Tony dipped a large gourd full of spirit water from the spring and ran back in the dark as fast as he could. "I got it. I got it, Ruth." He was so excited he stumbled and splashed some of the cymbee water on Ruth.

"Watch out! You're wasting it."

"I spoke good and loud so the cymbee could hear me. 'I'm getting water for a man hurt in the battle,' I told the cymbee, 'a very young man who looks like he's a very good man, too.'"

"I know the cymbee doesn't like a war raging around his spring, but I'm awful glad you got back as soon as you did, Tony, for me and him, too. He *is* a handsome man."

Tony looked hard at the dying man. "Seems like I've seen him somewhere before, Ruth. Hard to say, it's so dark." Tony knelt down and squinted his eyes up close, but it was almost pitch dark now. "Can't see but it seems like he may be that young Irish lieutenant at the rear guard near Huger's Bridge and at Quinby Bridge with the howitzer. I followed him down from Orangeburg with Rawdon after Ninety Six. He may have seen me when Timothy Withers sent me to the rear of the small corps going from Orangeburg to Goose Creek. And on to Moncks Corner, Hugers and Quinby. I just never met him."

"Forget all that now, Tony. What are we going do with a British soldier, whether you recognize him or not? Looks like he's taking nicely to the cymbee water right away, but we can't just keep on nursing him right here on open ground, even if you do want to help him."

"He's awfully weak, and he ain't going to live unless we help him. That's a fact. So let's get him back to my cabin if it's still standing—give him a chance for a good rest, lots of cymbee water, some biscuits and sorghum, if we can find any, keep him clean and patched up, and I bet he'll be fine in no time. But he's sure a sorry looking sight now. Beat like a rented mule."

Tony's rescue of Lord Edward Fitzgerald from the battlefield at Eutaw Springs was written down in the regimental record:

"So close, indeed, and desperate was the encounter, that every officer engaged is said to have had personally, and hand to hand, an opportunity of distinguishing himself, and Lord Edward, who we may take for granted, was among the foremost in the strife, received a severe wound in the thigh, which left him insensible on the field. In this helpless situation he was found by a poor negro, who carried him off on his back to his hut, and there nursed him most tenderly till he was well enough of his wound to bear removing to Charleston. This negro was no other than the 'faithful Tony,' whom, in gratitude for the honest creature's kindness, he now took into his service, and who continued devotedly attached to his noble master to the end of his career."

··•◆◆•··

"How are we going to keep him from being captured?" Ruth asked. "We're going to get ransom money? No telling how many rebels still around here, looking out to see if Redcoats are going to pursue 'em. And I'm sure they would love to capture an officer. Good ransom money, this one."

"Then we got to move and get over to the cabin right away. We got to save him before somebody pushes us aside and strips him of his gear. It ain't far from here. Come on. Help me with him."

Trying to walk on each side of the wounded soldier, Ruth began to laugh. "Looks like we're all drunk."

"Fact is, he can't walk at all. I guess I've got to sling him on my back if we're going to get anywhere, get out of this clearing before too much dark and too much dawn. Stop laughing. This ain't funny."

With Lord Edward on Tony's back, Tony and Ruth stumbled on toward his family's cabin a hundred yards away. It was still standing.

"This man needs our help for the rest of the night," he told a group of surprised men, women, and children who were in the cabin taking refuge.

"Where's my family? Don't worry. This wounded soldier ain't going to hurt anybody."

"They took off with Miss Maggie heading to Bracky on the Santee," one of them replied as he slipped out the door.

After convincing the more skeptical men in the cabin that they would be safe from reprisals—a promise he could not keep—Tony helped Lord Edward gently to the floor and gave him a blanket and some food.

"There, he's comfortable enough now. He's weak as a new-born calf. Hasn't said a word. Ruth, I bet some soup and cornbread will bring him around. You can sure tell the cymbee water saved his life. Looks like he's about my age."

"He's *very* handsome," Ruth said. "Looks like an angel."

Ruth went outside and got a bucket, washed it out, and began to punch holes in the bottom.

"Whoa, that's a good bucket. You're ruining it."

"Get me a rope, Tony. We're going to tie up this bucket on the roof beam over this angel and let the water drip on his wound little by little by little all night 'till it's good and clean. In the morning he'll be fine. Something I heard a woman do for her wounded husband last March at Guilford Courthouse."

The next day was Sunday and rainy enough to keep the ground muddy. The Carolina sun was trying to break through the clouds but hesitant to start up more trouble, to give more men more light for more mischief. Some in the cabin went out early, saw no activity, military or otherwise, and came back to tell Tony that Stewart's army retreated only to Ferguson's Swamp and was still hanging around, not yet marching toward Fair Lawn and Moncks Corner. Elements of a British rear guard anticipating a renewed attack by Greene were nearby.

"We've got to get loose of Greene's army and find a horse for this man, get him as far as Wantoot," Ruth told Tony as they left the cabin with their wounded British officer, now well enough to limp along with help. "I think he rested pretty well during the night 'cause I watched over him. The drip, drip, drip of the cymbee water from the bucket helped a whole lot with the pain."

"He can't ride a horse, Ruth. Got to find a wagon. The Brits destroyed all the rum and other stuff way before the battle, but they've still got wagons around here. And—can you believe it?—folks in the cabin say he left about seventy of his wounded, just like somebody said."

After they struggled to reach a road about a quarter of a mile from the cabin and near the battlefield, Tony squinted his eyes toward a figure coming directly toward them. From his point of view, it was barely moving, a haggard old black man in a wagon that looked as if it had been thrown together from parts of broken wagons left on the battlefield. A salvaged horse was pulling it, as tired of war as men were. Tony smiled at his good fortune.

"Hold on there, mister. We sure could use that wagon. We need to take this British officer to Wantoot." Tony pointed to Lord Edward leaning against a tree. "You wouldn't be headed down St. Stephens Road or down the Moncks Corner Road, would you?"

"I can get anywhere any way you want, especially if he's really a British officer. Sure looks like he is, and in sorry shape, too. Maybe they'll pay good for him. And I ain't a spy or I'd be riding backwards." Using his best grin, the old man looked around for an appreciative audience. He let the reins go slack and picked up a jug from the floor planks.

"There's a rat's nest of egos amongst those British officers, so I really don't rightly expect to get anything for my labors. But I ain't doing the work. My old mule Drum's doing the hauling." After a swig from his jug, he looked from face to face, drawing out the grin left over from his spy joke. "Just keep him alive, and old Drum will do the rest."

The ride to Wantoot was rough. Lord Edward winced in pain as he bounced around on the rough planks. "Here you go," Ruth said, and offered him a blanket. "And a little whiskey the driver kindly lets you have—not as good as cymbee water, but it'll do. You're leaving pain behind now." She stuffed the blanket around his back leaning against the side of the wagon and handed him the jug. "You don't talk much, do you? Embarrassed to be whupped by rebels and saved by blacks?"

Within a short time, they were spotted by Stewart's rear guard which was composed of a detachment of the flank battalion commanded by Major Majoribanks. When he saw Lord Edward's bright scarlet tunic with one gold epaulette, Majoribanks himself stopped the wagon.

Without Ruth's help, Lord Edward carefully climbed down from the wagon bed, saluted as best he could, and embraced his battalion commander.

"My, my," Ruth whispered to Tony, "If I knew he was in that good a shape—what, to get out of the wagon on his own like that!—I would have told him to get in it on his own and kept the blanket for myself."

It was clear that Lord Edward was regaining strength quickly, only twenty-four hours after suffering from dehydration and a life-threatening thigh wound. The appearance of Major Majoribanks, on the other hand, caught Ruth's eye. "The major looks worse off than our young officer. Looks weak and feverish. He could do with some cymbee water, too, if we had any left. I saw you finish it off, Tony, nursing that tooth."

"It's easy to see they're both worn out. Yesterday was fighting in a skillet."

After a short exchange with Majoribanks regarding movement of Stewart's army, Lord Edward looked proudly at Tony. "I was miraculously saved by this wonderful man. Thanks to him—and in equal measure to this kind woman—I am ready for further duty."

Ruth smiled and glanced at Majoribanks, then at Tony who was equally surprised and pleased to hear their invalid speak so well of them and the care they gave him. This was the first time Tony and Ruth heard him say anything other than yes and no in response to their questions about his health. But they also realized that at that moment, their roles as saviors would change immediately to roles as servants, and that they would be sent forward to join other blacks in Stewart's column to cut down trees to block the road as the British retreated.

Ruth changed her mind about cutting down trees and wanted to do just that. For Tony, however, it was another matter. From the time he saw him lying helplessly on the battlefield, Tony sensed a need to protect the young Irishman. The feeling grew stronger from hustling after cymbee water, carrying him on his back, feeling the sheer weight of the man, stumbling in the dark—all creating a bond through human suffering and aspiration. Instincts of affection from mutual exertion and escape from danger arose to assert themselves over lifeless guns and armor and to recreate a selflessness lost in the conflict. The feeling was set apart from a general restoration after battle of the natural order he loved about the Lowcountry. It was personal. He could no longer envision going back to Miss Maggie's.

Turning to the young black man about his same age, Lord Edward noticed him in a contemplative mood, and said, "My good man, may I ask your name?"

"Tony Small. The woman who helped me take care of you is Ruth. That's Ruth over there."

"How do you do?" Ruth politely said. "And what's your name?" Her surprising bold inquiry was not viewed as impertinence by the young lord whose life, he knew, she helped to save. All others for the moment also gave Ruth easy license to be herself.

"Lieutenant Lord Edward Fitzgerald." He smiled and handed her the blanket from the wagon, struck by her beauty and her dazzling array of teeth as she smiled broadly in return.

"Now, Tony Small," Lord Edward said, "I will need some help. I have just been given charge of escorting prisoners to Charleston. If you would manage the daily chores required of my office, I should be extremely grateful."

Tony was dumbfounded and exhilarated at the same time. He could only smile broadly and say, "I'm glad to."

Major Majoribanks heard Lord Edward's remark, and in a quiet voice added, "You must now be charged with another duty as well, lieutenant. I must give you the responsibility of serving as the officer escort of the very man you captured at the thicket."

Entirely forgetting his own wound by now—and putting side his description of Washington as a "fat bastard" in the heat of battle at the thicket—Lord Edward immediately replied, "Major, I gladly accept the honor of escorting so gallant an enemy to Charleston."

By this point in the conversation and realizing that only Tony was invited to go along with Lord Edward, Ruth looked at Tony as if to say, "Good for you. I want to go with the others, anyway. I'll fend for myself. See you in Charleston." Yet, Tony could tell she was fearful and apprehensive of the future. She stepped back and took no further part in the conversation.

Tony went over to her and whispered, "This is good for both of us, Ruth. Go along with the others. I'll find you in Charleston, and we can live free together. I love you, Ruth. I'll find you. Don't worry."

Ruth said nothing. She smiled, reached up and kissed Tony on the mouth to signal that both knew they reached another plateau in their great adventure. Lord Edward saw them part as she quickly joined other blacks who watched the reunion.

"Lieutenant Colonel Washington tells me that he is a friend of Daniel Ravenel of Wantoot," Major Majoribanks told Lord Edward in an unsteady voice. "It is there the advance column is headed, if Colonel Stewart has not arrived already. I shall not, however, be able to catch up with you in time to enjoy the comforts of Wantoot. I must lag behind to protect the rear and keep only the progress allowed a very sick man."

"We cannot permit you to remain behind in this exposed position, sir," Lord Edward replied respectfully. "You do not look well, sir, if I may say so. Come ride in the same wagon with our prisoner to Wantoot."

"I cannot go with you to Wantoot in a wagon, lieutenant. My orders are to guard the rear after our entire column has withdrawn. I shall follow you on horseback."

"Very well, sir."

Turning again to his new friend, Lord Edward said, "One thing more, Tony Small. Perhaps you just heard that I have the honor of personally escorting Lieutenant Colonel William Washington. I should appreciate it if you help me attend to the American officer's needs as well. He is a highly valued prisoner, a Continental officer of some renown."

"I'm ready to go, Lord Edward. We thought you were going to Wantoot. Ruth's gone on with the army all the way to Charleston."

By the time the wagon and the rear guard detachment of Major Majoribanks' flank battalion finally reached Wantoot, Majoribanks' fever worsened to such an extent that he could not go any farther. Seeing that the flank commander's condition was extremely critical, not from a wound but from sickness, Lord Edward approached Tony for help.

"Can you find a black man or woman—someone you know and trust— who can give immediate care to the major? Someone who can take him back to his own cabin and secretly nurse him back to health, just as you did for me, without alerting the Ravenel family?

"The major simply cannot risk capture in his incapacitated condition. The rebels could be watching even now and move on Wantoot as soon as we withdraw—or even before. They will certainly capture him if he's not hidden among the black community."

"I'll find somebody."

"Good man. I have only a small detachment to escort the prisoners. We barely repulsed Colonel Eggleston on the way here. I suspect Hammond and

Maham are just waiting for a chance to attack our train and free Lieutenant Colonel Washington. I'll wait for you."

They both looked at Majoribanks. His tall frame, leaning against a wagon wheel, extended beyond the blanket laid out for him, and another barely covered his chest. Perspiring and shivering, he was clearly in pain. Disease, which killed more soldiers than combat, now lay claim to a particularly valiant one.

"I'll find somebody—I think I know just the man—my father knows him—and I'll be sure to tell him that whatever he does, don't let on to master Ravenel that the major is here at his plantation. Yes sir, I think I know just the man."

"Master Ravenel Secundus of Wantoot is a rebel. He joined Marion's men when he was very young and was probably on the line with Marion yesterday. If he survived, he'll turn in any British soldier resting here. Fact is, he's probably out there looking at us now. There's more than one fox in the swamp."

"It might be hard to find somebody who's going to be against what he thinks master Ravenel wants. Nobody much runs away from this plantation because they get treated as good as a black man can expect."

Within a very short time Tony returned. Lord Edward stood by Major Majoribanks who was asleep. His ashen face sharply contrasted with his scarlet tunic and emblems of rank. Strong enough to show resolve under extreme discomfort, his hands held steadily to the cover thrown over his torso. The noise of troops already on the move made whispering impossible.

"This is Primus Button," Tony announced to Lord Edward. "He promises to take good care of the major and not tell anyone. And folks in his cabin won't talk, either."

Lord Edward looked at the large black man, heavy set and over six feet tall. "That's right," Primus said without first being spoken to by Lord Edward. In his left hand he held a hat crumpled along the same creases as if taken off again and again. He was dressed well and wore a good pair of shoes, the first thing Tony noticed. "They won't talk, and I'll do my best to fix him up and have him back on his feet in no time. I won't leave him."

It was still raining. Deer flies and humidity assumed battle positions. Lord Edward realized this is why nobody wants to fight a war in the Lowcountry. Natural defenses of the local inhabitants are insects and humidity, and their unrestrained desire for independence which, funneled through the narrow spigot of revolt, runs in a thousand different directions at once.

Hearing nothing more from Lord Edward, and after a long look at Majoribanks, Primus Button said, "But don't you think we need to get him over to my cabin? Annie Belle is there. It's not near the big house. He looks mighty poorly."

Leaving his flank commander behind in the midst of enemy troops was gut-wrenching for Lord Edward. He looked hard at the major, then with a glance at Primus and another black man who by then came to help carry the major, Lord Edward knelt near the ear of his commander. "We shall soon see you at the garrison in Charleston, sir. We will send a secret escort, faster than the small corps that took Rawdon to Charleston. I'm confident you'll regain your strength as your fever subsides. You'll be back with the battalion within a week."

He stood up and looked at Tony who was shaking his head. Primus Button put his hands on his knees and leaned forward to look at his patient. Seeing that Majoribanks was too weak to respond to his parting works or perhaps even to hear them, Lord Edward said, "Mr. Button, he's yours. Tony, let's go. Our prisoner is waiting."

Moving south along Murrays Ferry Road from Wantoot Plantation, Lord Edward with his small detachment guarding several hundred prisoners, including William Washington, was hindered by having to move aside or maneuver around fallen trees. At Moncks Corner Lord Edward caught up with the main army. Major John Doyle, who arrived with support troops from Charleston, was the senior officer in charge of seeing that their valuable rebel prisoner was properly cared for. After Lord Edward assured Doyle that he was no longer seriously hampered by his own wound and that he could adequately care for Washington, Doyle turned the job completely over to the young lord. Tony rode in the wagon with Lord Edward to Charleston. Washington rode in a separate wagon.

"He's important," Lord Edward told Tony, "relative to his kinship as second cousin once removed to the American Commander in Chief, General George Washington. By now, you have certainly heard of that great Virginian."

Tony smiled as Lord Edward's words were jostled up and down by the bumpy wagon going over the rough road. Lord Edward, too, was amused at his own shaky voice. For the first time in his life, Tony was now sitting completely at ease next to a white man. It wasn't like talking to Miss Maggie or to the Sinkler brothers or to Job Marion, and far different from talking to an overseer. Now Tony could talk as he pleased. Ask questions and say what's on his mind. He could help a white man by what he knew, not just by what he could do. And speak his mind, he did. Comedy created by both of their bumpy voices offered a cover more comfortable than a blanket.

"I hear that William Washington didn't escape when he was left alone. He could have after he was caught at the thicket, when nobody was watching him in all the confusion during your scramble back to Miss Maggie's—the brick house, I mean."

Lord Edward knew that Tony was one of the people living at the battle site. What he didn't know was that he would now hear more about Tony's area of expertise on the McKelvey Plantation—horses—namely, Carolina marsh tacky horses. A member of one of Ireland's most aristocratic families would now yield the bumpy floor to Tony Small to talk about what they both loved.

"Of course," Tony continued, "he wouldn't have been taken prisoner in the first place if he was riding Miss Maggie's Eagle or one of Marion's marsh tackys. Those marsh tackys can get through thick underbrush with ease because they got narrow chests and narrow faces with big eyes and can see everything and weave through all the blackjack. It's like having a weapon the enemy doesn't know about. You could even say that Tarleton would have caught the Swamp Fox if the British were riding marsh tackys in Ox Swamp—in spite of what I hear Tarleton thinks about our tackys."

"You're a talker, Tony Small. That's good. But I never heard of these tacky horses—tacky because they're cheap to buy, right?"

"Lots of things here I bet you never heard of."

Amused and delighted to realize their mutual love of horses and Tony's easy, open manner, unintimidated by racial difference, Lord Edward addressed the more serious issue of parole that Tony raised. He never talked down to his new black friend, and Tony never spoke obsequiously to the Irish lord.

"The honorable concept of parole is one of the risks of war, Tony. As important as Washington is to us, we allowed him to remain alone in the brick house. He was quite capable of escape, of course, notwithstanding the cannon and musket fire all around him. And at one time there were several Americans around, trying to get inside."

"He would have stayed put anyway from what I saw about him. He's a man of his word, and when you caught him and didn't offer parole, he was stuck here with you no matter what. That's the way everybody sees it. Sounds like a man married to his sword and honor. Sword and word just have one letter difference, if I know my letters right. 'S' that 'snake' begins with. So the sword is not mightier than the word, just longer, and it doesn't wiggle as much."

Lord Edward laughed out loud. "You have a way of getting straight to the point, Tony ... of a sword." Tony joined another burst of laughter, but not quite as loudly. Neither man was afraid of telling lousy jokes.

"Of course you must know that he escaped after being captured by Lieutenant Colonel Tarleton at Moncks Corner in April of last year," Lord Edward countered, "so I don't know if the man's word is as good as you think. And he's a sneaky fellow, really. With his trick using a log as a fake cannon, a 'Quaker' cannon—admittedly, an old ruse—to deceive Colonel Rugeley into surrender last December, he ruined a good loyalist officer's career. So we still have to watch him."

"Maybe. He knows you're not going to give him parole, anyway. You need him as hostage if the rebels hang any British officer to pay 'em back for hanging Colonel Hayne last August. Oscar, Marion's man, told us about all that. Folks in Charleston didn't like that at all. That's what I hear. He's a good one to have around."

Lord Edward sat quietly as the wagon bumped along, sometimes wincing from the pain he still felt from the wound in his thigh. A small amount of blood continued to drip through the bandage. He looked at Tony intensely. "How do you know about Oscar? Anything about Francis Marion, for that matter?"

Tony's eyes widened and his mouth dropped open to draw in a short deep breath, not knowing if he made a major blunder. Lord Edward caught his reaction and kept a firm eye on him. Tony straightened his shoulders and spoke in a firm voice. Being embedded with the Americans was a secret he could not keep forever, or wanted to.

"Ruth and I met him at Mt. Tacitus, Henry Laurens' Plantation. I was sometimes with Marion's men in the battle." He crossed his ankles and pulled his feet underneath him. He fidgeted slightly but never took his eyes from Lord Edward. He knew his future was in the balance.

"Did you carry a weapon? Did you fire at His Majesty's troops?"

"No."

"Tell me more."

"I was on both sides. I was on your side at Ninety Six. On your side till captured at Huger's Bridge with all the other loyalist blacks and regimental stuff in the rear guard. I saw you there but didn't know who you were. I went with you from Orangeburg to Goose Creek with Rawdon's small corps on the way to Charleston. Then after you left Rawdon and took off for Moncks Corner, I was with black folks walking in the rear to join Stewart. After we were captured I was with rebels at Quinby and Shubrick's. I saw you there, too. I never fired at anybody. Neither side. Never carried a gun or sword. The rebs know that. Then I went home to Miss Maggie's and back to work for a while. But then Ruth and I took off for Thomson's place, and Laurens', and Burdell's. Stewart and you already went past Laurens' place by the time we got there. Then we followed Greene right back to the Eutaw springs, where I live, like going in a circle. We found you wounded at Miss Maggie's after the battle. I never had a gun or sword at Eutaw or anywhere else. I never fired at Americans or British the whole time from Ninety Six on."

Tony ended the recital of his adventures with both chin and eyes turned up toward his interrogator, but his tone of voice was never assertive.

"Very well," Lord Edward said, continuing with a steady gaze at Tony. He looked Tony up and down as if looking for a weapon hidden in his clothes, then calmly said, "Very well. We'll talk about all you've seen and heard at another time. You appear to be neither a soldier nor a spy. You look and sound imminently trustworthy, I must admit." Lord Edward took his hand off the handle of his sword where it rested throughout Tony's narration, convinced that Tony was as unpracticed as he in the art of deception and shared a child's discernment of truth.

"Perhaps this will be the end of your moving back and forth between the lines as a non-combatant. And maybe I'll teach you how to shoot, so you can make a fool of yourself like the rest of us."

Tony's sigh of relief was audible, as if he had been holding his breath for an hour. The wagon continued to bump along, now and then hitting a large boulder that sent their rear ends into the air as high as their voices. The uses of adversity along the rough route helped to encourage communication rather than squelch it. After more laughter and a further period of silence to mark the official end of Tony's psychomachia, Tony quickly put the conversation back on the rails about William Washington. He smiled and spoke in the same kind of bouncy, almost comic, voice which put the new friends on a level road which they would now begin to travel together.

"Washington's good to have around."

"That's the point. Yes, he's a good one to have around in case we need him for political bargaining. It is Lieutenant Colonel Stewart's position all along that parole for Washington is out of the question. However, that doesn't mean that he can't do most of what he wants to do once we get to Charleston. Lieutenant Colonel Washington is a mighty impressive fellow whom, I am sure, we will not harm while in our custody. I characterized him quite differently, however, as he rushed us at the thicket."

"You'd hang him in a minute if something happens to Rawdon."

Lord Edward smiled. His new friend was feisty. "Yes, perhaps you're right. Perhaps. But Washington is not of Rawdon's rank. If we hang anybody, he'll be of higher rank. Maybe you."

Tony returned a weak smile.

"As it turns out, Admiral DeGrasse, to whom the privateers gave Lord Rawdon, refuses to turn him over to the rebels. That's the good side of his adventures on the trip back. The bad side of the story is that all the records of the American campaign by the regiment were tossed overboard to keep them out of the hands of the privateers. But, again, happily his Lordship and Lieutenant Colonel Doyle—the other Doyle—and their wives, I might discreetly add for the sake of Rawdon, are with the French for now."

"Their women will take care of 'em. But why's the written stuff so important? It won't matter to me, at least, till you teach me to read—if I'm going to be any good to you, I mean if you keep me around. I know a few letters, 'J' as well as 'S,' but that's all. Even Miss Maggie wouldn't teach me to read."

"Yes, that's the law here. The answer is that the regiment now has very few documents to help in setting strategy for further action in the West Indies. England, as you should very well know, continues to do battle with France in an even more southern venue, the West Indies. We need to know which plans were successful, which were not. Our real enemy is France, of course, all over the world, and Spain is always in the mix, but not this little bunch of rebels in America.

"Now Colonel O'Hara in his new command will have to rely in our officers' best recollections to make sound decisions for the regiment. The West Indies is different—but not much—from the Lowcountry. The damned heat. The damned humidity. The damned insects. They say you have to get drunk just to sleep at night. The first English settlers from Barbados brought aspirations for sugar, then for inland rice, but they probably just wanted a better chance to get a good night's sleep."

"Whatever crop it is, it takes a lot of black folks to do it all, especially rice. My folks came from Barbados. My momma says we're one of the first families in the Carolinas, black or white."

"And I already know that the 19th Foot is bound to be sent to Barbados and Antigua and ultimately to St. Lucia, if we ever get out of being boxed inside that terribly unhealthy city of Charleston."

"Well, if what's up here is like what's down there, sounds like you'll be jumping out of a rebels' frying pan into a French fire."

"'We,' not 'you.' 'We.' I need to keep you close by, Tony Small, in case I need to exchange you for a nice fat goose, if not to hang. One can get mighty hungry inside the garrison in Charleston."

Tony broke into a wide grin, comfortable enough this time, and looked to see the town on a flat horizon as the military column drew near. "And here we are. The holy city."

The two men grew silent as they approached Charleston. Tony suddenly jumped up in the wagon to get a better look and unconsciously steadied himself with a hand on Lord Edward's shoulder. Lord Edward smiled and looked up at him and said, "This wonderful city—it's on the tip of a detumescent peninsula that hangs down into the ocean."

"Rivers on each side to form the Atlantic Ocean," Tony said loudly over an increasing racket of the military column as it picked up its pace. He quickly sat back down as their laughter in the bumpy wagon made their comments that much more ridiculous.

"Of course, prosperous plantations do flourish up and down each river, far away enough from the salty tidal water to allow rice to grow in fresh water. And the town is for the most part loyal to the king. But, Tony, by your expression, I have a feeling that's not the first time I'll be telling you something you already know."

After sorting out numerous details in transporting a military detachment of prisoners and finding suitable accommodations for William Washington, Lord Edward and Tony settled into their own quarters in the garrison. Lord Edward busied himself with arranging his few personal provisions and regimental documents in the common room that separated their two bedrooms. His modest desk and uncomfortable, wobbly chair looked like furniture swapped for more comfortable accommodations that were there prior to arrival. He waited for Tony in the common room.

"Now let me tell you something you probably don't know. I will give you a brief look at what to expect in Charleston. You need to know what to expect if you are to be of help to me. I barely know the town myself, having been here only three days in June, but this is what I've heard. The key to running Charleston during our occupation is the Board of Police, not the British army. Nobody realizes that simple truth. The Commandant of British military forces in the Charleston garrison was initially and briefly Brigadier General James Patterson. Now, of course, it's Colonel Nisbet Balfour. Charleston is incorporated, so there's no municipal government for the town. It's been under martial law, enforced by British soldiers, since it fell in May of last year.

"So you need to remember that the Board of Police, rather than the Commandant and other military authorities, is the governing body in virtually all civil administration. The head of the Board is known as the Intendant General."

"A funny name."

"It's not a complex system of government, and you have to know it to be useful to me. He's appointed by military authorities. Lately, the Intendant Generals have been Lieutenant Governor William Bull who replaced James Simpson in February. I'm not sure if he's still on board. Maybe Sir Egerton Leigh or Thomas Knox Gordon has taken over. Whoever it is, you need to be aware of him. As my man carrying correspondence, you represent me."

"You're going to have to tell me all this again, Lord Edward, because I can't take it in all in at one time."

"Yes, you can. You're just like me, and you can listen just once. Know about William Bull in all circumstances. He's a good subject of the king. Lives on Meeting Street. And just know that the Board of Police runs a quasi-municipal court system to hear grievances and civil cases and to regulate markets, streets, contracts, debts, commerce, property disputes, care of the poor, sanitation, and the like, and burials—burying blacks in separate cemeteries from whites, for example. And tell your black friends that the Board also governs unruly conduct of Negroes, houses of public entertainment, and the sale of liquor. I want you to make friends with as many blacks as possible. An easy task."

For the eight months between 8 September 1781 and 5 May 1782, when the 19th Regiment of Foot evacuated Charleston, Lord Edward Fitzgerald and Tony spent most of their time in the British garrison in Charleston, a town utterly destitute of sanitary arrangements. Lord Edward's primary duty in Charleston remained that of a lieutenant in the 19th Foot to secure the safety of the city. He and the other eight lieutenants in the regiment led excursions outside the garrison for necessary provisions to sustain an army surrounded by rebel troops. At times, Tony went with them but never carried a weapon. At last he could see for himself the big oaks in Charleston, but as his mother told him, they were not a mile around.

Lord Edward's secondary duty was to continue his care of Lieutenant Colonel William Washington. For this duty, Tony was essential. He could more freely move outside the city, whereas Lord Edward's scarlet uniform usually kept him near the gates. But there was a more influential force at play in Washington's recovery, someone whom both Lord Edward and Tony welcomed.

Jane Reily Elliott, beautiful, clever, and rich, looked out the window at Sandy Hill Plantation, just north of Charleston. It was the morning of 26 March 1780, a few days after her 17th birthday and a year and a half before the Battle of Eutaw Springs. She heard from one of her father's servants that the dreaded Lieutenant Colonel Banastre Tarleton and the dashing American cavalry commander Lieutenant Colonel William Washington were in the area. With her father she rode seven miles to Rantowles Bridge where they both hoped to see military action from a safe distance. Stopping well short of the bridge, Jane asked who the important looking British officers were as they sat on their fine mounts at the bridge.

"That, indeed, is Clinton and Cornwallis in their scarlet jackets, but I don't recognize the third officer," Colonel Elliott replied. "Looks like a German. They're expecting to meet someone, I suppose." He looked at his daughter whose face could scarcely hide her excitement as she sat sidesaddle in a bright blue dress, ready for a party then and there. Her father's plantation house, also known as Hyde Park or Elliott's Savannah, and its thousands of acres with hundreds of enslaved blacks, was only a short half-day ride to the seasonal balls in Charleston.

"This could be an interesting day, Jane dear, but we're much too close to what's to come."

The day turned out to be exactly what Jane hoped for—a clash between Tarleton and Washington. "The American dragoons were riding toward Bacon's Bridge," she said, trying to catch her breath as she described to her father in her own words what they both saw, "when their commander saw the green jackets of none other than Tarleton's Legion bearing down on them. But our brave patriot commander turned and fought hand-to-hand with Tarleton and beat him back. The foolish British thought they could charge toward us on one little narrow causeway. We were waiting, our brave commander and his cavalry. We got the best of Tarleton personally, too."

"'We'? You and Lieutenant Colonel William Washington?" The colonel laughed and smiled at his daughter. "Jane, that was General Washington's cousin from Virginia. You must control your love of battle, my dear—and of warriors. The former becomes you only in limited circles, say, in the company of Athena and Diana."

Jane blushed but smiled broadly when her father added, "But you will soon get to meet your handsome warrior. I have included him among others I shall entertain at Sandy Hill within the coming days. And by the way, Lieutenant Colonel Washington missed catching Cornwallis and Clinton at Rantowles Bridge by only a few hours."

The courtship of William Washington and Jane Elliott began a few weeks later and moved toward genuine affection and love at a pace typical of those who seem to be made for each other. Jane was known to all not only for her beauty and youth, but also for her good manners, keen perception, and natural frankness. The Virginian, eleven years her senior, was very manly, and to some, even majestic in person, if a bit stout. His strength of character was obvious. Socially, he was taciturn and retiring, little more than a decorated wall flower.

Jane Elliott was anything but a wall flower. Sometime before the Battle of Cowpens on 17 January 1781, she heard Washington express regret that his regiment did not have a flag. Quick witted and generous, Jane cut a square of heavy crimson silk damask from a curtain at Sandy Hill, put it on a hickory pole, sewed on a gold silk fringe, and said, "Here's you flag, colonel."

··••◦❈◦••··

In the fall of 1781 after Eutaw Springs, as Washington lay wounded in the British garrison in Charleston, Jane made numerous visits to nurse him back to health in obvious ways.

"That's all it takes," Tony said. "I don't know anything more sustaining and salutary than the love of a good woman. Better than cymbee water." William Washington fully recovered by January 1782. Jane's father died the year before, leaving her several plantations, including Sandy Hill and the adjacent Live Oak Plantation.

Washington's presence at the garrison gaol and Jane's visits drew four distinctive personalities together. After numerous visits by Jane, the four became more and more comfortable in the company of each other. On one occasion the aristocratic young woman, about Tony's age, spoke about an issue seldom if ever raised by whites on front of blacks. She was standing near Tony as she spoke, not at all in a condescending manner.

"I cannot for the life of me, see why free blacks like Tony should not feel anything but satisfaction to serve the patriot cause. If I may speak freely, Lord Edward, your man Tony should by rights be on the colonel's side, not the king's. After all, you must see that his better future lies in service to those of us who are soon to win this war and be done with the British yoke."

Jane's willingness to engage the Irish nobleman and, indirectly, his black manservant in a frank and feisty conversation about slavery reminded Tony of Ruth's equal measure of boldness. Tony surmised that Jane heard of his conversations with Lord Edward and Washington.

"If I may speak freely," Tony replied, as if with the pun to completely take over the exchange from Lord Edward. He looked quickly at Lord Edward, but respectfully added, "I don't see what you mean by my 'better future lies in service.' I heard Lord Edward and Colonel Washington discuss the future of America after the war is over, and I don't see a future of freedom here for people of color. But they both like what Mr. Thomas Paine says. I do, too. Lord Edward reads parts of it to me."

Even though she started the conversation, Jane glanced at Lord Edward with a look inviting approval for Tony to speak directly to a white woman. Each remained standing calmly side by side, neither backing off and both literally standing their ground.

"I don't know if I ever had a country after my people left to make that long terrible voyage over here. The middle passage. My friend Ruth tells me that my place is here with her and our families and friends on all the McKelvey places, but I don't see much freedom here. I'm about the only one that's free, and then not completely. My parents, my two brothers, and me. That could change anytime."

Tony adjusted his shirt by the top button. "I could be enslaved as long as there are white men who steal free black folks to sell 'em. I heard all about those proclamations of freedom for us—Lord Dunmore's and Pendleton's in Virginia six years ago and Clinton's a couple of years ago in New York—but so what? Some folks got certificates of freedom, but if we're still enslaved, what's that to us? What then?"

"'What then,' Tony, my boy," William Washington exclaimed in a loud impatient voice, "could depend on many things in the future of these several colonies, South Carolina as well as Virginia. Let me first say that you are the first black man with whom I've entertained the possibility of discussing a rather more economic, even intellectual, subject than you think. I fancy you deem yourself somewhat of a renaissance man for being able even to broach the subject in moral terms."

"We black folks talk about things that are happening to us a lot more than you may think," Tony replied quickly, quickly enough not to interrupt and remain respectful.

"Well, indeed... Nonetheless, Tony, you are correct to say that I admire Mr. Paine—I would pay out of my own pocket to see that his works are published—but I have no plans to free any of the blacks who belong to Miss Elliott, that is, after I begin the administration of her twelve thousand acres. Why, the inland rice fields alone could never be properly managed without enslaved labor. What would we do at Orange Parish, Craven County,

Granville County, and Ninety Six District, to say nothing of our largest holdings at St. Paul and St. Bartholomew Parish? What then, I ask?"

That was the first time anyone heard of a definite engagement for an Elliott-Washington wedding—a welcomed momentary interruption. Jane moved over to her fiancé and kissed him on the cheek as he took her by the waist and swung her around in a circle. Lord Edward jumped forward to steady the American as he almost lost his footing to everyone's delight, especially Jane's.

But after a burst of congratulations and cheers subsided, Tony doggedly continued with what, oddly, the three others in the room were still committed to hear.

"Yes," Tony replied, still mindful of place and time, "but I heard that Dunmore didn't even free his own enslaved folks. I heard from some of my Virginia friends that Dunmore's Sarah ran away to join the Black Pioneers, and that was a year after Dunmore issued his great proclamation. In fact, I heard of only one enslaved person ever being freed by Lord Dunmore— Roger Scot—there could be more—and he immediately joined the British forces. But that was in Virginia. The whites here in South Carolina ain't as good."

Everyone enjoyed a good laugh at that, Washington's lasting the longest.

As tension eased and to spare Tony any further discussion of freedom which might escalate into a verbal altercation—which Tony would certainly lose at peril of losing even more—Lord Edward stepped in to offer a convivial middle ground.

"At least," he said, "we do all agree that *Common Sense* and *American Crisis* are works of a first-rate mind, however the direction our different responses may take us. And however the irony of Mr. Jefferson's declaration is, with regard to its meaning to thousands of blacks in irons at the time of its writing and now."

Jane Elliott and William Washington exchanged looks as Lord Edward continued. "Even so, it is at least the case under His Majesty's laws that whoever steps foot on English soil is himself an Englishman, as free as any man can be, and he cannot be sent back against his will to wherever he came from. That's thanks to the *Somerset* case only a few years ago. But we are not on English soil, and within months we will be pitched off these colonies entirely."

With that aggressive declaration by Lord Edward, the discussion of slavery ended. After a pause, Jane cheerfully said, "I wish you could make a toast at our wedding, Lord Edward. It will be the 21st of April, next. It will be a gay and happy affair, and I for one shall miss all my British friends among the officers attending."

"I regret not being able to attend. I suspect the Black Dragoons might object."

"I am sure General Leslie will be good enough to send Tony to accompany the colonel to Sandy Hill," Jane continued, giving no notice to Lord Edward's reference. Then, as if in an afterthought, but in the forefront of her thoughts all along, turning to Tony she said, amid hardy laughter by the colonel, "After he arrives at Sandy Hill, Tony, he's mine."

Several days after Tony's exchange with Jane Elliott, Lord Edward brought up the topic of Tony's own social life. Tony could tell the master prankster was setting him up for something. Probably something to get even with him for previously setting a bucket of water on the top of his door, slightly ajar, so that when he fully opened it, water came splashing down.

"Tony, this place is alive at night with unruly conduct. Do you think that you might like to have someone here with you? Perhaps your friend Ruth, if you can find her, or perhaps someone else?"

"I'm always on the lookout for her, inside and outside the city. I don't know where she went after we left the battlefield at the springs. She went on ahead with Colonel Stewart, remember? Probably stayed in Charleston, hiding from old man Snow, but I'm still trying hard. I just ain't seen her."

"Well, I hope you don't see her at the Ethiopian Ball," Lord Edward said and roared laughing.

"That ain't funny. I love Ruth. You know that. Anyway, Charleston's half black. The white enlisted men bring black women into the city where they get all dressed up like their white mistresses and dance till four o'clock in the morning. You know what goes on. The Board of Police won't stop it, either. I found that out. In fact, that's just one way of handling idle soldiers. Lots of bad things go on here."

"Very well," Lord Edward said, still chuckling at his own joke, but cautious not to extend it to the point of hurting his friend's feelings more than he had already. Both men were well above keeping personal accounts.

"You're right. I apologize. Meanwhile, we must see to it that at least our guest Lieutenant Colonel Washington is comfortable enough. He will be allowed what books his contacts provide. He has told me already of his request to have several titles from Mr. Izard's collection, which I am told is one of the best in America, outside that of Mr. Jefferson's in Virginia. You may go and find them as the colonel directs you to do so."

"And if he sneaks a gun or sword in, will you be blaming me?"

"Tony, if he sneaks a horse in, let me know. As you well know, I have begun to trust you enough already to allow you to attend Lieutenant Colonel Washington outside the city walls, whenever Lieutenant Colonel Stewart permits it, that is, whenever he and General Greene use our prisoner in person to exchange messages. Greene is right outside our doorstep now."

"Why me?"

"Because you are the perfect fellow to do so. The rebels would not permit me or, for example, Lieutenant Crofton or anyone of a captain's rank, to be present in the company of so thick a scene as might gather around Washington when he visits Greene's headquarters and be among his former comrades whilst still our prisoner."

"Crofton's an arrogant fellow," Tony observed. "I've met him. Nothing's ever out of place with him, so he expects everybody to know the place he gives 'em."

"Never mind that. There's to be an exchange of prisoners, as well, that will allow you to tag along whilst messages are sent regarding terms of exchange for prisoners of war.

"Now listen, these terms are tricky. They were drawn up between Lieutenant Colonel Carrington for General Greene and Captain Cornwallis on behalf of Lieutenant General Earl Cornwallis, done at the house of Mr. Claudius Pegus on the PeeDee—last May third, I think it was. You need to know all of this, just like you need to know about the Board of Police. This is not back-channel communication, Tony. By consent with other officers, including Lieutenant Colonel Stewart, you are privileged to be present at an official communication by flag of truce. It's not an uncommon procedure at this time of the war when we want our officers and men returned, and Greene wants the release of many of the rebel officers taken prisoners in the siege of Charleston and the pitiful men still suffering on our boats in the harbor.

"But to the point, my faithful friend, you will accompany back to this garrison one of His Majesty's officers amongst those being exchanged, a certain Captain Henry Barry of the 52nd Regiment of Foot. Be advised, Tony, that although you will serve only to tag along and be of general service in the exchange, please know that Captain Barry is one of our officers we desperately want exchanged. We want him back safe and sound without any mumbling about Lieutenant Colonel Hayne. Tend to his every need."

"Primus Button tells me the major has died of the fever" was the first thing Tony told Lord Edward on the morning of 25 October 1781. "He died three days ago. Primus and Annie Belle did all they could. He just was never able to pull out of it, is how they sent us word."

Lord Edward remained composed. He turned away from Tony and stood quietly for a moment, arms folded. He spoke to whatever lay out beyond the room, out the window. "He was one of the finest officers in the entire regiment. I must inform Lieutenant Colonel Coates at once. A terrible loss." He turned back toward Tony and sat down in a nearby chair. He leaned forward, resting his chin on his right hand, his elbow on the arm of the chair, his left hand holding onto the other arm in a posture Tony never saw before.

"It got real confusing for Primus," Tony continued. "He thought he was going to be punished or even worse for hiding the major, but Mr. Daniel told him that if he knew Major Majoribanks was there, he would have brought him in the house and got Mrs. Ravenel herself to take care of him. That kind of surprised Primus and hurt Annie Bell's feelings, because they knew nobody could have done any better than they did to take good care of the major. Lord Edward, it looks like you're staring straight through the floor boards. Are you all right?"

"Wantoot served as British headquarters for a short time. Maybe the Ravenels knew the major from just such an occasion." Lord Edward leaned back in his chair. "They are also friends of William Washington. Obviously, they like him, but, remember, the two generations of Ravenels, eighteen-year-old Secundus and his father, are both rebels resisting us."

"That's what Primus told me. But he also told me that Major Majoribanks saved Mrs. Ravenel's china and crystal and other valuable stuff when soldiers were tearing up almost everything in the house and going wild. Major Majoribanks put a stop to the ruckus."

"I didn't know that. That no doubt endeared him to them both, as it would anyone whose property is saved from looters. Perhaps Mr. Ravenel didn't hear that it was Major Majoribanks who helped turn the tide for us at Eutaw Springs."

"I think he was thinking of something else. Some say it was Major Majoribanks, not you, who saved Lieutenant Colonel Washington from being bayoneted in the thicket."

"That's of no moment, whatsoever."

"Well, anyway, Primus told me that the major wanted to be buried in the woods in a secret place, but Master Daniel, Secundus' father, dug a grave right by Black Oak Road, not too far from the big house so he could see it at a distance. Says it's not just a little ordinary grave, either. It's an honored place, nearly as nice as he would have in England."

"Very good, but I doubt that."

"Yep, I heard troops say that if a marker was placed for every British soldier like Majoribanks, the whole world would be covered with granite. Wow, they're a rat's nest of egos, all right, just like that old wagon driver said who got us to Moncks Corner."

••◦◦❈◦◦••

In late December 1781 William Washington made a bold proposal to Lord Edward as he and Tony entered his room a few days later. After getting up to greet them, Washington returned to his desk and sat down. He took out his pipe and lit it, again filling the small room with a sweet odor of Virginia tobacco.

"You must meet a friend of mine. His name is John Laurens."

"Same man whose daddy owns the plantation Ruth and I visited on the way to the springs?" Tony asked.

"Well, I don't know about that, and I don't even know who Ruth is," Washington replied, somewhat irritated that Tony jumped in with a question before Lord Edward could respond. "General Greene's army stopped at his plantation on the way to Eutaw Springs last September. You both may know that he's the son of Henry Laurens who is the holder of several other rice fields in Upper St. John's Parish. He's one of the so-called rice barons. He was president of the Continental Congress in Philadelphia."

"Of course, I've heard of them both," Lord Edward replied. "An arch rebel and his very rash son, but, I grant you, admirable for his zeal to your cause."

"I think I can arrange a parley between you two enemies. I met him briefly only yesterday on a short trip outside of Charleston, one made with your permission. I met Laurens quite by accident. He's back from England and France. He's due to return as aide-de-camp to General Washington. There's much to do after Cornwallis' surrender at Yorktown."

Tony stepped closer to hear better, a step or two behind Lord Edward. A clean white piqué shirt gave him more assertive confidence with Washington than before.

"Lieutenant Colonel Laurens is here while en route to address the South Carolina General Assembly, and he agrees to meet me in private to exchange ideas about what to do after the war. You may already know of Laurens' military service at Brandywine, Germantown, Monmouth, Newport, Charleston, Savannah." Washington was careful to include British victories in the litany. He saw Tony's excitement at the prospect of meeting such a man.

"Wounded four times, six months as a prisoner of war. I'm told he left Yorktown on the fifth of November and arrived in Charleston in early December. I assume you already know that since General Leslie is occupying Charleston, the state legislature is gathering in late January at the Masonic Lodge in Jacksonboro, about thirty-five miles south of Charleston, to pass the Confiscation Acts. At least that's the plan. I know your spies have told you all this."

"Nothing so large in its political intent can be hidden for long. And I have heard something special about the man which I like and fear at the same time. Tony tells me about something he's heard—that John Laurens will speak to the governing body of this colony on behalf of enslaved blacks who wish to be free men. Very unsettling to the British army. More men to fight."

Lord Edward approached a nearby chair, put his hand on the back of it and bade his older republican friend to move from behind his desk and sit down beside him near one of the two windows in his cell. Lord Edward looked out the window on an enormous oak tree, big enough to serve as a gathering point for rebel radicals. As if talking to the tree, he continued. Tony remained standing. This time there was no raucous crow outside the window.

"Laurens proposes to arm some three thousand blacks with arms—three thousand! Tony says he asked Congress for five thousand but didn't get that many. And, after the war is over, he proposes to grant them freedom for their service. He's been pushing this idea on at least two previous occasions and—happily for us—been soundly denounced in South Carolina at each try."

"That's well known," Washington replied. "Rutledge's strong opposition to Laurens, the son I mean, is perhaps pay-back for these kinds of efforts by young Laurens that provoked Lowcountry planters so much that they even offered to surrender Charleston after the fall of Savannah if Whitehall would permit the town to remain neutral." Washington laughed out loud. Turning to Tony, he added, "There's no Patrick Henry in Charleston."

"General Greene hopes that you rebels will do the sensible and sound strategic thing and arm blacks. Tony has already told us both about the loyalist black soldiers he saw at Ninety Six and the black patriot soldiers at Eutaw Springs, mainly from North Carolina, Virginia, and Maryland.

To hear him talk, he must have met them all, and he claims they're all good fighters."

Looking over at Tony, Lord Edward added, "And he can even remember their names! Says it's part of history. Tony, you never seem to tire of telling us their names and what they did. You make it sound as if the lieutenant colonel here, and Greene, Marion, Pickens, Lee, Williams, Sumner, Stewart, Coffin, Majoribanks, and I—all of us are doing little for either side, and even pale in comparison."

The two men burst out laughing again and looked over at Tony who only smiled and nodded approvingly.

"Happily for us," Lord Edward said, "arming South Carolina blacks as rebels will not happen if Rutledge continues to have his way over young Laurens. Happily for us, the cruel exercise of Sumter's Law has failed and, moreover, a scheme to enlist rebel blacks will never be executed."

Washington quickly got up from his chair to change the subject. "As I've told you, my friend, I well know about the book you so fondly speak of whenever we talk about liberty and freedom and the common aspirations of men. Tony confided to me that Thomas Paine, whom you admire greatly, is also admired by John Laurens. How Tony knows that, I have no idea. How Tony knows anything confounds me. Probably made it up."

Once again, both looked at Tony as if he were an official censor, but Tony simply smiled again and said nothing. He was happy to let his two superiors continue until the most opportune time arose for him to jump in again, as respectfully as he could.

"Perhaps that is what we have in common," Lord Edward replied. "That and the strategic need for both sides to arm blacks. The few years between Laurens and me, as between you and me, are relatively small, not a whole generation, about ten or eleven years. We all are men who appear to some as young radicals, but to Paine as merely men with common sense. Laurens' proposal to arm blacks is common sense that envelops a grander idea of seeing the common humanity in us all."

"Hold on now," Washington said. "You speak a language not understood by those of us fighting for freedom ourselves. Jefferson's 'all men are created equal' does not, of course, mean in every circumstance. Common sense includes reason, and reason arises from economic realities. I have no plans to free my blacks in Virginia, as I've told you. Nor does the Commander-in-Chief himself. Or Jefferson, for that matter. And you might be surprised to know that of the total of some three hundred enslaved blacks in all the Henry Laurens' plantations, only about forty are fit for military service, even if called upon."

"We all have reputations as bold aggressive men in battle, hotheads, and you and Lieutenant Colonel John Laurens are far more experienced in battle than I, certainly. But Laurens has taken the spirit of seeking fame on the battlefield into the legislature as well. There he uses it to espouse the equally just cause of freedom, a cause for everybody, blacks and whites. Of course, I don't know if he would ever free his blacks and go bankrupt in the short run, but, philosophically, at least, it's simply common sense. You win the war with the help of black troops, and blacks become better citizens after their freedom. That's the moral economics of it. It's a bigger way to think about liberty than the way you're thinking about it. Liberty that includes everybody's personal freedom, not liberty to protect personal property of just white male land-owners, but liberty that includes black people, too, and *their* property. Greater economic prosperity will follow—for everybody. You'll see a Charleston tide that raises all ships."

"We have already won the war, even if it's not completely over," Washington said after a pause and a sincere smile that quickly lapsed into pressed lips. He shuffled papers on his desk that were shuffled before, never read, the usual complements to a deliberate if not disheveled mind searching for a key to further deliberation. "It's been over since Yorktown, really since Eutaw Springs that knocked you out of the South. You and Major Majoribanks saved the day at Eutaw Springs, you can tell your grandchildren, but England's grand efforts are not enough. Your government remains miserly, freely feeding off our bounty. Your fat king is crazy as a loon. You're throwing money away you need to fight France and Spain. You and everyone else in the garrison know that, but, happily, realists outnumber cowardly abolitionists in your country. South Carolina is already prepared for the future, prepared in mind and resources. Economics is the basis of morality."

Tony jumped in. "'Morality?'"

Ignoring Tony's interruption with a violent wave of his hand and a look to indicate that he was really pushing his luck this time—his own friend and Lord Edward's faithful servant or not—Washington continued. "At any rate, Lieutenant Colonel Laurens is coming to see me. He just suffered a military disappointment this month to catch your Lieutenant Colonel Craig and his cattle herd at New Cut on John's Island. He's not in a good mood, even though he did successfully help Greene protect Jacksonboro from a British raid.

"When he left Yorktown on November fifth, he went to Philadelphia before being sent by Washington and the Continental Congress to the Southern Campaign. He's been in Charleston since early December, as I mentioned, and is expected to take his seat in the House of Representatives in Jacksonboro tomorrow to introduce his foolish notion of establishing three battalions of Negroes. General Greene, as you may know, supports the idea, but Rutledge and all the planters strongly and wisely object." Washington paused. "Will you join me to meet him?"

Tony looked at Lord Edward and finally sat down in a straight-backed chair near the windows to wait for his response. Lord Edward got up as if to search for an idea momentarily—and happily—lost. He looked over at Tony who throughout the long discourse gave no strong indication of his own thoughts, other than in his brief interruption of Washington when he made reference to morality. Finally turning again toward Washington, Lord Edward spoke as if divulging classified information.

"We take you for a man of your word to return as our prisoner. Whitehall has all but shut down its directions in the colonies and will soon redirect His Majesty's resources to the West Indies. So a meeting with Laurens is of little moment strategically.

"But if I am to meet him, I must do so quietly. We three are known for our rashness in not following orders, and I have no orders to meet with him, or not, so I must be careful. You will remain under my care. Tony will come with us, as usual. I'm sure he, too, wants to meet the young idealist from Charleston."

"He's one of the best there," Tony said, breaking his silence. "Polydose told me about John Laurens. Clinton returned her to Robert McKenzie in

Jacksonboro after she ran away, and she's been all eyes and ears there ever since. If you set us all free, we won't be telling on you."

··◦·❊··

The date was 20 January 1782. After riding north a few miles in darkness toward the Charleston Neck, the three men met up with Laurens near defensive Charleston city tabby walls. Made of oyster shells, they were nearly as effective in repelling cannon balls as the spongy palmetto logs used in the first, unsuccessful siege of Charleston six years earlier. Each man surmised that theirs was not the first clandestine meeting to be held on that spot. The grass was high, and big live oaks stood nearby, their branches touching the ground. A little copse served well to give sufficient cover. It was a spot far removed from Rawdontown where Tory refugees from Ninety Six camped.

When they rode up, John Laurens looked surprised to see that his friend William Washington brought along a British officer and his manservant. Laurens was accompanied by a black man about Tony's age. Washington began the conversation. "Greetings, my friend." He waited till all steadied their mounts. "This is Lieutenant Lord Edward Fitzgerald of the 19th Regiment of Foot in the Charleston garrison. I asked him to come along to meet you. He, too, loves liberty, but just not ours." No one laughed, but the immediate introduction helped put Laurens at ease.

After Lord Edward and Laurens acknowledged each other with a polite nod, each man got off his mount, Washington first, then Lord Edward and Laurens, then Tony and, last, the black servant, obliged to hold the reins of his master's horse. Tony marveled at the horse's beauty and apparent strength. Laurens, slightly smaller in stature than Lord Edward, but equally handsome with an air of discipline and authority, was dressed in his finest republican blue waistcoat. He carried an impressive sword and side arm. Lord Edward in scarlet tunic carried the same. There was no display of showy martial airs.

Washington addressed his fellow American. "I was told earlier that you would oblige a secret meeting in the interest of a meeting of minds and concern for the future of the republic, now that the war has taken this downward spiral and is all but over. I apologize if I arrive with others, unexpected. Lord Edward wants to meet you and, if nothing else, to share his admiration of Thomas Paine."

"The war is most certainly not over," John Laurens replied politely to his patriot comrade and extended his hand to the enemy officer. "But I offer my hand to this esteemed gentleman in friendly parlay. I take William's word that we both love freedom and the right to discuss it in any forum. I gather that you have not brought anyone else with you other than this Negro man." Laurens turned to Tony with an outstretched hand and steady look.

As surprised as Ruth was when Oscar politely addressed her at Burdell's Tavern, Tony shook his hand. "I'm Tony Small, here with my master and friend Lord Edward. He's told me about Mr. Paine, the Englishman."

"What do you know about him, Mr. Small?" Laurens asked.

Everyone was completely caught off guard. Why was Laurens immediately turning to Tony? And 'Mr. Small'? What difference did Tony's knowledge about Thomas Paine make to the future of the republic? Laurens skipped over a member of Ireland's most esteemed peerage to talk first to a black man he never heard of.

Washington and Lord Edward were about to intervene in a short gap in the exchange as Tony was trying to comprehend the moment as well, but the two officers held back. It was clear that John Laurens wanted to hear from Tony Small. His black servant stepped closer. Laurens wanted to take the measure of a man the likes of whom he would soon be celebrating in his effort to get the legislature to arm blacks.

"Is there anything you would like for me to tell members of the General Assembly? Anything you feel not ever expressed enough? Black men are rarely allowed to speak for themselves."

"That's what I'd say right away. I'm a free man, coming from the McKelvey place on the Santee, but I can't prove it down here in Charleston. Lots of time, if I'm by myself and not on Lord Edward's business, I can't travel around like I can back home. But I can prove that I can shoot just as good as any white man if I was taught. Same as reading and writing. Same as anything."

"My efforts to put rifles in the hands of black men are based on people like you who think they could be as good a soldier as a white man, black men who are not beaten down into thinking they don't deserve to be free, the same freedom any white man wants for serving his country. I must admit that it remains a question if blacks are equal to whites in every instance, but as armed soldiers, blacks can certainly be taught the art of warfare, and to that extent be equal to many of our white soldiers and perhaps be used on the front lines as they were at Eutaw Springs. No man is uppity if he asserts his manhood in defense of his country."

Tony did not add his own thoughts about the use of Sumner's black soldiers to fill in the gap left by Malmedy's withdrawing militia. Instead, he said, "Well, giving us guns is right, but I ain't ready to say this is my country."

The two Americans showed concern about this, not so much at the content of the statement but more at the boldness with which a free black spoke. Even Lord Edward did not expect so grand a moment to be put at risk by Tony. Nor was anyone ready to interrupt Tony who, they could tell, knew this was a very important time in his life. He found himself free to talk with a member of one of the most illustrious families in South Carolina, only because of the extraordinary circumstances of this very odd meeting among combatants.

Listening to their exchange was a member of one of the first families of Virginia. Tony knew that, too. And he already knew all about the House of Leinster, Ireland's most noble family, and the Geraldines who virtually ruled Ireland during the Middle Ages. But he also knew that his own family was of proud lineage from Africa. Tony was not thinking about the contents of *Common Sense* by Thomas Payne. Tony was, instead, thinking of all the black men he and Ruth talked to and all the other black men they saw as they marched from Burdell's Tavern through the woods to Eutaw Springs. Those at Star Fort, Huger's and Quinby Bridges and Shubrick's Plantation. They or their ancestors came from Africa, as enslaved men and women, certainly, but he would insist still proudly so, as blacks, as proudly as the present white company came from England and Ireland, blacks with a unique pride born in a crucible of suffering, humiliation, and death.

"Not until all of us get freedom," Tony said, "not just the ones who fight for South Carolina. I don't think we should have to *do* anything to be free. We're *born* free. You can't *give* anybody something when it's not yours to give."

Laurens shifted his weight from one foot to the other and unconsciously placed his hand on his sword, a gesture that did not go unnoticed by Lord Edward. But both he and Washington stood still. Tony looked over at Laurens' servant who continued to listen to every word.

"Your Mr. Jefferson says so, too, even if he does have some enslaved blacks himself. I'm treated better by Lord Edward so far than by any white person I know, including Miss Maggie McKelvey. And I know a lot of black folks like me who thought they were free when they got safe behind British lines and then found out they were just sold again to somebody else. Fact is, I can't trust anybody just now till I see how this war plays out. And even then, I'd be a fool to trust 'em. Colonel Washington tells me for sure y'all are going to win, but so far my best friend is Lord Edward, and no telling how long he can protect me. Meanwhile, I wager that taking up arms for the rebels could go either way for black folks, freedom or not, after this whole war is over. I mean, we all ain't plain stupid."

All three white men stood quietly after Tony stopped talking. All three smiled at Tony's remark, "I mean, we all ain't plain stupid." Tony was, indeed, more typical of blacks than many whites liked to admit. Laurens' black servant nervously looked at his master, as if to say, "Let's go." He fumbled with his own horse's halter.

Laurens raised his eye brows wide, pursed his lips, and gave an upward thrust of his chin as if to think about it all, then slightly and quickly shook his head to register his surprise at the clarity of Tony's response and its unavoidable call to action. No one said anything. He thumped the pipe he was smoking against his boot and let the tobacco, still burning, drop to the ground. Finally, he looked at Washington, not Lord Edward or Tony, and said, "I understand. A former enslaved man of mine named Jemmy ran away from me after Sir Henry Clinton landed near Charleston last year. He joined the Engineers Department of British Army." Turning to Tony, he added, "Perhaps you know him, Mr. Small."

"No, sir, I do not."

"Did you by chance know my devoted servant Pompey and his friend Tom Peas who was owned by my father? They both died of the fever a few years back."

Again, Tony said he didn't know them, as if to imply respectfully that not all blacks knew all other blacks. He took Laurens' questions about blacks he knew as typical of a white's response to racial questions. Did he hear what I just said? Is he just making small talk because he's got nothing better to say? Tony braced for more discourse that missed the point. It was like listening to someone talk about the kind of wood and strings of a banjo instead of the music it makes.

"Sadly, two good black men, Doctor Cuffee and March were punished terribly by my father. It was over an altercation with another planter, John Lewis Gervais. Both were given sound whippings for speaking their minds, expressions, I suspect, made in perfectly acceptable manners, if only they were white. March was put under strict supervision and sent to my father's plantation at Mepkin. Doctor Cuffee was sold to a planter in Orangeburg. My father told me that each needed a well-deserved correction, but I must say that I doubt that."

Now self conscience of the place in the conversation he gave to Tony and not to his black servant, Laurens turned to his servant and said, "This is a British officer of a noble family, Lord Edward Fitzgerald. Lord Edward, I am familiar with your family, sir, from the years spent in London both as a student in the Middle Temple and in service on behalf of the Continental Congress."

To his black servant he added, "And you may have heard of this Virginian, Lieutenant Colonel William Washington, who is a cousin of our Commander in Chief, whom you met while I was the general's aide at Valley Forge. And this is Tony Small who speaks for himself."

Only Tony stepped forward and shook the hand of the black servant who stood frozen, silent and still nameless—a failure that illustrated a deep divide among blacks, one which Tony in this instance was reluctant to correct. If Ruth were there, she would have asked his name. Washington and Lord Edward nodded to the servant.

Laurens turned to get back on his mount without having a discussion with Lord Edward about a shared sense of liberty and Thomas Paine. His horse became agitated and reared up. Lauren's servant could do little to calm the horse. Tony moved forward and took the reins.

"Now, big boy, steady, steady. Easy, easy, easy. You're Liberty, hard to get a-holt of. There, you've lost that wide-eyed look already."

"He's a stallion," Laurens said. "His name is Pacer, but I like the name you've given him." He smiled and took the reins from Tony and swung into the saddle.

The servant came over and whispered under his breath to Tony, "Boy, you're good with horses, but you best keep all that high thinking about freedom to yourself. You'll get us all in a mess of trouble."

"We have thirty-five miles to ride before the legislature begins its session tomorrow," Laurens said. "I'm told the Swamp Fox himself will be there with Lieutenant Colonel Maham and, of course, many stubborn politicians— that's probably topsecret information I am giving to the enemy.

"Please give my regards to Miss Elliott, William. I have heard that she is taking good care of you while in custody. I myself have been wounded four times. It is not a pleasant experience. It's a shame I never had my Martha by my side.

"I doubt if the issue even gets to a vote. These South Carolina planters would rather risk having a treaty that will allow the British to keep Charleston under *uti possidetis* than fight with a greater degree of certainty in winning. So for now, at least, Tom Paine will be kept in a book that might as well be a box."

"Lord Edward, there's a man here to see you," Tony announced in his quarters several days after their meeting with Laurens. "Calls himself Captain Marsh but says you may know him as Captain Marsh Kingston. Says he won't take much time."

Tony opened the door and nodded to an unassuming, capable looking black man. The man took off his hat and looked around the room. He adjusted the strap of the croker sack slung over his shoulder. He carried no side arm. Lord Edward looked up from his desk and signaled Tony to stay in the room.

"Lord Edward, I really want to talk to Tony here but know I first have to talk to you."

"No, not at all."

"Then I reckon I'll just get right to it, sir. We want your man Tony to join us in the Independent Troop of Black Dragoons in the British Provincial Army in South Carolina. That's a mouthful but it's the official name for us. General Leslie calls us the Black Dragoons. Some folks along the Congaree call us Black Riders."

"I'm familiar with your unit, Captain Marsh. I heard it discussed by the general himself. Your unit, since its formation in November last, does His Majesty great service. Captures renegades who wish to desert the garrison." Lord Edward got up from his desk and without shaking hands with Marsh, went over to a smaller table as if to look for specific references or letters. "I'm aware of all that, but you must also be aware that an aggressive role of blacks making excursive attacks on the enemy's surrounding positions is a radical idea which may backfire on us. Even some loyalists hate you."

Marsh continued to stand rigid but not at attention. He answered by a simple gesture of putting his hat under his arm, quietly inviting further comments from Lord Edward.

"Tory owners of the enslaved are as passionate as Whigs about keeping black men, women, and children as their property essential to their economy. As a matter of fact, Tony and I had a conversation only recently about the efficacy of forming all-black battalions. General Greene is aware that General Leslie and you are doing just that, and, to counter us, you might be interested to know, Lieutenant Colonel John Laurens is making an effort to form battalions of black rebels. "So I, too, will get right to it, Captain Marsh. A decision Tony might make to join you is entirely his own." He looked at Tony with a look of apology for not letting him have the first word.

Tony raised his eyebrows and made a short clicking noise with his clinched teeth, then took up the conversation. "Tell me about your Black

Dragoons, Captain Marsh. Lord Edward's already told me that you're not official, even if Benjamin Thompson has landed in town. He has, hasn't he?"

"Right. He's Lord George Germain's man, straight from London, so what he says about his King's American Dragoons up in New England goes for us Black Dragoons down here, too. We're legitimate, even if we're mainly off the books."

"Perhaps off the books because General Leslie himself hasn't gotten permission from his superiors in New York," Lord Edward added.

"Well, I'm the CO. Our officers include Robin our Quartermaster and Garrick our adjutant. Lieutenant Mingo rides with me as second in command. He's an excellent horseman, as I hear you both are."

"What's your total strength in numbers?" Tony asked.

"Three noncommissioned officers and twenty-one enlisted. Scippio, Daly, and John Mayham are the sergeants. We already hit William Matthews' place on the seventeenth and scared him silly. Matthews said he was neutral, but we didn't believe him. Told him we would have cut him to pieces if he wasn't an invalid. We're the nightmare this war's been waiting for—if it needs another one. We're not always trained, but we're learning, and we're all good horsemen from the start. I said that already. Most of us reared in the stable, like you."

"Well, you know Lieutenant General Charles, Earl Cornwallis, took our regular cavalry to Virginia," Lord Edward said, "so, if you're implying that Lee and Marion have an advantage we need to deal with, you're right— even if Lieutenant Colonel Washington's horse is much reduced after Eutaw Springs. That is, notwithstanding the fact that elements of his 3rd Regiment are still very much in action, as we expect to see shortly. And we didn't even have enough cavalry at Eutaw Springs—that's why we could only hold the field. Are you aware of all that?"

"Can't say I am. We're just hungry to make things right, Lord Edward. Everybody knows that. We're men, same as you. Our women and children have been suffering too long, too hard. If we can kill as many rebels as a pistol and sword can get to, we're happy. Got nothing to lose and can hope for freedom after we kill 'em, too. Got nothing to lose." He looked at Tony. "Got nothing to lose."

"I'll think about it," Tony said. "Lord Edward's 19th Foot is not a foraging unit. We protect the garrison. All those excursions are usually left to loyalist provincials, to the 30th, the 17th, other foot regiments, the 84th, and even the 64th that fought at Eutaw. We do go out occasionally, however. But I don't know now if I want to take the risk and leave the 19th here. That's Colonel Coates's decision, anyway. I know we need to eat and we need matériel that we can get only outside this garrison we're pinned into. But this war's over. And I don't know if I want to kill anybody. Just not sure. I don't think freedom is guaranteed to a black man, no matter what killing he does for either side. That's the heart of it."

"Better hurry and stop dreaming. You're a free man already, Tony Small. You saw all those free black men fight at Eutaw Springs. We've got to take the offensive if we're going to survive. I bet you already heard of our success at Smith's Plantation a few days back. Lieutenant Mingo, the boys and me helped whip 'em good. Jumped all over them rebs. We're proving ourselves but need some more men who can ride good like you, Tony."

"Lieutenant Colonel Washington told us about the Reverend Robert Smith, if that's whose plantation you refer to," Lord Edward said. "He's the vicar at St. Philips here in Charleston. But, again, ultimately, this is Tony's decision. I can say, however, that Tony is of great use in our effort to maintain the garrison in his role as Lieutenant Colonel Washington's servant as well as mine."

A few days later, Tony met the Black Dragoons on a very fine charger which Lord Edward loaned him. He found them in the middle of recounting past successful expeditions and immediately preparing for another. All were on their horses within the walls of the garrison in a small area more appropriate for bivouacking than for getting ready for an expedition. Chickens and an occasional goat and pig dodged the hooves of their horses. Several women with water and rations grumbled and fussed as they pushed aside the flanks of horses to get to the men they were trying to serve. A few of the younger men purposefully moved their mounts in the way, adding to the merriment that arose from shouts bouncing first on one side, then another, depending on where the women were. "Over here. Not there. I need water over here."

Most ignored the new manservant of an Irish lord, a black man without combat experience. Others shot quick glances at someone they reckoned would be their weakest link.

"Colonel Benjamin Thompson sure surprised 'em yesterday at Brabant's, didn't he," Aberdeen, a slight but muscular man, said to other privates nearby.

"When Major John Doyle charged Marion's men, and they all got bunched up and went scampering across Wambaw Bridge like scalded dogs, I almost split a gut laughing," Private Hammond added. "The whole bridge just fell into the creek. Thompson sure surprised 'em." Hammond always spoke after Aberdeen, and if left nothing to add or improve upon, simply repeated what Aberdeen said. He was too big to be interrupted or teased.

"I wish we had been more in the middle of it all," said Private Dawey, the smallest but not the youngest dragoon. "Colonel Thompson could have used us more, I reckon. We could have really made those rebels run."

Lieutenant Mingo rode up and heard the men boasting. "He'll use you today, and you'll get your chance this time, but you might be that scalded dog today. Turns out, we were fighting men under Colonel Archibald McDonald and Benton's Dragoons yesterday. We even captured a big patriot—a planter named Charles Cotesworth Pinckney. He's been complaining about the murders we've been committing all over the country, just like what Bloody Bill Cunningham does. But today we're going to Tydiman's Plantation. We're fighting Colonel Marion himself who's come back from Jacksonboro to take command of his men."

"The Swamp Fox has still got short-timers and reformed Tories who don't want to fight anymore," Captain March said as he, too, rode up and joined them. "They'll run for sure, just like they did yesterday." He glanced over at Lieutenant Mingo and nodded. "If you follow my orders, shoot straight, and don't run away, we'll do fine. We'll have Major John Coffin with us, too. He knows Marion from Eutaw Springs.

"Watch me. I'll be following Bloody Bill Cunningham's Dragoons. You—over there, Dawey, Cane, Aberdeen, Charles, Dick, Gilbert—call Isaac, Tom, Jamie, January—call 'em all over here so everybody can hear me. January, you and Primus, Lynch, Toney, Hammond, and Jeffry, you ride behind Sergeant Mayham. Cane, you and Charles, Dick, and Gilbert ride behind Sergeant Daly. Stay in formation. Don't get scattered. Do your job. Yesterday was a practice run. We just watched from the rear. But this is real, and we'll be smack dab in the middle of it. The rest of you ride with Sergeant Scippio, and that includes you, Peter, and the other Peter, and Pompey, Samuel, and Prince. You, too, Jacob."

Captain March then turned to the horseman near his side and said, "Tony Small, you ride in the rear and tell your master what you see, if we get out of this alive. If you lose sight of me, stick near the 30th Foot. You'll recognize some of those Irish boys, I'm sure, and I expect your Lord Edward will get reports from them as well as from you, if you make it through."

The date was 25 February 1782. The expedition of little moment came and went safely for Tony, but that would change a couple of months later for the Black Dragoons.

On 21 April 1782, the day of the Elliott-Washington wedding at Sandy Hill, Black Dragoons were far away in a skirmish near Fort Dorchester and the Quarter House between loyalists and Lee's Legion. Shortly after that time, Tony had pressing news of both events. He burst into Lord Edward's room, much less interested in giving a report of the wedding he attended than in telling Lord Edward about a fresh report of the skirmish.

"Captain Marsh and Lieutenant Mingo had about thirty Black Dragoons with 'em to help Captain George Dawkins' Loyalists, about a hundred of 'em." He paused, stumbling over his words. He took a deep breath. He dabbed at tears with his sleeve and sat down in a chair laden with papers.

"They were up against Captain Ferdinand O'Neal, the officer you saw at Quinby, the one who turned around at the bridge instead of jumping over the loose planks. O'Neal had about thirty dragoons with him, all from Lee's Legion.

"Dawey, Cane, Aberdeen, Charles, Dick, and Gilbert—I knew 'em all— dismounted to set up an ambush of O'Neal's cavalry patrolling the east side of the Ashley River near Bacon's Bridge." At that, Tony jumped up from his chair and shouted. "They were on one side of the road with Sergeant Daly.

Sergeant Mayham, Primus, January, Lynch, Toney, Hammond, and Jeffry on the other side. Sergeant Scippio with Isaac, Tom, and Jamie were still mounted, like Captain Marsh. You know Scippio, one of my best friends. We would talk and talk about what was going to happen after this war."

"Calm down, Tony, calm down. You're speaking too fast."

"I don't know what went wrong. Captain Marsh had the two Peters, Pompey, Samuel, Jacob, and Prince. The two Peters were so young, so good and strong. Funny, too. Used to say, 'No, that's him,' even when we got it right. They always took it well when everybody, including me, got 'em mixed up, meaning to or not. I wasn't told how they all got themselves in such a mess.

"The ambush was only part-way successful. O'Neal and Captain John Rudolph, who was with him—that's Michael's brother, the one at Quinby Bridge—ran right through it down Gaillard Road, but they took a lot of casualties from the Black Dragoons."

"How did we know to ambush the rebels in the first place?"

"Don't know. It may have been a cooked-up plot to capture General Greene—I don't really know. Don't even know how to explain it to you."

How best to deal with such terrible news, to present it to one who is so dear to me, yet whose race is the cause of such misery to mine. Is his heart like mine, the same color as mine, his blood the same color? How can we get more and more freedom if our color doesn't ever change?

"The rest of what happened is terrible. They saw some of the Black Dragoons and went after them with a fury. I think they caught Pompey and Jacob. I bet those two big strong men gave 'em a good fight, though. Some others I ain't heard about. Rudolph caught Captain Marsh in the swamp trying to escape. No quarter's ever given to black folks. Rudolph cut off Captain Marsh's head with one blow. Some say it was a man named Smart who got his head cut off, but I know they're talking about my friend Marsh. They were getting even with black folks they call 'vile dragons.' They were trying to teach us black folks a lesson."

Tony stopped talking, then calmly said, "I don't think we all got the message."

Tony looked straight at his friend and said, "Such a terrible thing might have been Cuffy's fate, too, if he had survived Eutaw Springs. I told you about Cuffy. He could have died at Eutaw by the sword of an angry white rebel, even though he was found with an American rifle in his hand—or by the sword of one of Marion's black rebels—who knows? Main thing is that they all got their color back after the fighting stopped. The color dead."

"I'm very sorry to hear this news, Tony. Very sorry, indeed." Lord Edward paused a long time, then went over to his friend, now sitting again uncomfortably on the documents in the chair, and put his hand on his shoulder. "Let's just sit here a while together."

After an hour or so of talking about the Black Dragoons, Lord Edward quietly raised the subject of Tony's attendance at the wedding at Sandy Hill.

"The wedding? The wedding … was ceremonious, a quiet affair. Not that many people, just important ones. They'll live on Legare Street in Charleston, not at Sandy Hill, for now, depending on General Leslie. I think they've gone to Kiddy-wah for their honeymoon."

"That's all nice to hear."

"At the reception after the ceremony, the colonel gave a toast to you for saving his life. Some rebel officers were very surprised to hear him talk so good about an enemy, especially somebody at the thicket, somebody with Major Majoribanks who turned the battle against 'em at Eutaw. Anyway, Lieutenant Colonel Washington gave a toast to you, but he omitted one thing. He should have said that anyone else who heard such a complement about himself would get a big head about it. But not you. You wouldn't even be listening.

"He said, 'I never knew so loveable a person, and every man in the army, from the general to the drummer, would cheer the expression. His frank and open manner, his universal benevolence, his valour almost chivalrous, and, above all, his unassuming tone made him an idol of all who served with him.'"

The lives of Tony Small and Lord Edward changed dramatically later in the spring of 1782. General Leslie ordered the 19th and 30th Regiments of Foot to depart Charleston on May fifth for the West Indies where British troops were needed to fight the French. Lord Edward's great adventure in arms took a different, inactive course, and Tony's life as servant and confidant on foreign shores began in earnest. The circumstances that lay behind the departure of Tony Small with Edward Fitzgerald's regiment in May 1782 were complex and intimately related to the role of blacks in the war.

That spring Lord Edward had a tough sell to Tony to make sense of the exploitation of blacks in the evacuation. "Voluntary arrival in British camps of those escaping from slavery," he tried to explain, "is never clearly determined as emancipation by London authorities, I'm sorry to say. Whitehall does not want to undermine the strength and support of loyalists, whose hapless enslaved men, women and children willingly fled to our troops expecting to be free."

"I know that," Tony said in a tone of voice that gave the strong impression that Lord Edward would never succeed with his explanation, regardless of his good-faith effort. Tony had Rudolph's decapitation of Marsh in the back of his mind.

"Well, now British officers are trying to take blacks with them, many because they have formed friendships or simply have grown accustomed to being waited on. But, as you know, many want blacks because they want to sell them in the West Indies."

"I know that, too. This ain't good for me. It just doesn't look good. Sounds like it doesn't matter if I'm born free. That's really always been the way it is."

In the departure from Charleston of the 19th and 30th Regiments, in troop ships bound for St. Lucia, Barbados and Antigua, General Leslie himself did not challenge Tony's status as a free black man and allowed Lord Edward to keep Tony as the two regiments sailed out of Charleston harbor. He no doubt did so only by virtue of the noble birth of Lord Edward and his role as former aide-de-camp to Lord Rawdon.

But other urgent arrangements were made on Tony's behalf. After a hard struggle against false claims made by loyalists to insist that Tony was an enslaved black, Lord Edward ended up paying a nominal sum for Tony's liberty. Nonetheless, at Tony's explicit request, Lord Edward never conceded that Tony was anything other than a man born as free as he himself was.

"Under the circumstances, Tony, paying blackmail is a more expedient way to settle this matter. It's a necessary concession. At any rate, I must continue to have you by my side. I would have gladly paid considerably more if more had been demanded. Even the price of a nice fat goose." Tony let that old joke slide. Now something else was on his mind.

On 5 May 1782 Lord Edward and Tony Small stood on Gadsden's wharf, an eight-hundred-forty-foot quay on the Cooper River at the mouth of Charleston harbor. Odor of oil and armor overwhelmed whiffs from tea olive bushes, just as the odor of gunpowder did at Burdell's Tavern after the Battle of Eutaw Springs. The mellifluent odor could not push through the humidity beyond the gardens along East Bay Street to reach the wharf. The sights and sounds of the bustle of conscripts and enslaved labor loading matériel onto the ships also generated their own inimitable odor, like that of men in battle. Tony looked at what he was about to leave behind forever.

On the way to the wharf he saw mostly non-native plants in the gardens south of Broad Street, different from the native plants he knew in Miss Maggie's garden. He knew he was about to leave a place like no other on earth. Charleston, the Holy City, a place that claimed both foreign and commonplace things uniquely as its own, as if to brand what is in fact universal. The birds were Charleston birds, critters were Charleston critters, even roaches and rats. The sun and moon fell within its orbit of ownership. The color of some houses was not green but Charleston green. People standing at a distance were people like none he would ever meet again. Mainly out for themselves but within a bond of civility like no other. Even the air was Charleston salty air that he would never breathe again.

His parents, brothers, and friends were already a thing of the past. Eagle would have another rider, he thought. He looked at Lord Edward without saying a word.

Both men were familiar with the flag Christopher Gadsden designed for the war, a flag with a rattlesnake in chopped-up parts for each colony and the words, "Don't Tread On Me." Gadsden built the wharf with a large exit ramp as if to underscore the words for British troops. As Tony feared, it would in future years come to serve as the main point of importation for thousands of enslaved men, woman and children who survived the middle passage over the Atlantic Ocean from West Africa.

Now Tony was using Gadsden's Wharf as a point of departure. The two men stood on the wharf as inconspicuously as possible. Lord Edward played no commanding role during the evacuation. A gang plank was lowered from a British warship for boarding. Brigadier General O'Hara and other senior ranking officers, including Coates, newly promoted by Leslie to the rank of brigadier, watched as staff and key personnel of the 19th and 30th Regiments of Foot boarded. The rank and file of other regiments then quickly moved forward in an orderly fashion. Troops looked over their shoulder as they boarded. The entire ordeal was an evacuation made under a great deal of duress and with a sharp sense of urgency.

When it came time for Lord Edward and Tony to board, Tony suddenly stopped. Fifty feet away stood Ruth. Tony had not seen her for eight months when she left him at Eutaw Springs to make her own way to Charleston. Lord Edward stepped back from boarding. Without a word, Tony went over to Ruth and kissed her.

"Phillis had her baby," Ruth said, before he could say anything. "I found out after we talked. Mariah. The baby's name is Mariah. Don't you remember? Phillis came with Rawdon into Charleston just to get behind British lines so her baby could be born free. Little Mariah is already three months old." She took quick short breaths throughout and nervously looked over her shoulder. Tony knew the birth of Phillis' child was not what she came to tell him.

"She's free, Tony. She's born behind British lines, so she's free."

"Yes, she's free. It's wonderful to see you again, Ruth. Where have you been? I've looked all over for you. I love you, Ruth."

"I love you, too, Tony Small." They suddenly locked together, body and soul. Troops continued to board. The commotion and agitation on the dock created an excitement in the air, military excitement, the kind they both knew at Henry Laurens' Plantation and Burdell's Tavern, yet very different. Amidst it all, each was trying to talk about love, the kissing cousin of war.

"I envy you, Tony. I envy you."

Tony hugged her more tightly and kissed her again and again. "Ruth, we've loved each other all our lives. You're my best friend, my dearest love, my faithful Ruth."

"I know," Ruth interrupted as if to avoid listening to his real words in favor of her own imaginary words which she recited alone for eight months, worn words she could continue to refashion for years to come, words all lovers create and keep for themselves, words which they put aside when not useful and pick up when they are, like protective clothing when it's cold.

"I love you, Tony Small. I can be free here, too, Tony, like you. The war is over. Things are going to change. You can get Lord Edward to buy my freedom from Mr. Snow, even if things don't work out the way they should and he tries to take me back. I've been trying to get away to see you in the garrison all this time, but just couldn't do it because of old man Snow. He came down to Charleston to get me. Now I ran away again. We can still have a life together here."

From a distance, Lord Edward saw his friend gently fold Ruth into his arms. He could not hear what either was saying. A great blue heron swooped down over the parting troops, then rose again and flew off out into the harbor.

"You are my only love, Ruth. What we both told each other ever since we used to play together as children in the McKelvey oak by the Eutaw springs—all that will never change. I know you love me as much as I love you. I will always love you, Ruth."

"This is your native land, Tony. You belong here."

"Leaving you behind is the hardest thing I'll ever do. Leaving my country is hard, too. This is my country. My heart will always be with you in the Lowcountry. But I have to go."

"They could still keep me enslaved, you know that, don't you, Tony? You don't trust white men any more than I do, Brits or rebs."

"Lord Edward can barely get me out with him, and I was born free. He can't take you. He just can't take you, or he would. I'll come back someday to find you and free you if, God forbid, you're still enslaved."

"I plan to get on any boat that'll take me," Ruth said.

"Then I'll trace records of passengers and find you. Everybody's supposed to be sailing to New York before the end of the year. Then Canada. That's the rumor. Lord Edward told me. You've heard it, too."

"I want to leave before then, Tony. I have to leave. I'm afraid of old man Snow. I'm just like you, Tony. We've been through so much together. I know you love me, and I know you're not a selfish man. Maybe you do have to leave me behind now. I don't know. I just don't think we will ever see each other again. I'm not sure what I think. I want you to save yourself if you can't save me, too, Tony Small."

Ruth looked up at the sky, raised both hands, spread her fingers wide, then clinched her fists and shook them. "Lord God almighty, help me. I'll never be enslaved again."

Lord Edward saw her kiss Tony and whisper something in his ear. He saw them part and Ruth run away.

Chapter 6

———⌀———

IRELAND

Tony Small sailed to St. Lucia in the Lesser Antilles with Lord Edward who within a year's time took his faithful friend with him to Ireland. Raised to the rank of major in the 19th Regiment of Foot, Lord Edward wanted to join the 90th Regiment of Foot to earn the rank of lieutenant colonel. But he also wanted to join the 90th Foot, in part for a reason at odds with his military ambition, one related to his growing friendship with the free black man who rescued him and carried him on his back at Eutaw Springs. Lord Edward wanted to transfer to the 90th Foot primarily because he wanted advancement in rank, but also because he wanted out of the Caribbean where Tony was constantly at risk of being stolen and sold without Lord Edward's knowledge or, worse, without his being able to do anything about it. Lord Edward wanted to return to Ireland and England, both to find better opportunities to seek fame and to allow Tony to live without fear of being enslaved. Lord Edward Fitzgerald for the first time consciously put his military ambition in context of his friendship with Tony Small and chose to move into other venues toward fame for himself and greater liberty for Tony. They became a team forged on American soil for the same purpose.

The cry of liberty, which Lord Edward heard in America and felt every day through his friend and manservant, began to assert itself in relation to his own country. The cry of liberty was less abstract upon his return to Ireland in 1783 when he was elected to Parliament to represent Athy, a market town in County Kildare southwest of Dublin. There it had already reasserted itself through thousands of his countrymen rising up against British rule. A need for military action for liberty in Ireland eventually replaced in Lord Edward a desire for military action with the British army for personal fame. But before he conducted any military action in Ireland, Lord Edward and Tony spent four years in Ireland, England, and the continent. Then another two in Canada.

Lord Edward missed the sheer excitement of battle, and he knew that anything less than heroic military action failed to provide the template on which he could promote his status as an ideal catch for a woman within his own social circle. He was a very handsome lady's man, quick to lose his heart to beauty from any direction, often from the ground up. His good looks and manners took him to the gates of success, but for lack of money no further. He was briefly infatuated with a young woman in 1783, a Miss Mathews, but nothing came of it. During the period of reelection of Fox over William Pitt in 1784, Lord Edward met Elizabeth Sheridan in London. He was twenty-one and she was thirty-nine years old, each at the time merely an acquaintance of the other. Before her marriage to the playwright Richard Sheridan, Elizabeth was known as Miss Linley, the most famous female singer in England. All the while, Tony listened when called upon. He was aware that the stiff breezes of romance shook his friend as powerfully as the winds of war. And he, too, had his own story.

More romance came for Lord Edward in 1786 from being besotted by Lady Catherine Meade, whom he called Kate, daughter and heiress of the first Earl of Clanwilliam, but he was eventually, and predictably, sent packing by her father. After recovery from that, Lord Edward was hit in quick succession with another solid rejection, this time by his cousin Georgiana Lennox, twenty-one years old, the youngest daughter of his mother's brother, Lord George Lennox, whose son Charles became the 4th Duke of Richmond. As the sister of a future duke, Georgiana was way out of reach for the impecunious Lord Edward. Her father's determination of that left Lord Edward with enough animosity to fuel resentment toward his own upper class. By 1786, however, he found his French mistress Madame de Lévis.

That same year, Lord Edward wrote of the strength Tony gave him during his struggle on the high seas of romance. "I was going to send Tony to London to learn to dress hair, but when he was to go, I found I could not do without his friendly face to look at and one that I found to love me a little."

In 1787 Lord Edward and Tony went to Spain, Portugal, and Gibraltar where Lord Edward visited his former commander at St. Lucia, General O'Hara who surrendered in place of Cornwallis at Yorktown. But taking ruins to ruins did less for the young romantic than sharing war stories about women with his servant and closest friend.

Tony never just tagged along. Gibraltar opened the door for him to tell his own story, to tell more of what went on between Ruth and him on Gadsden's Wharf when the 19th Foot departed Charleston five years earlier. After a drab day full of the kind of administrative nonsense that triggers reflection on important events, the two retired to their quarters. Tony looked about the sitting room which served as Lord Edward's office. Objects faded into darkness at end of day before he lit the lamps. Lord Edward thanked him and continued to read, oblivious to the moment.

"I had to leave Ruth behind, you know."

Lord Edward remained seated at his desk, took his pipe out of his mouth—he rarely smoked it—and looked up to see Tony standing idly in a dark corner, leaning on a window sill. Tony held a vase in one hand, studying the figures as an archeologist would to give it a date and provenance. He looked at the curves of the vase. He turned it this way and that, as if to impose motion on its figures.

"She wanted me to take her with me or stay with her in Charleston."

"What?" Lord Edward got up from his chair. "You could have told me. I could have tried to find a way for her to leave with us."

"No, not really. Not really." Tony put the vase back on the window sill. He avoided looking directly at Lord Edward and stared out the window, moving his head this way and that, but with a fixed look on a specific object, in spite of the darkness and in spite of the static figure that could not be moved with his hands in the same way he moved the figures on the vase. He continued to give the impression of one determined to look critically at a subject from all perspectives, or as one who saw something he recognized. He squinted his eyes, then looked at the terra firma of the Rock of Gibraltar itself, but he might as well have been looking at the diaphanous and shifting clouds floating by in the faint light of dusk.

"General Leslie wouldn't let that happen, especially at the very last minute as we were about to board. You know that. I didn't want to raise false hopes. I didn't know what to do. I mean you were lucky just to get me out. I couldn't stay."

His friend did not interrupt. After a while Tony looked straight at him and asked, "Was I selfish?" He turned away to answer his own question in a round-about way, to stir up enough issues out of which he might gain some perspective to find an answer, fearful of finding enough selfishness that would tilt the very ground beneath him.

"That's the worst thing in the world, to be selfish. Loving somebody and claiming to be practical about it just doesn't work, does it? Or want more than you need. I mean when you fool yourself and think what you're doing is practical when it's really just selfish. I thought we both couldn't have freedom with you at the same time, in the same way."

Lord Edward walked over to where Tony was standing. He aimlessly picked at a loose thread on his scarlet tunic to signal that "these things happen" and that Tony need not pursue the matter if it were too difficult. He then moved toward two large chairs, thinking that Tony might want to sit down. After Lord Edward's comment in Charleston about the possibility of Ruth being at the Ethiopian Ball, neither ever made insipid remarks about the other's love affairs. He slowly sat down and waited for Tony to continue.

"It would have been selfish of me to bring her along, even if she could have—just to risk seeing her disappear and sold once we got to St. Lucia. I was afraid she would be sold if she came with us. She would never have the protection I had living with you, and she and I would have been vulnerable living apart from you. She couldn't live in the barracks. You couldn't help her if she lived alone."

"I never knew this, Tony. It's terrible, not knowing what your future might have been with someone you love. It's one of the worst feelings in the world. In its own way, worse than unrequited love. Maybe I could have gotten her safe quarters, as I offered to do in Charleston. But maybe not.

"Do you remember, Tony, the day I asked you to be my manservant and attend me on my duties in Charleston?"

"I do," Tony replied and smiled.

"That was a happy day for us both, was it not? I mean for both of us. I deliberated whether to take you with me to St. Lucia, too.

"It was that little gesture you made in helping Lieutenant Colonel Washington into the wagon as we left Eutaw Springs that told me who you are. And the care you gave Major Majoribanks in helping find the Buttons to take care of him at Wantoot. Ruth knows you love her, Tony. She sees what we all see in you."

"She told me on the wharf."

"Told you what?"

"She told me on the wharf when we left that she was going to have a baby. That was the last time I heard anything. Maybe she got away to New York and on to Canada. Maybe Oscar got Colonel Marion to buy her from Snow. I'll always see her coming 'round the corner. Said if it was a girl, she'd name her Dido."

After serving in the 90th Regiment of Foot, and ignoring a possibility for greater political status, Lord Edward joined the 54th Regiment of Foot in 1788 to seek military adventure in Canada. He took Tony with him to Halifax in Nova Scotia, St. John's and St. Anne's in New Brunswick, to

Quebec, Montreal, Detroit, the Great Lakes, and down the Mississippi to New Orleans. At some points, Tony seized upon the opportunity to search for Ruth. His inquiries of David George, a black leader in Halifax led nowhere. Black refugees from Charleston, Kate, Nancy, Will Hicks, and Bristol, knew nothing about Ruth. Neither did John Brown, Punch, Peter Hume, Thomas London, John Williams, Peter, and William Simpson, all of whom sailed from Charleston to Halifax for a new life.

Tony's search in St. John's for anyone arriving on a boat fleeing Charleston was also futile. Tim, Daphne Shields, Silvia Bailey, Ned Huger, Besse, Kitty, John and Jacob Lynch knew nothing. Manifests of ships which sailed from Charleston to Canada with blacks seeking freedom were of no help—those of the *Midsummer Blossom*, the *Duchess of Gordon*, the *Little Dale*, the *Sovereign*, the *Two Sisters*, the *Ester*, the *Elizabeth*, the *Mars*, the *Spencer*, and the *Lady's Adventure*.

In St. John's the most important South Carolinian was a runaway from none other than the Swamp Fox himself, a black man named Abraham Marrian. Tony caught up with Marrian at his home, sitting in a rocking chair, smoking his pipe. He was about thirty years old but looked twice his age. His rugged broad shoulders were drooped from a perpetual posture of either picking up or putting down a heavy burden. His enormous hands stuck far beyond the ragged edges of his checkered shirt sleeves. He had several pipes, all good ones, status symbols, and used them like promiscuous lovers, two or three alight at one time, favoring one, then another. At least one was guaranteed to be faithfully burning.

"There were several of us on the *Lady's Adventure* who worked for soldiers," Marrian told Tony. "I'm just the one who sticks out because everyone remembers my master Colonel Francis Marion. Somebody told me you were looking for me. I know Tim. He's the only one here from the famous DeLancey's Brigade."

"Tell me, Marrian, why did you change your name a little? You don't go by Marion—M, A, R, I, O, N—anymore," Tony said, proudly spelling it out by way of explanation.

"When I ran away in 1782 to join the British. I first worked for Lieutenant Simon Tarbell of the King's American Dragoons. After the war ended, I made it up here to St. John's with the British evacuation of New York. I liked the Swamp Fox—that's what they called him. I liked the colonel, I really did. Some called him a general after his rank on the Continental Line. He was the best they had on how to whip British dummies standing in a row in their bright red coats. Hide like an Indian. Hit and run. That was Greene's way, too. He was a good man, as far as it goes for somebody who enslaves other folks, if that makes any sense, so I want to keep a little bit of him around. But all the rest I want to leave far behind in the pluff mud of Carolina."

"Well, can you tell me if you've seen a black woman named Ruth from the Lowcountry?"

Marrian looked pensively at Tony, and after a pause, replied, "Afraid not. I heard you were looking for her. I met a lot of black folks in all that time, but nobody named Ruth." He tugged at his sleeves, thumped ashes from his pipe against his boot, then the palm of his hand to knock out a few slightly burning still inside. The hot ashes meant nothing to the calluses on his hand. He blew forcefully through the stem making the sound of a decoy, Tony thought, as if to lure tobacco leaves to fill his pipe again.

"Well, if you hear of her, let me know, or maybe try to get word to me. I would sure appreciate it." Tony started to leave, then for some reason he looked back at Marrian and saw Marrian looking hard at him. He waited a while longer, then turned around and started to walk away again.

"Wait up, Tony Small," Marrian called out. "I'm not being completely honest with you. I just don't want to hurt your feelings or say something that ain't so." Tony came back and sat down without a word. Marrian looked down at the warm pipe still in his hand, then straight at Tony.

"I did hear something about a woman named Ruth. It was at a time when a lot of Redcoats were leaving Charleston. I don't know if it was your woman, but I heard an old man named Snow came down to Charleston from the Santee and sold a runaway girl that was giving him lots of trouble. They were watching her all the time she was saying goodbye on the dock to her Redcoat friends in the summer of '82. They grabbed her as soon as they could and sold her the same day. Said she fought like a wild cat. Called her an arch bitch. Said her name was Ruth."

Marrian looked at Tony's face and went on, just to keep a drone of sound alive for Tony's sake. "Said she was really something. If that was your Ruth, then I'm powerful sorry."

Without a word, Tony got up, turned and walked down the dusty little road leading back to town. Marrian kept his seat but soon called out, "Wait up. Don't feel too bad, Mr. Small. That ain't all. I heard after that, my old master the Swamp Fox himself ended up owning Ruth. Bought her going to have a baby. Oscar wanted him to."

After three weeks in St. John's, Lord Edward and Tony set off again, this time for St. Anne's, about one hundred miles farther west in New Brunswick. There Major Lord Edward Fitzgerald assumed his duties as one of the officers at a fortified outpost of the 54th Foot. Tony found no evacuees from Charleston at St. Anne's—and none farther west at Quebec, their next destination, or anywhere else—so he completely put aside his search for Ruth for the remaining time in Canada.

They left St. Anne's in early 1789 and traveled southeast in deep snow for nearly four weeks to arrive in mid-March in the frontier town of Quebec. "This snow is like nothing at the springs," Tony told Lord Edward along the way as they both struggled in snow shoes. "The ladies better get here fast."

"The ladies?" Lord Edward asked.

"April, May, and June."

Along the route they hunted moose and elk and saw some of North America's other magnificent wild animals, wolverines, wolves, beavers. If they had seen the mighty grizzly bear—*ursus arctos horribilis*—Lord Edward would have told his mother.

After spending two weeks in Quebec, they launched canoes on the St. Lawrence River and, again meeting Native Americans all along the way, arrived in Montreal, two hundred miles southwest, by late April 1789. Lord Edward and Tony continued down the St. Lawrence to Lake Ontario where they boarded a schooner to arrive at Fort Niagara by May 1789 and, later, traveled farther south to Fort Eire. At Fort Eire Lord Edward and Tony met the famous Mohawk chief Joseph Brant who was well known to both the British army and government. Brant was kindly received by Lord Rawdon and Charles Fox during a trip to London, so he was very happy to welcome Rawdon's former aide-de-camp and Fox's cousin.

"We're invited to accompany Chief Joseph," Lord Edward told Tony a few days later, "and go along the southern coast of Lake Eire to Detroit. From there we'll head north on Lake Huron to the outpost at Michilimackinack. Tony, it's clear to me now that my interest now lies more in exploration, not the army."

"That's very clear, to me and moose, too."

In late June 1789, back in Detroit, under the auspices of David Hill, a Mohawk and Europeanized chief like Brant, Lord Edward received an extraordinary honor bestowed on only a few other Europeans.

"You are to be congratulated and admired," Tony said. "You are a Chief of the Bear Tribe, of the Seneca. 'Ye sayats Eghnidal.' When we return to your home town, I will call you 'Eghnidal.' Now, honorable one, let's get down the river to New Orleans and catch a boat to Dublin. I'm told it will take us a month to make out way just to the headwaters of the Mississippi."

As time progressed, both men became fully aware that they were living in an age of revolutions, the American, 1765–1783, the French, 1789–1799, and the Irish, 1782–1798.

In the winter of 1789–90, Lord Edward and Tony Small in Ireland and England zealously took up the French war cry of liberté, égalité, fraternité. Arguments with his fellow officers in the 54th Regiment of Foot stationed in Portsmouth were not at all well received. A year later he fell in love again.

Lord Edward knocked on Tony's door in Portsmouth and rushed in. "Tony, I have two passions, really one—my passion for the army is waning. You know I'm enamored of Elizabeth. Met her before we left for Canada, but wasn't obsessed with her as I am now. I simply must be with her as often as I can. To hear her sing. To make love—don't look at me that way! She's in love with me, too."

"Elizabeth Linley Sheridan is a beautiful woman." Tony knew his response would mean little beyond that fact. "But, don't forget, she's also the wife of a powerful politician who's a friend of your cousin Charles Fox and a popular playwright, as well."

Rake and serial lover, Lord Edward waved both hands in the air. "In matters of the heart, Tony, she is none of them. She is moving to Southampton to be near Portsmouth, so I can be with her more often. And it may interest you to know that I am not playing the scoundrel. Her husband Richard plays that role, and she has given him up for it."

"'Scoundrel'? In South Carolina a man who steals a good friend's wife while he's out of town is found in a ditch with a bullet in his brain."

Events took a rapid turn. By the end of March 1792 their child Mary was born. By May, Elizabeth died. Lord Edward confided to Tony, "My beautiful songbird is gone ... dead from childbirth, our child." He slumped down in an easy chair, crying, his eyes open, looking straight at Tony as if he were praying. To see his friend in such pain, Tony wept also, but after a while went over to his desk to arrange the usual clutter in the usual way. A messy desk served nearly as well as a window as a place of emotional retreat when neither man could be outdoors. Lord Edward buried his face in his hands. Tony came over to him and put his hand on his shoulder but said nothing. Still with his head down, Lord Edward spoke in a muffled uneven voice.

"Before she died, she gave our little Mary to a woman in Bristol to rear legitimately with Richard. Tell me again, Tony, how you feel about not being able to see your child, the child Ruth told you about when you left Charleston. I like to think it was a girl, like my Mary. She would now be in her tenth year, a young girl full of fun and mischief like her mother and father."

"She may be Oscar's child, Lord Edward. It's not something I like to think about."

"That's the reason I want to know how you handle your own circumstances. I don't know what I'm going to do."

Lord Edward got up and went to his desk. He paused, looked at the same clutter of papers, then at other pieces of furniture scattered about as if he, too, wanted to spend time rearranging everything, to put everything in order to prompt an orderly mind. Tony waited quietly to hear if the brash young officer would again take unreasonable action and rush into a dangerous situation.

Lord Edward looked at his hands, those of a soldier who could handle both pistol and blade. "I will not interfere," he said quietly.

•••

Months later, in October 1792, Lord Edward and Tony returned to Paris as a guest of Thomas Paine who published *The Rights of Man* the previous year when they first visited him.

"Tony," Lord Edward confided as they walked in the rain down a busy street near the Tuileries Garden, "now that I have returned by expeditions in Canada and my Elizabeth is gone, my enthusiasm for the army fades more and more. My failure to rise to the rank of lieutenant colonel and commanding officer of the 54th Regiment is, I'm sure, partly responsible for my lack of enthusiasm. But even if promoted, I doubt if I could last much longer." He paused just long enough to reflect briefly on what he said and what more he wanted to say, then added, "I shall refuse any more military duties."

"I'm not very surprised," Tony said. As they continued to walk along, he thought his friend's mind would change when the rain stopped and the sun came back out. But with one look at Lord Edward's face, Tony could tell his decision was as firm as his rigid jaw and pressed lips. He had seen that look before.

"Be careful," Tony said. "They think you're going to take all that republican zeal back to Ireland with you and cause some real trouble some day. That's what they're worried about."

"Right. From radical to republican, Rousseau to Paine. You as well as I share an enthusiasm for the revolution that's going on in France. Can you image that our brothers among the Iroquois would ever think that a leveling doctrine is something to be feared?"

"Well, if they can't, John Rutledge sure can. You're in the same boat you were in South Carolina, except now you're rowing in the opposite direction. Both times up stream."

Lord Edward laughed as Tony turned around on the crowded sidewalk, bumping into passing strangers, to take long steady strokes with an imaginary oar. Tony then stopped and squatted down as if sitting in a boat—or on a commode, as one passing Frenchman muttered. "A Jacques," Tony replied.

A month later Lord Edward renounced his title at a dinner party and became an ordinary citizen, "le citoyen Edouard Fitzgerald." To the armies of France, he toasted, "May the example of its citizen soldiers be followed by all enslaved countries, till tyrants and tyrannies be extinct." And to, "The speedy abolition of all hereditary titles and feudal distinctions."

"The company you keep at the Jacobin Club," Tony told Lord Edward, "the likes of Lord Semphill, John and Henry Sheares, and Thomas Paine, all those kinds of people, do nothing to lessen your reputation as a republican. Your fellow officers think you're encouraging an invasion to bring a revolution to Ireland. I told you that before."

"Not to worry about my reputation on that score. The regiment court-martialed me last month and kicked me out of the army. I just didn't want to bother you with that bit of news, but everyone knows it. I'm glad it's done."

Three days later, the nephew of the Duke of Richmond and great-great-grandson of King Charles II met Pamela, the illegitimate daughter of Madame de Genlis and Louis Philippe Joseph d'Orléans, also known as Philippe Égalité. For his republican sympathies, Pamela's reputed father called himself "Citoyen Égalité." The following month, the quintessential romantic pair got married.

The Parisian sun shown bright on the morning four days before Christmas in December 1792. "Lord Edward, I've never been in the company of so many big shot French people as I am today. Don't tell me who's coming to the wedding. Tell me who's not—it'll be a shorter list. You're twenty-nine and she's just sixteen. And she's got no money, either, just like you. Will there be a royal baby sitter for her at the wedding?"

"Enough, Tony," Lord Edward replied as Tony continued to help him get dressed for the ceremony. "Suffice it to say that Louis-Phillippe d'Orléans, Pamela's half-brother, will be here with their father Philippe Égalité. Pamela's mother served as governess to him. But don't be obsequious—something you're incapable of, anyway. And clearly, you must not speak of or react to any reference to Philippe Égalité's vote for the execution of his cousin Louis XVI three months ago. We can only rejoice silently today that his death began the republic. And, no, there will be no royal baby sitter, only one black smart aleck guest."

Tony beamed and looked into the eyes of his friend as he straightened Lord Edward's white tie. "If Ruth could see me now," Tony replied. He turned to get himself dressed up for the occasion.

"You, my faithful friend, will be my essential guest, but if you're a star gazer, it might amuse you to know that Pamela is third in descent from Phillippe II, Duke of Orléans, the Regent—kind of like an acting king—of France for King XV when he was a little boy. That was a long time ago. Phillippe II was the son of Phillippe I, younger brother of Louis XIV, the Sun King who ruled from Versailles. Of course, that's by virtue of an illegitimate line through her father. Similar to my being fourth in decent from Charles II along an illegitimate line through my mother, as Lord Rawdon reminded me."

"Then I'd best not react to any reference to bastards," Tony said. "I might be the only one in the whole room who knows his momma and daddy."

"That's what I mean by an essential guest," Lord Edward replied and laughed. "Someone legitimate, even if a smart aleck."

Tony smiled at that comment throughout the wedding ceremony. He observed with pride the union of his best friend to the most beautiful woman in France, La Belle Pamela, in her glorious coiffeur topped by the Bonnet Rouge, symbol of the Revolution.

After the ceremony, when he had a minute alone with Lord Edward, Tony looked into the future of all three of them with a brief observation.

"Lord Edward, you have now on your right side, Pamela who represents a French revolution, and on your left, me, who represents an American revolution. People are bound to see that in the middle of us both, you yourself represent an Irish revolution. Let's *all* be careful."

Pamela and Tony formed a close friendship from the moment they met. The common bond of love for Lord Edward was strong enough to resist the passion of jealousy that would have divided people of lesser qualities. It did not take long for Pamela to share Tony's recognition of her husband's impulsive drive toward danger. Both were deeply concerned for Lord Edward's safety.

When Lord Edward, Pamela, and Tony returned to Ireland the following month, January 1793, they moved into Leinster House in Dublin, ancestral home of the Fitzgerald family. After ten years representing Athy in Parliament, Lord Edward's attention now turned to the United Irishmen, founded by Theobald Wolfe Tone in Belfast in October 1791 to resist British rule.

"I won't deny that my praise of republicanism in France creates suspicion among my colleagues in parliament," Lord Edward confessed to Pamela and Tony as they sat down after supper to discuss the events of the day, which included a controversial vote cast by Lord Edward. Although accommodations for the three in Leinster House were spacious, they sat close to each other by a fireplace, each participating in equal measure to the conversation, but with Tony careful not to talk too much. A recent product of her seemingly ceaseless occupation, Pamela's dress was modest, as always. Lord Edward's and Tony's were much improved from their buckskins in Canada, but they also were such that one could not discern Lord Edward's social station from his clothes, nor see from Tony's that he was a servant. Lord Edward's distain for grand houses and fancy dress was well known.

"I bet they didn't miss the irony of someone like you voting not to restrain a radical group like the Volunteers from assembling to discuss politics," Tony said. "Volunteers is a radical name. Tennessee volunteers were the Overmountain Men at King's Mountain who hammered a bunch of loyalists. Parliament looks to you here in Leinster House to maintain things the way they always have been—with the Brits on top and everybody else on the bottom."

"The Protestant Ascendancy on top, Irish Catholics on the bottom," Pamela added.

"Parliament can't look to me for that," Lord Edward replied. He shrugged his shoulders and turned toward a large open window. A short burst of sunlight hit at just that moment. "Look how beautiful the grounds are here. Come, both of you. Look here. What a privilege to be who and where we are. What glorious gardens—just look!" There was still enough light for a good view.

"And look at the gardener," Tony said.

"Yes," Lord Edward said, "look at the gardener, too."

"Well, he's not as well off as he should be, is he?" Pamela said and looked at Tony. "He works as hard or harder as any man around. Certainly, harder than most of your colleagues in the Irish Parliament."

"So you're both now in cahoots with each other, are you?" Lord Edward grabbed Pamela with a big hug and began kissing her. "Most of my friends in the United Irishmen were born in the 1760s and were teenagers, like me, during the American War of Independence," Lord Edward said in a muffled voice between kisses buried in Pamela's neck and hair. After releasing Pamela, giggling and squirming from his grip, he suddenly dove back into her hair, amid Pamela's higher squeals and his own words spoken in the same muffled voice as if to divulge secret information in code. "Wolfe Tone, Oliver Bond, the Sheares brothers, Archibald Hamilton Rowen, and, close to my heart, Arthur O'Connor. I'm the only war veteran among that lot." Lord Edward pulled back as if gasping for air.

In all this playfulness, so typical of Lord Edward, only Tony could turn the conversation to the heart of the matter. "They won't be much help in an armed rebellion, if that's what you're thinking of as the only thing that'll work to set up a republic here."

"I am," Lord Edward replied and released Pamela, still laughing. "Only armed revolt can lead to the creation of an Irish republic. That's what it took in America. That's the only language the British speak."

"Careful with that," Pamela advised. "The blade swings both ways. I know that as well as anyone. Matters can easily get out of hand among the rabble. And you must think of your family now." She paused. "Yet, I know your dear family includes all of Ireland. God, God, save us all."

••◦►§◄◦••

Eleven months later, Pamela's father Philippe Égalité was guillotined following Robespierre's *coup d'état* and Reign of Terror. Fear for her father came true. She became unusually distraught at hearing the news and wept openly.

"Come, let's go tend the garden at Frescati," Lord Edward said, trying to comfort her with a retreat to the family estate situated in the seaside villa of Blackrock, just outside Dublin, the place of his Rousseau-based education. "There we can try to put this terrible event behind us as we sort out our future. Pamela, you can rest there." He picked her up from a sofa and held her in his arms.

After their arrival by coach on the short trip to Frescati, Lord Edward said, "I'm afraid that working side by side with Tim the gardener bothers some of my colleagues in Parliament, but I can't wait to start getting dirty again. That's as far into the future as I want to go for now. A border of primroses, polyanthus, with hyacinths, jonquils, pinks, cloves, narcissuses, as merry a garden as Tony ever had at Eutaw Springs."

"When you work side by side with Tim, Protestant land owners see you as making a political statement of your leveling doctrine," Pamela said quietly. "I have lost a father. I don't want to lose a husband."

"Tim, Tony, and I will just put the seeds in the ground, water them, and watch them grow. That's hardly a political statement."

"It is, if you're not exploiting Roman Catholic cottiers at the same time," Tony added, "like lots of your colleagues in Parliament are doing. That's why you see all your flowers and plants ripped out of the ground. I know what that's like. Cuffy did it to my garden. He wanted to be level with the whites. Ripped up even Miss Maggie's garden—that is, before you and Major Majoribanks stomped it good and made a mess of it trying to put down a revolt."

Tony returned Lord Edward's steady look in response to his comment about Miss Maggie's garden. "Lord Edward, you're like Cuffy trying to scrape up muskets, rifles, and swords. You slink around like he did. The only difference is that you don't get run off when somebody sees what you're trying to do—not yet, that is."

Lord Edward smiled. "And I am particularly incensed that my social and political class objects to my entertaining 'ordinary folk,' as they call them."

"Your class simply thinks that you are doing more than dancing and drinking with ordinary folk," Pamela said. She laughed and did a pirouette, and Tony joined in to make it a little jig, circling around Lord Edward.

"They know you're charming—we all do—and they think you're raising support for a revolt," Pamela said, laughing as she and Tony continued to dance. "I can't wait till we move into our little house in Kildare, but Frescati is wonderful for a while."

"That'll do," Lord Edward said and laughed. "Enough! Both of you. That'll do for now." He seized upon the moment to grab Pamela and dive back into her neck and hair.

In 1794, about a month before Pamela was to have their first child, Lord Edward, Pamela, and Tony left Frescati on the coast and rented a pretty, quiet, and comfortable house in Kildare southwest of Dublin. Sophie, Pamela's new French maid, and a few other new servants came with them. Edward Fox Fitzgerald, little Eddy, was born in Kildare among the ordinary folk. "In her little American jacket," Pamela stayed busy after his birth planting sweet peas and mignonette. There, also, Lord Edward began to make practical applications of his revolutionary ideas as he continued to move back and forth among Frescati, Leinster House, and Kildare. Tony joined Lord Edward during times he went to Leinster House.

"You are, indeed, a charming man," Tony said in a light-hearted manner to Lord Edward who was about to leave Leinster House one bright morning shortly after joining the United Irishmen, which by now attracted more and more attention as a rebellious faction of nationalists and republicans. "But I have to tell you again and again that your charm will not win a rebellion if one ever comes.

"We've always agreed that it will take arms and good intelligence. We know that from the siege and assault of Star Fort at Ninety Six. And you were surprised by Light Horse Harry Lee while foraging in the potato patch right before Eutaw Springs. No good intelligence. I go on and on about America because I think you're forgetting the lessons learned there. All those regimental records of the 19th Foot lost at sea, you once told me, were useful because they contained important lessons on tactical and strategic experience. You may be forgetting details now even though you agree that only an armed revolt will free Ireland. Why won't you tell me what you're doing? You creep in and out of the house without a word. You're beginning to live a life apart from me. Don't you trust me with secrets? I can help if you let me."

Lord Edward looked at his faithful friend. He turned as he left the house after hearing Tony's last few words. Tony stood at the door, a few feet higher from the stone pavement leading away from the house. Lord Edward looked up, raising his eyebrows in a concerned expression becoming more and more common. His somewhat rumpled jacket, not properly adjusted to his shoulders, showed the haste with which he was leaving.

"Tony, for the present time, I am doing what I do for your own protection and for Pamela's. I know if I tell either one of you anything, I am telling both of you. If ever you—and she—are asked any questions about me, you both can honestly say that you do not know anything. There may be secret handshakes and code words that attract your curiosity as you watch visitors come and go, but Arthur O'Connor and I wish to conduct business within the narrowest circle possible. It's not a question of trusting you and Pamela with secrets. But if you must have a role, I beg you to look out for Pamela and little Eddy—and alert me of any Castle government spies you feel have infiltrated this house."

Tony made his usual short clicking noise with his teeth. He shook his head, unsatisfied with his friend's response, but he agreed to let it go at that. He did not query Pamela about what her husband may have told her but presumed that she also remained in the dark.

Nonetheless, Tony and Pamela accompanied Lord Edward when Lord Edward and Arthur O'Connor went to Hamburg two years later in May 1796. The two revolutionaries were in Hamburg on a secret mission to solicit the French Directory to invade Ireland in support of the United Irishmen's revolt against the British controlled Castle government in Dublin. During all this intrigue, Lord Edward and Pamela left Little Eddy in London with his grandmother Lady Emily—a woman familiar enough with children after her own two dozen pregnancies and nineteen births. In Hamburg, Lord Edward left Tony to watch over Pamela and her new baby, their second child, little Pam.

Lord Edward also went with O'Connor to Basle, Switzerland, for meetings with the French. Primarily, Lord Edward met with Charles Reinhard, the French minister in Hamburg, while O'Connor negotiated with General Hoche, the proposed leader of no less than a planned French invasion of Ireland to aid Irishmen in their rebellion against British rule. Hoche wanted to get even for Pitt's three previous expeditions against France. Watching such a life of intrigue unfold, even at a distance and even with much left unspoken, was as exhilarating for Tony as it was for Pamela. Yet, both fully realized the risks of so monumental an undertaking.

"I may not know what exactly you are doing all the time, but I am little more than a serious liability to you, Lord Edward," Tony told him in Hamburg. "Showing my black face is like waving a red flag. I know I'm the one who all the British spies in Paris will see first if I ever go to France with you—no cover of darkness like I had with Pompey Grant, Ned Zanger, and Lazarus Jones when we naked blacks slipped out of Star Fort to get water at Ninety Six—and they'll look for you and suspect that you're up to something secretive with French agents. They might even think I know something. I can't even leave Kildare with you."

"True enough," Lord Edward said, amused at Tony's comparison of his experience at Ninety Six with a visit to Paris. "I would rather stay out of Paris to sort out details of the invasion."

"You're always wearing a green or red cravat—the one for Irish liberty and the other for bloodshed in France. That's saying, 'Look at me, look at me. I'm a trouble-maker.' You should wear a neutral white cravat. You might as well wear a red coat with a cross-barred white 'X' on it."

As they prepared to return to Kildare in September 1796, and it was clear that Eddy would be separated from his mother and father, Tony quietly took little Pam's new nursemaid aside. Julie, a bright young woman with beautiful Irish green eyes, good sense and charm, recently joined the family servants.

"Julie," Tony said in a tone of voice as if to make the conversation strictly business, "we all know that little Eddy is a delight. I used to take him to Mrs. Fisher's garden in London to see all the flowers. He loves that garden, but he loves his father's garden even more. He's as much a gardener as his father, really. Little Eddy always loves to hear from me about the flowers in his father's garden that other people call weeds, and even Lord Edward sometimes wonders just how those kinds of flowers get into his garden."

At that Tony laughed softly. Julie saw that it was nervous laughter. What was he nervous about? Did he pull her aside to talk about weeds? And why so business-like?

"I told Lord Edward just the other day that all those ordinary folks he mixes with are what some upper class people think of as weeds in a garden, but I told him they're really not weeds at all, no more than Sayey, an enslaved friend in Carolina, is a weed. You don't know Sayey, but she was lots of fun to tease. Like his father, little Eddy loves all kinds of flowers.

"And his mother and father love him dearly. They taught him how to love. That's what most folks don't ever learn. So please don't think of Lord Edward too harshly or judge him too unsympathetically. Everything going on is extremely painful for him, as it especially is for Lady Pamela. We're facing terrible times. I know you'll come to love the family as much as I do."

Julie remained quiet during all of Tony's long explanation of what was going on in the family. She sensed that his nervousness arose not from talk about flowers and weeds but from simply being near her. She looked at Tony with complete awareness of the circumstances, and he knew immediately that she had flushed out his true intentions with ancient feminine art. He had previously done his best not to pay much attention to her, although they both were aware of occasional moments when she glanced at him only to catch him looking at her. Now he knew that he was not talking merely to a nursemaid, but rather to a kindred spirit of his own station, of any station.

Tony put aside further discussion of the relation each had with the Fitzgeralds. He immediately responded to what he clearly felt in his heart from that moment on. He began to speak more slowly.

"I see a kindness about you, Julie." Then in a very tender way as if to mock the business tone he began with, said, "That makes me think that you and I will be much more than just friends in the future." Everything suddenly changed for both of them.

In the following months, Tony's memory of Ruth began slowly to give way to the kindness in Julie's eyes. At Kildare, he and Julie began a serious romance. Family life at Kildare, which was created by Lord Edward to present an air of indifference to politics and thus to disguise his revolutionary plans, created the perfect setting for Tony and Julie to fall in love. Lord Edward's convivial parties set the stage with dances, dinners, drinks, and fires. Great fires in the hearth and heart. Tony learned Irish jigs and songs and joined in the fun with Julie.

Visits by Arthur O'Connor also continued to stir the passions of Lady Lucy, Lord Edward's youngest sister, by now a solid republican like her brother. Love, the ultimate revolution, was in the air.

At one point in all the excitement, Julie cautiously approached her mistress. "Lady Pamela, do you know Lord Edward's man Tony very well?" She paused. "Is he a good man?"

Pamela, who was busy arranging a dress she hoped to wear later that evening, put it down and looked sweetly at her young child's maid. She moved a sewing kit from a nearby chair and patted the seat gently to invite Julie to sit down.

"Ah, Julie, I have noticed an exchange of glances between you and Tony. So has Lady Lucy. Rest assured. He is a good man. All of us know that he is as kind and caring as anyone alive. I permit Tony to call me by my first name, not as Lady Fitzgerald. Lord Edward permits the same, but Tony never calls my Edward by just his first name.

"The likes of my Edward would not have kept him around for all these years if Tony were not the best man he knew. And Tony would have left my husband's service long ago if he had not seen the best qualities of a man in Edward."

She looked at Julie and smiled. "But be on your guard, Julie, Tony's playful around those he likes best—just like my Edward."

Julie nodded at what she already knew, and both women left their brief exchange, sharing the same confident smile of being able so succinctly and in such short order to sew up and capture a man to the very quick of his being.

That evening Tony saw Julie standing alone outside little Pam's nursery. Unmindful of anyone who might happen to pass by, he boasted, "Julie, I'm very happy now. I'm happiest when I'm with you."

Caught off guard with such a sudden bold and direct declaration, Julie replied, "You are like no one I have ever met, Tony Small. You're usually so indirect, so oblique in the way you show a fondness. I know you do because I've caught you staring at me. But you seldom say anything directly about your feelings. You're like so many men in England and Wales and Scotland and Ireland. You show your feelings only indirectly, and seldom say them out loud. I like that. That's the way we both are. But now you're very bold. I never even met an American before I met you."

"And never heard such a strange accent, either," Tony said and smiled. He handed her a small little rosebud.

"Thank you, Tony Small, thank you very much. I guess it goes without saying that this rose is meant for me? Or is it a weed?"

"That is a direct rose bud."

"Sometimes I simply can't understand what you are saying. You say so many words that I don't understand. All Americans—it's hard to understand all Americans, but you're the most difficult."

"It's called 'Gullah-Geechee.' I sometimes speak 'Gullah-Geechee. It's the dialect we Lowcountry blacks speak. It's a mixture of English and African dialects. But that's only with you. With Lord Edward and Pamela and everyone else, I try to speak only in the clearest best Lowcountry southern accent I can muster. I still make mistakes, but not always." Tony was laughing as he spoke, purposefully making it even harder for Julie to understand him.

"Lowcountry southern? Not Irish southern or English southern? I just can't understand what you say half the time. And I never saw a black man until I saw you. Are all black men as handsome as you?" she asked in a teasing way.

Seeing that Tony was thinking about what to say, she smiled and continued. "If the British had won the war, they would have made you Americans learn to speak English. Maybe English like Lord Edward speaks it. Or Pamela, with a French accent. Or me with an Irish accent."

After a long pause, Tony looked at her and said, "Gal, you sho' nuff got muh eye tie up."

"What?"

"Do you understand?" Tony was still smiling broadly and suppressing a warm laugh at the same time.

"What did you say?"

"You hab muh eye tie up!"

"Well, if you don't want to talk plain English, then I guess I'll have to get back to the nursery to see if little Pam is still asleep." Julie stuck out her tongue to make a funny face at Tony and turned to walk away.

"I love you, Julie," Tony said, dropping his Gullah accent and taking her gently by the arm. He tenderly turned her around to face him directly as he spoke softly. "It means 'I love you' in Gullah .... Will you marry me?"

Julie took a short audible breath, and her beautiful green eyes again widened in a way that gave her good heart away. She smiled. "Yes, I will, Tony Small. Yes, I will."

Within a year, a lovely daughter was born whom they named Moirico, and the center of Tony Small's life shifted to the well being of his own family.

Christmas Day 1796 celebrations at Leinster House gave way to a loud cry from Lord Edward's study. Tony rushed to find out what was happening. He noticed through a cloudy sunless day the departure of a stranger who had been visiting with Lord Edward.

"I did not know about any of these plans of Hoche's—none at all! The fools!" Lord Edward yelled moments after receiving bad news of an aborted French invasion.

"I was told they would be here in the spring of '97—in the spring!—with eighty thousand muskets and fifteen thousand men. Damnation! And they were supposed to land at Galway Bay, not Bantry Bay. Of course, we weren't there to meet them. What a waste! How greatly disappointing—utterly disappointing! Disastrous!

"Tony, this is what happens when a commanding officer—Hoche—keeps his cards too close to his chest."

"This mess wouldn't have happened under Lord Rawdon, or Lieutenant Colonel Coates, or Major Majoribanks, or Lieutenant Colonel Stewart," Tony replied.

Lord Edward, knowing something about a fair fight, and a lot about the vicissitudes of fortune, let out a long sigh, looked at his faithful friend from Eutaw Springs and replied, "Yes, of course not. You're right. But I regret that all of the commanders you mention are, or were, in the same army we now are fighting, or trying to fight."

The two men stood silently for a long time. Each knew as well as the other what the lack of French support meant to the success of an Irish uprising. After a while, Lord Edward looked a short distance away at his sword, the one replaced by the 19th Regiment of Foot after he broke his sword on the back of an American patriot at Orangeburg. He walked across the room, picked it up without drawing it from its sheath, and replaced scabbard and blade on the back of a chair. He picked up his side arm lying in the same chair, looked at it for a long time and calmly put it down. Then as if he were talking to no one, observed, "I hope this is not our Yorktown. Theirs must come again."

•••◦❖◦••

By the beginning of 1797, Lord Edward was being watched day and night by the Castle government in Dublin.

"They are everywhere, wherever we go," Tony complained to Lord Edward as they walked down Grafton Street. Tony was trying to keep up with the rapid pace his friend was setting. People on the street recognized them both and gave way as they approached. "Spies from the Castle government," Tony muttered, trying to catch his breath.

"If my short republican hair cut and my blood red cravat don't get their attention, perhaps it's you they spot before they recognize me," Lord Edward replied. "Your black face sticks out here as much as it would in Paris. Didn't we talk about painting yourself green?"

"This ain't a joking matter, Lord Edward. You have to drop your good nature and begin to think like you did at Quinby Bridge and Eutaw Springs," Tony said. "They're at war even if you ain't."

"You know, Tony," Lord Edward observed, "we tried to buy George Washington in 1780, before I arrived in America. "'Washington is certainly to be bought—honors will do it.' That's what an Englishman said before we came to realize that your man deals in different currency. I just don't see myself as a field commander like Washington leading an entire insurrection. I must make it clear that a Frenchman must serve in that capacity."

"But you have so many military skills. What you learned about war from the Americans in the Lowcountry is now the kind of warfare you can conduct against the Redcoats. And you do have lots of qualities of Washington himself."

"I learned how to fight a battle, but only from a battalion level. And for goodness sakes, don't compare me with George Washington."

"Then you're like the next greatest general in the American war, the Swamp Fox himself. You can harass the British from the rear and surprise detachments with superior numbers, just like Francis Marion did to Coates when the 19th Foot high-tailed it from Biggin Bridge to Charleston."

"You're making more of it than it was."

"No, I'm not. Lots of us black folks saw what you did to the rebel's rear guard when you came flying back to fight off Lee at Huger's Bridge and help Colin Campbell and Bell at the rear of the baggage train when the rebs were pillaging the regimental silver. I know Campbell was captured, but Lieutenant Bell told everybody of your exploits. You're probably the reason Sumter gave Bell's books back to him after he took them with the silver and all those guineas in the regimental paymaster's box. Sumter was afraid you'd come to get 'em."

Lord Edward joined Tony in a good laugh at the absurdity of that thought. Between the two men, after all, there was nothing that was not a laughing matter, if only for a short time. Both good-hearted men enjoyed a world of laughter from their infancy, and that, together with sharing tough times together and having an innate sense of compassion, born of their mothers' love, was the binding force for the love and affection they had for each other. But now Tony continued in a stone-cold voice.

"And if your new friend Thomas Reynolds—I don't trust that man—if he doesn't believe it, you can go back to Carolina and ask Agner Croy, Robert Stedwell, Will Waring, and lots of other black folks who saw you—Nancy and Frank Peters, my friend Jack, and Ballifo. That's the truth. Me, too, even if I didn't know exactly who you were then."

"This is different, much different. You're trying to outhunt the dog, Tony, as our friend William Washington would put it."

"No, it's the same kind of warfare," Tony insisted before Lord Edward could say more, "except here and now you're going to be acting like the rebels did against you when you were fighting with the British against them.

"Quinby Bridge, too. I talked to a lot of other black folks who saw how brave you were at Quinby. You can't deny that, can you? You held your own against what Aaron Spelman, Jim Capers, and Old Sandy said was the most outrageous act of courage they ever saw—me, too—when rebel cavalrymen Armstrong and Carrington and Macaulay jumped the bridge to get at you and Colonel Coates. I was on the other side with the rebels. You and the

19th held the bridge. I sang a little song about that. We all saw it with our own eyes. It's legendary—heroes on both sides. You fought hand-to-hand against men under some of the greatest officers America ever had.

"You held your own at Shubrick's Plantation, too. Marion, Lee, and Sumter themselves, all great commanders, were just on the other side of the Creek. Y'all looking straight at one another, spitting distance. Probably did spit. And if you've forgotten that, then you're the only one on both sides of the ocean who has."

Lord Edward's efforts in the summer of 1797 to convince the French to make a second invasion matured into only a distant prospect and eventually withered away. General Hoche was dying of consumption, and the French were beginning to see Ireland not so much as a staging ground for harassment of London than as an insignificant land to the west. Bonaparte did not have the enthusiasm of Hoche toward Ireland. Ireland was no longer on the French map, but Lord Edward was slow to fully grasp the reality of the situation.

"We've got to continue to hope that France will help us with another effort to invade," he confided one morning with Tony without initially disclosing the particulars which he and the United Irishmen devised. "But if we must, with or without them, we have to press on."

"Your own family, other than your sister Lady Lucy, won't help the cause, anymore than the other elite Irish families will, right? I mean they're just not going to stick their necks out like you're doing. Church of Ireland or Church of England necks, either one."

"Yes, you're probably right about that, too."

With his hands flat on the top of the desk, Lord Edward continued slowly to look at open documents on his desk, those he instructed Tony not ever to try to read. He straightened himself from a momentary slump, pushed his shoulders back, and without looking up said, "I'm secretly training soldiers who are ordinary Irishmen, mostly Roman Catholics, some Presbyterians, dissenters. Most of them are as inexperienced as the American rebels von Steuben trained at Valley Forge, and very few are as experienced as the black troops we faced at Eutaw Springs. I've done my best to teach them coordination between hand and eye initially by simply throwing a stone at a tree, the way the Indians in Canada learned coordination with a bow and arrow. They all look to me as an example of Irish nobility, albeit Anglican, on their side."

Lord Edward continued to share strategic and tactical information with Tony. This brought Tony fully into the conspiracy to overthrow the Castle government.

"With your own eyes," Lord Edward said, "you see how remarkable this alliance is, one made of Roman Catholics, outcasts of the State, and dissenters, Presbyterians in the north, all victims of the Castle establishment, all sharing a love of Irish freedom. Indeed, most of the leading people in the conspiracy are Protestants. But the fact is, revolutionary fervor is abated in Belfast and the north. After martial law was declared, we no longer have the armed men we once had. Apart from pikes, we have about six thousand muskets and the guns and muskets the French may bring us, these five years after they declared war on England. We're all very insistent about what role France will play if they do come to help us—they will consent to act under the direction of our new republic, as Rochambeau did in America."

Tony began to take in the full measure of United Irishmen's strategy for the uprising. He was getting an insight far greater than that which Lord Edward gave him about Charleston sixteen years ago. He quietly waited to see if Lord Edward was going to continue. He didn't budge, despite his discomfort, and looked hard at his friend and master as Irish history unfolded.

"But now, alas, after seizure of our weapons in the north under General Lake's Proclamation and a full year after Hoche's disastrous mess of trying to make an invasion, my dear friend Arthur O'Connor has left for France, disgusted with our lack of militancy. I must hold onto a very thin possibility that the French will try again to help us, or we must lead with what little we alone have. I fear in a very short time, it must be the latter."

••◦►✤◄◦••

At the beginning of 1798 only Pamela and Tony knew where Lord Edward was, and even they did not know all the time. On one of his short excursions from Dublin to Kildare, Lord Edward and Tony met in the parlor to discuss when to start the revolution. Tony and Pamela were more and more beginning to be brought into Lord Edward's secret concerns. The weather was lovely on a day in which reason might have its best shot at success. Pamela and Tony were dressed in their finest country garb, as if ready to celebrate reason itself.

"I know the French have told you that *maybe* they will be here in April, but you should wait until you have greater assurances, even if it's not until August," Tony said. "Start the Rising then. Wait till you have support that's real." Pamela nodded her agreement.

"We may have to go it alone this time," Lord Edward replied without looking at either one. "The committee has talked it over. The people are restless. I can't hold them back. Our minds are set on a May Rising. MacNeven's United men and men from Wicklow and Kildare will hold Dublin—the Castle itself, Trinity College, the banks, and the Customs House—till our advancing armies from the coast can get here." His voice conveyed a determined point of view as if he were speaking to a large group of men.

"The French failed us before when they did not disclose their advanced schedule. The Americans were simply lucky that Count de Grasse showed up at Yorktown at the right time, as if the French were just dropping by to save a republic. I love the French, of course, but they can't be counted on in this case. They're not going to drop by to save us. This is now Ireland's own fight for freedom and Ireland's alone."

"That's foolhardy, Lord Edward. You're acting the same way you acted at Ninety Six, and when you got wounded at Eutaw, too. You rushed into rebel pickets without support approaching Ninety Six and even broke your sword on a rebel's back—there and at Orangeburg, too. You were lucky to have Welbore Ellis Doyle appear on the scene to save you. The only time you were smart was when you skedaddled when you came across Greene's whole army, the time you were guarding the sweet potato foragers near the springs. Use your experience, for God's sake.

"You're way ahead of yourself now, too. It's different if you're fighting the kind of battle you fought at Quinby. There you had to take a stand. Fought it out hand-to-hand. You had no choice when you had no support. Same as in the thicket at Eutaw Springs, for a while at least, before you and the major pulled back to save the day. And even that was planned." Almost exhausted from his frustration, Tony paused to watch Lord Edward's reaction. "I keep telling you this, time and time again. I keep telling you that you have gifts of a great commander, but a great commander knows when to fight, like Greene and Marion."

Is he even listening? Thank God for windows. Better than mirrors. You can see yourself better through a window than in a mirror. We both long for the present to be over and the future to start. To be somewhere something other than just the weather happens. To have something to do, other than to wait for yesterday. Somewhere outside the room we're in. Big windows or little ones, big rooms or little rooms, all the same, because it's what's outside that's always bigger. Can't trust a man who doesn't look out of windows.

Tony continued in a reasonable tone of voice. "Here, in this situation with no weapons to speak of, you've got French support coming in August. They're not going to make the same stupid mistake twice. You shouldn't either. Don't be like William Washington and rush into the thicket without waiting for Hampton and Kirkwood—or like Sumter at Shubrick's without waiting for Singleton's artillery. That's foolish. Wait till you hear a certain date from the Directory. Think like the Swamp Fox. Like Greene."

Lord Edward sat down and motioned for Tony to do the same. Pamela continued to sit quietly. He was tired of Tony's preaching about his version of American engagements. He now would give his own. He knew the French were not coming in time to seize the moment, if they came at all. He calmly looked at the few fixtures in the room, paintings on the wall, furniture, the fireplace, and again out the window as if once again he were gathering artifacts as facts to arrange in order to create in his own mind an impression of considering all possibilities.

He took a deep breath. "No. We've got to act this spring. This is what I learned in America. I'm taking pages out of Francis Marion's and Nathanael Greene's play books and using them to our advantage. We'll harass escorts of ammunition, cut off detachments of foraging parties and make the king's men know they're in a foreign country. I've told MacNeven and his United men that it takes patience to conduct guerilla warfare.

"At Eutaw Springs, Greene put the South Carolina militia and state troops on the front line, and the North Carolina, Virginia, and Maryland Continentals on the second line. They had to rush forward when the first line collapsed. We also will keep our best men in reserve on the second line. On the streets in Dublin, as few as three, and no more than sixty, British troops will make up their front line on some very narrow streets. Streets like Aungier, Camden, and Wexford. Digges, Bishop's, and Peter's Row, too, all at the bottle neck of Redmond's Hill. They'll fire their muskets and withdraw, we hope without hitting too many of us. Before the second British row can take their place and move up on the front line, the first line of United men will rush the British with ten-foot pikes and create havoc. That's more or less how Cruger and Sheridan punched a hole in Malmedy's front line at Eutaw Springs, with their bayonets—so we're taking lessons from the British as well—but we're going to do it with speed, not raw fire power or bayonets, but with pikes. British bayonets can't match our ten-foot pikes. British troops will be too crowded in the narrow streets of Dublin to fight against them.

"Puts them in the same tight fix we heard about when the Black Dragoons were in the skirmish near Fort Dorchester and the Quarter House between loyalists and Lee's Legion. Same as when Marion got the Black Dragoons in a squeeze at Fair Lawn Plantation on the Wadboo River near Moncks Corner after we left Carolina. Same kind of pincer squeeze Majoribanks and I set up at the thicket, although that was at an angle. A large British regiment can't maneuver in tight spots. This is street fighting. The British soldiers will be dreadfully galled from the housetops by a shower of bricks. Tony, I'm not like John Laurens at Tar Bluff. I won't put men in an impossible situation.

"And British soldiers will not be able to hear their officers' orders amidst all the noise and clamor of a popular tumult. I barely heard Majoribanks pulling back from the thicket. And as at the bridge at Quinby Creek and Stewart's retreat from Eutaw Springs, people will tear up the roads and barricade them with implements of husbandry. Pikes give us the advantage."

"You're gonna lose," Tony said.

Tony returned with Pamela and the family to Dublin from Kildare. The pace of life grew rapidly. Fear for Lord Edward's safety intensified. Tony's sense of impending danger was honed from observing the shifting troops at Eutaw Springs, and even before, from watching Armstrong's and Blount's Regiments in Greene's army organize themselves at Mt. Tacitus. In the Canadian wilderness he was careful when he saw moose, wolves, and bears. Whenever he walked the streets of Charleston and St. Lucia, he was on the look-out for someone who might steal him to sell. He could see danger coming around the corner, so when he heard a servant open the front door to Leinster House late one afternoon to admit the sheriff, Tony rushed to Lord Edward in his study.

"Sheriff Oliver Carleton from the Castle is in the house looking for you. Somebody—the butler—must have let him in not knowing what he's after. But he's looking for you."

"What?"

"Hush. Not so loud. Keep quiet. You've got to get out of here now. Now!"

"I have to leave you here with Pamela. You're a magnet, you know."

"Go to Merrion Street, into the dark. Now go! I'll hold back the sheriff as long as I can."

Sheriff Carleton rushed into the hall to find Tony standing near the door as it shut behind Lord Edward. The sound of an empty bucket rattled at the foot of the steps. Fortunately, under the circumstances, all the water which Tony precariously placed in a bucket perched at the top of the door, slightly ajar, had dripped out of a hole in the bucket. Lord Edward was able to escape Tony's favorite trick as well as the sheriff.

"Where's your master, Small. I know you're hiding him. Get out of my way."

"He's not here. That was a servant who just left. You can search every room if you wish."

The sheriff pushed Tony aside and, seeing only a dim light attached to the back of Leinster House, turned back and tried to fling open the door of the nearest room. To his surprise Tony stood in his way. "He's not in this room—believe me!"

Sheriff Carleton looked firmly at Tony. "I know you're his man, Small, and I know you are well aware where I can find him. I'm threatening you with arrest for obstructing justice if you don't tell me right now where he is." He spat on the floor.

Tony just looked at him without a word.

"You'll die in gaol as a traitor. Or hang," the sheriff screamed as he knocked Tony to the floor. Shoving Tony farther aside with his foot, Carleton rushed upstairs to search more of the premises. He ignored Pamela's screams as he barged into her bedroom and began pulling out draws and overturning furniture. Carleton quickly found enough incriminating evidence of insurrection to convict Lord Edward of treason.

He then turned on Pamela herself. "Where's your rebel husband, a malicious traitor to his country? Tell me now, or else!" Little Pam began to cry. Pamela picked her up without saying a word. Julie and Sophie stood trembling and wondering if they would be thrown into prison for treason.

"Sheriff, I must insist that you cause Lady Fitzgerald no unnecessary distress," Tony warned Carleton as he caught up with the sheriff in Pamela's room. Blood dripped from a cut on his mouth. "As you see, she's pregnant."

The sheriff shrugged his shoulders. "Another little revolutionary bastard." He left the room with an armful of documents. The house shook with an awful racket as he went clamoring down the main steps of the house and out one of the side doors, cursing as a bucket of water fell on his head.

Tony and Pamela thought that Lord Edward fled to France. Instead, aided by his friend Mr. Lawless, he fled to Mr. Kennedy's house on Aungier

Street, then to the house of another friend, Mrs. Dillon, at Portobello by the Grand Canal on the outskirts of Dublin. There he stayed for nearly a month, seemingly oblivious to the danger. A dangerous game of hide and seek in houses began that included Mr. Gannon's at 22 Cornmarket, up and down Thomas Street to Mr. McCormick's at number 22, Mr. Moore's at number 119, and finally to Mr. Murphy's at 153 Thomas Street.

"You really must not go out for strolls along the canal, Lord Edward," a worried Mrs. Dillon said. "Such anxiety and suspense! I know how much delight you take in my flowers. You should be content to cultivate my garden without going outside. Stay here within its walls. And you're much too loud. It's as if you want to be captured. Everyone can hear you laughing and playing with the children in the neighborhood when you go out."

Shortly thereafter, Lord Edward in disguise made his first secret visit to see Pamela who moved with Pam from Leinster House to a house on Denzille Street. Tony, Julie, and Sophie went with her. For the government, Lord Edward's ghost was everywhere, and nowhere to be found.

The British were ruthless in their efforts to defeat the United Irishmen. "I can't help but compare what the British are doing to Irishmen to what they did to patriots in the Lowcountry," Tony said. "And what American Whigs did to Tories and Tories to Whigs was as bad. General Lake's taken a page from the torture book of Tarleton and Bloody Bill Cunningham."

Pamela did not want to hear anything further, but Tony carried on with what amounted to a rant.

"I can only hope Lord Edward isn't tempted to come out of hiding and act in a crazy way to stop the picketing and pitch-capping of croppies. They're two kinds of tortures that Lake's inflicting on anybody who opposes him. Lord Edward has got to have patience to stop all that—strapping men to a tripod and whipping 'em, sticking a cap of burning tar on their heads, slicing off ears, raping women, burning homes, taking cattle and poultry, and splitting up families."

"Oh, Tony, please stop."

"I'm sorry, Pamela, but there's a big difference. There weren't as many patriots in America who suffered as bad as these nationalists here."

Pamela looked up from her seat on the sofa. The beautiful young woman spoke as if she were standing before hundreds of revolutionaries. Her voice grew stronger. "And in America cruelty by an oppressive government didn't work, did it? The patriots there had guns to stop it, not just pikes. That's the heart of it all, isn't it, Tony? Guns?"

⚬⚬⊰❈⊱⚬⚬

"Lord Edward!" Tony said a short time later as he opened the door where Pamela was staying on Denzille Street. "Is it safe for you to be here? And look at you, disguised as a woman again. Are you a revolutionary because you like to dress up as a woman?"

Lord Edward smiled at his good friend's effort to lessen the anxiety. "Not to worry, Tony. I have but a while to see Pamela. I'll go straight to her rooms."

"She'll be as happy as she'll be surprised, but be careful. I bet you're going to remind her you're not a woman. I'll watch the door."

After Lord Edward left a few hours later, Tony saw Sophie and Julie hurrying about the house in an excited manner.

"Are you running around because you think government officials arrived?"

"Not that," Julie yelled over her shoulder as she ran toward the butler's pantry. "Lady Pamela is having a baby—much too early, and all over the excitement from Lord Edward's visit."

"They must have discussed giving the baby a name," Tony shouted as Julie continued to run down the hall.

"Lucy."

"He'll never see her," Tony muttered sadly. "Or hold Pamela, little Eddy, and Pam in his arms again."

⚬⚬⊰❈⊱⚬⚬

Lord Edward's luck finally ran out. He was captured shortly thereafter, on 19 May 1798, four days before the Uprising was set to begin. What Pamela and Tony feared most had come to pass.

"Pamela," Tony said as the two of them sat awkwardly in straight back chairs on Denzille Street, "I know enough now, after the treachery took place, to tell you what I heard about the capture of Lord Edward. Do you want me to tell you?"

"No," Pamela replied. "No, I don't. In my mind he's always free."

"Mine, too," Tony said, "but in his own mind he knows he is not."

After a while, she quietly said, "Tell me." She looked out the window as often as Tony and Lord Edward, this time in a daze.

"On May nineteenth, the day after Lord Edward avoided capture, the rat Magan dropped by to see Miss Moore, hoping to pick up any scent or see tracks of his prey. Poor Miss Moore didn't know Magan was being paid by the government to catch Lord Edward, so she blurted out that Lord Edward was at Murphy's house. Major Swan and Captain Ryan—both pure scum—went with a bunch of soldiers straight to Murphy's."

"Make this quick, please, Tony, and stick to the story and spare me the horrible truths of bloodshed."

"Very well, but you should know of Lord Edward's valor which he's always had in times of crisis and effusion of blood.

"He was upstairs calmly reading a book, *Gil Blas,* even though he heard troops outside his window. He's always calm in times of danger. The greater the danger, the calmer he is. I saw him fighting rebels at Quinby Bridge, slashing his sword back and forth as if he was just exercising.

"Then they tell me he joined his friend Neilson and his host Murphy for dinner in a back drawing room. For some reason, Neilson left the room. Major Swan then stormed in. Lord Edward jumped up like a tiger."

Pamela turned her gaze from the window and looked at the floor, then Tony, then the floor again, as if her Edward were lying there.

"I have to go on, Pamela, because you need to tell Eddy, little Pam, and Lucy someday how brave their father was. Ireland is England's Negro. Everybody knows Pitt just nursed this whole Uprising along so he could stomp the Irish. Wasn't ever going to be a Reform. Anyway, Swan fired a small caliber pocket-pistol at him but missed. Lord Edward slashed him across the hand with a dagger. Another bucket of scum named Ryan came in and stabbed his sword cane into Lord Edward, and Lord Edward fell back onto his bed. Ryan grabbed him around the waist to stop him from getting up and escaping. Lord Edward turned his own dagger on Ryan, and Swan rushed to help Ryan. The three men wrestled on the floor in puddles of blood almost as deep as they were at Eutaw Springs.

"Then in comes Major Sirr. I never liked him when I saw him at Gibraltar. Neither did Lord Edward. You can tell a lot about a man just by the way he laughs and sneezes. That cowardly rascal fired two shots point blank at Lord Edward and got him in the right arm near the shoulder. Lord Edward didn't even have a gun. And worst of all, even though they all knew Lord Edward was too seriously wounded to go anywhere, two soldiers came into the room and battered him down to the floor with their muskets. A cowardly drummer took advantage of the moment and wounded him on the back of the neck as soldiers held him down. That's six men it took to capture him."

Tony stopped and waited for Pamela to raise her eyes from the floor to give some indication to continue. Pamela wept silently and looked up. She raised her handkerchief to her eyes in an absent-minded gesture.

"The first doctor to see Lord Edward in custody, Dr. Adreen, told him that his wounds weren't serious. They tell me that Lord Edward said,

'I'm sorry for it.'

"That's so pitiful to hear, isn't it, Pamela? Pamela, are you all right? I can stop now. He's at Newgate Prison. We'll go see him."

Without ever being allowed to see her husband, Pamela left Dublin on 25 May 1798 and went to London with little Pam and infant Lucy, Sophie, and Tony with Julie and their daughter Moirico. Only twenty-two years old, Pamela arrived disheveled and miserable from not being allowed to stay in Ireland where she could maintain at least the hope of being by the side of her wounded husband in gaol.

Tony came to her room, knocked and entered. The London house was far removed from comfortable lodgings they enjoyed in Ireland. A bed, two chairs, desk, armoire, and wash basin and stand took up most of the room. A suitcase, as if ready for immediate use, lay open in the corner.

"You have done all you can, Pamela. You would have been arrested as a spy if you stayed a minute longer in Ireland, and they would only put you back on the boat if you tried to return. It's terrible back in Ireland. From what I hear, thousands of United Irishmen were killed by the British after the May Rising failed."

Tears streaked Pamela's cheeks for so long that she no longer bothered to catch every drop with her handkerchief. The white collar of her dress was wet with tears. Tony saw his remarks caused Pamela further distress, and he quietly left the room.

"Lord Edward," young doctor Armstrong Garnett said as he entered the prison cell, "I am asked by Dr. Lindsay to be by your side during your final hours." Taking out his diary, and thinking little of how callous his remark and manner were, Garnett began to record Lord Edward's moods as they swung back and forth between being violent to peaceful. Lord Edward lay on a hard bed, his wounds untreated.

"I am writing down your every word for posterity, Lord Edward. I cannot hear all of your statements—your voice is weak—but so far I have written that you are happy in the persuasion that you are dying for your country, and that you feel that God will receive you for having contributed to the freedom of your country. Is that right?

"But what should I write regarding your military service in America? Do you want me to record anything about your wartime experiences there? The British high command is well aware of your record in America."

Lord Edward turned to look at the man sitting by him with his diary and pen in hand. He then looked toward the wall by his bed. Names and dates were scratched into the stone. There was no low window in his cell, only one high up with bars.

He paused and calmly uttered, still facing the wall, "You may say what you wish, but for me I hope God will forgive me."

Expecting more, Garnett quickly jotted down what he heard and waited for further comments on the battles and skirmishes which Lord Edward faced in the Southern Campaign, as one might expect of a soldier on his death bed. But Lord Edward, head of the United Irishmen Military Committee with at one time as many as three hundred thousand men under his command, was silent or made only delirious ramblings, common to combat officers in their last hours, about militia and numbers. He faded in and out of consciousness.

"What's that?" Lord Edward suddenly cried out, as he raised up from his bed. In his weak state of mind, he could hear from his cell the sounds of hanging a prisoner named Clinch. This was to remind him that the gallows waited for him, if on the odd chance he survived his wounds.

Finally, he said, "Dear Ireland! I die for you! My country, you will be free!"

Report of Lord Edward's final words copied down by Dr. Garnett got back to Pamela and Tony. They heard that he died at two o'clock in the morning on 4 June 1798. They also heard that fearing reprisals from the rabble, a despicable relative by marriage, Lord Castlereagh, convinced Lady Louisa, Lord Edward's aunt, to have the body moved at night and interred secretly in the crypt at St. Werburgh's Church near Newgate Prison.

Several days after Lord Edward's death and burial, Tony again knocked on Pamela's door in London. She invited him to enter. This time Pamela was sitting quietly in a small cushioned chair, her eyes red from crying. She looked intently at Tony as he came into the room. Not unkempt, she nonetheless no longer bothered much about her appearance.

"Pamela, I heard that a British sergeant major who knew Lord Edward at Ninety Six, Eutaw Springs, and Quinby Bridge made a visit to Lord Edward before he died, as he was suffering from his shoulder and neck wounds in Newgate Prison. I want you to hear about it, if you want to. May I tell you what I heard?"

Pamela looked up and smiled. She silently motioned for him to sit down in a nearby chair.

"The two went through hand-to-hand fighting against the Americans and saw lots of their comrades get killed. They remembered Lieutenant Hickman at Eutaw Springs and, especially, Major Majoribanks. The sergeant major knew that Lord Edward was a brave and courageous officer at Eutaw Springs. He knew about me rescuing Lord Edward, too, about how I took care of him, but he never heard about how Ruth and I gave him cymbee water from the springs at Eutaw. I guess he wouldn't know about that, anyway.

"At first, Dr. Lindsay wouldn't let the sergeant major speak to Lord Edward. The doctor was afraid he would praise Lord Edward and make him feel better. That was real nasty mean, wasn't it? He knew that everyone who served with him loved him. But the sergeant major persisted and finally got to see him.

"I know how precious such a visit would have been to you, if only you and little Pam were allowed to see him. I think my black face prevented me from getting a chance to see him. I wish I could have taken him some cymbee water, if I had any. Or just been by his side in his agony as I was in my cabin at Miss Maggie's.

"He told me that Lord Edward said very little as he reminisced about the times they spent together in South Carolina. He reminded Lord Edward of his thigh wound at the Battle of Eutaw Springs and how that wound was in service to the king and different from the wound he was suffering from now.

"But Lord Edward stopped him and said,

'Ah! I was wounded then in a very different cause; that was in fighting *against* liberty—this in fighting *for* it.'"

Tony waited a long time to hear if Pamela wanted to say anything, but she remained silent, still looking intensely at him, occasionally looking toward the door as if she expected Julie to bring little Pam into the room.

"Pamela, I also heard a lot of the details about how Majors Sirr and Swan and Mr. Ryan captured Lord Edward on the nineteenth. Same number as his old regiment—he would have liked that irony. I think he all along was trying to avoid capture by just common sense. We know how many times he resisted efforts by London and the Castle government to get him to leave the country. They would have just let him go free if he left Ireland. And he was so popular and beloved by everyone, the rustics and simple people he loved. The weeds, I call 'em.

"I think he appreciated just how important it was always to keep moving from place to place. He picked that up in the Lowcountry from Colonel Francis Marion, I think. That rascal Tarleton could never catch the Swamp Fox because he never stayed in one place more than two nights. And Lord

Edward did the same around Dublin, moving from one safe house to another. It's just plain common sense, really. But unlike the Swamp Fox, Lord Edward was surrounded by traitors and really did not make every attempt to conceal his whereabouts—as if he wanted to get caught. Do you think he did?"

Tony was trying to do his best from just going on and on comparing everything with American experiences. But he couldn't. That was the crucible. Pamela continued to look at him, sometimes smiling, at other times weeping silently. She never moved, other than to wipe tears with her handkerchief.

"I think he fought against Sirr and Swan and Ryan the same way he fought against those rebels who had the audacity to ride over Quinby Bridge straight into Coates and Lord Edward. He was at his best in hand-to-hand combat. Sirr and Swan found that out. Ryan paid for it with his life. And all those soldiers with 'em saw the kind of fighter they say he was at the thicket at Eutaw Springs. Some men are just born fighters. I wasn't up close to him there like I was at the rear guard near Huger's Bridge and at Quinby Bridge, and I didn't get to see him myself at the thicket. I told Lord Edward about all this not too long ago, how great he was in battle. I didn't see him fight at Orangeburg, either, when he broke his sword on the back of one of William Washington's dragoons about a week after Shubrick's Plantation. Ruth and I fixed up his thigh wound at Eutaw Springs. It was real bad. He must have put up a fierce fight against the rebels who gave that to him somewhere near Miss Maggie's house."

Pamela remained patient with Tony's report as it wandered back and forth from South Carolina to Dublin. She had heard some of it before. She knew that Tony was again and again reliving his whole life with her beloved husband, the only way Tony now could deal with his own loss. This was for Tony's sake, for his reckoning how his own fight for freedom ended up.

"He was eager for fame in America, and here, for freedom. He wasn't afraid of being wounded or dying for it, either. He didn't want to die on the battle field at the springs, though. I just wish I was there to help him. I sure would use a gun then.

"I know I'm talking too much about Lord Edward and me in Carolina, Pamela. Please forgive me. It's just that he was left alone to die, and I wasn't there with him. I'm kind of afraid of what's going to happen in the future, too, now that my faithful friend of seventeen years is gone. You know I was with him more than anyone in his life.

"I was fighting for more freedom the whole time after I met Lord Edward, but I never really had a country when I lived in America. You don't have a country when you and most folks like you don't have complete freedom—or any freedom at all. But I told Ruth on the wharf when Lord Edward and I left Charleston that Carolina was my country. I guess in my heart it always will be. Julie knows that. But now maybe Ireland is, next maybe France, then England, but it's home only if we all are free. That was true in Canada, too. In America I was a man without a country because the country never saw me as a man."

Pamela continued to listen to the heart of her beloved husband's best friend as he tried to make sense of his life in relation to her husband's, and she gleaned from his words the life of her husband's as well.

"I mean, I'm always fighting, but with words and ideas, not with guns and swords. I'm always at war, my own personal war, for more freedom, no matter what country I'm in, and fighting for all of us, too, especially against folks who don't see that if somebody's in chains, everybody's in chains. Mental chains, too, I mean. Not even knowing you're in chains. It's my own war going on all the time in all the wars in America, the Indies, and now Ireland, too. I fight when I'm treated different no matter where I am. Countries are just people who get along with each other. We all have got to love each other or die, don't we?

"Oh, Pamela, I saw first-hand the ebb and flow of history move on a vast field of battle. I saw great men in the company of Lord Edward spur on what's going to be remembered for a long time, and now I see the fall of Ireland's best. And all the time, Pamela, I've been pursuing my own fortune, rushing headlong at great price and thinking all the time about the people I love. I've survived to bear witness to what's good about us as friends.

"Pamela, I couldn't have loved Lord Edward as much as I did if I didn't love freedom more. I think he knew that. And he loved me for the same reason. And I think at the end of his life he knew that people looked at him the same way he first looked at me in my hut at Eutaw Springs and said to himself, 'That's what freedom means.' Friendship and kindness. For everybody. All the time."

After Tony's long litany was over, neither spoke for a long time. Even if not at the usual peak of her appearance, Pamela was beautiful in her cream-colored dress with scarlet trim, a dress like one she made for little Pam. She put it aside, exhausted in a calm and serene way, not so much by reason as by emotions. Her future was in the air as much as Tony's, her fears as real, if not more so.

Tony began to laugh softly. "Lord Edward taught me how to read and write, but when he wrote out Major Majoribanks' name for me and pronounced it "Marsh-banks," I almost gave up. Somebody with the word Majoribanks got a-holt of the alphabet and wouldn't let go. The letters don't always fit the sounds in English, do they? Kind of like words and meaning. He always told me to be sure to think through everything, too, so I asked him, if you think through everything do you come out on the other side?"

With that, knowing it meant little sense, Tony became somber, his right elbow resting in the palm of his left hand as his fingers slowly rubbed his cheek—a customary posture when he discussed serious matters with Lord Edward. Now he unconsciously stood in the same way at the widow. "My greatest regret is that they wouldn't let me patch him up in that terrible prison and save him like I did on the battlefield at Eutaw. Ruth could have saved his life in prison if she had been there with a gourd of cymbee water and been able to push those devil doctors out of the way."

By the following August, Pamela and little Pam left London to return to Hamburg. Tony, his wife Julie, and their child Moirico went with them. Pamela married an American consul, Mr. Pitcairn, in Hamburg a year and a half later.

Tony knocked on the door of Pamela's room in Hamburg, and after hearing her invitation to enter, he walked in and stood quietly as she finished tidying up new sewing, including yet another dress for little Pam, a red one this time. She turned from a small table, delighted to see her good friend. "Faithful Tony, do please sit down."

"Pamela, I have here something that was written by General Sir John Doyle about Lord Edward. I think you'd like to hear it. He was the major then, after Major Majoribanks, who turned over William Washington to Lord Edward—and me—after the Battle of Eutaw Springs. Here it is. You can read it or I'll try to read it to you."

"You read it, Tony, please." Pamela also helped teach Tony to read, and she suspected correctly that he practiced for this moment. And this time, lacking the dreadful sadness shortly following Lord Edward's death, she was braced for whatever Tony had to say.

"He said,

'Of my lamented and ill-fated friend's excellent qualities, I should never tire in speaking. I never knew so lovable a person, and every man in the army, from the general to the drummer, would cheer the expression. His frank and open manner, his universal benevolence, his *gaieté de coeur*, his valour almost chivalrous, and, above all, his unassuming tone, made him the idol of all who served with him. He had great animal spirits, which bore him up against all fatigue; but his courage was entirely independent of those spirits—it was a valour *sui generis*. Had fortune placed him in a situation however difficult, where he could *legitimately* have brought those varied qualities into play, I am confident he would have proved a proud ornament to his country.'"

Tony looked up from the page and saw Pamela's broad smile, but she said nothing.

"Pamela, I was with Lord Edward for many years. Some of that time was spent when the two of you were married. And I have been with you and little Pam alone here in Hamburg for eighteen months. Now that you've married

Mr. Pitcairn, I feel that I've long enough been faithful to you, Lord Edward's widow and my own good friend." Tony paused as Pamela continued to take in what was just read to her and now to listen to Tony's announcement. Perhaps, Tony thought, he is rushing news of his departure after hearing so great a eulogy of Lord Edward.

"Pamela, everything said or written about Lord Edward falls short of the man we both knew, and I would love to stay by your side to remind me of him. But Julia and I have to leave you now. We've already been in touch with some black folks who may help us set up a tailor's shop in London. You know that she's a skillful seamstress. We want our little Moirico to grow up in England. I'll try to work with horses."

Pamela sat up straight. With her lovely arms and delicate hands she put down the fabric of little Pam's red dress on the table. She smoothed out invisible wrinkles and creases and patted it as if little Pam were already wearing it. Although she was no longer as beautiful as she was in happier days, she was not at all a pathetic figure and evoked no pity. After all, for five years she celebrated life with a man who blurred the lines of fact and fiction.

Tony continued to hold the floor. "I saw lots of sorrow in my life," Tony said, "and, as you know, I saw many happy days with Lord Edward. I followed him wherever he went. I did what he did and helped him with things he had to do. I left behind what I loved in South Carolina, my family, my friends, and the life I hoped to share with 'em in the Lowcountry. I hoped for the best in South Carolina. Now I feel lucky to have Julie and Moirico here by my side.

"I don't even know what happened to 'em all—what happened to my parents, what happened to my friends who were enslaved by the McKelveys and the other planters. They all have names, but I bet few are remembered. Maybe to somebody. Dick and his wife Molly and their children Jesse, Nancy, Dick, Plenty, and Hesey. Tom, who was also a carpenter, and his two children Frank and Tom. And Aleck who was just a young fellow, but very smart." Tony laughed at his own joke.

"Jacob, John, Phebe, Silvia, Josse, Clarinda, and Stepney. I used to tease Stepney about her name. Have you ever heard a name like Stepney? Sayey had a funny name, too. She was my little flower. Whenever Miss Maggie brought flowers from the garden into the living room, it was like she brought in my friends. They were all owned by Mr. James and Miss Maggie McKelvey. And lots, lots more people, too. Seems like there were hundreds I didn't even know. Josse was a wonderful little lady. She took such pride in doing things well. Jacob was a leader. Plenty was plenty of trouble to his momma." And again he chuckled at his skill in remembering names and flipping one around, this time drawing a smile from Pamela.

"As I sailed away from Charleston with Lord Edward over ten years ago, I stood on the deck of the ship and watched the shore of the Lowcountry get fainter and fainter. Those great oaks and tall stately palmetto trees on the beach are still in my mind. I didn't know if I was deserting people I could help if I stayed, and I asked myself if we are all in this together or is it everybody for himself.

"And Sally. I wonder what happened to Sally. She was as pretty as Jenny and Rinah. Chloe, too. Sarah and Venus, too. They were all smart, smarter than the boys. I used to play with Abraham and Prince at the big live oak. And Hercules and Hester. I played mostly with Ruth, but she wasn't owned by Miss Maggie. Old man Snow owned her.

"There, I just barely mentioned Ruth. But Julie knows how much I loved Ruth. How hard it was to leave her in Charleston and how I tried to find her in Canada. I guess I still love her and always will.

"I wonder what happened to Hagar and Isaac. Paul and Ben, and Katy and Bob. Some of them were in the cabin when Ruth and I brought Lord Edward from the battlefield. McKelveys owned all of 'em.

"The best of the lot was Cuffy. He died at Eutaw Springs."

"I shall miss you, Tony Small," Pamela said after she could contain her feelings no longer. "I shall truly miss you. What little remains of my own family will never forget what you meant to us and to their father." She continued in a steady voice.

"My husband told me never to be jealous of his friendship with you, Tony, and I have not been. Nor will I ever be. You have been my faithful Tony, as well, and I trust I have been a faithful friend to you, too.

"Surely, you know Lord Edward loved you. He was so fond of telling me how he was later surprised at his own sudden decision to take you with him when he left the battle ground at Eutaw Springs. He told me that he needed you to help him escort all those prisoners and Colonel Washington. But it was more than that. He told me that it was almost by instinct that the two of you became friends. He never tried to explain it any further."

At that, tears came to Tony's eyes, and he looked away.

"Love is not measured out. If it is, we all thought Lord Edward loved us more than anyone else. He had such an infinite capacity to love. He told me that you held a special place in his heart and mind—in his mind, too, Tony. He not only loved you dearly as someone he could trust and who served so nobly as his manservant. That was your lot that you both embraced with mutual dignity in the times we live in. But he loved you as a friend, too, as an absolute equal. A true friend. A good man. I think you always knew that.

"You left one revolution only to become a part of another, and you have witnessed in my life yet a third. France and American succeeded but, alas, our dear Ireland failed."

Tony was quiet as he listened to the wife of a great romantic figure recite what it was like to be alive in such an exhilarating age—ah, to be alive in any age.

"Tony, he told me that he felt so often that he waited on you—that you were the master and he the servant. That was because he was so firmly devoted to leveling all social places and degrees, and he listened to everyone. You were for him the very incarnation of the brotherhood of man, the belief that we are all alike. We *are* all in this together. But it was also because of what your good sense meant to him, your level-headedness. What you literally stood for. The spirit of American ideals which you brought in your very being to Ireland. Freedom. Liberty. Justice for all. Equality. Fraternity. Law—good laws that reflect all that. Good men enforcing them. They would have been abstractions to him if, as he told me, he were not able to see your black face day after day.

"Tony, you're an Irish Lafayette.

"He wanted Ireland to have what America has, or promises to have, but you were not just a simple reminder to him, Tony. He told me you completely embodied the very political and philosophical ideals he chased all his life. By your birth and early life in South Carolina, where nearly all blacks are still enslaved, you already attained a wisdom that Lord Edward sought. He had to revolt. He had to throw off his own birthright and entitlements to reach the state of mind you were born with. You taught him what love of brotherhood and sisterhood means, what living together peacefully means. How good and pleasant it is.

"His mind and heart never left that sweet adversity, the Lowcountry of South Carolina where democracy so ironically began with guns and slavery."

Days later the Smalls sailed for England, keen on a better life. Moirico was old enough to be enchanted by the waves breaking over the bow. Doing her best to keep Moirico as dry as possible, Julie let her look out over the channel from a safe distance.

"Let her hold onto the rail," Tony said.

"Your daughter is too rambunctious for that. You know as well as I do, she'll jump in and try to swim to England."

With Moirico finally asleep in a nearby deck chair, Julie approached her husband who was standing at the rail looking out. The waves were mesmerizing, putting both their minds in a suspenseful mood that invites casual truth-telling among close friends. "Tony, why were you so faithful to Lord Edward? I sometimes thought you loved him more than you love your own family."

Tony turned and gently took her by the arm in the same way he did when he asked her to marry him. He then wrapped both arms around her waist. He closed his eyes and kissed her. "You must never think that, my dear Julie. He was my friend, just as Pamela and little Pam are. You and Moirico are my heart." Julie nestled into his chest.

"I'm not the only one who idolized Lord Edward. We all felt the same way. An old groomsman once told me that he and all the other servants at Leinster House would gladly lay down their lives for him. Just as I would a hundred times over. He had no faults of character that I could see. He was Eghnidal, a Chief of the Bear Tribe of the Seneca Indians. But he once told me that I always pestered him about writing home—and I did. If I hadn't made him write so many letters, no one would have ever known that he was safe and sound in Charleston, the Caribbean, and Canada. Everyone is glad I pestered him to write. And another time he said I was avaricious—that was my biggest fault, counting money that we saved in Canada. He got the money and I counted it."

Tony laughed softly and looked out over the waves. He kissed his wife's lovely brown hair. "Well, he was wrong then, too. We had to save money to get down the Mississippi to New Orleans and back to Dublin, and I was the only one who wasn't always giving money away to anybody he thought needed it more than we did. I guess that and the letter-writing business are the only faults he ever had. And they were both about me, so maybe I caused them."

Julie snuggled her head further into her husband's chest and hugged him tightly. She heard his heart beat through his overcoat and the sound of his chuckle after saying he was the cause of Lord Edward's faults. She looked up and softly kissed him on the cheek and nestled her head back on his chest.

"He took up arms and fought hard against powerful enemies. He hated bullies. About that kind of person, he used to say his mother told him, same as my momma told me, that some people just don't know how to act."

Tony returned to his first skill of training horses when he arrived in London and went looking for a job. He avoided mentioning any connection to Lord Edward's family while interviewing for a position, but if the subject came up, he never denied it. Without success he approached the Conollys, Hollands, Foxes, and Fitzgeralds. He sought out positions among other families known for their large stables.

He tried to pick back up what he was weaned on at Maggie McKelvey's stables, to regain what he lost for lack of consistent riding at Leinster House, Frescati, Kildare, and Carton House. He could still talk to horses, the way he did to Eagle. He could work well with English and Irish thoroughbreds, like those he saw briefly at Secundus Ravenel's Plantation at Wantoot. He longed to import marsh tacky horses to England, a proposal dismissed out right by everyone.

"Tony," Julie quietly said one morning, "I'm real sorry to see you work so hard to get a good job, but we really do need more money. I didn't take you for a husband just for the money you could make. You know that. I took you to love. Just loving you is a good living. And if something ever came up between us, I'd let you know ahead of time so we could work it out. But Moirico needs more now that she's growing up. We all need more, Tony, even though we scrimp and save and work hard, and we sure aren't spendthrifts."

"Life's hard," Tony replied. "Hard. 'For better or for worse, richer or poorer' means a lot. Family is everything." He took her in his arms and kissed her. Tony continued to hold her and waited a long time to continue. He looked over her shoulder at the cramped and cluttered room which was both tailor shop and living quarters. He saw clothes that could pass for rags and rags that could pass for clothes. Julia loved bright colors and intricate designs, material set aside in a separate pile.

Eventually, he looked kindly in her eyes and said, "If you leave me to find a better provider—a man with a nice house by the river with a nice carriage—I'll understand. You're so pretty, Julie. You can do that if you feel insecure and want more things for yourself and Moirico."

"You know I'll never leave you, Tony. I'll never leave you. I'm not selfish. I could never find a better man, anyway. I know you can't provide well, and you're in poor health, Tony, but I'll always love you and be by your side. But you should ask for help from the Fitzgeralds. It's only fair that they help you now. Tell them that you had to give up work with horses, and that you can now only help in my tailor shop. Tell them everything."

"Lady Louisa Conolly and Lord Henry both visited Lord Edward in prison shortly before he died, but I don't think they will help me. Maybe I should write a letter to Lady Sophia."

"Yes, Sophia. She's the perfect one to write. Lord Edward and Pamela gave little Lucy to Sophie. She'll help us. I know she will."

To figure out exactly how to broach the subject of asking for money, Tony first got in touch with Arthur O'Connor's servant Jerry O'Leary. O'Leary was a well-know figure in London with prosperous friends. If any black knew how to get about in the city, it was Jerry O'Leary.

Tony called on O'Leary unannounced. O'Leary met him at the door of an impressive but small brick addition to the back of a larger house off Fleet Street. O'Leary was neatly dressed with polished shoes and looked at the stranger to find that he, too, was well-kempt. After Tony introduced himself and mentioned a mutual friend now living in London, William Snow from Charleston, O'Leary greeted him warmly.

Tony recited his exploits with Lord Edward and the delicate purpose of his visit. "How does somebody ask for money? I've never done that."

"Lord Edward was your friend," O'Leary said, "more than your master. That's why you can ask for money. You earned every farthing the two of you ever shared."

"Lady Sophia will look at it as a hand-out. That's what I'm afraid of."

"She knows it's not a hand-out, Tony. I know her. She knows you've earned whatever you ask her for—kind of like back pay. Kind of like getting money from a pension fund you earned in America after saving his life. My goodness, man, you saved his life! Isn't that worth something to these Fitzgeralds? It's for being a faithful servant and friend, like Francis Barber was to Dr. Johnson. He got lots of money, a £70 annuity plus £1,500 inheritance."

Tony thanked the sophisticated Londoner. As he walked to the front door and turned to shake his hand, O'Leary said, "By the way, Tony, you look like a man who keeps the right kind of company. If you know of a good woman for me, I'd be much obliged. I'm looking for a good strong black woman who can take care of herself. I hear black women from America are like that."

"I'll turn that job over to Julie."

Signing his letter as Anthony, sometime in 1803 Tony wrote Lady Sophia:

> "My Lady,
>
> I hope you will pardon the Liberty I take in writing, but having a great favour to aske and knowing your Ladyships goodness, makes me take this freedom. I am at present in a very bade state of health and not able to do anything to support myself or family. I apply'd to Mr. Oglovie some time ago for what is owning to me by Lawler and he told me as soon as the Estates in Ireland would affort it he would let me have a hundred pounds,

now being so ill and having no money I am drove to the greatest distress, for what little money I have been spent Docktors. the Favour I have to aske of your Ladyship is if you could make intress for me in the Family to make up a sum of money for me so that I might be able to keep our business for my wife and children which is my greatest trouble or if it was in your Ladyship's power to advance me some, I make no doubt but Mr. Oglovie will pass his word for it for realy if I was not in the way as I am I would not trouble your Ladyship on any account or the family—I am at present under the Hands of Surgeon Heavisides George St Hanover Square. He gives me every hopes of recovery he desires me to take all the nourishing food possible and take but little Exericse—I hope your Ladyship is well and Miss Lucy.

I remain your Ladyship's faithfull servant

Anthony Small

PS My directions are No. 10 Air Street Piccadilly"

Months passed with only a small sum sent by Lady Lucy Fitzgerald. Nothing was ever forwarded from Lawler or Ogilvie.

"That's fine," he told Julie. "We all simply have to carry on for now, but I fear that you and Moirico must soon make do without me."

Several months passed. Noticing a certain peacefulness about her husband one morning, Julie saw in his tired eyes that he was thinking about the Lowcountry of South Carolina, about his most adventuresome days with Lord Edward, and about all the friends he left behind. Tony went to the window to look out once again.

After a while he said, "I saw Cuffy the other night. Stood right by our bed. He looked big and strong as ever. Cuffy smiled at me and said, 'We'll all get through this together.'"

Julie watched him turn away from the window and take determined steps toward the front door.

"I must go lie down now, Julie. I'll be out yonder under the big tree. I'll get back up after a while, 'cause when I feel like I can't ever hold my head up high again after Lord Edward's death, when I remember him and what he stood for, I straighten up and hold my head high, same as when we used to walk together on the streets of Charleston and Dublin. I'll get back up after a while.

"I first carried him on my back at Eutaw Springs, but after that we carried each other a long way toward freedom."

On a late autumn afternoon, a few years after Tony died, an attractive young girl finishes her work at a shop in London and walks southwest on Piccadilly toward Green Park. She walks slowly as if to look especially hard at places that are particularly attractive to her. Corners, nooks and crannies, even gutters. Her only diversion is to stop at an occasional equestrian statue. At times she picks up something and puts it in her pocket and walks on to cover as much distance as the waning daylight allows. At one point on her route she gives a wide berth to drunken soldiers spilling themselves and their liquor out of a pub.

Suddenly the young girl almost stumbles upon what appears to be a large bundle of rags under which she sees a rather haggard-looking woman of African descent.

"My, my, what's happened to you?" the young girl asks and laughs in a good-natured manner. "You look terrible."

At that, the much older woman sitting on the curb looks up. She, too, laughs to indicate that she takes no offense. Her broad smile shows a dazzling array of beautiful white teeth that shine like the stars.

"I've been hurt bad," the woman says in a weak voice. "Mighty kind of you to stop."

The young girl looks at her and deliberates whether to continue on her route before it gets too late.

"We've got to get you some help, ma'am," the young girl says. "You wait right here. The sun's about to go down and we need to get off the streets right away, but you wait right here and I'll be back as soon as I can."

Moments later the young girl returns with a flask of water. "Here, drink it. It's good water. It'll give you some strength back. Then we've got to get you out of here. It's plain spooky around here at night and dangerous for two women to be out on the streets alone."

After she gets on her feet, the woman asks, "What were you looking for? I saw you scrounging around the street like you were hunting for gold."

"Well, I was," the young girl says and laughs again. "I do every evening after work before it gets too dark. Little bits of treasure, you known, left along the way by drunk soldiers and busy people who might drop a penny or two. Bits of anything, really. Buttons, whatever. Helps make ends meet."

"And no telling who you meet," the woman adds. "Where're we going?" She fades in and out of consciousness, barely able to walk.

The young girl carries much of her full weight as they struggle along. Both began to chuckle at what a funny sight they look like to passersby.

"What's your name, ma'am? What should I call you?" the young girl asks. "You sound like an American."

"Yes, but I don't go by my American name any more." They continue to stumble along the sidewalk, dodging horses and carriages as they cross streets. The woman speaks with difficulty.

"All I ever had was a first name, anyway, but I don't go by that, like I said. Call me Miss Heron."

As the young girl arrives at the tailor shop where she lives, she seems not to hear the woman ask the same question of her.

"We need to get you into nice clothes and feed you some soup and let you rest in a good bed. I'll tell Momma you're here, and she'll help you, too. Tomorrow you'll be up and about, I'm sure. Tomorrow is another day. I can help you get a job. I know lots of black folks here in London."

"But what's your name?" the woman asks again.

"My name's Moirico. Moirico Small."

The woman smiles and looks into her eyes. "You're Tony's girl, ain't you?"

PART II

Afterword and Appendices, Historical Notes, Exhibits, and Maps

AFTERWORD

A fter the British took Savannah in December 1778 and Charleston
in May 1780, they thought they could continue their campaign,
following their success at Camden in August 1780, and flank
George Washington from the South to force surrender. But they lost at
King's Mountain in October 1780 and at Cowpens in January 1781. They
had only pyrrhic victories at Guilford Courthouse and Hobkirk's Hill in
March and April 1781 and in skirmishes during Raid of the Dog Days in
July 1781. They held the field but gave it up at the Battle of Eutaw Springs
in September 1781, having lost thirty-five percent of their army. British
failure and American success in the Southern Campaign led to Yorktown
in October 1781. Washington slipped down from New York. The French
arrived. Greene denied Cornwallis supporting troops from the South. To
some extent, the Southern Campaign won the war for the Americans. Like
white Whigs and Tories, white patriots and loyalists, African Americans
played active roles on both sides throughout the campaign.

The two major battles at Ninety Six and Eutaw Springs and the running
skirmish of Raid of the Dog Days are necessarily described in some detail to
afford an opportunity to name and give creative narratives to the historical
African Americans who, according to Moss and Scoggins, did fight or could
have fought in them. Among the names in Appendix I are also those of black
men and women who are plausible on-lookers at particular times and places

while Lord Edward is in the Lowcountry. Throughout the book, no more than a half dozen major characters are white.

About five thousand blacks fought on the patriot side during the war, and at its end, one in twenty American servicemen was black—an extent of integration not matched until blacks fought for the Union in the Civil War and in larger numbers in the Korean War.

Tony Small is virtually unknown to history. His name does not appear in any major historical publication and rarely appears in on-line references. He is seldom if ever discussed by amateur or academic historians. That fact alone supports writing the lengthy historical information that follows the creative nonfiction.

The only historical primary source for Tony's identity as an African American who rescues Lord Edward from the battlefield at Eutaw Springs, South Carolina, is the Thomas Sumter Papers, Lyman C. Draper Manuscript Collection, 6VV321, State Historical Society of Wisconsin. A primary source for the friendship of Tony and Lord Edward after Eutaw Springs is the collection of Lord Edward's letters, but there is nothing in the letters that provides an historical narrative of Tony in South Carolina. Certainly, not enough exists for a biography. Tony's friendship with Lord Edward lasts seventeen years in South Carolina, the West Indies, Canada, Ireland, England, France, and the continent.

In her 1997 biography of Lord Edward, *Citizen Lord*, Stella Tillyard identifies seven collections of letters, including those at the National Library of Ireland and the British Library. Correspondence that runs about eight hundred items from the 1770s to the 1830s is in the National Library of Ireland. The most controversial letters regarding the capture of Lord Edward were released as late as 2012. There are one hundred and fifty items from 1798 alone.

This book could not have been written before publications of the Moss and Scoggins compilations of African-American names in the Southern Campaign. The method here of writing about Tony and Lord Edward, one inclusive of black soldiers and civilians, is determined in part by the Moss and Scoggins roster of names and short historical biographical information. First, from my own research I identify the battles and skirmishes in which Lord

Edward is a participant, or in which he arguably is a participant. That places Lord Edward at no fewer that twelve military actions in South Carolina. Next, I match all the names of African Americans in Moss and Scoggins who are also definitely at the same engagements, or reasonably could have been, and use their historical biographical information to provide fictional narration. That allows Tony and other blacks a role in historical events as participants and eye witnesses.

Nor could it have been written without using the research of Richard Watkins and James Queen who, in their research of land genealogy, identify past and present owners of land on which the Battle of Eutaw Springs was fought (Appendix II). Watkins and Queen suggest the owner at the time of the battle may have been Maggie McKelvey who took ownership of the plantation after the death of her husband James. The McKelveys owned several plantations with thousands of acres around Eutaw Springs and along the Santee River. Placing the historical Tony Small as a free black man, rather than enslaved, on Maggie McKelvey's Plantation at Eutaw Springs, and placing the battle on ground around her brick house is a reasonable historical conjecture. No primary source characterizes Tony as either free or enslaved. No other research identifies the plantation as belonging to anyone specifically.

Sometimes, it is a stretch to place named blacks at particular events. For example, Ned Zanger [L360] and Lazarus Jones [L169] are players who help to narrate the action following the Second Siege of Ninety Six. Moss and Scoggins simply list Zanger as a guide and a member of a company of Black Pioneers "acquainted with part of the Carolinas." And Lazarus Jones simply uses his team and wagon prior to 19 July 1782 to haul flour "from Summer's Mill on the Broad River to British forces at Camden." This creative nonfiction fleshes out their roles. All narrations do not, however, wander far from standard histories, conflicting as standard histories are.

Generally speaking, if a relation or incident is not referenced in the historical notes or is not commonly known in American history, it is fictional. Most significant fictional events, for example, are Tony's activities at the McKelvey and other lowcountry plantations and his conversations with Maggie McKelvey, his interest in Cymbee water, his travels and activities other than his factual rescue of Lord Edward at Eutaw Springs as narrowly described in the Draper manuscript, and creative narratives around his departure from Charleston with Lord Edward. Ruth's relation with Tony is fictional, as are Tony's meeting with John Laurens, his meeting with Abraham Marrian, his conversations with Jane Elliott and William Washington, his actions with the Black Dragoons, his consolation of Pamela, and most of his conversations with Lord Edward. Washington, according to Roger Chapman, former curator of the Green Howards Museum (19th Regiment of Foot), influenced Lord Edward as much as Tony.

Tony's activities after leaving South Carolina are broadly borne out in Lord Edward's letters. While very few readers on either side of the Atlantic know about Tony Small, Irish, English, and Canadian readers know a great deal about Lord Edward, and French readers know about Lord Edward through his wife Pamela, Lady Fitzgerald.

This book introduces readers to Tony Small, a major figure in African American history. It is the first to write at length about Tony Small and Lord Edward. Part II is essential to the history of Lord Edward in South Carolina, and for the most part Tony creatively rides along with or near him during particular historical events in Part I.

Part I is necessarily a work of creative nonfiction, a curious animal: nonfiction in that all the characters, except a few unnamed, and all major events are historical; creative in that the narrative and most minor events are possible if not probable. One may ask, time and again, where pure history stops and creative nonfiction begins. The historical apparatus in Part II allows readers to find answers to that question. For example, facts taken from Appendix I, the biographical entries in Bobby Gilmer Moss and Michael Charles Scoggins in *African-American Loyalists in the Southern Campaign of the American Revolution*, 2005, and *African-American Patriots in the Southern Campaign of the American Revolution*, 2004, support the story in Part I.

Furthermore, division markers throughout Part I (and below) separate and highlight historical quotations taken from Lord Edward's letters and Moore and MacDermott from the author's creative narratives.

Some of the historical details may be entirely unfamiliar to most readers. At the same time, and not included in the notes and appendices but rather written in the text, are familiar historical events—events in which Lord Edward very likely or certainly played a role, and, creatively, Tony Small as well. To that extent, the parameters of the story are more defined than in a work of pure fiction.

For example, in the first paragraph of Chapter Three, "Raid of the Dog Days," Lord Edward is probably in Rawdon's detachment going from Orangeburg to Goose Creek where Lord Edward leaves the detachment to go to Moncks Corner to join his regiment while Rawdon travels on to Charleston. This likely scenario is based on historical research of others. Tony's role, however, of following along with Rawdon's party to Goose Creek and then following Lord Edward to Moncks Corner is creative. Since the paragraph is mixed with an historical event in which Lord Edward may have taken part and a creative action by Tony, it is included in the text, not referenced in the purely historical notes.

Such markers in the Notes are meant to indicate where pure history stops and creative nonfiction begins, but if even they are ignored and the entire book is taken as historical fiction or even a novel, little is lost of Tony and Lord Edward's historical importance. Lawrence Hill in his novel *Somebody Knows My Name,* a "work built on the foundations of history," uses "fictional characters who are drawn from real people having the same names." New York: WW. Norton, 2017, p. 473. Tony and Lord Edward's story is told very differently.

Although some historians may disagree, the twentieth-century "troubles" and the 1969–2001 Irish Republican Army (IRA) activities share the same issues in the public imagination with Lord Edward and the Uprising of 1798.

Tony's history is recorded mainly by Lord Edward in letters to his mother and others, but nothing tells of Tony's life in South Carolina. Tillyard's biography of Lord Edward has only four pages based on the Draper Manuscript about Tony in the Lowcountry. This book was written, off and on, over a period of thirty years in Charleston, the only place it could have been written.

The Memoirs of Lord Edward Fitzgerald, a biography by Thomas Moore, was published in 1831. Moore mentions Tony about fifteen times. Moore was a close friend of Lord Edward's uncle and aunt, Lord and Lady Holland, whose personal accounts of their nephew are given almost entirely to the Irish lord's political and social life, not his military activity, in Ireland and England. Letters by Lord Edward as well as letters about him, many of which are printed in Moore's cleaned-up Whig biography, revised by Martin MacDermott in 1897, give Tony his last name.

When he was an undergraduate at Trinity College, Moore never gets over seeing Lord Edward one day walking on the streets of Dublin—when a proper man of the Protestant Ascendancy would have been riding his horse. In his preface, Moore observes that Lord Edward is, "except for O'Connell, the best known of any Irishman whatever," and writes,

"As an instance of this, I may mention the following anecdote, related to me by a well-known author. Taking his son, a schoolboy, recently to spend his vacation in Ireland, and arriving at Kingsbridge Station in Dublin, he hired a car, telling the man to drive round to the places best worth seeing in the city. Five minutes later, finding that the driver had stopped before a dingy old brick house in a back street, he asked him—'Well, what's this? Where are we now?'—'Sure, sir,' says the man, pointing up with his whip, 'this is Mr. Murphy's house, where *Lord Edward* was took.'"

Any story that arises from the American Revolutionary War, or the War for American Independence as the British call it, can get sucked into a rehashing of well-known battles. Any orbiting story that gets near the life of Lord Edward Fitzgerald can easily be drawn in and consumed by a figure steeped in romanticism, political intrigue, revolution, military exploits, and sheer adventure. This Scylla and Charybdis the book hopes to avoid as it gives an account of Tony Small's life.

It is not, however, a struggle to give the life of Tony Small its due. An Irish scholar identifies "faithful Tony"—as Lord Edward describes him—as Lord Edward's "constant companion and symbolic talisman of the universal brotherhood of man." Lord Edward's life is without parallel in an age when individuals played great roles on the world stage, and Tony Small is at the center of it, both before and after Lord Edward's marriage to Pamela. Pamela and Tony, with their families, flee Ireland together after the death of Lord Edward.

The revolutionary mind which Lord Edward brought to the United Irishmen makes little sense without an account of his experiences in the American Revolutionary War. Lord Edward, head of the Military Committee, was the only leader of the uprising in 1796–98 with combat experience in a large campaign. He witnessed the successful effects of partisans in guerrilla warfare conducted by Marion, Sumter, and Lee and knew the devastation of civil war waged in the backcountry by American Tories and Whigs. As aide-de-camp to Lord Rawdon, a senior British field officer in the Southern Campaign, Lord Edward was exposed to strategic as well as tactical military operations. Most significantly, however, he tasted a new birth of freedom for his own native land, in part through Tony Small.

Early in their relation, Lord Edward says that Tony cannot write, but apparently he learned how on his own or with help. Apart from a letter he wrote, asking for financial support when he was ill in London in 1803, Tony himself leaves no written record. Further research in London and Dublin could, of course, discover more about this famous man and his family.

"Tony, Negro [SC]" appears on page 327, identified in Appendix I as [L327], in a list of two thousand eight hundred African Americans in Moss and Scoggins' *African-American Loyalists in the Southern Campaign of the American Revolution*. A list of eight hundred African Americans appears in their *African-American Patriots in the Southern Campaign of the American Revolution*. "The scope of African American service during the Revolutionary War is nothing short of amazing," they write in the introductions. Lord Edward Fitzgerald's name does not appear in biographical notes regarding blacks in either volume of Moss and Scoggins.

Stella Tillyard's biography of Lord Edward includes a painting identified as a portrait of Tony Small by Thomas Roberts (1748–1778). W. A. Hart, however, says that identity is unlikely. Roberts could not have been commissioned to paint the portrait in the 1780s. Instead, Hart claims, the Thomas Roberts painting is one of a nameless East Indian black man in a portrait shown at the Society of Artists in Ireland in 1772, "Portrait of Bold Sir William (a Barb) [name of the horse], an East Indian black, and a French dog, in the possession of Gerald Fitzgerald, Esq." Hart also mentions that the painting could be a portrait of a North African visitor to Dublin in 1783, Ahmet Ben Ali, made by an unknown artist. The portrait by Thomas Roberts was among works shown in a special exhibit at the National Gallery of Ireland, 28 March–28 June 2009.

If the Roberts portrait is not of Tony, the Draper Manuscript and Lord Edward's letters are the extent of primary sources on Tony Small. However, like the Moore and MacDermott biography, the Revolutionary War historical novels of William Gilmore Simms are here given weight as major secondary sources. *The Forayers, Eutaw, The Partisan: A Romance of Revolution, Mellichampe,* and *The Scout: Or, The Black Riders of the Congaree,* for example, cannot be dismissed out of hand as irrelevant historical documentation. Simms' main source is a Charleston patriot who lived during the Southern Campaign—his grandmother.

Modern English spelling and grammar are almost always used. No orthographical effort is made to reflect eighteen-century black pronunciation (orthoëpy and cacoëpy) and dialect in the Lowcountry of South Carolina, or white pronunciation and dialect in Colonial America, Canada, Ireland, England, and France. Gullah is used once, when Tony talks to Julie. Typical subject-verb disagreement is used sparingly. "Y'all," "ain't," "'em" ("them"), and several Lowcountry Southern idioms are sometimes used. Courtesy titles for nobility are in keeping with usage in DeBrett's.

———∽———

NAMES OF HISTORICAL AFRICAN AMERICANS APPEARING IN *TONY SMALL AND LORD EDWARD FITZGERALD*

A s well as names of those who do not appear in the book but who, with few exceptions, also could have been present during Lord Edward Fitzgerald's twelve battles in the Southern Campaign, or during his and Tony Small's residence in the British garrison in Charleston, their travels in Canada, and Tony's residence in London:

P = page number in Bobby Gilmer Moss and Michael Charles Scoggins, *African-American Patriots in the Southern Campaign of the American Revolution*. Blacksburg, South Carolina: Scotia-Hibernia Press, 2004. For example, Evans Archer appears on page 11.

L = page number in Bobby Gilmer Moss and Michael Charles Scoggins, *African-American Loyalists in the Southern Campaign of the American Revolution*. Blacksburg, South Carolina: Scotia-Hibernia Press, 2005. For example, Aberdeen appears on page 1a.

Repetition of names indicates different people with the same name. The list includes about 283 or 8% of the 3,600 names compiled in Moss and Scoggins.

A
Aberdeen [L1a], Black Dragoon
Abraham [L1c], Gadsden's Wharf
Adams, Emmy [L1], evacuated to Canada
Alexander, Sawndy [L2], evacuated to Canada
Amoretta [L3], evacuated to Canada
Anthony [L6], son of Phillis, Goose Creek
Archer, Evans [P11], Black Pioneer, Ninety Six, Eutaw Springs
Artis, John [P14], Eutaw Springs

B
Bailey, Silvia [L10], evacuated to Canada
Ballifo [P16], Biggin Church
Bass, Elijah [P19], Eutaw Spings (KIA)
Bella [L15], Gadsden's Wharf
Benjamin [P133], Eutaw Springs
Benjamin [L16], evacuated to Canada
Besse [L18], evacuated to Canada
Bibby, Absolom [P23], Eutaw Springs
Bibby, Solomon [P23], Eutaw Springs
Billy [L20], Gadsden's Wharf
Black, Cesar [P26], South Carolina Line
Blackmore, Thomas [P27][L25], Black Pioneer to Ninety Six
Blake, Prince [L25], evacuated to Canada
Bob [L27], evacuated to London
Bristol [L32], evacuated to Canada
Britain, John [L33], Goose Creek

Brown, John [L35], evacuated to Canada

Brownguard, Jasper [P36], Eutaw Springs

Burnett, William [P39], Eutaw Springs

Burton, Jenny [L39], with Stewart at Eutaw Springs

Button, Annie Belle [*Cemetery Records*], cared for Majoribanks

Button, Primus [*Cemetery Records*], cared for Majoribanks

C

Cadar [Ravenel, *Recollections*], saw a cymbee

Cain [L43], Gadsden's Wharf

Cane [L45], Black Dragoon

Capers, Jim [P43], Biggin Church, Eutaw Springs

Carney, Thomas [P44], Ninety Six

Case, Joseph [P48], Eutaw Springs

Charles [L49], Black Dragoon

Charles [L50], St. John's Parish

Chavers, Drury [P53], Eutaw Springs (KIA)

Chloe [L52], evacuated to Canada

Coff, William [P60], Eutaw Springs

Coleman, Edward [P61], Ninety Six

Collin [P62], Cowpens

Collins, Nancy [L56], Goose Creek

Cooper, William [L59], Ninety Six, evacuated to London

Crowell, Sambo, Goose Creek

Croy, Abner [L62], Bacon's Bridge

Cudjo [P67], "faithful driver"

Cuffee, Doctor [P68], Orangeburg

Cuffy [McKelvey, *Index to Inventories*], McKelvey enslaved foil to Tony

D

Davy, Sergeant [L69], Black Dragoon

Dawey, Private [L70] Black Dragoon

Dick [L73], Black Dragoon

Dick [L74], evacuated to Canada

Desbernays, Peter [P77], South Carolina Line

Dublin [L80], Gadsden's Wharf

E

Elijah [P134], Eutaw Springs
Ellis, John [P82], Eutaw Springs
Ely [L85], Gadsden's Wharf
Everly, Judith [L87], evacuated to Canada
Everly, Sam [L87], evacuated to Canada

F

Fenwick, Peggy [L88], with Stewart at Eutaw Springs
Ferguson, Andrew Jr. [P84], Ninety Six
Flora [L90], saw a cymbee
Frarde, Angres [L95], Goose Creek
Frederick [P134], Eutaw Springs
Furman, Shadrack [L97], London

G

Garrick [L98], Adjutant, Black Dragoon
George, David [L102], evacuated to Canada
Gibson, Charles [P95], Eutaw Springs
Gibson, Prince [L103], His Majesty's Field Train of Artillery
Gilbert [L103], Black Dragoon
Godfrey, Kitty [L108], evacuated to Canada
Gray, Ben [L114], evacuated to Canada
Greenard, George [L114], evacuated to Canada
Gibson, Prince [L103], His Majesty's Field Train of Artillery
Grant, Pompey [L113], Ninety Six
Gums, George [L115], His Majesty's Field Train of Artillery

H

Hammond, Private [L118], Black Dragoon
Hammonds, Isaac [P107], Eutaw Springs
Harman, Edward [P109], Eutaw Springs

Harris, Edward [P110], Eutaw Springs

Harris, Edward Jr. [P110], Eutaw Springs

Harris, Drury [P109], Eutaw Springs

Hercules [L129], saw a cymbee

Hicks, Micajah [P121], Eutaw Springs

Hicks, Will [L129], evacuated to Canada

Hill, Agrippa [P121], Ninety Six

Hood, Charles [P123], Eutaw Springs

Hooker, John [P124], Eutaw Springs

Howard, Nancy [L132], Dorchester

Huger, Ned [L133], evacuated to Canada

Hume, Peter [L133], evacuated to Canada

I

Isaac [P135], Eutaw Springs

Isaac [L136], Black Dragoon

Isham [Ravenel, *Recollections*], saw a cymbee

J

Jack [L141], Dorchester

Jacob [L147], Black Dragoon

James, Jeremiah [P135], Eutaw Springs

Jamie [L148], Black Dragoon

January [L151], Black Dragoon

Jefferies, Jacob [P137], Eutaw Springs

Jeffry [152], Black Dragoon

Jemmy [L152], Engineers Department of British Army

Joe [L157], evacuated to Canada

Johnny [L160], Gadsden's Wharf

Johnson, Diana [L161], Goose Creek

Johnson, Thomas [L166], Eutaw Springs

Jones, Hannah [L168], evacuated to Canada

Jones, Lazarus [L169], Ninety Six

K

Kate [L174], evacuated to Canada

Kate [L175], evacuated to Canada

Kitty [L180], evacuated to Canada

Kneller [P146], Eutaw Springs

L

Lamb [P147], South Carolina Line

Leah [L184], Gadsden's Wharf

Lomack, William [P151], Eutaw Springs

Lomax, Will [O'Kelley, Vol. 3, p. 540, fn. 593], Eutaw Springs (WIA)

London, Thomas [L191], evacuated to Canada

Lucretia [L192], evacuated to Canada

Lynch [L193], Black Dragoon

Lynch, Jacob [L193], evacuated to Canada

Lynch, John [L193], evacuated to Canada

Lynch, Phebe [L193], evacuated to Canada

M

Mary [L199], evacuated to Canada

Manly, Moses [P154], Eutaw Springs

Mariah [L196], daughter of Phillis, Goose Creek

Marion, Oscar or Buddy [P176], Francis Marion's servant and friend

Marrian, Abraham [L197], evacuated to Canada

March [P156], enslaved by Henry Laurens

March, Captain [L195], CO, Black Dragoon

Mason, Patrick [P158], Eutaw Springs

Martin, Absalom [P157], Eutaw Springs

Mayham, John, Sergeant [L201], Black Dragoon

Mills, Daniel [P161], Eutaw Springs

Mingo, Lieutenant [L209], Black Dragoon

Mitchel, Dinah [L210], evacuated to Canada

Mitchel, Frank [L210], evacuated to Canada

Mitchell, Henry [L210], evacuated to Canada

Morris [L215], Black Pioneer

Mott, Rosania [L218], evacuated to Canada

Munro, Hector [L219], evacuated to Canada

Mills, Daniel [P161], Eutaw Springs

Mott, Rosania [L218], evacuated to Canada

N

Nancy [L221], evacuated to Canada

Nancy [L221], daughter of Phillis, Goose Creek

Nancy [L222], evacuated to Canada

Nelson [P169], Eutaw Springs

Newsom, Moses [P170], Eutaw Springs

Nickens, James Sr. [P172], Eutaw Springs

O

Old Sandy [P208], Biggin Church

Old Dick [P78], Ninety Six

O'Leary, Jerry [*Dictionary of Irish Biography*, "Small, Tony"], London

Overton, Daniel [P176], Eutaw Springs

P

Paris [L229], evacuated to Canada

Peas, Tom [P180], enslaved by Henry Laurens

Pebbles, Andrew [P180], Eutaw Springs

Perkins, George [P182], Eutaw Springs

Perkins, Jacob [P183], Eutaw Springs

Peter [L236], evacuated to Canada

Peter [L237], Black Dragoon

Peter [L237], Black Dragoon

Peter [P185], Eutaw Springs

Peters, Frank [L239], Biggin Church

Peters, Nancy [L239], Biggin Church

Peters, Thomas [L240], London

Pettiford, Drury [P186], Eutaw Springs

Pettiford, Elias [P188], Eutaw Springs
Pettiford, George [P187], Eutaw Springs
Pettiford, George [P188], Eutaw Springs
Pettiford, Philip [P189], Eutaw Springs
Pettiford, William [P190], Eutaw Springs
Pinckney, Thomas [L242], His Majesty's Field Train of Artillery
Phillis [L241], Goose Creek
Polydose [L244], Jacksonboro
Pompey [P192], enslaved by John (or Henry) Laurens
Pompey [L245], Black Dragoon
Primes, Record [P194], Eutaw Springs
Primus [L248], Black Dragoon
Primus [L249], Gadsden's Wharf
Primus [L249], Black Dragoon
Prince [L250], Biggin Bridge
Prince [L251], Black Dragoon
Pugh, David [P195], Eutaw Springs
Punch [L254], evacuated to Canada

Q

R

Ranly, Joseph [L259], His Majesty's Field Train of Artillery
Reed, Benjamin [P199], Eutaw Springs
Reed, Willis [P200], South Carolina Line
Reid, Shadrack [P200], South Carolina Line
Rice, Thomas [L262], His Majesty's Field Train of Artillery
Robin [L267], Quartermaster, Black Dragoon
Robinson, James [L268], evacuated to Canada
Robinson, James [P203], Eutaw Springs
Robinson, John [L269], London
Rutledge, Flora [L272], evacuated to Canada
Ruth [L272] [P206], "arch bitch," [friend and lover of Tony Small in this
creative nonfiction]

S

Sam, Miller [L277][P207], Huck's Defeat

Sampson, Samuel [L279], evacuated to Canada

Sampson, Stephen [L279], evacuated to Canada

Samuel [L289], Black Dragoon

Sarah [L282], Black Pioneer

Sayey [McKelvey, *Index to Inventories*], enslaved by McKelvey

Scippio, Sergeant [L286], Black Dragoon

Scot, Roger [L288], joined British forces

Scott, Emanuel [P210], Eutaw Springs

Scott, Isom [P211], Eutaw Springs

Simpson, William [L295], evacuated to Canada

Shields, George [L292], evacuated to Canada

Shields, Thomas [L292], evacuated to Canada

Shields, Daphne [L292], evacuated to Canada

Shingleton, Archy [L292], His Majesty's Field Train of Artillery

Shingleton, Charles [L292], His Majesty's Field Train of Artillery

Shingleton, Jesse [L293], Royal Artillery Department

Shubrick, Patty [L293], Shubrick's Plantation

Slain, Tom [L295], His Majesty's Field Train of Artillery

[Small], Tony [L327], "faithful Tony"

Smith, Jacob [L297], His Majesty's Field Train of Artillery

Smith, James [P214], Eutaw Springs

Snow, William [L300], London

Solomon [L302], evacuated to Canada

Spelman, Aaron [P217], Black Pioneer, Ninety Six, Eutaw Springs

Stedwell, Robert [L304], Bacon's Bridge

Stepney [McKelvey, *Index to Inventories*], enslaved by McKelvey

Stewart, John [L306], evacuated to Canada

Stone, Joe [L308], evacuated to Canada

Stringer, Mingo [P222], Eutaw Springs

Sweat, Abraham [P223], Eutaw Springs

T

Taburn, Joel [P225], Eutaw Springs

Talbot, Joseph [L313], evacuated to Canada

Talbot, Nancy [L314], evacuated to Canada

Titus, Ishmael [P233], Camden

Tom [L325], Black Dragoon

Toney, John [P237], Eutaw Springs

Toney [P326], Black Dragoon

Tony [Small][L327], "faithful Tony," as described in the Draper manuscript

Tim [L321], evacuated from Canada

U

V

W

Waite, Amy [L331], evacuated to Canada

Ward, Linus [L335], His Majesty's Field Train of Artillery

Waring, Will [L338], Dorchester

Warwich [L336], evacuated to Canada

Wedder, Sam [L339], Goose Creek

Williams, John [L352], evacuated to Canada

Williams, Sally [L353], evacuated to Canada

Wilson, David [P250], Black Pioneer, Ninety Six, Eutaw Springs

Withers, Timothy [L356], Goose Creek

Wright, Samuel [L357], evacuated to Canada

X

Y

Z

Zanger, Ned [L360]

———— ⟡ ————

IDENTITY OF TONY SMALL

Tony was probably born free since he was free to travel, specifically to wander about on the battlefield after the Battle of Eutaw Springs, as he did according to Draper Manuscript, 6VV 321 (**Exhibit 1**). Also, Tony was probably free since Lord Edward's letters do not mention any difficulty in getting Tony out of Charleston with him. After he replaced Clinton as commander-in-chief, Sir Guy Carlton ordered Leslie to make a list of blacks who were expressly taken, rather than freed, by the British army. The list by Leslie accounts only for black loyalists who belonged to patriots whose estates were stripped by the British. Carlton's order to Leslie makes no mention of black loyalists who joined the army by proclamation and whose continued freedom was not guaranteed.

The list by Leslie has not survived, unlike *The Book of Negroes*, Carleton's own more famous list of approximately three thousand blacks who sailed from New York for various British colonies, mainly Nova Scotia.

Approximately one thousand two hundred blacks, ill treated in Nova Scotia, left ten years later to settle Freetown, Sierra Leone.

The Small family is not listed among the approximately six hundred families in Paul Heinegg, *Free African Americans of North Carolina, Virginia, and South Carolina from the Colonial Period to About 1820*, Vols. I and II, 5th edn. Baltimore: Clearfield, Genealogical Publishing Co., Inc., 2005.

Of course, Tony could simply have escaped slavery and, after saving Lord Edward Fitzgerald, been evacuated from Charleston with Lord Edward on 5 May 1782. No record states that Lord Edward paid a price to anyone who might have owned Tony before Lord Edward was permitted to leave Charleston with him. No one named Tony is listed among the McKelvey inventory of enslaved people, below, and notes to Appendix I.

There is, however, a record of a black man named Tony who purchased his own freedom in 1777 from John Rose. This Tony may have been Tony Small before he took a last name. In any event, whether Tony Small is born free or whether he is the certain Tony who bought his own freedom, the effect is the same at the time when Tony Small meets Lord Edward.

According to Brent Howard Holcomb, a professional genealogist and editor of *The South Carolina Magazine of Ancestral Research*, little or no evidence exists in public records about African Americans during the time of the Revolutionary War. Such is especially true on the loyalist side. Nearly all South Carolina records are based on ownership of property, and since Tony Small probably owned no property, no public record of him exists.

South Carolina Miscellaneous Records, Main series, turns up no evidence of Tony Small. This series begins in 1729 and continues until 1825. It covers the entire province or state of South Carolina until 1791 at which time the Columbia series begins, covering the upper division of the state. Holcomb found no evidence of Tony Small or of simply Tony in the "S" entries from 1775–1790 (pages 39–95 of the "S" entries) and the "T" entries from 1773–1790 (pages 11–30 of the "T" entries). Holcomb found no entries in the period for anyone named Small, but he did find one entry for a man named Tony in Miscellaneous Records, Volume RR, pages 555-556 (South Carolina Archives microfilm ST374A). In 1777, this Tony paid a certain John Rose of Charles Town £580 for his freedom:

"To all Christian People to whom these Presents shall come, be seen or made known, I John Rose of Charles Town in South Carolina, Gentleman, send Greeting. Know ye that for & in consideration of the Sum of five hundred & Eighty Pounds lawful current Money of South Carolina to me in hand before the Insealing & delivery of these Presents well & truly paid by Tony a Black Man (and at and immediately before the delivery hereof my Slave), the said John Rose have made manumitted, Liberated & set free the said Tony, & for myself and Heirs Executors & Administrators do covenant & grant to & with the said Tony that neither myself, the said John Rose, nor my heirs Executors or Administrators shall or will at any time or times hereafter Claim or Demand any manner or Right or property in the said Black Man Tony, but of and from the same shall be forever barred by these presents. And I do declare and make known by this present Writing that the said Tony is absolutely entitled to all the protection of the Laws and every immunity by the Constitution or Customs of South Carolina granted to free Black Men, Mustizoes or Mulattoes. In Writing whereof I have hereunto set my hand and Seal at Charles Town this fifth day of September in the Year of our Lord One thousand seven hundred & Seventy Seven before Credible Witnesses Testifying the same. John Rose LS"

About a year later, on 22 September 1778, the document is witnessed by Philip Tidyman and Ripley Singleton and proved by oath of Ripley Singleton before William Nisbett, J. P.

Tony Small, c. 1760–1804, lived and died around the same time as Lord Edward who was born on 15 October 1763 and died on 4 June 1798. Small left no footprints in South Carolina other than those he left on the battlefield at Eutaw Springs. No burial records of family members or anything else exist in state or local records in South Carolina. Apart from military excursions with Lord Edward in the West Indies, Gibraltar, and Canada, Small lived in Ireland, France, Belgium, and London where he is probably buried. No record of his life is known to exist outside of Fitzgerald family letters, the Draper manuscript, and references in Moore and MacDermott. Our Tony Small is mentioned once in the Revolutionary War romance novels of

William Gilmore Simms. In the late eighteenth century, there were between three thousand and five thousand blacks living in London, or about one percent of the population. In all of Ireland there were between one thousand and three thousand.

Like Dubliners, Londoners certainly would have taken notice of Tony. His residence at No. 10 Air Street, Piccadilly, London, between Sackville Street and Piccadilly Circus, is a short distance from St. James Church, Piccadilly. William Blake who wrote "The Little Black Boy" in *Songs of Innocence*, 1789, lived not too far away on South Molton Street, Mayfair. If Tony were ever in the company of Dr. Johnson's servant Francis Barber, who died shortly before Tony, or in the company of other blacks in London, there is no known record. Evidence of Tony's existence in London remains the task of further research.

Limited research on Ancestry.com by Pamela White, Northampton, Massachusetts, shows an entry in the parish register of St. Mary's Wimbledon, that an Anthony Small, the name Tony used to sign his letter to Lady Sophia, was buried on 14 May 1804:

"Anthony Small, a Black, aged 40, buried."

Surrey History Centre; Woking, Surrey, England; *Surrey Church of England Parish Registers*; Reference: *P5/1/8.*

Wimbledon is about six miles from Air Street, Piccadilly. In the early nineteen century it seems to have been largely rural with some grand estates. Tony Small might have been visiting someone there in search of employment with horses when he died. Without money, he would not have been returned for burial at St. James, Piccadilly.

Both Tony Small and the land of Raphoe Barony and adjacent property in South Carolina on which the Battle of Eutaw Springs was fought and on which Tony may have been born have a shared uncertain genealogy. As set out in John Locke's (and Lord Ashley's) 1669 *Fundamental Constitutions of Carolina*, the nobles who received grants of land from Charles II, pursuant to a charter dated 24 March 1663, were Proprietors, Landgraves, and Cassiques. The Proprietors and local nobility took forty percent of each county, leaving sixty percent for the freemen and settlers of each province.

Locke's five drafts of his *Constitutions* are deemed "an extraordinary scheme of forming an aristocratic government of a colony of adventurers in the wild woods, among savages and wild beasts." After the *Constitutions* were abandoned in 1700 or 1705, having never been adopted, and after the Lords Proprietors transferred their interests to the crown in 1729, the existence of Proprietors and provisions for Landgraves and Cassiques ceased altogether. If a barony did exist, however, it would have been an estate actually granted or agreed to be granted by 1729 to a Landgrave or Cassique. Nonetheless, some Lowcountry properties continued to be described, as they are today, sometimes inaccurately, as baronies. Baronies around Charleston included the Wadboo, Quenby (aka Quinby), and Fairlawn Baronies, and the Ashley Barony named for Anthony Lord Ashley, Earl of Shaftsbury. Moncks Corner was named for George Monck, Duke of Albemarle.

To find out more about the McKelvey land on which Tony Small may have lived, and on which the Battle of Eutaw Springs was fought, one must look further into the land genealogy of Raphoe Barony (**Map 1**). John Bayley, Esq., a Landgrave and Irishman from Tipperary, paid the council of the Lords Proprietors the sum of £100 on 16 August 1698 and received a plat for forty-eight thousand acres along the Santee River near Eutaw Springs. At his death, his landgrave's patent, along with his landgraveship, descended to his son and heir of the same name. He, too, never came to South Carolina to see his property, but instead gave Power of Attorney to Alexander Trench of Charleston to sell it all. Trench arranged with the Surveyor General to have the land surveyed prior to sale, pursuant to general directions of the council of the Lords Proprietors. However, Trench did not follow through to make a direct application to the council, but instead simply surveyed out a parcel of land and then annexed the plat to a deed of conveyance from himself, as attorney for John Bayley, to the purchaser. The purchaser took the land to which Bayley was entitled under his patent. No direct grant from the Lords Proprietor appears for that specific parcel of land.

Most old records of such plats prior to 1732 have disappeared. Consequently, titles from John Bayley cannot be traced back to a definite grant from the Lords Proprietors. They simply commence with a deed of conveyance from Trench who bargained off a parcel of land and conveyed the land to the purchasing party. That party necessarily bought land that had not yet been surveyed by Trench. The upshot of all this is that it is unknown when the Raphoe Barony was surveyed out. No grant for it is on record. No record of transfer of the barony exists from John Bayley or anyone claiming under him.

Although some of the Battle of Eutaw Springs occurred within Raphoe Barony, the main battle ground at Eutaw Springs does not lie within lines of Raphoe Barony, but instead lies in adjacent acreage to the west. As in the case of acreage within the barony itself, as determined by John Bailey, no record exists of a conveyance of the adjacent property by the Lords Proprietors to John Strode (aka Stroud). Nonetheless, previous to the laying out of the barony on 15 September 1705, John Strode was issued, by an unrecorded party, three grants of four hundred acres. Each lay to the west of the barony and, like the barony itself, south of the Santee River. Strode's property formed a solid body of land of one thousand two hundred acres in total. In the eastern most grant were at least two springs known as the Eutaw springs, one big and one small. The old plat spells it as "Hutaw." It is the actual land on which Tony Small may have been born and reared some sixty years after John Strode was issued his grants.

Understanding the relation between Barbados and the Lowcountry of South Carolina is crucial to understanding the history of both black and white families, including Tony's. Settlement of the Lowcountry of South Carolina was by way of Barbados when English planters and their servants and enslaved blacks, undetermined by name and number, landed at Albermarle Point, today called Charles Town Landing, in April and May 1670. Soon thereafter these planters formed the Goose Creek Men.

The name of the settlement by 1671 was called Charles Town and remained such when it moved across the Ashley River ten years later to Oyster Point. When it was incorporated on the peninsula in 1783, the name of the town was changed to Charleston. The present narrative uses only the name Charleston and thus ignores the historical distinction between Charles Town and Charleston.

Some of the first settlers may have spent little time in Barbados en route from Great Britain to South Carolina, or "South Carolana" as it was then called, but their life style quickly adapted to Barbadian customs. Barbados heavily influenced the development of society in South Carolina. The social order in Barbados was based on African slavery. A gentleman from Barbados—if not utterly destroyed by vanity and fashion—was civil, generous, sociable, and well supported on the backs of no fewer than seven or eight hundred enslaved blacks. Early South Carolina was thoroughly English as traditions and customs of the mother country continually landed on its shores from Barbados, along with enslaved blacks brought from Barbados with their masters.

The names of some of the first settlers, if not the very ones who landed at Albermarle Point in 1670, are known. They were sent by the Proprietors from Barbados—men and women named Colleton, Yeamans, Middleton, Gibbes, Foster, Robinson, Elliott, Fenwick, and others, including Strode. (Strode may have descended from the family of "Philosophical Strode," to whom the fourteen-century English poet Geoffrey Chaucer dedicated his long poem *Troilus and Criseyde*.)

No one knows the total number of Barbadians who arrived in the 1670s and 1680s, but by some accounts approximately two or three hundred Barbadians with their hundreds of enslaved blacks migrated to Carolina between 1670 and 1682. By other accounts, approximately fifty-four percent or seven hundred twenty-five of the one thousand three hundred forty-three white settlers who immigrated to South Carolina between 1670 and 1690 were probably from Barbados. Eighteen members of a family by the name of Small are recorded in Barbados baptismal records between 1637 and 1800. Other Small family members are recorded among wills and administrations and marriages that make no distinction between blacks and whites.

The Barbados sugar planters of the seventeenth century introduced Negro slavery to South Carolina. They brought with them a commercial, materialistic, and exploitative mentality. Yet, these Anglican Barbadians—whom Mathew Arnold would have called barbarians—were of a higher sort socially and economically than the families who later came directly from England and Europe. For their boom-or-bust way of life, getting and spending, laying waste their time, living recklessly and dying young, migrants from Barbados created the first real "wild west" in America.

Extant records of the first families from Barbados suggest that their history is nearly as unreliable as that of the families of enslaved Africans they brought with them. In any event, Tony Small's ancestors may have settled in the Lowcountry as enslaved labor brought from Barbados with Hugh or John Strode in 1670 or sometime shortly thereafter. The Small family is, of course, never mentioned by name, and members of the family may not at that time have even taken the sir name of Small. None of the names of blacks in Raphoe Barony at the time of Strode are known. The point is that their numbers were probably quite small—giving them a rather elite status in comparison to other blacks who arrived later—until rice was introduced from Angola to South Carolina in the early 1690s. Then thousands of enslaved blacks were imported to work in the labor-intensive industry, and the first black Americans began to be absorbed into the total black population.

Tony's ancestors may have arrived as men and women of mixed race, since numerous such people in Barbados indicate widespread miscegenation at that time. Also, South Carolina had a higher incidence of interracial sexual unions than that of other colonies.

At the time of the Battle of Eutaw Springs on 8 September 1781, Tony's family may have been working for over a hundred years on plantations that passed from Strode (to McPherson) to Kinloch to McKelvey/O'Neal/McKelvey. If so, Tony's lineage establishes him among the very first families in America. Furthermore, his family's initial association (albeit as master and servant, enslaved or not) with an upper class Anglican Barbadian family, and with subsequent land owners, might explain how this remarkable black man (by that time probably free) could retain the friendship and devotion of an Irish lord. He and Lord Edward, who was at the top of political and social ranking among the Anglican Protestant Ascendency in Ireland and England, may have shared a cultural affinity. Although Strode was English, McKelvey was Irish.

Tony was an individual who was smart, ambitious, and possessed a flexible sense of place, as all smart people do, white or black, regardless of their station and sense of pride. The present narrative presents a Tony who speaks his mind, as in creative exchanges with Jane Elliott and William Washington, and is informed of contemporaneous events, notably in his conversation with John Laurens. If Tony seems too much a renaissance man for his sophistication and knowledge of the times and issues, one must ask, why not?

His family history to some degree may account for his talents. Among the first families of blacks and whites in America, Tony and his family may have had a sense of genealogical superiority over others who arrived later in the Lowcountry, just as blacks and whites in genealogical societies have today. The truly first Americans who were on Kiawah Island near Charleston at least four thousand years ago must look on such a concept of place as bitterly ironic.

A sense of self-confidence and statue could easily have been conveyed by Tony's family, even amid the humiliations of slavery, at least for the first few generations after Strode's grant. Also, oral accounts of Tony's family could have been brought from Africa to embellish claims of prestige and power in the new world.

That coherence and claim of elitism within a black family like Tony's could have continued up to the American Civil War of 1861–1864 when much black oral history was lost and black family unity was almost totally destroyed. Shirley Small, a current resident of Eutaw Springs who, along with her brother Tony may or may not be a descendant, acknowledges that her family history begins after the Civil War. Lord Edward probably admired in Tony a personality and character that matched his own far better documented nobility. He saw nothing superficial or foppish in the African American and, later, in aboriginal Canadians, qualities of the white ruling classes in Dublin, London, and Paris that so repulsed Lord Edward. Tony matched Lord Edward as a man with many qualities. In short, Tony was more than an ornament, a romantic "noble savage," or a practicum from Rousseau's *Emile*, Lord Edward's primer in his youth at his family's seaside villa, Frescati, on Dublin Bay. The two recognized each other as kindred spirits on equal moral grounds.

The John Strode who held grants of one thousand two hundred acres west of Raphoe Barony on which Tony was probably born began to acquire land in the South Carolina Lowcountry as early as 1695 when he was granted five hundred acres of land on Fosters Creek. When he died prior to 1712,

John Strode left his widow Susannah an estate of about one thousand six hundred acres which he acquired by grant or purchase. At that point, three tracts of Strode land of four hundred acres each, or a total of one thousand two hundred acres, may have passed to John McPherson of Charleston before passing to the Honorable James Kinloch, son of Sir Francis Kinloch Bart, of Gilmerton in East Lothian, Scotland, who married Susannah; or the Strode grants and purchases passed directly to Kinloch by virtue of his marriage to Susannah. In any event, it is these one thousand two hundred acres lying to the west of Raphoe Barony that were the original relevant Strode acreage.

On 26 December 1749 James Kinloch conveyed two hundred acres, namely the southern half of the eastern most grant of four hundred acres of the original one thousand two hundred Strode acreage, to Margaret McKelvey O'Neal, widow of Charles O'Neal. (She is identified in this book as Maggie McKelvey.) Those two hundred acres conveyed to Margaret O'Neal included the two Eutaw springs, the big and the small. It is this tract of two hundred acres in the northeast section of the original Strode grant that is the center of the battle site thirty-one years later.

The remaining one thousand acres of the original grant of one thousand two hundred acres to John Strode, were conveyed by James Kinloch on 5 February 1750 to his son Francis who on 2 December 1756 conveyed the remaining strip of the eastern most Strode grant, namely the two hundred acres north of Margaret O'Neal's property and the part fronting the Santee River, to George Austin. As the original Strode property of one thousand two hundred acres stood at the end of 1756 and approaching the time of Tony Small's birth, two hundred acres were owned by Margaret O'Neal, two hundred by George Austin, and the remaining eight hundred acres by Francis Kinloch.

When in 1753 Margaret McKelvey O'Neal, widow of Charles O'Neal, married her cousin James McKelvey, the combined O'Neal-McKelvey plantations spread out over thousands of acres. Along the Santee and within Raphoe Barony, one O'Neal-McKelvey plantation, Brackey Plantation, was nearest to the original Strode grant. Prior to the Revolutionary War, neighboring plantations running down the southeast edge of the Santee River included Old and New Dorchee owned by Kinloch-Gaillard, Walnut

Grove owned by Gabriel Marion, Francis Marion's brother, and Pond Bluff owned by Francis Marion. A plantation owned by Thomas Sumter was among those lying just across the river to the west.

Just off the southeast corner of Raphoe Barony lay Lawson Pond, the grounds of which were conveyed in 1799 and 1800 from Margaret McKelvey's four daughters and joint heirs to Philip Couturier. Lawson Pond remains in the Couturier family today.

While parts of the Raphoe Barony lay vacant, Francis Kinloch on 4 May 1757 conveyed the remaining eight hundred acres of the adjacent Strode grants to Thomas Lynch (probably the second Thomas Lynch of that name, Thomas Lynch, Sr., 1726–76, father of Thomas Lynch, Jr., 1749–79, who married Thomas Shubrick's daughter Elizabeth and who signed the Declaration of Independence). Twelve years later, on 19 April 1769, Thomas Lynch and Isaac Motte (to whom Lynch, married to Hannah Motte, apparently conveyed partial title) conveyed title of all eight hundred acres to brothers Peter and James Sinkler. At some time the Kinlochs, Lynches, or Sinklers gave the name "Belvidere" to the eight hundred acre tract. The Battle of Eutaw Springs was fought on much of Belvidere, including some one hundred thirty-five acres which continue to be owned by descendants of the Sinkler family.

In light of numerous contemporary accounts of the Battle of Eutaw Springs and recent research on land genealogy by Richard Watkins and James Queen, existing foundations within the state park commemorating the battle may be traces of a brick house on a McKelvey Plantation. A central part of the action at the Battle of Eutaw Springs was fought around such a brick house which was situated at the head of the lower of two springs of Eutaw Creek that flowed into the Santee River. The name, if it had one, of the McKelvey Plantation is unknown.

An 1854 map or plan of William H. Sinkler's land shows "Remnants of Old Brick House" near the two spring heads and a pair of cross swords marking "Battle fought 8 September 1781" (**Map 2**). The Old Brick House was probably Maggie McKelvey's brick house, site of the battle. It was built on McKelvey land rather than on Belvidere. The entire plan that includes

Map 1 and others were donated by the Sinkler family to the Caroliniana Library in Columbia, South Carolina.

None of the Sinklers lived in the Eutaw Creek area during the Revolutionary War, but by 1808 William Sinkler's Plantation was up and running. The Sinkler "Negro Houses" shown on Map 5 could have been in place near the McKelvey brick house during the time of the battle, but they more likely were built by William Sinkler after the battle. Sinkler did not build his house where Map 2 marks the "Remnants of an Old Brick House" where the "Battle [was] fought 8 September 1781."

A map by William Faden and William Gerard DeBrahm in 1780 indicates that a "tavern" once stood near the banks of the Santee not far from Nelson's Ferry (**Map 3**). Map 3 also shows "Bourdel," Burdell's Tavern, through which the American army passed en route to Eutaw Springs which is not shown. A tavern located near the ferry would have been a good place for passengers to have a drink while waiting to get cross the Santee River on their way from Charleston to Camden.

White's Tavern is shown on the map of Charleston District, South Carolina, surveyed by Charles Vignoles and Henry Ravenel in 1820 and improved for Mills' Atlas in 1825 (**Map 4**). It is located several miles southeast of the battle site. Map 4 shows Eutaw Springs and a Sinkler house, southeast of Eutaw Creek, at a road crossing of the Nelson's Ferry Road. Map 4 is held in the South Carolina Room, Charleston County Library. Drawn forty years after the battle, it shows the route possibly used by Lieutenant Colonel Coates as he withdrew from Moncks Corner to Charleston.

The first of two maps or plans, both dated two years earlier on 20 May 1818, shows a tract of land conveyed by Colonel J. B. Richardson to William Sinkler that indicates "Negro Houses" adjacent to Sinkler's house just south of Eutaw Creek (**Map 5**). (A second plan dated 20 May 1818, not shown here, indicates Mrs. Margaret Sinkler's house that sits farther north between Eutaw Creek and the Santee River, but no Negro houses are indicated.)

In any event, the foundations of the brick house on the battleground site, which commemorates only a fraction—about eight acres—of the entire area on which the battle was fought, is probably not the foundation of a tavern.

According to David Reuwer who has done extensive study of the foundations of the brick edifice on the battle site, whether house or tavern, exact measurements cannot yet be determined. According to Reuwer, it had two stories and a garret and rested on piers. Only one basement brick pier of the edifice has been dug out, and the rest is yet to be excavated (**Map 6**).

Charles Fraser's *A Charleston Sketchbook, 1796–1806*, incorrectly identifies the McKelvey brick house as a tavern, although Sinkler family tradition still maintains the structure was, indeed, a tavern (**Exhibit 2**).

The gist of all this is that privately owned maps, now donated to the Caroliniana Library by the Sinkler family, support the research of Richard Watkins and James Queen on land genealogy. Watkins and Queen suggest that the battle may have been fought on land owned by Maggie McKelvey. If that is the case, a plausible scenario is that the brick house at the center of the battle was at the time one of several McKelvey plantation houses, probably abandoned by Maggie and most blacks as Lieutenant Colonel Alexander Stewart's British army approached. The "Negro Houses" shown in 1818 on Map 5, however, are not mentioned in any report of the battle and are not shown on any map of the battle itself. If any existed at the time of the battle, they were insignificant compared to the brick house. Negro houses were a prominent feature on maps to indicate the wealth of the plantation owner and usually lined the access road to the plantation house to show visitors how many enslaved workers the owner had. They were badges of prestige and clearly visible for the owner to keep an eye on them. In battles and skirmishes such as the one at Shubrick's Plantation Negro houses were a prominent feature. Even so, Tony took Lord Edward to his hut to tend to his wound after the battle, and he could not have traveled far from the battle field to his house with his noble patient on his back.

———— ∽ ————

LORD EDWARD'S TWELVE MILITARY ACTIONS IN THE SOUTHERN CAMPAIGN

T he twelve military actions in which Lord Edward Fitzgerald participated during the Southern Campaign of the American Revolution, or the War for American Independence as it is known in Great Britain, framed Lord Edward's military mind which helped direct the United Irishmen's Uprising of 1796–98. These actions, in turn, frame the creative nonfiction of Tony Small and other African Americans in the Lowcountry who observe and participate in them.

During the eleven months from the time he landed in Charleston on 3 June 1781 until the time he sailed away on 5 May 1782, Lord Edward Fitzgerald was in South Carolina with the 19th Regiment of Foot. He was definitely at Greene's Second Siege of Ninety Six where he was aide-de-camp to Rawdon and definitely at the Battle of Eutaw Springs where he was wounded and saved by Tony Small. Lord Edward very credibly was in other battles or skirmishes during Raid of the Dog Days in the Lowcountry in July 1781. British military action in the Southern Campaign in which Lord Edward and all or elements of the 19th Regiment of Foot participated includes the following. *A New and Accurate Map of the Province of South Carolina in North America, 1779* is used here to indicate Lord Edward's military actions (**Map 7**). An asterisk indicates no shots or sword play by Lord Edward:

Second Siege of Ninety Six (approximately 17 – 19 June 1781)

Pursuit of Greene's army after Ninety Six (21 June – 22 June 1781)

Friday's (aka Fridig's) Ferry (route from Ninety Six, after 21 June 1781, prior to Orangeburg)

Orangeburg* (approximately 8 – 10 July 1781, but no later than 12 July 1781)

Goose Creek* (15 July 1781)

Moncks Corner* (15 July 1781)

Biggin Church (16 July 1781)

Huger's Bridge (17 July 1781)

Quinby Bridge (17 July 1781)

Shubrick's Plantation (17 July 1781)

Siege of Orangeburg (25 July 1781)

Eutaw Springs (8 September 1781)

[Charleston, September 1781 to May 1782]

These events took Lieutenant Lord Edward in three general directions (**Map 8**). Between 7 June and 18 July 1781, leaving most of Stewart's 3rd Regiment, the 30th Regiment, and Coates's 19th Regiment of Foot at British Headquarters in Moncks Corner and in the garrison in Charleston, Lord Edward first went with a Light Infantry Company to Ninety Six, South Carolina. The Light Infantry Company was one of the two flank companies of the 19th Foot which, combined with flank companies of the other two regiments, formed Rawdon's flank battalion under the command of Major

John Majoribanks. Rawdon arrived in Ninety Six in time to relieve loyalist commander Lieutenant Colonel John Harris Cruger, forcing Greene to give up his assault on Star Fort at Ninety Six on 19 June 1781. Greene withdrew shortly before Rawdon arrived. At Ninety Six, Lord Edward was Rawdon's aide-de-camp.

Second, after arriving with Rawdon at Ninety Six on 21 June 1781, Lord Edward and the two flank companies of the 19th Foot initially went with Rawdon to chase Greene who may have gone northeast as far as the Enoree and Tyger Rivers in a circuitous route back to the High Hills east of the Wateree River. They may have failed to catch him by a few hours at a ford on the Enoree near its confluence with the Broad River. They turned around a day later on 22 June. Then, returning to Ninety Six and abandoning Star Fort, Lord Edward left with Rawdon and the two flank companies of the 19th Foot to go to Friday's Ferry en route back to Orangeburg. There they met nominal resistance. At Orangeburg Rawdon met Cruger, who came down after evacuating Ninety Six, and Stewart, who came up from Moncks Corner and Dorchester on 8–10 July. No skirmish or battle likely took place at Orangeburg at that time (but William Gilmore Simms, below, writes about a skirmish involving Lord Edward). Greene could not entice Rawdon into a fight before Stewart's reinforcements arrived and, in any case, both sides were too weakened by their action at Ninety Six and long marches thereafter to do much more fighting.

Lord Edward then left Orangeburg, probably on 10 or 11 July, and went with Rawdon and a small detachment of his corps on a secret mission to take Rawdon, who was ill, to Charleston as soon as possible in order to evacuate him to England. Their route may have included Dorchester and Moncks Corner where Fitzgerald separated from Rawdon.

Lord Edward's progress en route from Orangeburg to Goose Creek and Moncks Corner was permitted by Rawdon who relieved Fitzgerald of his duty as aide-de-camp in order for Fitzgerald to return to his regiment and help Lieutenant Colonel Coates withdraw from the British garrison at Moncks Corner to the main one in Charleston. Military actions in which Lord Edward took part may include actions at Goose Creek and Moncks Corner, and possibly Dorchester and Quarter House, between 12–15 July 1781. Raid of the Dog Days is what William Gilmore Simms calls the action by patriots on Coates and the 19th Foot saw all along their route as they evacuated the British garrison at Moncks Corner and withdrew to Charleston.

More certainly, during Raid of the Dog Days, Lord Edward was with Coates at Biggin Church on 16 July and in the battles at Huger's Bridge and Quinby Bridge and Shubrick's Plantation on 17 July 1781. Ruins of Biggin Church still stand (**Exhibit 3**). The east branch of the Cooper River is formed by the confluence of Huger Creek and Quinby Creek where modern bridges replace those near the battle sites. The day after the battle at Shubrick's Plantation, Lord Edward probably returned to Charleston with Lieutenant Colonel Coates and the 19th Foot. Reinforcements under Colonel Paston Gould, which were sent to Shubrick's Plantation, retreated with them. These were the British impending reinforcements of Colonel Gould sent by Colonel Balfour that forced Sumter to attack too soon and without artillery at Shubrick's Plantation.

Third, Lord Edward almost immediately marched from Charleston back northwest to Orangeburg where he joined Lieutenant Colonel Alexander Stewart's army and took part in action there on 25 July 1781, about a month after first passing through Orangeburg from Ninety Six with Rawdon. He was again among the two flank companies of the 19th Foot under Majoribanks, but he may have been detached to the 96th Regiment of Foot at Orangeburg which had been left by Rawdon on or about 11 July to protect Orangeburg. Sometime after 25 July in Orangeburg, Lord Edward returned to duty with the 19th Foot and marched with Stewart to Eutaw Springs. The final major action Lord Edward saw was at the Battle of Eutaw Springs.

After the Battle of Eutaw Springs, Lieutenant Colonel Stewart and relief troops sent from Fairlawn and Moncks Corner under Major Archibald McArthur, 71st Regiment of Foot, made a hasty retreat back to the British garrison at Charleston, their exact route unknown. Nothing more is recorded of any military activity by Lord Edward in the Lowcountry. It is possible that after fully recovering from his wound, Lord Edward may have participated in foraging parties and skirmishes around Charleston between October 1781 and May 1782. He took Tony Small with him when he evacuated Charleston with the 19th Foot and sailed for Barbados, Antigua, and St. Lucia on 5 May 1782.

————— ∽ —————

Lord Edward Fitzgerald in the Historical Novels of William Gilmore Simms

I n writing his Revolutionary War romances between 1835 and 1867, *The Forayers: Or, the Raid of the Dog Days*; *Eutaw: A Sequel to The Forayers*; *Mellichampe: A Legend of the Santee*; *The Partisan: A Romance of the Revolution*; and *The Scout: Or The Black Riders of Congaree*, among others, Charleston native William Gilmore Simms (1806–1870) talked to members of the African American communities near Eutaw Springs whose oldest members were participants in the war. Simms created the phrase "Raid of the Dog Days" in his novels to describe the series of patriots' engagements in July 1781 against the 19th Regiment of Foot as it withdrew from Moncks Corner to Charleston. American militia, cavalry and infantry, dogged

Coates's troops in one long continuous string of skirmishes and battles in insufferable heat unfit even for dogs.

Simms is among the first to write about the Revolutionary War from the point of view of ordinary people, poor whites and blacks. For modern readers, his support of slavery is reprehensible. Nonetheless, in his narratives of the eighteenth-century civil war between Whigs and Tories, Simms is close to at least one oral history still recited by present-day black Charlestonians, namely, the story of "Lord Edward" told by the manager of Belk-Robinson Department Store in Charleston in the 1940s and 50s. By his own account, Simms learned local history from his grandmother who witnessed events of the war. He also picked up stories "at the knees of those who were young spectators in the grand panorama of our Revolution ... and each had details of the local struggle which were as interesting as they were veracious." He interviewed members of Francis Marion's brigade, among others, and talked to an eye-witness to Isaac Hayne's hanging. "In 'helping' history he merely supplied 'from the *probable*, the apparent deficiencies of the *actual*.' The finished product was not romance, but history enlivened or made dramatic by art."

Simms is an historian as well as story-teller in his Revolutionary War romances. He firmly places Lord Edward Fitzgerald at Huger's Bridge and Quinby Bridge and Shubrick's Plantation on 17 July 1781. In *Eutaw*, Simms explains how Lord Edward gets from Orangeburg to Moncks Corner while transporting Lord Rawdon to Charleston for evacuation:

"Meanwhile, Lord Edward Fitzgerald has been required to join his regiment, the nineteenth, at Moncks Corner. His lordship no longer found it pleasant to serve as aide to a general whose liver is so much out of order as Rawdon's; and, being of an enterprising disposition besides and hearing vague rumors of a movement of Sumter's below—the movement on Murray's Ferry had reached his ears—he signified his desire to join his regiment, to which Rawdon readily listened. With a corps of forty horses, badly mounted, and mostly Loyalists, Fitzgerald succeeded in getting to Moncks Corner at the lucky interval, when all the American light parties, having struck down for the Ashley river and Goose Creek country, he found the roads tolerably clear."

Lord Edward's presence at Huger's and Quinby bridges and Shubrick's Plantation does not, however, rest on the Revolutionary War novels of Simms alone. That Lord Edward was at Huger's and Quinby Bridges and Shubrick's Plantation is also based on a report in Nisbet Balfour's letter book. The book of letters and dispatches includes a copy of a report, one Balfour made on behalf of Rawdon, to Sir Henry Clinton dated 20 July 1781, with a copy to Lord Germain. At the time Balfour writes from Charleston, Rawdon is already suffering from exhaustion and is evacuated the following day. Balfour writes that he is filing a dispatch that Rawdon would ordinarily have written himself. Rawdon is unable to write while he is at sea, but Rawdon himself will write at a later time when, Balfour says, "free communication with Lord Rawdon is open." Balfour's report summarizes major military actions conducted by Lord Rawdon from the landing of Irish reinforcements on 3 June 1781 to the eve of Rawdon's departure from Charleston on the *Warwick* on 21 July 1781.

Balfour attributes Sumter's withdrawal after the battle at Shubrick's Plantation on 17 July 1781 to the arrival of Gould's troops who marched from Charleston in response to news of the battle:

"On receiving this Intelligence, Colonel Gould, with about 700 men, marched from hence to sustain the 19th Regiment, and on his approach the enemy retired, but as Lord Rawdon is come down, with a small part of his Corps (Colonel Stewart being left in command of the rest), to Goose-Creek, I have some hopes he [Gould] may be able to intercept any Parties of them, that may attempt to get off that way."

This means that Rawdon—and his aide-de-camp Lord Edward Fitzgerald—already moved south from Orangeburg "with a small group of his Corps" and were in Goose Creek en route to Charleston sometime before 20 July and, possibly, as early as 13 July, the day after Greene gave up any thought of attacking Orangeburg. It was a decision that allowed Rawdon to hasten to Charleston. As Rawdon made his way to Charleston to be evacuated to London, Lord Edward traveled with him only as far as Goose Creek and from there went northeast to Moncks Corner, if not west from Goose Creek to Dorchester prior to its evacuation on 15 July, the day after Lee, Washington, Marion, and Sumter began to appear in force.

At Moncks Corner, Fitzgerald rejoined his regiment, the 19th Foot, under Lieutenant Colonel Coates and was in the middle of Raid of the Dog Days. He was in the running skirmishes at and along the road from Biggin Church to Huger's Bridge and on to Quinby Bridge and Shubrick's Plantation as the 19th Foot withdrew to Charleston. Lord Edward was in one constant fight all the way with no less than America's most famous cavalry units in full pursuit—Thomas Sumter, Francis Marion, "Light Horse Harry" Lee, Wade Hampton, Peter and Hugh Horry, Hezekiah Maham, Thomas Taylor, and Edward Lacey. No more famous adversaries in the war were more closely face-to-face.

In *Eutaw,* Simms offers a strict account of Lee's and Maham's attack on Coates's rear guard at Huger's Bridge and the skirmishes at Quinby Bridge and Shubrick's Plantation. It reads like an history text book and is presented without dramatic dialogue. It includes the heroics of Armstrong, Carrington, and Macaulay riding across the partially dismantled Quinby Bridge into Coates's howitzer waiting on the other side. Simms is writing as if he were a field officer filing a battle report.

Later in *Eutaw*, Simms' characters Porgy and Captain Peyre St. Julien discuss what might happen after it gets too dark for the Americans to fight at the skirmish at Shubrick's Plantation. For Simms, Lieutenant Lord Edward Fitzgerald is important enough to serve as a foil to his fictional patriot Captain St. Julien. One may even argue that Simms accedes to the fact that no real life American exists to match Lord Edward:

"'And what tomorrow?'

"'Sufficient for the day!—But we must go the rounds. If Coates be at all enterprising, he may beat up some of our drowsy sections with a warm bayonet tonight.'

"'Not he! But he has that dashing young Irishman, Fitzgerald, with him, who has spirit enough for the attempt. By the way, St. Julien, you had a pass or two with him today, at close quarters—that is to say, across the fence.'

"'But a pass!' said the taciturn St. Julien. 'It is the second time that we have crossed blades unprofitably.'

"'You have both reason to beware of the third passage,' said Porgy, 'I believe in the fate of threes! And so let us sip a little of this punch, which unites the sweet, the sour, and the strong! It would be almost justification for a man to get drunk tonight, particularly on such liquor, after so many mortifying disappointments today.'"

Simms is familiar with "the mournful history" of Lord Edward in Moore's 1831 biography, but Simms and Moore are independent sources arriving at generally consistent accounts. Simms's over-all account of Lord Edward must be given the same weight afforded to Moore's, simply because Simms interviewed South Carolinians who corroborate—and, at times—correct Moore.

In a note at the end of Chapter 27 in *Eutaw*, Simms corrects Moore who has Quinby Bridge and Shubrick's Plantation coming before the Second Siege of Ninety Six, not after it. But Simms thinks Lord Edward was not in the rear guard with Captain Colin Campbell, as Moore does, when the regimental silver was seized by Lee's Legion and Maham's dragoons. Speaking of Moore as "*our* historian," Simms comments:

"He does not indeed *say* that he saved the guard and the baggage, but he leaves this to be inferred, and this inference will be drawn from his statement by everyone who reads the passage in ignorance of the events. He is right as presenting Lord Edward at the bridge, and as being spiritedly engaged in covering it; but he again misrepresents him as being the person in command at the spot; when, in fact, Colonel Coates himself was present, and to his presence *our* historian ascribes much of the success of the British in saving the army. Fitzgerald was *in the rear of the main body*, but the rear-guard and baggage was a mile in his rear, and these were not saved, but lost; the Americans making large booty on the occasion; capturing the army chest with all its treasure, a thousand guineas, with a large body of stores besides, of the most useful description." Italics in the original.

But just as Simms himself varies from other sources—in this instance on the number of guineas taken: it was probably seven hundred and twenty, not a thousand—so does the present creative nonfiction take the liberty to follow Moore rather than Simms in putting the spirited Lord Edward in the middle of action in the rear guard.

Nonetheless, Simms must have interviewed those, including African Americans, who saw Lord Edward at Huger's and Quinby Bridges, Shubrick's

Plantation, and Orangeburg, just as Moore interviewed Irish and English contemporaries who knew Lord Edward. A notable difference is that Moore quotes extensively from letters to and from Lord Edward, whereas Simms has no such written sources. His sources are oral interviews of which he makes no independent record.

Simms mentions Tony only once, and his use of Lord Edward may be the only mention of Fitzgerald by name in any American source on the Revolutionary War. Most major historians today have never heard of either Lord Edward or Tony.

In *The Forayers*, Lord Edward is a suitor of Colonel Sinclair's daughter Carrie who has stolen his heart. With both men contending for the hand of Carrie, Simms again puts Lord Edward in direct conflict with Captain St. Julien in a fight between suitors. In early July 1781 during Rawdon's return from Ninety Six to Orangeburg where he meets Stewart and Coffin coming up from Charleston, Fitzgerald is put in command of a small corps of dragoons. Confronting St. Julien on patrol, he taunts him as the "gallant of Carrie Sinclair" before the two cavalry officers clash in an "embrace of sabres." Fitzgerald scatters when all combatants are surprised by the sudden arrival of Marion's men. This fictional account is the only American record of military action involving Lord Edward during the period between 8 and 10 July in Orangeburg, and the author of it is a Charlestonian. Simms admired Lord Edward enough to put him in direct conflict with his fictional hero St. Julien, just as Fitzgerald was in fact in conflict with Simms's real hero the Swamp Fox.

Lord Edward's reputation as a lady's man in Simms extends beyond Moore's Irish and English sources to include "a Miss Sanford, a lady of great beauty and wit, with whom he so flirted, just before coming to America, at the castle of Lord Shannon." And as "the story goes in Charleston, she is about to follow him to this country!" Miss Sanford is probably somebody Simms created for good measure, but his description of Lord Edward as "a young cavalier of very flexible affections" serves his purpose well.

Simms's fiction reflects a credible history of Lord Edward's activity in the Southern Campaign. Without a doubt Simms admired Lord Edward. He saw Fitzgerald as a man on a mission to gain fame, as well as a romantic lover.

American historians have simply lost what Simms knew about Lord Edward from oral traditions which were alive in the early nineteenth century. Most certainly Simms would have talked to African Americans, such as members of the Small (also, Smalls) family, a family whose descendants still live in and around Eutaw Springs generations after the battle. Yet even Simms is nearly silent about a member of that family who sailed away during the war with the Irish nobleman.

NOTES

———∽———

N otes exclude commentaries and histories of black patriots and loyalists found in Bobby Gilmer Moss and Michael Charles Scoggins, *African-American Loyalists in the Southern Campaign of the American Revolution*, 2005, and *African-American Patriots in the Southern Campaign of the American Revolution*, 2004. Notes cite less well-known sources or those of particular significance. Because some entries are based on pension applications made years after actual dates of service, Moss and Scoggins acknowledge that "statements contained in these documents are not always historically accurate," notably those of Jim Capers, *Patriots*, p. x, and William Cooper, *Loyalists*, p. viii.

NOTES TO PART I

NOTES TO CHAPTER 1: TONY'S WORLD

p. 7: The two-story house had two chimneys. Plus garret on piers. David Paul Reuwer, email to author, 16 May 2014.

p. 8: Eagle. The name of one of McKelvey's horses.
McKelvey, *Index to Inventories, Record of Wills and Miscellaneous Records of Charleston County*, 1687–1785, Vol. II (L–2). Charleston County Public Library, James and Margaret McKelvey, Vol. 99–B, p. 396.

p. 9: "I'll be back after a few more chores and have another look at you."
Belvidere was the name of the Sinkler tract of eight hundred acres conveyed on 4 May 1757 by Francis Kinloch to Thomas Lynch who on 19 April 1769, with Isaac Motte, Jr., a co-owner by that time, conveyed it to James Sinkler. Peter Sinkler (1728–1781), a patriot who rode with Francis Marion, died in prison in Charleston and did not own land near Eutaw Creek. His plantation in Pineville, Lifeland, was ravaged by the British. His brother James Sinkler died in 1800. He purchased the land for Belvidere but never lived there. His widow lived at Belvidere after moving from their plantation (Old Santee) on the Santee River near St. Steven. Their son William founded Eutaw Plantation and built a home in 1808. Much of the Eutaw Springs battlefield

lies on land still owned by the Sinkler family. Norman Sinkler Walsh, email to author, 20 May 2014.

pp. 11-12: Sayey... Stepney... Cuffy. McKelvey, *Index to Inventories*, p. 396; three names randomly taken from a long list of enslaved "Negroes." Monetary value is given by each name, for example, Clarinda and Stepney, £1,800.

p. 13: "You two rascals messed up one of the dikes." Rice kings began to flourish on enslaved labor from 1720 when rice became the main export crop, essential to the economy of the Lowcountry. Richard Porcher and William Robert Judd, *The Market Preparation of Carolina Rice*. Columbia: University of South Carolina Press, 2014. Porcher, email to author, 1 October 2014.

p. 14: "Lofty, Fish Eye, and Iron Side, too." McKelvey, *Index to Inventories*, p. 396.

p. 15: Belmont, Blue Hole, Limespring, Numertia, Brush Pond, Black Jack, and Ash Hill ...The Rocks ... Walworth. Nearby plantations. Author's telephone conversations with Norman Sinkler Walsh.

p. 16: "You're even trying to learn to read and messing with the cymbee." Henry Ravenel, "Recollections of Life on a Southern Plantation." *The Yale Review*: A National Quarterly, 1936, Summer edition, "The 'Cymbee' [Simbi] Water Spirits of St. John's Berkeley". Natalie P. Adams, *The African Diaspora Archeological Network*, June 2007, diaspora.illinois.edu. Ras Michael Brown, *African-Atlantic Cultures and the South Carolina Lowcountry*. Cambridge, U.K.: Cambridge University Press, 2012. Isham and Cadar are not in Moss and Scoggins. Recovery of four British soldiers is also attributed to the waters of Healing Springs near Blackville in Barnwell District after the Battle of Windy Hill at Slaughter Field, 22 December 1781. Terri W. Lipscomb, *Names in South Carolina*, South Carolina Revolutionary Battles, Part Ten, Vol. XXX, Winter 1983, pp. 10, 11. Charleston *Post and Courier*, 25 December 2014, A9.

p. 23: "I got black folks up there in Ninety Six around Star Fort." Star Fort at Ninety Six was a British post on the old Cherokee trading route that extended from Charleston through Orangeburg and farther north into the backcountry. About two hundred miles northeast of Charleston, Ninety Six was so named because it was the location of nine creeks flowing in one direction and six in another, or, as others claim, because it was ninety six miles from Kecowee or Keowee, the main Cherokee Indian "lower town" on the Kecowee River across from Fort Prince George, held by the British from 1753–1768. The fort served as a staging point for the British in the French and Indian War from 1755–1763. At one time or another, the American commander of the Southern Campaign, Major General Nathanael Greene, had as many as a thousand six hundred men, many of whom were Continentals, for his siege and assault of Star Fort. The five hundred fifty defenders of the fort were made up of three hundred fifty tough veteran provincials under the forty-three-year-old loyalist commander Lieutenant Colonel John Harris Cruger from New York. Colonel Lord Francis Rawdon, the British commander of field operations, arrived in mid-June to help Cruger. The total number of two thousand five hundred and fifty British and loyalist troops at Ninety Six outnumbered the patriots by nearly a thousand at that time. On 22 May 1781, Greene began his siege of the Tory fort. Patriots Brigadier General Andrew Pickens and Lieutenant Colonel Henry "Light Horse" Lee both arrived at Ninety Six on 8 June with their troops and about three hundred prisoners.

NOTES TO CHAPTER 2: NINETY SIX

p. 40: "Look at those boys staggering off all those ships." On 3 June 1781, a squadron of British warships escorted seventeen troop transport vessels under Colonel Paston Gould into Charleston harbor. The two thousand two hundred fresh troops from Ireland consisted of the 3rd Regiment of Foot (The Buffs, or Buff Howards), commanded by Lieutenant Colonel Alexander Stewart; the 30th Regiment of Foot (The Triple X; later, The Cambridgeshires), commanded by Colonel Paston Gould; and the 19th Regiment of Foot (The Green Howards), commanded by Lieutenant

Colonel James Coates. Each of the three regiments had two flank companies plus eight "hat" companies, a total of ten companies in each regiment. The six flank companies among the regiments were separated out to make up a light infantry and grenadier battalion, or flank battalion—the best soldiers—under Major John Majoribanks. Many in the hat companies were raw recruits who had never seen battle. Roger Chapman, "*The Newsletter*," The Friends of the Green Howards Regimental Museum. "With the 19th Foot through the American War of Independence, 1781 to 1783," September 1999, Issue 8, pp. 2–11; "Lord Edward Fitzgerald," p. 7. This is the best collection of short articles on Fitzgerald, the 19th Regiment of Foot in South Carolina, and British perspective on the battles of Quinby Bridge and Eutaw Springs. Chapman published a companion article on Lord Edward, "British Soldier to Irish Patriot: Major Lord Edward Fitzgerald, H.M. 19th Regiment of Foot, 1781–1783," *The Green Howards Regimental Museum*. Richmond, N. Yorkshire, n.d.

p. 47: "It was, indeed, supposed that the American general was not a little influenced in his movements by the intelligence which he had received." Moore and MacDermott, pp. 15–19.

p. 47: "Among the varied duties that evolved upon me as chief of staff." Moore and MacDermott, pp. 15–19; Italics in the original.

p. 48: "these half-savage people of Carolina." Fortesque, p. 239.

p. 50: "Say nothing, and let's follow Cruger to Orangeburg." The siege and assault of Star Fort at Ninety Six lasted from 22 May till 19 June 1781, but Rawdon's futile chase after Greene lasted only a few days. Rawdon was exhausted, his health in serious jeopardy, after marching about a hundred miles from Ninety Six, possibly first going east over the Saluda River and northeast toward the Tyger and Enoree Rivers, then marching southeast to Friday's (aka Fridig's) Ferry near Fort Granby at the confluence of the Broad and Saluda Rivers (modern-day Columbia), then marching farther south to Orangeburg. He made plans to retire to Charleston, via Goose Creek, leaving Lieutenant Colonel Alexander Stewart in charge of field operations in Orangeburg. The six flank companies under Major Majoribanks remained at Orangeburg with Stewart until late July. Lord Edward went with Rawdon's detachment from Orangeburg as far as Goose Creek, then Lord Edward went up to Moncks Corner to join Coates and the rest of the 19th Foot that did not go to Ninety Six. As the British felt more and more pressure from partisan action, Coates got orders to withdraw from Moncks Corner to the Charleston garrison. Coates's long evacuation column presented the Americans with opportunities for continuous guerilla attacks, in days too hot even for a dog. As a cavalry officer in Coates's withdrawal, Lord Edward participated in Raid of the Dog Days between 15–17 July 1781. After that he returned to Orangeburg by 25 July to rejoin Majoribanks' flank battalion and march with Stewart to Eutaw Springs.

NOTES TO CHAPTER 3: RAID OF THE DOG DAYS

p. 58: After everything of value was put inside the church. Coates's exact route to Charleston is unknown. From Biggin Church Coates went south to cross Wadboo Bridge. His cavalry probably separated and headed to Charleston via Bonneau's Ferry to cross the East Branch of the Cooper River before Wade Hampton could catch them. Coates may have continued south on Doctor Evans Road to Strawberry Chapel, St. John's, Berkeley, Biggin Church Chapel of Ease at Childsbury, then turned east (on Carriage Road to Quarterman Branch Road) to cross Huger's Bridge. Charles Baxley, email to author, 7 July 2013.

p. 62: "The nineteenth regiment, being posted in the neighborhood of a place called Monk's Corner." Moore and MacDermott, pp. 16, 17. "In the neighborhood" of Moncks Corner is Huger's Bridge. Quoting Major Doyle, Moore and MacDermott erroneously attribute Lord Edward's actions approaching Huger's Bridge during Raid of the Dog Days to his earlier actions at Ninety Six. Lieutenant Colonel James Coates, commander of the eight hat companies of approximately five hundred and sixty raw Irish recruits in the 19th Regiment of Foot not taken by Rawdon to Ninety Six, marched from Charleston to hold the garrison at Moncks Corner on 12 June 1781, nine days after the troops landed from Ireland. The small garrison of the 19th Foot at Moncks Corner was located about two miles west of the West Branch of the Cooper River, approximately thirty-five miles north of Charleston. Just to the north was Biggin Church. Nearby was the bridge over Wadboo Creek. As Moore correctly has it, Lord Edward was given the opportunity to demonstrate his bravery when Lee's Legion attacked the rear of Rawdon's column shortly after the 19th Regiment moved from its headquarters at Moncks Corner. But this event, in which regimental baggage, medicines, ammunition, and paymaster's chests that were left in the rear of the column and were taken by Lee (and Sumter and Marion), actually occurred 16 July 1781 during Raid of the Dog Days, not approaching Ninety Six after the 19th Foot landed in Charleston with the 3rd and 30th Regiments. Major Doyle's reference to the break up of a bridge is, later, to Quinby Bridge, not Huger's. Both Moore and William Gilmore Simms interviewed participants in the incident. Unlike Moore, Simms correctly places the action at Huger's Bridge, but he also claims that Lord Edward was not in the rear of the column. Chapman, *Newsletter*, Editorial, p. 2. Appendix IV, below.

p. 66: "What the …? Those rebs are all dressed up in British cavalry uniforms. Where'd they get 'em?" Robert "Rabbit" Lockwood, Longwood Plantation, telephone conversation with author, 26 June 2017.

p. 70: "Black folks' cabins, too, all built up in a row, some of 'em made of mud." Robert "Rabbit" Lockwood, telephone conversation with author, 26 June 2017. Max (Macky) Hill III, formerly of Middleburg Plantation, telephone conversation with author, 10 July 2017, suggests that cabins for enslaved blacks may have been similar to those at Middleburg Plantation excavated by Dr. Leland Ferguson, University of Wisconsin, in the mid-1980s, having clay floors and thatch-roofs and post-supported, wattle-and-daub walls. Without artillery, patriots could not damage the clay walls which absorbed rifle balls with only a thud, somewhat like British cannon balls as they bounced off palmetto trees used to construct Fort Moultrie in the first siege of Charleston in 1776. Like the McKelvey Plantation, the two-story Shubrick house was probably made of brick and built on piers. As a barony house, Shubrick's was probably more monumental with sixteen-feet ceilings.

p. 75: Quickly withdrawing to Charleston the next day. The house at Shubrick's Plantation (also known before and after as Quinby Plantation) no longer exists. A two-story house built in its place in 1800 was moved to nearby Halidon Hill Plantation one hundred and seventy-five years later. Richard Coen, telephone conversation with author, 28 June 2017. After three hours of fighting, darkness ended Sumter's assault. The 19th Regiment of Foot successfully held its position to mark the end of Raid of the Dog Days. The next day, Coates withdrew to Charleston under support of Gould's column of seven hundred men which landed four miles from Shubrick's Plantation on the morning of 19 July 1781. Coates arrived safely in Charleston on the 22nd. Lieutenant David John Bell, 19th Regiment of Foot, letter to Lieutenant Charles Masterson, 19th Regiment of Foot, Charlestown, 11 August 1781. *The Green Howards' Gazette*, Autumn 1976, p. 18. After Coates's main elements of the 19th Regiment of Foot made their withdrawal from Shubrick's Plantation to Charleston, Lord Edward Fitzgerald left his regiment and immediately went back up to Orangeburg to return to his detachment with the flank companies of the 19th Foot under Majoribanks and the rest of the British army under Stewart as they prepared to meet Greene at Eutaw Springs. Stewart's army moved out of Orangeburg on 30 July 1781 and by 4 August arrived at McCord's Ferry near Fort Motte on the Congaree River. About three weeks later, on 23 August 1781, General Greene left the High Hills, traveled up the northern bank of the Wateree River and crossed it near Camden. After leaving Camden and crossing the Wateree, Greene swung around to the southwest and crossed the Congaree River at Howell's Ferry. The Americans pressed on along the south bank of the Santee toward a British army whose commander thought he was safe from attack. Exact numbers of combatants at Eutaw Springs vary. After leaving two hundred men at Howell's Ferry where he crossed the Congaree, Greene brought to the field at Eutaw Springs about two thousand two hundred men, Continentals and militia. Stewart had about one thousand nine hundred, plus those in the rooting party of three hundred who made it back to the British camp. Jim Piecuch, "One of the Most Important and Bloody Battles That Ever Was Fought in America: The Battle of Eutaw Springs," http://southerncampaign.org/newsletter/v3n9.pdf [Sept. 2006], including a map of the battle by David Reuwer; *Southern Campaigns of the American Revolution*, Vol. 3, No. 9, Sept. 2006, pp. 25–37, 29. Jim Piecuch, "The Evolving Tactician: Nathanael Greene at the Battle of Eutaw Springs." *General Nathanael Greene and the American Revolution in the South*, Gregory D. Massey and Jim Piecuch, ed. Columbia: University of South Carolina Press, 2012, p. 220. Patrick O'Kelley, *Nothing but Blood and Slaughter: The Revolutionary War in the Carolinas*, Vol. 3, 1781. Blue House Tavern Press, 2005. Dunkerly and Boland, p. 25, Appendix Two; Swager, pp. 74–76; Lumpkin, p. 213.

NOTES TO CHAPTER 4: EUTAW SPRINGS

p. 81: Sometime before September fourth, Tony Small left Miss Maggie's Plantation. Out of one hundred and thirty-seven battles fought in the Revolutionary War in South Carolina, from 28 June 1775 to 14 November 1782, black soldiers fought in a sizeable number of which there is scant record of their service. Walter Edgar, *South Carolina: A History*. Columbia: University of South Carolina Press, 1998, p. 237. Cornwallis marched into Virginia two months before the running skirmishes of Raid of the Dog Days and the battles at Quinby Bridge and Shubrick's Plantation. He turned his back on the Southern Campaign, not because he was assured of victory in the South, but rather because he would have no more of it. Although the Americans lost almost every battle, their guerilla, hit-and-run tactics—only to return and continue the fight behind another bush or tree—simply did not fit British strategy of warfare by long lines of Redcoats in open conflict. Cornwallis left field command to Rawdon who in turn left the hot potato to Stewart. In July 1781, Colonel Paston Gould relieved Lieutenant Colonel Nesbit Balfour as the senior officer in South Carolina. Just around the corner in September was the Battle of Eutaw Springs. Between 29 July and 3 August 1781, prompted by a lack of provisions, the flank companies with

Lord Edward and the rest of Lieutenant Colonel Stewart's troops moved to Thomson's Plantation located near the confluence of the Congaree and Wateree Rivers that forms the Santee, about a mile below Fort Motte and near McCord's (aka McCant's) Ferry. In late August, General Greene moved toward the British forces, forcing Lieutenant Colonel Stewart's troops to march thirty-five miles farther southeast to Eutaw Springs near the Santee. Greene tracked Stewart from Thompson's Plantation to Henry Laurens' Plantation to Burdell's Tavern to Eutaw Springs.

p. 82: They began to retrace their steps down River Road a short distance to Mt. Tacitus, Henry Laurens' Plantation. According to plats and deeds in the State Archives, Henry Laurens bought Mt. Tacitus Plantation from Tacitus Guillard. Mt. Tacitus was not owned by Charles Pinckney. Charles Baxley, email to author, 2 June 2017.

p. 84: "I love Eagle, too, but tackys are what built the Lowcountry. What's going to save it, too." Informed by Lish Thompson, Charleston County Public Library, South Carolina Room, in conversation about Chico, her eight-year-old gelding marsh tacky. "Tacky" means "cheap," not costing much money (until recently). Charleston County Public Library, South Carolina Room file "Animals—Horses—Marsh Tacky." *The John's Island Stud (South Carolina) 1750–1788.* Fairfax Harrison, privately printed. Richmond: Old Dominion Press, 1931, pp. 54, 55. D.P. Lowther, Folly Ridge Farm, Ridgeland, South Carolina, reluctantly auctioned his rare herd of marsh tackys on 2 July 2016.

p. 98: "I'd just as soon not be at a place that lets Redcoats take a clean shot at you." The bulk of Stewart's army was initially drawn up in the woods in front of the cleared field and abandoned brick house. A few wooden outlying houses lay to the southeast of the house, near the two spring heads. British encampments with their tangle of tents and ropes were pitched on the open ground to the south and west of the brick house. After all elements arrived from Laurens' Plantation, General Nathanael Greene's army positioned itself at Burdell's Tavern on 7 September 1781 to advance toward Stewart at Eutaw

Springs. Greene's army was composed of infantry and cavalry units from North Carolina, Virginia, Maryland, and Delaware Continentals, North and South Carolina state militia, and South Carolina state troops. Greene left Burdell's at four o'clock in the morning of 8 September 1781 to attack Stewart seven miles farther down the road at Eutaw Springs.

p. 99: Tony continued with the American army as it moved from Burdell's Tavern toward Eutaw Springs. This sequence of battle follows Jim Piecuch, "The Evolving Tactician," and Lee F. McGee, "Most Astonishing Efforts: William Washington's Cavalry at the Battle of Eutaw Springs," http://southerncampaign.org/newsletter/v3n3.pdf; maps by John Roberts [March 2006]; *Southern Campaigns of the American Revolution*, Vol. 3, No. 3, March 2006, pp. 15–33. A thorough study of the battle by Dunkerly and Boland was published after the final draft of the present work was written; nonetheless, as much of Dunkerly and Boland's narrative as possible is followed, most of which is consistent with that of Piecuch and McGee.

p. 100: The loud gunfire drew the attention of another group of British soldiers nearby. Lord Edward Fitzgerald may well have been in a nearby foraging party sent out under guard by Stewart in the early morning hours to gather sweet potatoes. About three hundred men of the 3rd, 63rd, 64th, and 84th Regiments of Foot and New York and New Jersey Loyalists, including sixty-two detached from Majoribanks' flank companies, were drawn into the action from the woods between the Santee and the Congaree Road. Like Coffin's cavalry and infantry, they stumbled onto the American army which killed or wounded a small number. Others in the foraging party escaped, but most were captured. Stewart attributed the loss of these men, along with the loss of British cavalry prior to the battle, to a failure to completely route the Americans at Eutaw Springs.

p. 101: Observing Majoribanks' distinct formation, American Colonel Otho Williams reckoned it as one "having some obliquity to the main line, forming with an obtuse angle." *Documentary History of the American Revolution*, R. W. Gibbes, "Battle of Eutaw, Account furnished by Colonel

Otho Williams, with additions furnished by Cols. W. Hampton, Polk, Howard and Watt." Columbia: Banner Steam-Power Press, 1853; rprt. Spartanburg, 1972, p. 148.

p. 106: "Better and not as valuable, both," Perkins yelled back. Eighty-two years later black troops of the 54th Massachusetts under Lieutenant Colonel Robert Gould Shaw at Ft. Wagner showed the same resolve.

p. 110: "Not too long ago they shot poor Billy when he was making like a hog." *The Fire of Liberty*, Esmond Wright, p. 227. John Chaney, "The True Tale of Billy Lunsford," in Chapman, *Newsletter*, p. 9.

p. 111: "Impatiently rushing into a fight won't help him here." "[William Washington] advanced with his accustomed impetuosity; but found it impossible, with cavalry, to penetrate the thicket occupied by Majoribanks." John Marshall, *The Life of George Washington, Written for the Use of Schools*, 10th edn. Philadelphia: James Crissy, 1844, p. 231. Marshall describes the battle at "Eutaw Creek near which stood a brick house, surrounded with offices, into which Major Sheridan threw himself with the New York volunteers," p. 231.

p. 112: "Hold your bayonet!" Accounts vary. Some just say a "British soldier," Colonel Otho Williams says "a British officer," and some say Majoribanks rescued Washington, an act for which Daniel Ravenel buried Majoribanks with honor at Wantoot, since Ravenel was a good friend of Washington's. Williams, in Gibbes, p. 153. Joseph Johnson, *Traditions and Reminiscences, Chiefly of the American Revolution in the South*. Charleston: Walker and James, 1851, p. 301.

p. 113: Following Majoribank's tactics used in Ireland. Roger Chapman, conversation with author.

p. 115: "Don't shoot him, it's only a Negro." Moss and Scoggins, L277, P207.

p. 115: "a completely chaotic tangle of American troops in the ropes, tents, and other matériel of the British army." The American charge did not fail because thirsty troops got drunk on British liquor left in the tents. Nearly half of Sumner's North Carolina Continentals, by far the most troops, died at Eutaw Springs. Dunkerly and Boland, Appendix Two.

p. 115: Campbell's Virginians and Kirkwood's Delaware men who now had moved from the thicket. Piecuch, "The Evolving Tactician."

NOTES TO CHAPTER 5: CHARLESTON

p. 121: An eerie silence escorted exhausted troops and horses back to Burdell's Tavern. By holding the field, the British claimed they won the battle, yet after four hours of fierce fighting, both sides pulled back and froze in position. Gradually withdrawing the next day at a deliberate pace to Charleston via Moncks Corner, Stewart was reasonably successful in escaping the kind of guerrilla action Coates suffered in his withdrawal from Moncks Corner to Charleston in Raid of the Dog Days. Of the approximately one hundred and thirty-eight Americans killed and three hundred and seventy-eight wounded, many were taken from the battlefield to be buried or nursed back to health. Most were buried where they fell. The British casualties included eighty-four killed and three hundred fifty-one wounded. More than seventy British soldiers were left on the battlefield. Piecuch, "The Evolving Tactician," pp. 214–37. Piecuch, "One of the Most Important and Bloody Battles That Ever Was Fought in America: The Battle of Eutaw Springs," pp. 25–37. On the day after the battle at Eutaw Springs, William Snow wrote to his overseer Mr. Rhodes to share his concern that Ruth and other enslaved blacks might attempt to run away from his plantation in St. James Parish on the Santee River. Snow warned Rhodes not to reprimand Ruth: "These negroes, if they are not well secured, will get away; have no mercy on these negroes or they will deceive you... P. S. If you say the least about Ruth, she will run off, for she is an arch-bitch." Moss and Scoggins, L272, P206.

p. 127: Both hovered over the British officer in his bright red tunic, white britches, and black leather boots, lying on his back in a pool of blood and mud. Stuart Reid, *Redcoat Officer 1740-1815*. Oxford: Osprey Publishing, 2002. Roger Chapman, email to author, 4 April 2017.

p. 129: "So close, indeed, and desperate was the encounter." Draper Manuscript, 6VV321. Thomas Sumter Papers, Lyman C. Draper Manuscript Collection, 6VV321, State Historical Society of Wisconsin.

p. 131: "Get me a rope, Tony. We're going to tie up this bucket on the roof beam." A procedure used successfully at Guilford Courthouse for an ancestor of Ted Williams, Bozeman, Montana; conversation with the author, June, 2018.

p. 131: The next day was Sunday and rainy enough to keep the ground muddy. A renewed attack never came, at least not from Greene's entire army, although Marion and Lee continued to harass the British column as it began to move in earnest toward Daniel Ravenel's Wantoot Plantation, twenty-five miles southeast of Eutaw Springs in St. John's Parish, and on to Moncks Corner. At Monck's Corner Stewart's army met support troops under Major McArthur arriving from Fairlawn. Colonel Gould sent these troops from the Charleston garrison to help Stewart withdraw and also ordered Major Doyle to make an official report after Greene moved out of the area.

p. 136: "This is Primus Button." *Cemetery Records: A Documentary of Cemetery or Burial Ground Reports and Grave Relocation by Santee Cooper from the Project Area, 1939–1941* (Lake Marion, Lake Moultrie), pp. 185–87. Prepared as a Public Service by The Berkeley County Historical Society, 1986, by Sara Jean DeHay Guerry, Jamestown, South Carolina. The arbitrary choice in this creative nonfiction of Primus Button as a black man who nursed Majoribanks at Wantoot until his death on 22 October 1781 is based on the following entry on unmarked graves in Wantoot Plantation Cemetery #16 (Black): "This cemetery on Wantoot Plantation in St. John's Parish, Berkeley County, SC, is located about three miles west of Bonneau and about six miles north of Pinopolis, on the Black Oak Road..." It is described on page 187 as "the old slave cemetery." It contains about one hundred and fifty graves, five of which are Buttons, five with stone markers and the rest unmarked. Primus' grave is unmarked. Across the road from the Wantoot Plantation Cemetery, which is referred to as "the old slave cemetery," was the Wantoot Smallpox Cemetery. Primus Button is not the Primus who escaped from Keating Simon's or William Maxwell's plantations, L248, L249.

p. 137: "Annie Belle is there." *Cemetery Records*, p. 186.

p. 139: "With his trick using a log as a fake cannon, a 'Quaker' cannon." Seabrook Wilkinson, *Charleston Mercury*, July 21, 2005; Charleston County Public Library, South Carolina Room, Biography File, Elliott, #1138.

p. 143: "And here we are. The holy city." The Lords Proprietors granted religious freedom in part to get settlers to come to the Lowcountry, deemed by some a hellish place for its climate. As a result, South Carolina was the most diverse in its population of all thirteen colonies. Dutch, French, German, Swedish, Welsh settlers as well as English, Scots, and Irish came— but Roman Catholics were not allowed. For a while the Jewish population was second in size only to New York. Also, twenty-five or so West African cultures and survivors of about forty native American cultures and languages lived in the Lowcountry. Walter Edgar, Foreword to *Reflections of South Carolina*, Robert C. Clark and Tom Poland. Columbia: University of South Carolina Press, 1999, pp. vi, vii.

p. 143: "it's on the tip of a detumescent peninsula." The Lords Proprietors brought rice to the Lowcountry in the 1670s. Rice kings began to flourish on enslaved labor fifty years later. The early wealth of Charleston was built mainly on this "Carolina Gold." In the heart of the Lowcountry, three thousand five hundred and forty miles from London and one thousand six hundred from Barbados, the coastal city of Charleston was one of the richest in the British colonies and well worth defending.

p. 145: Charleston, a town utterly destitute of sanitary arrangements. Geoffrey Powell, *The History of the Green Howards: Three Hundred Years of Service*. London: Arms and Armour, 1992; Pen and Sword, 2nd edn., 2002. Ferrar, pp. 102, 103.

p. 145: He and the other eight lieutenants. Ferrar, p. 102. The "savage nature" of the Black Dragoons was to blame for their reputation. James Piecuch, *Three Peoples, One King: Loyalist, Indians, and Slaves in the American Revolutionary South*. Columbia: University of South Carolina Press, 2013, p. 317. After Lieutenant Hickman was killed in action at Eutaw Springs, the remaining lieutenants in the regiment included Richard Gem, George Taggart, Marcus Lowther Crofton, William Sray, Matthew Scott, Conway Blennerhasset, William Vincent, and William Beamish.

p. 145: Jane Reily Elliott. Charleston County Public Library, South Carolina Room, Biography File, Elliott, #1138.

p. 145: She heard from one of her father's servants. Rev. J. D. Bailey, *Some Heroes of the American Revolution*. Spartanburg, South Carolina: Band & White, Printers, 1924, p. 54.

p. 148: "What would we do at Orange Parish." *Biographical Directory of the South Carolina Senate*, 1776–1985, Vol. III (Sinkler-Index), by N. Louise Bailey, Mary L. Morgan, and Carolyn R. Taylor; N. Louise Bailey, ed. Columbia: University of South Carolina Press, 1985, p. 182.

p. 150: "Well, I hope you don't see her at the Ethiopian Ball." George Smith McCowen, Jr., *The British Occupation of Charleston, 1780–82*. Columbia: University of South Carolina Press, 1972, p. 104.

p. 157: "You're throwing money away you need to fight France and Spain." Alan Taylor, *American Revolutions: A Continental History, 1750–1804*. New York: W.W. Norton, 2016, p. 297.

p. 165: "We want your man Tony to join us in the Independent Troop of Black Dragoons." Incidental to Dunmore's plan for armed loyalist black troops in the Lowcountry, Lieutenant Colonel James Moncrief proposed forming a brigade of black soldiers, something General Leslie felt "will soon become indispensably necessary shou'd the war continue ... in this part of America." Lieutenant Colonel Benjamin Thompson was dispatched to New York to sell the idea to Clinton. Thompson had commanded black troops in Charleston since late 1781. After training a small number in mounted tactics and basic military discipline, Thompson took his black cavalry to Dorchester where the unit defeated a rebel band and took prisoners. By January 1782, this unit became known and feared throughout the Lowcountry as the Black Dragoons, one of the most active British units in the last months of the war. Because of their success, the Black Dragoons provoked outrage among whites in the Lowcountry. James Piecuch, "The 'Black Dragoons': Former Slaves as British Cavalry in Revolutionary South Carolina," *Cavalry of the American Revolution*, Piecuch, ed. Yardley, Penn.: Westholme Publishing, 2012, pp. 213–22.

p. 167: "ultimately, this is Tony's decision." On 24 February 1782 the Black Dragoons observed from the rear the fierce action at Brabant's Plantation, also called Durant's, near Strawberry Ferry, eight miles south of Moncks Corner on Wambaw Creek on the west branch of the Cooper River. The next day they were eager to be in the van and a major part of an engagement at Tydiman's Plantation.

p. 168: "But today we're going to Tydiman's Plantation." Patrick O'Kelley. *Unwaried Patience and Fortitude: Francis Marion's Orderly Book*. West Conshohocken, Penn.: Infinity Publishing.com, 2006, p. 584; *Marion's Brigade Engagements*, #66, map by Colonel George Summers, Francismarionsymposium.com.

p. 169: Captain March then turned to the horseman near his side. Colonel Benjamin Thompson's defeat of General Marion at Tydiman's Plantation on 25 February 1782 decimated Colonel Peter Horry's dragoons and reduced

Marion's men to about sixty. The British forces killed some twenty patriots, a sizeable number of casualties in a skirmish. The 30th Regiment of Foot took part in both skirmishes at Brabant's and Tydiman's. After the skirmish at Tydiman's, Greene sent Lieutenant Colonel John Laurens in support of Marion's Brigade which withdrew north of the Santee. As a result of British success at Tydiman's Plantation, the British could forage at will in the country side from the end of February till April 1782. Expeditions were supported by Captain Marsh and his Black Dragoons who made sure that lines of supply into Charleston were unobstructed by patriots. Deserters from the British garrison were either shot or returned in disgrace. However, the usual flight of personnel went on throughout the war, as ranks of the opposing combatants switched sides routinely. Patriots switched sides to join the British. Regular British soldiers, Hessians, and loyalists switched sides to join the Americans. Whigs switched sides to join Tory ranks, each side trying to guess how the conflict would end. "Which side am I supposed to be on?" remained a question about liberty that characterized an age of decision for white men and women as well as for men and women of color. Even though the British were fairly confident of their ability to forage around Charleston, Greene's army still had them pressed with their backs to the Atlantic. Marion was on the Cooper River watching the British right flank; Harden watched between Charleston and Savannah; Sumter kept post from Orangeburg to Four Holes Swamp; Hampton kept lines open between Greene and Marion; and Lee kept British scouts from finding out just how weak Greene's army really was.

p. 171: 'vile dragons'. Lewis Morris to Ann Elliott, 1 November 1782; 28 November 1782, "Letters from Colonel Lewis Morris to Miss Ann Elliott," *SC Historical and Genealogical Magazine*, Vol. 41, No. 1, January 1940, 6, 10.

p. 171: "I never knew so loveable a person, and every man in the army, from the general to the drummer, would cheer the expression." Washington's toast quoted in Chapman, *Newsletter*, "Lord Edward Fitzgerald," p. 7.

p. 172: The lives of Tony Small and Lord Edward changed dramatically later in the spring of 1782. Prior to the departure of about two thousand British troops to Jamaica from Charleston in December 1782, General Leslie hoped to use all blacks who were in the possession of the British as bartering chips to offset the property losses which loyalists suffered from confiscations by the Whigs. To this end, it was imperative to hold on to as many blacks as possible if loyalists were to regain as much of their confiscated lands as possible. Leslie, therefore, tried to prevent most officers from leaving Charleston with blacks whom the officers wished to declare free outright or emancipated by virtue of their voluntary arrival in British camps or personal service. On 3 May 1782, Leslie wrote O'Hara, "As I apprehend a number of Negroes the property of Persons in the Province which were allowed as Servants to the Officers of the 19th and 30th Regiments, are now embarked on board the different Transports contrary to a general Order of mine; I must request You will give the most positive Order to have them sent on shore immediately." Leslie demanded that officers' enslaved personnel be turned over to Colonel Ballingall, the commissioner of claims for Negroes. It didn't happen. Five months later, well after Lord Edward and Tony left Charleston on 5 May 1782, Leslie's brief articulation of a method of dealing with blacks was elaborated upon in a failed declaration on 10 October 1782. That declaration was meant to serve for all blacks being evacuated with the British from Charleston in December. All sequestered enslaved blacks, the declaration stated, in the possession of the British who belonged to Whigs were to be "restored to their former Owners ... except such Slaves as may have rendered themselves particularly obnoxious on Account of their Attachment and Services to the British Troops, and such as have had specifick Promises of Freedom." Enslaved blacks who voluntarily fled to the British and who thus fell into the exception clause were to be "fairly valued by a Person to be chosen by each Side" and their owners compensated by the British. The declaration made no provision for free blacks. Eventually, the agreement of 10 October was dissolved by Governor Mathews, but only after a vast number of enslaved blacks was already on British warships in Charleston harbor in December 1782 or under protection of British troops. However, many were in the wrong place at the wrong time. The realistic business of dealing with enslaved blacks in their possession grew intense as many British soldiers took advantage of the market and sold "the first Negroes they meet with ... for whatever money they can obtain" right off the boat or pier to Spaniards who sailed from Havana. Francis Marion was powerless as he heard from an informant that enslaved black were being deceived by the British and carried to the West Indies, into "a Thousand times (if Possible) worse Bondage, than they Experience here." William Moultrie accused Moncrief of taking over eight hundred South Carolina enslaved blacks to the West Indies for personal profit. Moultrie estimated that over twenty-five thousand, or one-fourth of the entire population in South Carolina, left the state during the Revolutionary War, most stolen by loyalists and nine thousand British soldiers who evacuated Charleston on 14 December 1782. By then, there were some thirty thousand fewer enslaved blacks in South Carolina than in 1775. Edgar, *History*, p. 244. William Bull estimated nine thousand left with the British in the final stages of the war. On balance, thirteen thousand may have left. Piecuch, *Three Peoples*, p. 323. Other estimates of all evacuees include four thousand troops, four thousand two hundred loyalists, one thousand five hundred freed blacks, and seven thousand enslaved. Taylor, *American Revolutions*, p. 314. On 27 October 1782 a large convoy of forty ships departed Charleston carrying most of the British Army and over three thousand seven hundred white civilians, many of whom were South Carolina Loyalists. On 14 December 1782, remaining elements of the British Army evacuated Charleston for good. The American Revolutionary War costs the British an estimated £115,000. South Carolina, with a white population of less than one hundred thousand, spent $5.4 million, and regularly met its financial obligations to the Continental Congress. In 1783, the year of its incorporation, it was the only one of the thirteen states to pay its requisition in full. Some forty-three thousand six hundred British and one hundred thousand Americans lost their lives in the war. *Leslie Letterbook*, Leslie to O'Hara, 3 May 1782; Piecuch, email to author, 2 February 2014; also, Piecuch, *Three Peoples*, p. 320–323; Lambert, pp. 174, n. 41, 178, 179. William Moultrie, *Memoirs of the American Revolution*. 2nd edn., 2 vols. Eyewitness Accounts of the American Revolution Series. New York: New York Times & Arno Press, 1968, 2: 351, 352.

p. 173: On the way to the wharf he saw mostly non-native plants in the gardens south of Broad Street. One would see mostly non-native plants in Charleston. One would see in the rural countryside mostly native plants, unless in a village where one would see a mix. Richard Porcher, conversation with author.

p. 174: Now Tony was using Gadsden's Wharf as a point of departure. Of the ten million blacks shipped out of Africa, roughly five hundred thousand—or one out of twenty—were brought for sale in North America, and forty percent of those brought to North America passed through Gadsden's Wharf. They were quarantined on Sullivan's Island, across the Cooper River from Charleston, before being brought for sale in the city. Edgar, Walter. Foreword to *Reflections of South Carolina*, Robert C. Clark and Tom Poland, ed. Columbia: University of South Carolina Press, 1999, pp. vi, vii; *Charleston Post and Courier*, 28 August 2014, p. A1. *The Life of Boston King*, Ruth Holmes Whitehead and Carmelita A. M. Robertson, ed. Halifax, Nova Scotia: Nimbus Publishing Limited, 2003.

NOTES TO CHAPTER 6: IRELAND

p. 177: Tony Small sailed to St. Lucia in the Lesser Antilles with Lord Edward. During the five years following his departure from St. Lucia, from 1783 to 1788, Lord Edward became active in Irish politics, enabled by his older brother William, 2nd Duke of Leinster, and his cousin Charles James Fox. He was elected a member of Parliament for Athy in 1783. Whether at home or in London, however, he still had a problem under the law of primogeniture. His estate in County Kildare, which he inherited when he became twenty-one years old, provided revenues of only £800 per year. His older brother William had it all—property, title, money that flowed with it, and Carton House. Lord Edward's share of their father's wealth was a pittance in comparison. This inequity that arose from a system that was arbitrary and irrational to Lord Edward compelled him to challenge the status quo. By late 1783 Lord Edward's cousin and kindred spirit Charles Fox formed a coalition with Lord North in a new government that no longer included Lord Edward's older brother William. But Lord Edward Fitzgerald was not an enthusiastic politician or "Foxite," even though fresh political advantages were available to him. He remained too much a child of Rousseau's *Emile* to share the cynicism and expediency required of public officials. His early education at his mother's sea-side villa Black Rock, or Frescati, was ultimately too formidable to yield itself to Ascendency life and London politics. His republican sympathies from his education by his stepfather William Ogilvie were now given full-throated opportunity to be heard. In short, the explorer and revolutionary man of action applied to his own life what he read in such works as Rousseau's *Confessions*, his *Discours sur l'origine et les fondements de l'inégalité*, and his *la nouvelle Héloïse*, Samuel Richardson's novel *Pamela*, Laurence Sterne's *Tristram Shandy* and his *Sermons of Mr. Yorick*, and Thomas Paine's *Common Sense* which inspired Americans toward revolution as *The Rights of Man* and *The Age of Reason* later inspired the French.

p. 179: That same year, Lord Edward wrote of the strength Tony gave him. Lennox papers, MS 35,004/20. Annotated. Begging Letter. Anthony Small. NLI Fitzgerald Papers. Kevin Whelan, email to author, 19 May 2014.

p. 181: After serving in the 90th Regiment of Foot. Chapman, "British Soldier to Irish Patriot," p. 9. Lord Edward and Tony's itinerary in Canada is taken from Daniel Gahan, "Journey After My Own Heart: Lord Edward Fitzgerald in America, 1788–90," *New Hibernia Review/ Iris Eireannach Nua*, Vol. 1, No. 2 (Summer 2004), pp. 85–105; and, Ruth Holmes Whitehead, *Black Loyalists: Southern Settlers of Nova Scotia's First Free Black Communities*. Nimbus, CA: Nimbus Publishing Ltd., 2013.

p. 185: "Now, honorable one, let's get down the river to New Orleans and catch a boat to Dublin." From Detroit Lord Edward and Tony traveled north on Lake Huron to the 54th Foot's most distance fort of Michilimackinack at the northern tip of Lakes Huron and Michigan and nearer to the southernmost part of Lake Superior. But then, without explanation or careful planning, Lord Edward decided to abandon his post and his regiment and, shirking further military orders, headed south with Tony. It took three months for Lord Edward and Tony in the company of five companions to travel down the Mississippi River to New Orleans, where they arrived in December 1789. In New Orleans Lord Edward and Tony got news of the Storming of the Bastille. By the time he arrived home in the spring 1790, almost two years after he left, he had already heard news of the marriage of Georgiana Lennox and the latest in controversies within the Regency government. He returned a man with points of view that would lead him to break ties with his social circle, political friends, and the British army. In a letter from New Orleans, he observed to his brother Lord Robert that from his experiences, including those in 1781 and 1782 in the Lowcountry, and in 1788 and 1789 in Canada, "I have seen human nature under almost all its forms. Everywhere it is the same, but the wilder it is the more virtuous." Moore and MacDermott, p. 117.

p. 186: Richard [Sheridan]. When Horace Walpole said Banastre Tarleton "boasts of having butchered more men and lain with more women than anyone in the Army," Richard Sheridan, who knew Tarleton as a student, replied, "Lain with! He should have said ravished. Rapes are the relaxation of murderers." Michael Pearfon, *Those Damned Rebels: The American Revolution as Seen Through British Eyes* (Da Capo Press, 1972), p. 334.

p. 188: "The speedy abolition of all hereditary titles and feudal distinctions." Moore and MacDermott, p. 129.

p. 192: "A border of primroses." Moore and MacDermott, p. 181.

p. 193: "In her little American jacket". Moore and MacDermott, p. 185.

p. 195: Hoche wanted to get even for Pitt's three previous expeditions against France. Moore and MacDermott, pp. 210, 211.

p. 196: As they prepared to return to Kildare in September 1796, and it was clear that Eddy would be separated from his mother and father.

By the end of September 1796, the Irish revolutionaries finished their negotiations with the French for what they hoped to be fifteen thousand soldiers and eighty thousand guns to be used in an invasion to be launched from Brest. Lord Edward returned to England with his wife, baby daughter Pam, and Tony. He took them to Lady Emily's summer retreat in Ealing, west of London. Anticipating the difficulties that lay ahead, if not his death, Lord Edward temporarily gave his and Pamela's first child Eddy, who had been staying with his grandmother, to the further care of the Duchess, Lady Emily. The decision was painful to Pamela but extremely pleasing to Lady Emily. Later, Pamela permanently gave little Eddy to the Duchess and the third child to be born, Lucy, to Lady Sophia, Lord Edward's sister who had no children. Lord Edward never saw Lucy. Of the three children, Eddy, Pam, and Lucy, Pamela finally kept only little Pam. Tillyard, p. 297. The family of one of Ireland's most famous revolutionaries suffered tremendously. Little Mary Sheridan died in November 1793. Based on letters in the National Library of Ireland that came to light in 2012, Lord and Lady Fitzgerald eventually gave up all three children to protect them, even little Pam to Lady Sophia. Kevin Whelan, email to author, 19 May 2014.

p. 200: "I did not know about any of these plans of Hoche's—none at all! The fools!" Lord Edward and Arthur O'Connor met in Hamburg, Basle, and Angers to plan a French invasion of Ireland to land at Galway Bay in the spring of 1797. An invasion never actually happened. It only tried to happen. Instead, on 15 December 1796, General Louis-Lazare Hoche sailed the French frigate *Fraternité* out of Brest harbor leading a fleet of forty-three ships. The entire invasion force numbered fourteen thousand soldiers and forty thousand weapons that included cannons, rifles, swords, and small arms, together with five thousand uniforms to be worn by members of the United Irishmen. To English vessels in the English Channel, Hoche appeared to be leading an expedition south toward Lisbon, so there was no cause for alarm. Hoche's obsession with secrecy, however, paid off only to that point. The remainder of his plans for landing in Ireland to rendezvous with the United Irishmen to start an uprising against British rule in Dublin ended in a classic military disaster. Fate was not on the side of the Irish and French.

Rough gale winds caused the troop ship *Seduisant* to flounder and sink, losing all one thousand four hundred men aboard. Hoche's ship got separated from the flotilla by fog and strong winds and was among several that were blown out into the Atlantic. The intact flotilla that first arrived off the Irish coast numbered only seventeen ships. Captains of the remaining ships that eventually arrived off the coast opened their instructions in the absence of Hoche and found that they had arrived at their correct destination, Bantry Bay—"correct" only in the sense that Bantry Bay was indeed the spot to which Hoche ordered them to sail, but not the correct point to reconnoiter with the Irish. Lord Edward and the United Irishmen not only expected them to arrive at a different spot along the west coast but also at a much later time. Without further instructions from the secretive Hoche—secretive even to the United Irishmen—the invasion force did not know what to do beyond that point. Some ships hugged the shore. More were blown out to sea. Sailors could not see lights from other ships. By 23 December 1796, only six thousand five hundred soldiers were aboard the ships gathered for disembarkation. Even the *Immortalité*, which replaced Hoche's flag ship, was nowhere to be seen. Howling, gale-force winds threatened to sink all the ships on Ireland's rocky shores. Failing to see any Irishmen at all waiting to rendezvous with them and march on British troops in Dublin, the French became disheartened, gave up, and sailed back to Brest without disembarking. Only four ships of the line arrived safely back.

p. 201: "Washington is certainly to be bought—honors will do it." Wright, *The Fire of Liberty*, p. 178.

p. 204: "Indeed, most of the leading people in the conspiracy are Protestants." Moore and MacDermott, p. 234.

p. 204: "We're all very insistent about what role France will play if they do come to help us." Moore and MacDermott, p. 209.

p. 207: "I'm taking pages out of Francis Marion's and Nathanael Greene's play books" Lord Edward's tactical plans for the Uprising were found in his writing box on the 12 March raid on Leinster House. However, he makes no explicit comparison with American guerrilla tactics used in the Southern Campaign. Moore and MacDermott, pp. 479–82. Streets named here in the "Dardenelles of Dublin" are those cited during and after the 1916 Easter Rebellion, not the 1796–98 Rebellion. Donal Fallon, "Come Here to Me," 6 October 2018.

p. 208: Tony returned with Pamela and the family to Dublin from Kildare. Lord Edward began to plot out more details of his strategy for war. The United Irishmen continued to conspire at Taylors Hall at Back Lane leading from Corn Market to Nicholas Street. In a paper handed over to Thomas Reynolds for delivery to the provincial committee of Leinster, Lord Edward described a country-wide revolutionary army of two hundred and eighty thousand men ready for the May Rising. But instead of taking the paper to the committee, Reynolds took it to the Castle government and even told them that the next meeting of the Leinster provincial committee was to be held at Oliver Bond's house in Dublin. On 12 March 1798, the Castle government raided Bond's house and arrested thirteen members of the committee. Among the five members of the executive, only Lord Edward avoided capture simply because he saw the arresting officer Major Swan, whom he recognized from his time in Gibraltar, enter the house. He quickly withdrew and remained free at Leinster House.

p. 210: Shortly thereafter, Lord Edward in disguise made his first secret visit to see Pamela. Lord Edward hid out at Mrs. Dillon's for about five weeks, on one occasion disguised as a very sick woman in bed. He kept moving to avoid arrest. Again with Lawless' help, he took up quarters at Mr. Murphy's house on Thomas Street. From his new safe house, late one evening Lord Edward made his second secret visit to see Pamela on Denzille Street.

p. 211: Lord Edward's luck finally ran out. Rather than take the Castle government's offer and flee to France to save his life, Lord Edward through the first week in May continued to shuttle back and forth from Mr. Murphy's house to Mr. McCormick's located a few doors down. He also returned for a while to Mrs. Dillon's. During this time, as always, he was anything but cautious. He continued to receive dinner guests without much scrutiny. Lord Edward set the May Rising to begin on 23 May 1798, according to the plan laid out in February, but fate in the form of further betrayal intervened. On 18 May 1798 Lord Edward barely avoided capture as he went from another safe house, James Moore's at 119 Tomas Street, en route to 20 Usher's Island, home of the Roman Catholic barrister Francis Magan.

p. 213: 'I'm sorry for it.' Moore and MacDermott, p. 313.

p. 213: Without ever being allowed to see her husband. The May Rising began without Lord Edward on 23 May 1798, but it, too, suffered from spies who gave the Castle government details of what was planned. British soldiers set up road blocks and occupied Smithfield Market which the United Irishmen designated as a rallying point. Armed with only pikes and a few muskets, the United Irishmen in Dublin waited for orders. In the absence of Lord Edward, none came. The rebel army in the city faded away. The Rising as it occurred in the countryside went even worse. About twenty thousand rebels marched into Wexford and declared independence from the British. Without Lord Edward or any other leader to organize them, they were brutally put down by Redcoats. At the end of the failed Rising, thirty thousand were killed. Thousands more died in its wake.

p. 214: "Lord Edward," young doctor Armstrong Garnett said as he entered the prison cell. The Castle government knew Lord Edward's wounds if left untreated would lead to his death, and that is precisely what the government allowed to happen. Rejecting medical advice by two doctors, Armstrong Garnett and Stone, to immediately operate on Lord Edward, a third physician, Dr. Lindsay, merely changed the dressings on Lord Edward's right shoulder and neck to permit the wound to fester. Septicaemia set in. Lord Edward suffered from severe spasms, nausea, and vomiting. Gross medical neglect, itself an effective method of execution, served to avoid the risk of inflaming the populace with a lengthy trial and certain conviction. The Castle government and Dr. Lindsay gladly consented to an inhumane form of torture that brought a slow but certain death. A midnight visit by Lord Edward's aunt Lady Louisa Conolly and his brother Lord Henry did little to ease his misery.

p. 214: But Lord Edward, head of the United Irishmen Military Committee. Moore and MacDermott, p. 245.

p. 215: He faded in and out of consciousness. Moore and MacDermott, p. 352.

p. 216: "I think my black face prevented me from getting a chance to see him." Moore and MacDermott, p. 282.

p. 216: 'Ah! I was wounded then in a very different cause; that was in fighting *against* liberty—this in fighting *for* it.' Moore and MacDermott, p. 22. Italics in the original.

p. 219: Tony became somber. On 14 June 1798, ten days after Lord Edward died, Lord Camden was replaced by a new Lord Lieutenant of Ireland who finally put down the Irish Rebellion on 24 September 1798. The cost of the Uprising to the government was twenty thousand lives and to the Irish insurgents fifty thousand. The new Commander in Chief was Charles, formerly Earl Cornwallis, now 1st Marquess Cornwallis, the same man defeated at Yorktown.

p. 220: "He said, 'Of my lamented and ill-fated friend's excellent qualities, I should never tire in speaking.'" Moore and MacDermott, p. 22. Italics in the original.

p. 221: "I don't even know what happened to 'em all." McKelvey, *Index to Inventories,* p. 396.

p. 224: "An old groomsman once told me." Moore and MacDermott, p. 372.

p. 226: To figure out exactly how to broach the subject of asking for money. Kevin Whelan, "Small, Tony (–1804)," *Dictionary of Irish Biography*; "New Light on Lord Edward Fitzgerald," 18th–19th–Century History, Features, Issue 4 (Winter 1999), The United Irishmen, Volume 7; https://www.historyireland.com/18th-19th-century-history/new-light-on-lord-edward-fitzgerald/ (Accessed 06 August 2019); Donal Fallon, https://comeheretome.com/2013/01/29/tony-small-the-escaped-slave-who-lived-in-leinster-house/ (Accessed 06 August 2019.)

p. 227: "I hope you will pardon the Liberty I take in writing." Letter to Lady Sophia Fitzgerald, sister of Lord Edward, to whom Pamela gave Lucy in August 1798. Lennox papers, MS 35,004/20. Annotated. Begging Letter. Anthony Small. NLI Fitzgerald Papers. Kevin Whelan, email to author, 19 May 2014.

p. 228: Months passed with only a small sum sent by Lady Lucy Fitzgerald. Donal Fallon, https://comeheretome.com/2013/01/29/tony-small-the-escaped-slave-who-lived-in-leinster-house/ (Accessed 06 August 2019.)

p. 228: "when I feel like I can't ever hold my head up high again after Lord Edward's death." Moore and MacDermott, p. 372. Tony Small died in London probably in 1804; Pamela died in Paris in 1831. Letter from Lady Emily Fitzgerald to Lady Lucy Fitzgerald, 29 May 1804, Strutt papers at Terling; Kevin Whelan, email to author, 19 May 2014.

NOTES TO PART II

⁓

NOTES TO APPENDIX I:
NAMES OF HISTORICAL AFRICAN
AMERICANS APPEARING IN *TONY SMALL*
AND LORD EDWARD FITZGERALD

p. 241: As well as names of those who do not appear in the book. Names other than those in Moss and Scoggins include McKelvey enslaved African-Americans in *Index to Inventories, Record of Wills and Miscellaneous Records of Charleston County*, 1687–1785, Vol. II (L–2), Charleston County Public Library; James and Margaret McKelvey, Vol. 99–B, p. 396, those whom Tony left behind, pp. 267, 268: Dick, Molly, Jesse, Nancy, Dick, Plenty, Hesey, Tom, Frank , Tom, Aleck , Jacob, John, Phebe, Silvia, Josse, Clarinda, Stepney, Sally, Jenny, Rinah, Chloe, Sarah, Venus, Abraham, Prince, Hercules, Hester, Hagar, Isaac, Paul, Ben, Katy, Bob.

Francis Barber was the faithful servant of Dr. Johnson. *Boswell's Life of Johnson*, R.W. Chapman, ed. J.D. Fleeman, rev. Oxford: Oxford University Press, 3rd edn. 1970. Michael Bundock, *The Fortunes of Francis Barber*. New Haven: Yale University Press, 2015.

Cemetery Records: A Documentary of Cemetery or Burial Ground Reports and Grave Relocation by Santee Cooper from the Project Area, 1939–1941 (*Lake Marion, Lake Moultrie*), pp. 185–87. Prepared as a Public Service by

The Berkeley County Historical Society, 1986, by Sara Jean DeHay Guerry, Jamestown, SC.

Henry Ravenel, "Recollections of Life on a Southern Plantation." *The Yale Review*: A National Quarterly, 1936 (Summer), "The 'Cymbee' [Simbi] Water Spirits of St. John's Berkeley."

NOTES TO APPENDIX II:
IDENTITY OF TONY SMALL

p. 251: Tony was probably born free since he was free to travel. Lisa Briggitte Randle, "East Branch of the Cooper River, 1780–1820: Panopticisim and Mobility," University of South Carolina Scholar Commons, 2018. Scholarcommons.sc.edu/cgi/viewcontent.cgi?article=5949&context=etd (accessed 25 August 2020)

p. 251: The list by Leslie has not survived, unlike The Book of Negroes. Lawrence Hill, *Someone Knows My Name*. New York: W.W. Norton & Co., 2007, 471–74.

p. 251: Carlton's order to Leslie makes no mention of black loyalists. R.W. Gibbes, *Documentary History of the American Revolution*, 2nd edn. Spartanburg: Reprint Company, 1853, 1972; 2: 153, 156, 164. McCowen, Jr., pp. 110, 145.

p. 254: In the late eighteenth century there were between three thousand and five thousand blacks living in London. Michael Bundock, *The Fortunes of Francis Barber*. New Haven: Yale University Press, 2015, pp. 32, 33. W.A. Hart, "Africans in eighteen-century Ireland," Irish Historical Studies 33 (129), May 2002.

p. 254: The Proprietors and local nobility. Henry A. M. Smith, "The Baronies of South Carolina," *The South Carolina Historical and Genealogical Magazine*, Vol. I (1927). Spartanburg, SC: The Reprint Co., 1988. Walter

Edgar, *South Carolina: A History*. Columbia: University of South Carolina Press, 1998, pp. 43, 44.

p. 255: Locke's five drafts of his Constitutions are deemed "an extraordinary scheme of forming an aristocratic government." Jonathan P. Thomas, "The Barbadians in Early South Carolina," *South Carolina and Barbados Connections: Selections from the South Carolina Historical Magazine,* Intro. by Stephen G. Hoffius. Charleston, SC: Home House Press, 2010, p. 8.

p. 256: Understanding the relation between Barbados and the Lowcountry of South Carolina. Walter Edgar, *South Carolina: A History*, pp. 35–46. Rhoda Green, CEO and Founder, Barbados and Carolinas Legacy Foundation, www.barbadoscarolinas.org (Accessed 07 August 2019); conversation with author 10 September 2014. Michael J. Heitzler, *Goose Creek, South Carolina: A Definitive History, 1670–2003*, 2 Vols. Charleston: History Press, 2005, 2006.

p. 257: Eighteen members of a family by the name of Small. *Barbados Records: Baptisms 1637–1800*. Compiled and Edited by Joanne McRee Sanders. Baltimore: Clearfield and Genealogical Publishing Co., Inc., 2011. *Barbados Records: Wills and Administrations*, Vol. I, 1639–1680, Vol. II, 1681–1700, Vol. III, 1700–1725. Houston: Sanders Historical Publications, 1979, 1980, 1981. *Barbados Records: Marriages*, Vol. I, 1643–1800, Vol. II, 1643–1800. Houston: Sanders Historical Publications, 1982.

p. 259: Shirley Small. In conversation with the author on the battlefield at Eutaw Springs.

p. 260: original relevant Strode acreage. Kinloch Memorial, 2 May 1733; Series: S11001, Vol. 3, pp. 405–07; South Carolina Department of Archives and History. The McPherson memorial was brought to author's attention by Richard Watkins; H. A. M. Smith, Vol. I, p. 113.

p. 260: conveyed the remaining strip of the eastern most Strode grant, namely the two hundred acres. H. A. M. Smith, Vol. I, p. 113; Charleston Deeds, Vol. GG, p. 25. Deed from Kinloch to O'Neal was brought to author's attention by Richard Watkins.

p. 260: As the original Strode property of one thousand two hundred acres stood at the end of 1756. H. A. M. Smith, Vol. I, p. 113.

p. 261: A plantation owned by Thomas Sumter was among those lying just across the river to the west. H. A. M. Smith, Vol. I, p. 114.

p. 261: Margaret McKelvey's four daughters. Richard Watkins and James Queen, "Land Genealogy," paper delivered at Francis Marion Symposium, Manning, South Carolina, organized by George and Carol Summers, 12 October 2012.

p. 261: The Battle of Eutaw Springs was fought on much of Belvidere. H. A. M. Smith, Vol. I, p. 114.

p. 261: traces of a brick house on a McKelvey Plantation. Author's conclusion from telephone conversation on 7 June 2009 with Norman Sinkler Walsh and from 10 August 2013 email from Harriet Sinkler Little, with whom the author toured the battle site on 13 December 2013; Sinkler family history, however, identifies the brick foundation as that of a tavern.

p. 262: a "tavern" once stood near the banks of the Santee not far from Nelson's Ferry. http://gaz.jrshelby.com/nelson.htm (Accessed 2010); William Faden's 1780 map supplied by Norman Sinkler Walsh, email to author, 6 May 2014. White's Tavern, a different tavern, is located on the 1820 Vernolles-Ravenel map several miles southeast of the battle site along the road between Nelson's Ferry and Moncks Corner.

p. 263: According to David Reuwer who has done extensive study of the foundations of the brick edifice on the battle site. David Paul Reuwer, email to author, 16 May 2014.

NOTES TO APPENDIX III:
LORD EDWARD'S TWELVE MILITARY ACTIONS
IN THE SOUTHERN CAMPAIGN

p. 267: Second, after arriving with Rawdon at Ninety Six on 21 June 1781. Balfour letter book, 20 July 1781 report to Sir Henry Clinton and Germain; copy furnished by Charles Baxley.

NOTES TO APPENDIX IV:
LORD EDWARD FITZGERALD IN THE
HISTORICAL NOVELS OF WILLIAM GILMORE SIMMS

p. 270: He also picked up stories "at the knees of those who were young spectators in the grand panorama of our Revolution." Sean R. Busick, "Simms as a Presenter of History through Fiction," *A Sober Desire for History*. Columbia: University of South Carolina Press, 2005, pp. 63–78, 70; 68, quoting from Simms, *The Lily and the Totem. The Revolutionary War in South Carolina: An Anthology,* Compiled by Stephen Meats from the Writings of William Gilmore Simms. Columbia, South Carolina: Southern Students Program, University of South Carolina, 1975.

p. 270: "In 'helping' history he merely supplied 'from the *probable*, the apparent deficiencies of the *actual*." Busick, p. 78. Italics in the original.

p. 270: "Meanwhile, Lord Edward Fitzgerald has been required to join his regiment." *Eutaw: A Sequel to The Forayers, or Raid of the Dog Days*. New York: Redfield, 1856; David W. Newton, ed. Fayetteville: University of Arkansas Press, 2007, p. 241. Simms mentions Fitzgerald nearly forty times in *Eutaw*, and Tony once ("Tony proved faithful"), Redfield, p. 523.

p. 271: Lord Edward's presence at Huger's and Quinby bridges and Shubrick's Plantation. Robert Charles Lawrence Fergusson Collection, The Society of the Cincinnati, No. L2001F617, Date 11/01; Charles Baxley, email to author, 30 April 2104.

p. 271: Lee, Washington, Marion, and Sumter began to appear in force. Balfour letter book, Fergusson Collection.

p. 274: In *The Forayers,* Lord Edward is a suitor of Colonel Sinclair's daughter Carrie. *The Forayers, or the Raid of the Dog Days*, New York: Redfield, 1855. David W. Newton, ed. Fayetteville: University of Arkansas Press, 2003.

p. 274: Fitzgerald scatters when all combatants are surprised by the sudden arrival of Marion's men. *The Forayers*, Newton, ed., pp. 432–35.

p. 274: Lord Edward's reputation as a lady's man in Simms. *The Forayers*, Newton, ed., p. 192.

Exhibits and Maps

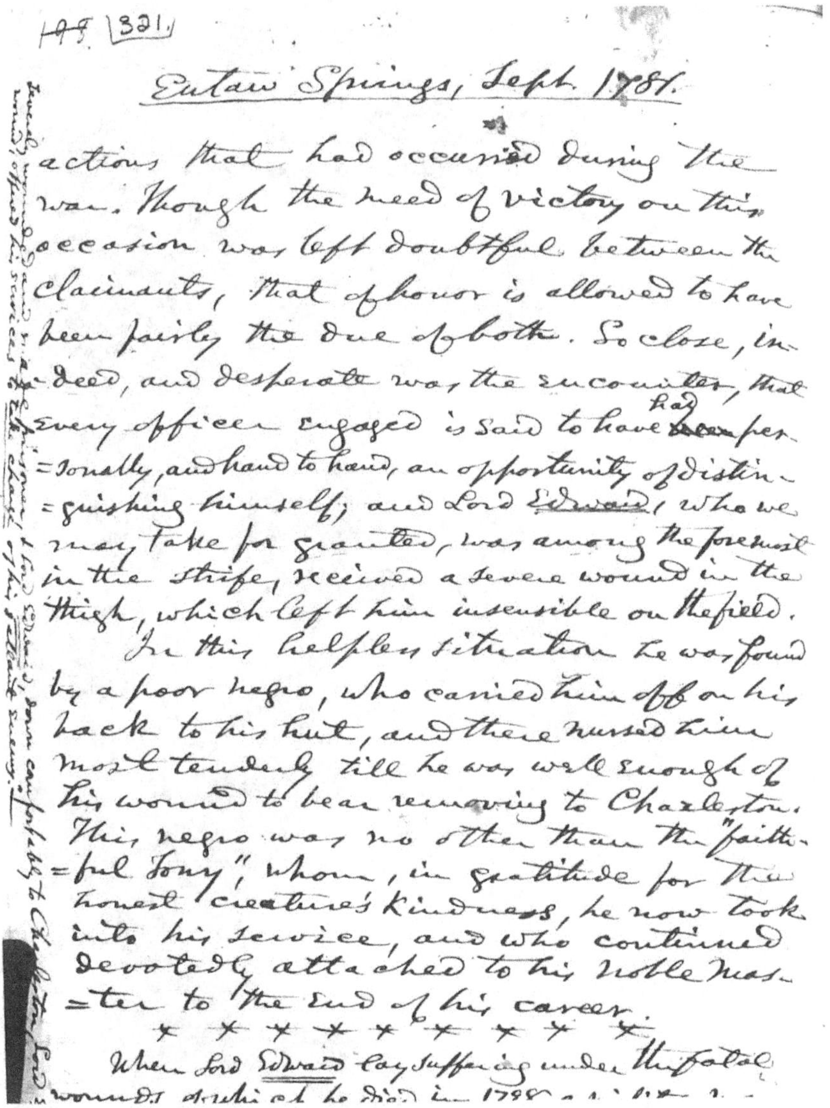

pp. 321.

Eutaw Springs, Sept. 1781.

actions that had occurred during the war. Though the meed of victory on this occasion was left doubtful between the claimants, that of honor is allowed to have been fairly the due of both. So close, indeed, and desperate was the encounter, that every officer engaged is said to have had personally, and hand to hand, an opportunity of distinguishing himself; and Lord Edward, who we may take for granted, was among the foremost in the strife, received a severe wound in the thigh, which left him insensible on the field.

In this helpless situation he was found by a poor negro, who carried him off on his back to his hut, and there nursed him most tenderly till he was well enough of his wound to bear removing to Charleston. This negro was no other than the "faithful Tony," whom, in gratitude for the honest creature's kindness, he now took into his service, and who continued devotedly attached to his noble master to the end of his career.

* * * * * * * * *

When Lord Edward lay suffering under the fatal wounds of which he died in 1798 . . .

Exhibit 1 Draper Manuscript, 6VV 321,
State Historical Society of Wisconsin

Exhibit 2 McKelvey brick house (c. 1800), Charles Fraser,
A Charleston Sketchbook, 1796–1806, intro. by Alice R.
Huger Smith. Rutland: Charles E. Tuttle, n.d.

Exhibit 3 Biggin Church, author's photograph, 2010.

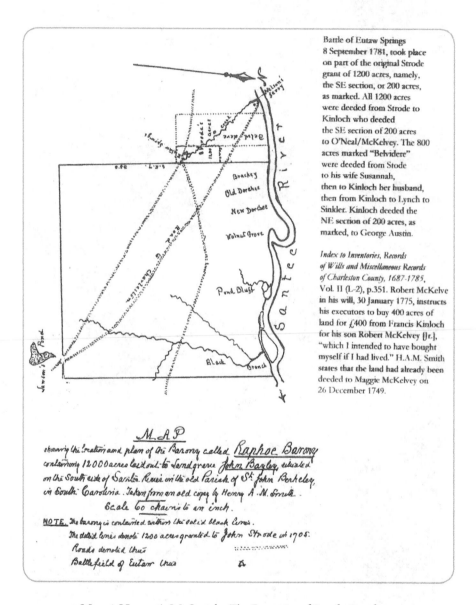

Battle of Eutaw Springs
8 September 1781, took place
on part of the original Strode
grant of 1200 acres, namely,
the SE section, or 200 acres,
as marked. All 1200 acres
were deeded from Strode to
Kinloch who deeded
the SE section of 200 acres
to O'Neal/McKelvey. The 800
acres marked "Belvidere"
were deeded from Strode
to his wife Susannah,
then to Kinloch her husband,
then from Kinloch to Lynch to
Sinkler. Kinloch deeded the
NE section of 200 acres, as
marked, to George Austin.

*Index to Inventories, Records
of Wills and Miscellaneous Records
of Charleston County, 1687-1785,*
Vol. II (L-2), p.351. Robert McKelve
in his will, 30 January 1775, instructs
his executors to buy 400 acres of
land for £400 from Francis Kinloch
for his son Robert McKelvey (Jr.),
"which I intended to have bought
myself if I had lived." H.A.M. Smith
states that the land had already been
deeded to Maggie McKelvey on
26 December 1749.

Map 1 Henry A.M. Smith, *The Baronies of South Carolina,*
Raphoe Barony. Spartanburg: The Reprint Co., 1988, Vol. 1, p. 110.

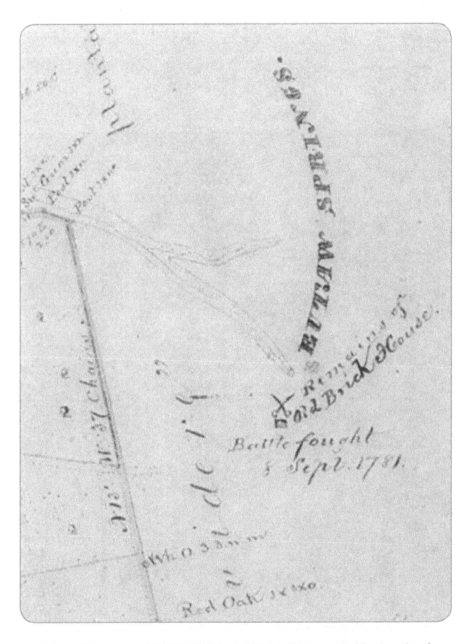

Map 2 "Remains of Old Brick House," Eutaw Springs, Sinkler Family of
Eutaw Plantation, Caroliniana Library, Columbia, South Carolina.

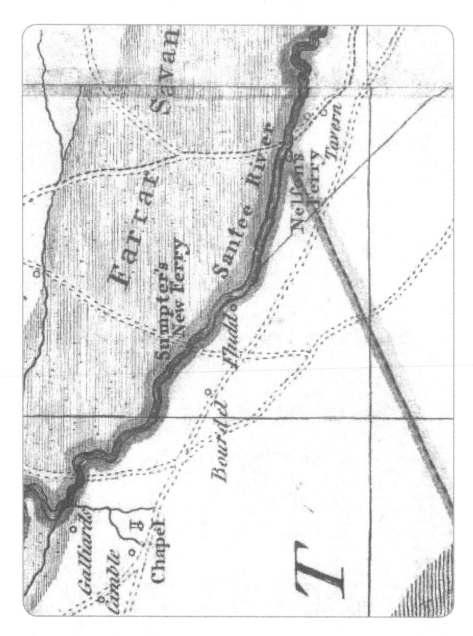

Map 3 "Bourdel," "Nelson's Ferry," and "Tavern,"
William Faden and William Gerard DeBrahm, 1780, in John A.
Robertson, et al., *Global Gazetteer of the American Revolution.*
http://gaz.jrshelby.com/nelson.htm (Accessed 2010.)

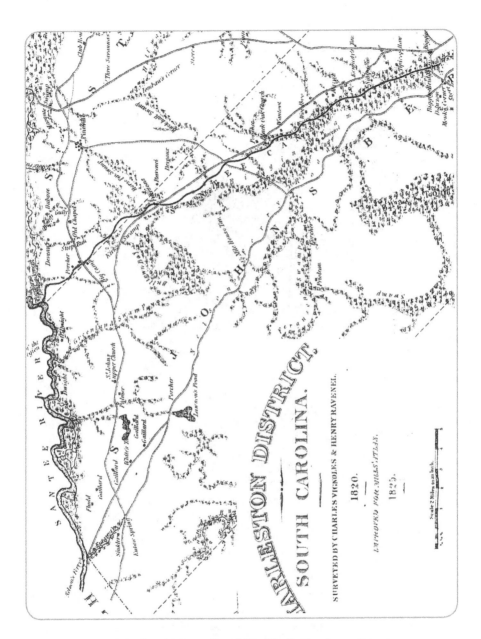

Map 4 "White's Tavern," and "Sinkler," *Charleston District, South Carolina*, surveyed by Charles Vignoles and Henry Ravenel, 1820, improved for Mills' Atlas, 1825; Library of Congress; Charleston Public Library, South Carolina Room.

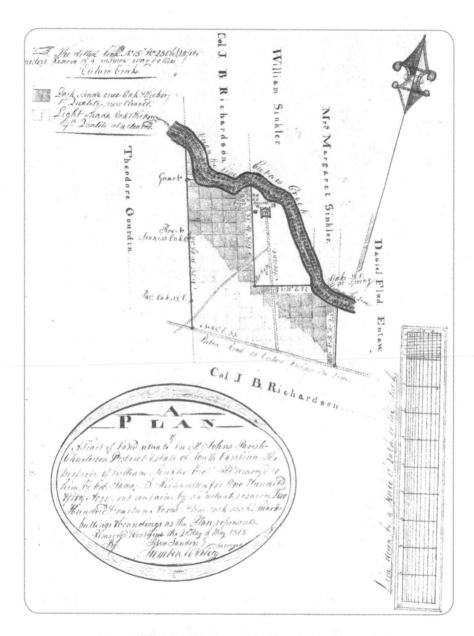

Map 5 "Negro Houses," *A Plan* for tract of lands of
William Sinkler, 20 May 1818, Sinkler Family of Eutaw Plantation,
Caroliniana Library, Columbia, South Carolina.

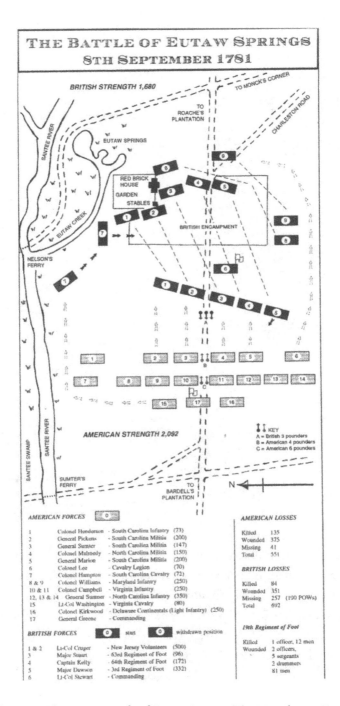

Map 6 Roger Chapman, *Battle of Eutaw Springs*, The Newsletter, Friends of the Green Howards Regimental Museum, September 1999, Issue 8, p. 9.

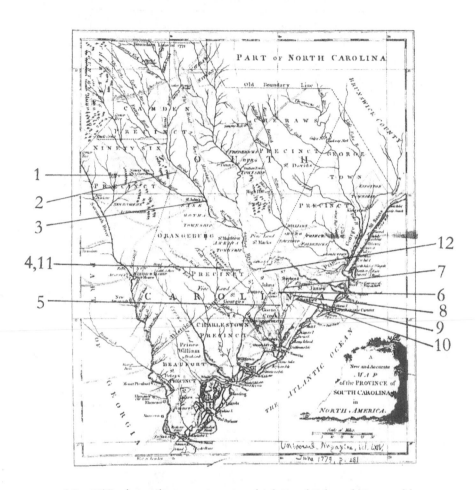

Map 7 Twelve military actions in which Lord Edward Fitzgerald
participated, as marked by the author on *A New and Accurate
Map of the Province of South Carolina in North America, 1779*
[loc.gov/item/2013593294]: 1. Second Siege of Ninety Six; 2. Pursuit of
Greene's Army after Ninety Six; 3. Friday's Ferry; 4. Orangeburg; 5. Goose
Creek; 6. Moncks Corner; 7. Biggin Church; 8. Huger's Bridge; 9. Quinby
Bridge; 10. Shubrick's Plantation; 11. Siege of Orangeburg; 12. Eutaw Springs.

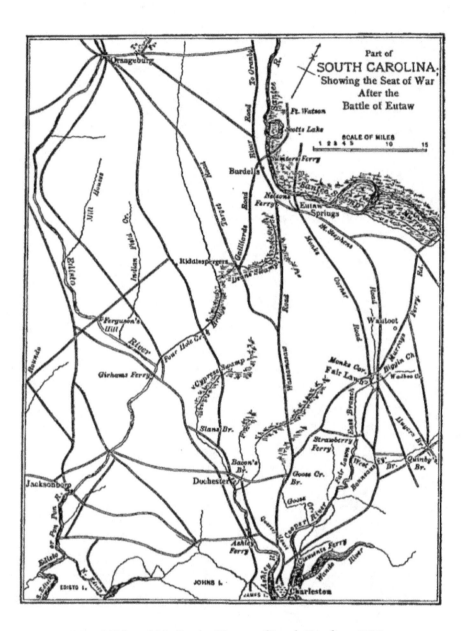

Map 8 Edward McCrady, *History of South Carolina*, 1780–
1783. London: MacMillan and Co., Ltd., Vol. 4, p. 481.

ACKNOWLEDGEMENTS

———⟨∽⟩———

Roger Chapman, MBE, retired British Army officer and former curator of the Green Howards Museum in Richmond, Yorkshire, is the inspiration for this book, and much is drawn from his own research and writing. Several years ago, Chapman made an effort in America to identify and retrieve the regimental silver which was lost to Lieutenant Colonel Henry Lee and General Thomas Sumter as the 19th Regiment of Foot (after 1744 called the Green Howards) approached Huger's Bridge in the early morning hours of 17 July 1781. Inquiries were made. Charlestonians knew nothing. One of Sumter's descendants merely observed to the author that if any silver were found on his groaning board, he would "stay fast and wait till this whole thing blows over."

Research on land genealogy by Richard Watkins and James Queen, compilation of names and research on black loyalists and patriots by Bobby Moss and Michael Scoggins, and the wide range of knowledge of the Southern Campaign by Charles Baxley and J.D. Lewis are lynch pins of the history in this book. Essential biographies of Lord Edward Fitzgerald are those of Moore and MacDermott and Stella Tillyard, *Citizen Lord: The Life of Edward Fitzgerald, Irish Revolutionary*. Useful general information is found in *A History of the Services of the 19th Regiment* by Michael Lloyd Ferrar, *The Fire of Liberty* compiled and edited by Esmond Wright, *The War for America, 1775–1783*, by Piers Mackesy, and *The War of Independence* by Sir John Fortesque.

Kevin Whelan, Director, Notre Dame Global Gateway, Dublin, offered timely information regarding Lord Edward's correspondence of about eight hundred items from the 1770s to the 1830s, released by the National Library of Ireland in 2012. Articles on line from Donal Fallon, "Come Here to Me," were very useful.

A work of fiction and fact, this creative nonfiction is based on much historical research. Book-length publications by Jim Piecuch, Gregory D. Massey, Patrick O'Kelley, Christine R. Swager, and most recently, Robert M. Dunkerly and Irene Boland are notable among many that provide current scholarship on the Southern Campaign. Hands-on experts in the field, authors, and contributors to numerous publications and web sites, namely, Charles Baxley, J. D. Lewis, Lee F. McGee, David Reuwer, Douglas Bostick, William Anderson, Robert T. Morgan, Steven D. Smith, William Gordon, Stephen G. Hoffius, Don Bracey, Charles M. Wallace, Chris Amer, Carl Steen, Scott Withrow, Greg Brooking, Mark Hill, Lish Thompson, Nic Butler, Robert McIntyre, D.P. Lowther, John Ramsey, and Donny Carson, and Pamela White generously shared their knowledge at key points. Baxley, especially, gladly helped to answer all questions and shared essential documents and information. Articles appearing in *Southern Campaigns of the American Revolution* (SCAR), southerncampaign.org, are authoritative. Brent Howard Holcomb, professional genealogist and editor of *The South Carolina Magazine of Ancestral Research*, kindly researched the name Tony Small among archives.

As well as familiar standard histories which account for the Revolutionary War in the Lowcountry, articles by H. A. M. Smith and those published in the *South Carolina Historical Magazine* were essential in understanding South Carolina and Barbados connections. Alphonso Brown, Gullah Tours, Charleston, supplied the Gullah language used by Tony. Rhonda Green and other members of the Avery Institute of African-American History and Culture at the College of Charleston, in support of the Avery Research Center, generously shared their expertise. Fred Stroble provided the anecdote of "Lord Fitzgerald" in the Historical Preface.

Macky Hill, Robert "Rabbit" Lockwood, Jack Bennett, and Dick Coen shared their knowledge of plantations on the east branch of the Cooper River.

My sons Will and John assisted in field excursions. Ed Zorensky, Stephen Hoffius, and Lee Barnett offered advice on how to write a good story.

The professional computer skills of Kevin Locke were essential.

Joseph Winkelman, PPRE Hon RWS, kindly created the original watercolour drawing for the front cover.

Author's photograph by Leslie Morningstar.

Back cover photograph by John Black.

I am indebted to the Sinkler family of Eutaw Plantation, Norman Sinkler Walsh and Harriet Sinkler Little, for several of the maps and plans. Eliza Couturier, Richard Porcher, and Daniel Ravenel IX, kindly addressed questions and shared maps and documents unique to their family lands and histories around the battle site. Conversations with Shirley and Tony Small of Eutaw Springs helped bring history to life.

THE AUTHOR

———⟨∽⟩———

For nearly forty years, Robert Ray Black lived in Charleston, South Carolina, where he taught English, practiced law and taught at the Charleston School of Law. He now lives in Bozeman, Montana, where he writes, skis, hikes, and camps with Cooper his Labrador retriever in the Rocky Mountains. He is the author of a law book, the coeditor of a medieval text, and a contributor to a book of poetry and several scholarly journals. He holds a B.A. degree from Sewanee: The University of the  South, M.A. degrees from Vanderbilt and Oxford Universities, a Ph.D. from Princeton, and a J.D. from The University of South Carolina. He taught at several universities. With a direct commission in military intelligence and the infantry, he served as a First Lieutenant in the U.S. Army in Korea and Germany during the Vietnam era. He is a former Inspector General of the Society for the Descendants of Washington's Army at Valley Forge. He is a past member of the General William Moultrie chapter of the Sons of the American Revolution and has participated in many local historical association meetings throughout the Lowcountry of South Carolina. Robert Black has two sons.

Web site: RobertRayBlack.com

CPSIA information can be obtained
at www.ICGtesting.com
Printed in the USA
BVHW092207220421
605633BV00013B/1737/J